A Steampunk Misadventure

written by
Josef Matulich

cover & illustrations by
Seth Lyons

Dalmatian Alley Books
2022

The Silk Empress
ISBN 979-8-218-06155-5

Written by
Josef Matulich

Cover & Interior Art by
Seth Lyons

Edited by
Elizabeth Parsons, lizmakesstuff.com

published December 11, 2022

Other books by Josef Matulich

Camp Arcanum
(Arcanum Faire 1)

Power Tools in the Sacred Grove
(Arcanum Faire 2)

The Ren Faire at the End of the World
(Arcanum Faire 3)

Squirrel Apocalypse

DEDICATION

To all those who spin stories, become consumed by them, and finally make sense of the world through them.

ACKNOWLEDGEMENTS

This book was written during a very difficult period of time for everyone on the planet. If not for my family, this sprawling, chemo-addled manuscript would never have been beaten into shape, nor would have I. Thanks also go out to my editor Liz Parsons and my beta readers Dave Goudsward, Sheldon Gleisser, and Evan Siegling.

Additional thanks to my coworkers in the Nationwide Asian Language Unit who provided much assistance: Hannah Park, Jessie Huang, Angie Li, Shirley Dajun, & Li Su.

And thanks to Stuart Sisk, who knows about yawaras and other pointy things.

This is a work of alternative history speculative fiction. Any resemblance to actual people, events, and political situations is purely coincidental.

ONE

16th of August 1889
The High Silk Road,
west of Hami, China

"Nǐ hǎo, muhafez," Feng Po McLaren muttered as he scanned the horizon through the magnifying lens of his high-altitude mask. Algie recognized the first two words as "Hello" in Chinese but had only the vaguest idea of the remainder. Since his mentor was still dangling by knee and ankle in the starboard rigging of the airship *Wu Zetian*, Algie assumed it had something to do with the air pirates rumored to be lying in wait for them. The two of them had been in the Fish's Mouth for the last two hours searching for them.

"They're out there, Pig, I swear to you," Feng Po said in English, rendered barely comprehensible by a thick Scots accent. "They're so close, I can practically smell them."

Algie Piggrem still flinched minutely at the shortening of his family name to a barnyard animal. He put up with it because it seemed to be the fate of a First Mate's apprentice.

"Shì de, lǎoshī," Algie said with a nod. That was the only Chinese Feng Po had taught him so far, something the equivalent to "Yes, O Enlightened One."

The thought of air pirates didn't frighten Algie at all. To the contrary, it excited him to have a chance to see the subject of so many of his penny dreadfuls firsthand. Even as a twelve-year-old boy, he was convinced he could go toe to toe with the worst of them.

Feng Po shouted something else and then whooped in victory. He lowered his mask and grinned. One side of his curled mustaches was crimped from the way he had held it to his face. Algie maintained an expression of respectful interest with some difficulty.

"I found them, Pig!" Feng Po waved for him to come join him on the rigging. "Come on out and have a look for yourself, *chong wu.*"

Algie felt another twinge of foul temper with that bit of Chinese. Chen Bo Lin, the very large crewman with the artificial hand, recently explained to him that *chong wu* was a term of endearment, one reserved for dogs, pigs, and other small pets. Though he chafed under Feng Po's constant goading, Algie knew the *Wu Zetian* was a better berth than the Home for Friends of Children or aboard the *Roscommon Venture* bound for the gold fields of Australia.

"Shì de, lǎoshī."

Algie smiled, nodded, and made to hop over the rails of the Fish's Mouth, the forward observation platform halfway up the *Wu Zetian's* gas envelope. A ridiculous name, unless the gas bag of your airship was fashioned to look like a gigantic red-and-gold lucky fish lantern. Then, it all made sense.

Algie clambered out onto the rigging as easily as any of the boys who were born to it. This hadn't been the case several months ago when he had just been taken in. The swaying ropes and bamboo deadeyes were far from steady, and the view straight down from a few hundred meters was both petrifying and liquifying. Then, one day Algie thought to himself: *What would Dale Daring, Boy Airship Pilot do?*

The answer was that the boy adventurer would just stroll out there as if he were crossing the high street. Algie had taken a deep breath, squared his shoulders, and clambered across the knotted hemp like any of the other *Lǎoshǔ*, and he never felt the slightest bit of fear again.

"Very good, Pig." Feng Po beamed as he handed over the mask, a garish red and white thing fashioned after a Chinese

Opera character. With his blue silk brocade waistcoat and the red and blue knotted cords on his belt, Algie's mentor was a pretty garish character himself, the middle-aged son of a Scots steamship engineer and a lady-in-waiting to the Chinese court. The long braid he wore in common with the other Chinese crewmen was bound up in blue cord knotted into lucky fish and dragons. He pointed to a gap between two mountains.

"Tell me what you see there."

Since the mask was sized for a European adult, it was big enough for one and a half of Algie. He closed his left eye and put his right eye behind the magnifier. With a bit of squinting and manipulation of the focus knob, Algie finally picked out their target. Centered between the two peaks and drifting on a loose anchor one hundred meters above the scrub and gravel of the Chinese desert, the small airship did its best to look like a piece of the landscape. Its topside was painted the mottled colors of dried dust and stone. The bottom of the canvas gondola and the airbag were a light sky blue. The *picaroons* packed cheek to jowl in the craft were all variations of a muddy greenish-brown. They clutched an alarming array of hooks, spears, and firearms. Alarming to Algie because the lot looked like gear you could buy at a Liverpool farmers market.

Algie lowered the mask and handed it back to Feng Po.

"So, that's what air pirates really look like." They resembled none of the flamboyant descriptions of the penny dreadfuls he'd grown up on. He'd expected striped pants, velvet coats, and satin sashes. This group looked the type to rob pig herds on the way to Newcastle.

"*Picaroons*, or *muhafez,* we call them. Well, you're most likely not seeing them on their best day." His mentor absently hung the mask back on its hook on his belt. "That's a twelve-man cutter, the kind you Brits would only use for delivering mail. The paint scheme is the type invented by Ayub Khan and his exiles. And there's nearly two dozen of them in that shopping basket. Has to be my old *muhafez* brethren. They're small, pack neatly, and travel well."

The older man chuckled raucously and sped down the rigging like a spider monkey with his braided queue waving like its tail. He threw himself back over the railing and punched out a code on the electric voicepipe.

"*Passerelle*," said the scratchy voice coming out of the machine. That was the French word for "bridge", one of the first specialized words besides "port," "starboard," and "water closet" that Algie had picked up in the ship's common tongue. The pronunciation was worse than his own, which meant that it was probably one of the American bridge crew on the other end.

Feng Po launched into a blazing fast monologue in French, which somehow still sounded Scottish. Algie only caught one word in ten. It took less than thirty seconds for the bridge man to lose his patience and interrupt.

"English, please."

"Of course, Your Lordship," said First Mate McLaren. He winked at Algie and then tweaked his mustaches into something resembling a matched set. He leaned into the mouthpiece of the voicepipe and spoke slowly and clearly in stilted English.

"May I please speak to the Captain? It seems we are all about to be ambushed and murdered. Thank you and please."

"Just a moment." The crewman's tone was halfway between put-out and panicked.

Feng Po lifted his finger off of the "talk" button and muttered something indecipherable. He was all smiles, though, when the Captain came on the line.

"Captain Strausser, here."

"First Mate McLaren in the Fish's Mouth. There is a *picaroon* cutter lying in wait for us about seven kilometers off the port bow."

"Air pirates?"

"So they are called in Adventure Stories for Boys. I usually just call them well-armed layabouts. Less pressure to live up to expectations that way."

There was a moment of silence on the line, long enough for a man to grit his teeth and count to ten under his breath. This happened quite often when these two men spoke. Feng Po was a personal favorite of Mme. Streif, the airship's owner, and she gave him *carte blanche* to say whatever he wanted to whomever he wanted. Otherwise, the Captain would have had the First Mate dangling by his heels behind the propellers from Peking to Vienna.

"So, what is your suggested course of action, Mr. McLaren?"

"Since there is only one of them, I would take it they will try to close and board to do as little damage to the merchandise as possible. Some larceny and light kidnapping. It would be excessive and unprofitable to try to bring us down."

"And so, you think we should do what?"

Feng Po chuckled.

"If that single ship is all we have to contend with, I would suggest climbing to a thousand meters and running away like scared rabbits."

"And if there are more?"

"If they catch us, we put a dress and lipstick on Ensign Bigsby and convince the *picaroons* that he has wealthy relatives. But barring that, I have a few effective stratagems in mind."

A bit of the background commotion on the bridge came through on the voicepipe, but Capt. Strausser drowned that out. Bigsby had always been sensitive about his inability to grow a mustache.

"I will take that under advisement," the captain said. "Sound General Quarters. Keep your eyes open, Mr. McLaren."

"Aye aye, sir."

Feng Po switched off the device and rubbed his hands together in glee.

"It seems today, Pig," he crooned, "is the day to lose your maidenhood. Shout out, if you would be so kind?"

Algie cupped his hands around his mouth and bellowed out "*Yeiban sush*", the Ships' Cant phrase for "Battle Stations, All Hands on Deck."

One of the *Lǎoshǔ* skittered by on the rigging immediately.

"*Olo parsima!*" Peng shouted as he tossed Algie the red rubber ball integral to the boys' games. Algie stuffed it in a pocket for safe keeping as his friend took up his station on the port wing.

He heard the *Yeiban sush* call taken up by the other *Lǎoshǔ* throughout the rigging. As the cry went up amongst the crew on the junk's decks below, Feng Po pulled his command baton from his belt loop.

The baton was a solid bit of wood with brass fittings and Chinese characters etched into it in rings. The top was a carved ivory dragon's head with red jewels for eyes. The stories said it was a personal gift from the Emperor or taken from the body of a provincial governor. Wherever it came from, it packed a nasty wallop. Algie'd gotten smacks across the buttocks from it in the way of discipline. It also took down the double handful of sailors pursuing him the day he had met Feng Po in Capetown.

The First Mate struck the control yoke that ran through the Fish's Mouth three times. Each blow let out a low ringing sound, something like a wooden bell or the sound of a distant drum. The hollow bamboo and lacquer ring ran all the way around the gas envelope at the center line to the control fins at the tail. The hemp and bamboo rigging connected the yoke to the hull and engine struts below. By the third blow, every part of the *Wu Zetian* hull, deck, and engine rang.

Feng Po tapped out the cadence for *yeiban sush*. First, a sharp blow with the baton flat across the control yoke:

Thrummm!

A second's pause and then three sharp blows with the brass tip.

Tot-tot-tot!

Feng Po paused for the time it took for the first series of beats, and then repeated again.

Thrummm Tot-tot-tot!

Algie saw members of the rocket crew, Hsu, Chen, and Ma, in line along the main deck's railing taking up the cadence with belaying pins and the handles of their launching mauls.

Thrummm Tot-tot-tot!

The bridge officers came out to the observation areas on either side of the Texas deck which held the flying bridge and officers' quarters. Their fancy uniforms of green and black braid made them look as rigid as the lacquered silk of the *Wu Zetian's* hull. They timidly joined in the tattoo with swagger sticks and fists on the railings.

Thrummm Tot-tot-tot!

The *Lǎoshǔ* scattered to the far points of the rigging, boys in little more than loin cloths for the noon day heat. They climbed the ropes like the rats they were named for and out across the wings and sails. Mateo, a Portuguese sailor's son, clambered out to the end of the starboard engine strut and tapped out the rhythm on the engine cowl with a wrench. Algie kept time stomping barefoot on the bamboo deck.

Thrummm Tot-tot-tot!

It sounded and felt like every member of the *Wu Zetian's* crew joined in with the *yeiban sush* cadence, from the Germans in the engine room amidst their spirit engines, to Liu Jean-Pierre the shipbuilder's son in his workshops, to Mme. Streif herself in the gardens and pagodas of the forward deck. Algie imagined her five Conversers in their fancy dresses and grim expressions joining the rhythm with boot heels and iron fans.

Thrummm Tot-tot-tot!

The cadence went on forever.

It only went on for thirty seconds.

Feng Po McLaren brought it to a close with six flat blows against the control ring. When the ringing stopped, every soul on the Silk Empress was in their place and in time with each other. Algie felt the beat go on in the blood in his head and the soles of his feet.

Master Huang, the old crewman that dispensed herbs and traditional cures to the Chinese crew that refused to be treated by Dr. Koslowski, stood high above the pergola that shaded the Conversors' silk gardens. He held a fist high in the air and shouted something in Chinese.

"What did he say?" Algie asked Feng Po.

"A very romantic notion." Feng Po's mustache cranked up on one side of his face as he smiled. "We will die for the Silk Empress, he said. Not sure if he means the ship, or Mme. Streif. Not that it matters: I hope to make my *muhafez* brothers-in-arms do the dying today, instead."

The First Mate pointed towards a lockbox below the control ring.

"Come here, Pig. I have something I'd like to show you."

Algie looked over his shoulder. The *picaroon* cutter was still a few kilometers away.

*

The lock of the armory chest was a beautiful brass mechanism of wheels and pegs and a circular hasp. Red Chinese characters were enameled onto each flat peg. Feng Po spun the wheels in seeming random ways until the lock popped open.

"Now, this is a thing of true beauty," he said as he gently lifted the lid. He removed a flat black box that looked to be slightly larger than Algie's family Bible. "The latest labor-saving device from Liu Chemical Industries: I give you the Mermaid's Purse."

Algie eyed the black box with its label in black and yellow Chinese writing and the ornate brass keyhole in its center.

"What does it do?"

"What does it do?" Feng Po cackled at the thought. "It makes enemies go away, especially the combustible ones. About a quarter stick of *Zhàyà*[1], some jellied spirits, and just a dollop of *Gǒng bàolù*[2] to start things off with a pop."

Algie idly examined the box, turning it over in his hands as Feng Po fished some other components out of the lock box.

The first mate took back the Mermaid's Purse and screwed quadruple fishhooks into the corners of the contraption.

He held up an ornate winding key for Algie to see.

"You fly above a deserving opponent's airship, like that *muhafez* shopping basket out there, and charge the mechanical fuse with three turns of the key. Throw it over the railing to let the barbed hooks snag the fabric of the gas envelope or the netting. You scull away as quickly as you can. Thirty seconds later you have a bonfire for their vanities."

"Wicked!" Algie exclaimed. He could hardly wait to see it in use.

"There are several other inventions from young master Liu's workshop they've asked me to field test. There's one particular item right there called the Monkey King..."

McLaren cut himself off as a commotion arose behind them. The Alert cadence, two short strikes and one long, rang throughout the ship over and over. The *Lǎoshǔ* on the fantail and dangling on the rigging shouted as they pointed at a patch of desert scrub just behind the airship. A dome of painted fabric and netting rose up from the ground with the sounds of engines and gunfire. It floated straight up, trailing loose debris and mooring ropes, until it was on a level with the *Wu Zetian*.

Feng Po dangled from the portside rigging to get himself a look. He didn't bother using his mask's magnifying lens. The ambush ship was close enough on their tail that Algie could see which of the air pirates had gold teeth.

"That's no flea bite British cutter, Pig," the first mate muttered. "That's a German cruiser. Probably one of the mothball fleet from when the *Qing* handed the European Cartel their collective asses at Palikao."

As they watched, more of the motley *picaroon* crew stowed the camouflage net to reveal the battered, but somewhat armored, hull of the airship. Gunmen crowded the forward catwalks as two men fussed with a one-pound gun on the prow.

Algie looked from the smaller craft still a kilometer or two ahead of them to the warship just behind.

"Are they as dangerous as they look?" Algie asked.

The *muhafez* touched off the one-pounder and struck the *Wu Zetian* a glancing blow on the portside stern. The load was grapeshot, which was lethal against crew and rigging, but less than effective on the stiffened silk hull. The worst casualties were the pigs and ducks kept in the external cages by the galley crew. The armored cruiser twitched off its course from the gun's recoil.

The alert cadence stopped suddenly. Everyone on board knew they were under attack now.

"There is some element of risk, I must admit." Feng Po clutched the rigging as the airship accelerated beneath them and began to climb. "Thank God! The good Captain Strausser has chosen to bravely run away."

The gunners on the German airship let loose another volley. The spray of lead shot passed off the port side in the gap between the engine strut and the forward control wing. Enough of it hit the wooden propeller to give it an unbalanced wobble as it spun.

Algie clutched the rope railing as the enemy chewed the *Wu Zetian* to death in little pieces. He had read every one of the Dale Daring and August Vogel airship stories, had thought the collected knowledge was as good as a term in the Queen's Air Academy, but he quickly realized this was all much more fun when it was in penny dreadfuls.

"Pig!" Feng Po shouted. The expression on his face said that he had shouted at Algie more than once.

"*Shì de, lǎoshī.*"

"Go forward, to the end of the platform and keep an eye on that shopping basket!"

Algie nodded vigorously.

"Make fast your tether, Pig. The road will get bumpy from here on out."

Algie walked hand over hand along ten-meter observation platform. He clung for life halfway out as the ship made an evasive maneuver hard to port. Their pursuer let off another round. Algie couldn't see where it hit, but he could feel the impact through his feet.

He screwed the carabiner at the end of his tether around one of the bamboo rail posts and uncoiled the rope that hung around his shoulder onto the deck. With his left wrist thrust through one of the safety loops, he felt secure enough to slide out to the very edge of the platform.

"They're heading right for us, sir!" Algie shouted. "Eight hundred meters out! Hard starboard!"

That was close enough to see the ragged *picaroons* aiming their squirrel guns and crossbows at them. Well, *him* actually, since he was an obvious target thrust out ten meters ahead of everyone else. The German cruiser on their tail was even closer and getting ready to blow them out of the sky. Algie looked down to where their wreckage was most likely to fall. It was all stony desert and scraggly brush, with nothing as soft as water or sand to land in as far as the eye could see. The only variable was the line of semaphore towers and telegraph lines that ran along the spine of the High Silk Road.

The mechanical arms and colored lights of the semaphore towers below them started to spell out a message:

"PICAROON WARNING. 6 MERCHANT SHIPS CONFIRMED LOST IN LAST 2 WEEKS."

"I think you're a bit late on that warning," Algie muttered to himself.

He kept looking at the ground below for more bad news. Algie saw another camouflage net that laid directly in their path, replacing a small section of the desert less than five hundred meters ahead. Their pursuer slowed for no good reason, letting the space between the German ship and the *Wu Zetian* grow quickly.

"AMBUSH!" Algie screamed as he pointed down at the blind.

"*Wáng bā dàn!*[3]" Feng Po shouted at once.

He took just a second to confirm with his own eyes and then began shouting orders into the voicepipe. Something about a Bastard Turn, an extreme maneuver Algie remembered executing at half-speed only once or twice.

The *Lǎoshǔ* and the internal hydraulic motivators pulled the two forward control wings into stiff opposition. The starboard fin cupped into the wind to brake that side of the airship as the port fin angled into the airstream and gathered lift. Power to the starboard engine was cut off completely as the damaged port engine roared and shuddered to push the ship into an impossibly tight right turn.

Algie held on for dear life. The gigantic red fish lantern and the ornate Chinese pleasure barge were only held together by a cat's cradle of ropes and flexible ductwork. The lower hull pitched and yawed from side to side during the wild maneuver. The gas envelope shuddered under the forces on the control ring. The oiled silk fabric rippled like a banner in a high wind. Their attempt to evade the ambush felt like it could wreck the airship just as easily as the *picaroons*.

As it was, the turn wasn't quite tight enough. The port wing and engine strut passed over the camouflage netting. Something beneath it burst into fire. A fountain of flame and spark and sharp-edged shrapnel burned through the blind and rose up into the sky well above their level. Half of the port wing simply disappeared. The engine strut, made of sterner stuff, bent in half and let the engine swing in toward the lowermost hull. The damaged propeller made a sound like a buzzsaw as it ground against the mounts for the keel fin.

"*Bidh do mhàthair a 'cadal leis na Sasannaic!*[4]" Feng Po roared at the *muhafez*. It was his fiercest oath, saved for only the most special of occasions, though Algie still didn't know what it meant. "You think you're so bloody clever!"

He waved Algie back from end of the platform and returned to the voicepipe. Algie saw no sin in retreating from the most exposed spot on the ship. By the time he made it back to the Fish's Mouth, the First Mate was already giving the Captain the benefit of his years of *picaroon* experience.

"A fusillade of rockets off the fantail would dissuade that German monster from getting too familiar with our hind parts, Captain," Feng Po said. "That'll give some breathing room to deal with that little *muhafez* cutter."

"The broadside crews are of no use to us where they are, for the moment," the Captain agreed.

Algie heard a few orders being given to someone else on the bridge. Feng Po reached out and tousled his hair with a smile.

"That was a sharp eye out, Pig," he said. "You probably saved all our lives. Now, it's for me to put them all back at risk."

Feng Po spoke into the horn of the voicepipe again. Algie saw the rocket crew below moving astern with their mallets and bellows launchers.

"How much control do we still have on just one engine and a wing?"

"We're not making another one of those turns, I can tell you that." The Captain grunted. "With a bit effort we can keep the ship steady and straight."

"And you still have control of the ballast valves?" Feng Po gestured for Algie to pick up the key and Mermaid's Purse from the locker.

"Ummm… Yes?"

"Then you need to make for a broadside on the cutter." Feng Po winked at the boy.

"But we're moving our rocketeers to the stern," the Captain sputtered. "What do you plan to do? Throw vegetables?"

"I said nothing about actually launching a broadside, but that is the maneuver my *muhafez* compatriots would be expecting. Once we're close enough, we would execute the Rising Cobra stratagem. It'll be page twenty-three in the little book Mssr. Patrouille and I wrote up for you."

Algie could hear the pages of that book fluttering over the voicepipe. Finally, the Captain spoke:

"You're insane."

"And that's what will save us all," Feng Po said with a smile. "We have about ten seconds before our friends out here realize we aren't going to fall out of the sky by ourselves. If you have a brighter idea, I will be glad to execute it."

The Captain spent five of those ten seconds in silence. He came back on the wire with a grunt and an unhappy tone.

"This is what Mme. Streif hired you for. You'd better be right."

"If I'm not, I'll be dead and wrong, and that should make you very happy in the Afterlife. Wait for my signal, sir. First Mate McLaren, over and out."

He let out a deep breath and a lot of his bravery and arrogance seemed to go with it. Algie stood beside him with the explosives and the winding key. He was scared, moving on towards petrified.

"*Guan Yin*, Lady of Mercy, pray for us," his mentor said. "We're really in the soup now, Pig."

"You don't think we can get out of this?" Algie asked.

Feng Po chuckled singularly without humor.

"Oh, I could get us out of this. I expect even *you* could get us out of this. I'm not so sure our American captain will get us out of this."

Feng Po looked over at the German cruiser behind them. It was showing signs of firing up their boilers and closing in for the kill.

"And we definitely don't have time to discuss it." He put a hand on Algie's shoulder. "Here's what you need to do, *chong wu*. Scamper out to the end of the platform with the Mermaid's

Purse and the key. In about a minute, we are going to be vaulting over the top of that little shopping basket. When we do, I need you to drop this on top of them. With luck, this will snag in their rigging and they will all be blown to the Hell of Screaming while Running around on Burning Ground."

"With luck?" Algie said. If their lives were depending on this trick, he didn't want luck to have anything to do with it.

"This is the first time it's been used in combat. No guarantees."

The first mate swatted Algie across the buttocks, but gently.

"Now, get out there, *chong wu*. And keep your head down."

Algie clutched the Mermaid's Purse close to his chest with both hands. He kept the arming key clenched tight in one fist. To keep from being bounced off the walkway, he bent low so the top rope railing was at the level of his shoulders.

The *Lǎoshǔ* had already unfurled the flying jib sail below him. The Captain was using it and the remaining engine to tack back and forth in a course parallel to the little cutter's. This rocked Algie from side to side, too, but it had yet to pitch him over the railing. Still, he was glad to hunker down at the end and wait for his chance.

His hero Dale Daring was always resolute, always sure and fearless. Algie tried to suppress his fears by asking himself again: "What would Dale Daring do?" As he crouched down at the end of the platform with a barbed time bomb in his hands, he had no bloody idea.

Algie heard the thump of hammers on the bellows of the launching tubes, one after another. In less than a second, he heard the high pitched "twang" of the inert rockets hitting the end of their ignition cords and pulling their mechanical fuses. Then, the whistling screech of the assault rockets came from the fantail. Less than five seconds later, explosions and screams came from the men on the catwalks of the German cruiser. The short time between launch and impact meant their pursuer was close. Close enough to throw rocks.

Or grappling hooks.

Another volley screamed out towards the warship. It may have taken six or seven seconds to connect. Two seconds longer, maybe two hundred meters farther back. That wasn't much, but he'd hang his hope on the slightest hook right now.

Up ahead, the cutter slowly turned towards the *Wu Zetian* to present the smallest target just as she was turning head-on to meet the cutter. Algie wondered what must be going through the *picaroons'* minds as they were being descended upon by the two golden dragons on the bow and the enormous banner-bedecked red and gold fish with a young boy and a Mermaid's Purse on the tip of its tongue.

The gunmen on the smaller craft opened fire with rifles and scatterguns. Evidently, their thinking was "Let's kill it and see if we can eat it!" Algie hugged the bamboo deck and prayed that a stray shot didn't set off the explosives underneath him.

"Get ready, Pig!" Feng Po shouted.

The *Wu Zetian*'s own gunmen opened fire from the prow, keeping the air pirates' heads down if nothing else. One let off a signal flare at the little cutter. It burned like a bright green comet and passed between the hull and the envelope without hitting equipment, rigging, or *picaroon.*

A total miss.

Knowing finally what Dale Daring would do, Algernon Piggrem stood and climbed to the top of the rope railings. In "Dale Daring and the Barbary Pilots," the boy hero had been in a similar situation: his airship crippled, his crew all overboard or dead, and the Tunisian air pirates' destroyer bearing down on the Sultan's defenseless air yacht. He said: "There is only one way to guarantee a direct hit". Then, he had jammed his airship down the air pirates' throats and leapt into the Mediterranean before the phlogiston holding the craft aloft burst into a mighty conflagration.

The *Wu Zetian* was nearly within stone-throwing distance of the cutter when the ship shuddered and began to pitch upwards. Far below him, Algie heard the rush of water as the forward ballast tanks released.

It was a matter of seconds now. Algie climbed over to the outside of the railing and held on with one hand. He leaned out past any other part of the ship, giving him an unobstructed view of the three-hundred-meter drop to the desert below.

There's no time for fear, he told himself. *Today you must be a hero.*

Once again, he had about three seconds to make a life-or-death decision.

The *picaroons* were wide-eyed in shock as the *Wu Zetian* rose up like a feather in the wind and it looked like they would be passing underneath this great lacquered box of a merchant ship.

"Let go, Pig! NOW!"

Algie turned the arming key three times and let go. Not from the Mermaid's Purse, but from the railing. He dove headfirst at the envelope of the cutter, holding the black box of explosives in front of him as he fell. It took less than three Picadillies to make contact.

Two sets of the quadruple hooks dug into the batten cloth of the gas bag. Algie continued to fall while the Mermaid's Purse stopped. His face hit the brass timing mechanism with a sickening crunch.

For the briefest of moments, he thought he'd set off the device prematurely as stars and flares of light crossed his vision. Then his sight cleared and he felt a sharp jolt as his twenty-meter tether went taut against his climbing harness. Algie twisted the hooks of the Mermaid's Purse into the oiled-canvas of the gas envelope before he could be pulled away. He rose up into the air like a rocket himself to look down upon the confused and angry faces of the *picaroons*, including the one that climbed to the top of the cutter's gas bag.

For some stupid reason, Algie waved goodbye.

They responded by firing their guns. He was swiftly rising up out of their range, but he felt two sudden stings, one in his right thigh and the other across his ribs on the left side. That felt like someone set a red-hot poker onto the flesh and bone under his arm.

Algie was shocked. All of Dale Daring's opponents were too busy leaping to safety or dying ignobly to take pot shots at the boy hero.

There must be something wrong with these air pirates.

1 "Dynamite", Mandarin
2 "Fulminate of Mercury", Mandarin
3 "Bastard", literally "turtle's egg" (Mandarin)
4 "Your mother is friendly with the English!" Scots Gaelic

TWO

28th of December 1888
Portsmouth, England

"Are you sure you can do this?" There was a definite quiver in Deirdre's voice, though what caused it Algie couldn't say. It could be fear from their being on the roof of the four-story dormitory building in the center of the Friends of Children compound. Or it could be the cold. It was a few days after a giftless Christmas and snow had piled up nine inches deep on the tile roof. Whatever the cause was, he was going to get them off this roof in the next few minutes.

"I've been preparing all week," Algie said. "If I'm not ready now, I'll never be."

Deirdre sighed, the sound of a long-suffering soul. She did not deserve the kind of life she endured here at the orphanage. Algie had promised the both of them would escape, just as Dale Daring had fled the French prison in *Dale Daring and the Island of Devils*.

Algie applied all his craft and cunning in his preparations. He traded a bird skull and a fist full of blue jay feathers to Eustace Penderghast for the screwdriver the older boy had nicked from the custodian. Stephen, Declan, and Morgan, thick-necked bullies and snitches the lot of them, were bought off with tins of sweets. Mrs. Billew thought candy was a terrible extravagance for foundling children and impeded their growth as contributing members of society. From reading the August Vogel books, Algie had learned to make *moulage,* a treat not for the weak of stomach. The secret process was to take scraps of bread, chew them up, and pack them in a discarded bootblack tin. In three days, the chemicals in his spit broke down the starches into a kind of sugar.

Only in a home completely without sugar could pre-chewed and partially digested food be considered a treat. At Mrs. Billew's Friends of Children home, Algie had a successful black market economy based upon it.

So he and Deirdre collected warm outer clothes, extra socks, mittens, scarves, loaf ends, assorted crackers, bits of salt pork wrapped in greasy paper, flint and tinder, broken candles, cleanish handkerchiefs, and five shillings three pence for their flight from Mrs. Billew's domain. With luck, they could even make Lee-on-the-Solent on the mainland.

For the more difficult breach of the security of the quad surrounding the dorm, Algie built many of the devices to his own specifications. Using the pilfered screwdriver, he had removed four heavy wire coat hooks from separate cloak rooms. Screwing them into a broken-off length of mop handle gave him the start of a serviceable grappling hook. Springs and struts cannibalized from his bed and mounted on a wooden shelf bracket from the back of the library became a serviceable crossbow-like launcher for the hook. In the upper story storerooms were a few windows that no one would open before spring. Deirdre and he collected yards and yards of sash cord and pulleys from inside the walls that would allow them to set up something like a breeches buoy across the courtyard.

It was midnight and Algie was beginning to feel a little shaky himself. He hefted the grapple launcher in his hands and pondered the chances that it would do anything besides explosively disassemble itself when the time came.

"The longer we stay here," Algie said in what he hoped was a heroic voice, "the more chances our enemies have to thwart us."

He wasn't sure if that was a direct quote from one of the Dale

Daring novels, but it should have been. Deirdre gave him a fragile smile and nodded her agreement. Or she shivered up and down in a meaningful way. They were both in danger of freezing to the spot if they didn't move soon.

Algie set the first coil of sash cord at his feet so it could unwind freely. He tied the end to the grappling hook and jammed the shaft into the launcher. The springs complained as they stretched and the struts clinked as they folded into their tightest form. It felt like he was setting a bear trap, with only a fifty percent chance of it locking into place. Algie hoped he would still have his fingers when he was done.

"Here goes nothing," he muttered.

The hook launcher fired with the sound of a cat falling into a grand piano. The grappling hook flew more or less like an arrow, wobbling along a high arc towards the chimney stack of the building across the courtyard. It flew over the clay pipes and disappeared on the other side.

Algie could have been knocked down with a feather. Everything had worked exactly as he had planned.

Deirdre beamed up at him and he tried to put on a face that would say that he never had a doubt. Unfortunately, that expression and all others were frozen out by the one that said: "Gawd, it's cold out here. I hope we won't die."

He bent low and collected the coil of sash cord and began reeling it in. Algie could hear the wire prongs scratching along the slate roof and then banging repeatedly on the brick chimney as he pulled up the slack. One could only hope there was no one awake in the upper story that might notice the racket coming through the attic.

Eventually, they saw the mop handle peek over the top. Algie pulled the cord more and more gently, treating it like a fish that still did not have the hook set in its mouth. Two of the prongs caught on the other side of the chimney.

Algie pulled the line taut. The hook didn't move.

He planted his feet and pulled with all his weight. The cobbled-together grapple might as well have been an anchor, it was that firmly in place. He handed the line over to Deirdre.

"Here, keep the tension on while I secure our end."

Deirdre looked as excited as he felt. Her blue eyes glistened with more than windburn and when she smiled, her cheeks looked like two red apples. He was so glad he could make her happy.

Algie carefully scaled the icy roof with the remainder of the coiled cord in one hand. Once he got to the peak, he pitched the line over the chimney stack and secured it the best he could. Not being very good at knots, he wrapped it around and tied it several times over. He leaned his weight on it then and it dipped just a little bit. Being maybe a story or two taller than the other end, the line pitched about twenty degrees. This would let them slide gently down to the other end.

If there were no problems, that is.

He climbed down carefully to where Deirdre and the rest of their equipment awaited.

"Well, so far, so good," he said.

"Isn't that what the man who fell out of an eighth-floor window said the first seven floors?"

Algie frowned.

"I have gone to great lengths to build every possible safety feature into this," he said.

"I know," Deirdre replied. "I was just trying to be funny."

Algie shrugged.

"I think that was the wrong joke for the situation."

Without further conversation, he took up the conveyor carriage and set it on the line above his head. Calling it a carriage made it sound much finer than it actually was. Primarily, it was two pulleys from inside a window sash mounted on a block of wood. A wooden coat hanger hung below that to act as a hand grip. Three discarded leather belts acted as a safety harness to wrap around the rider's torso.

"I'll go first," Algie said. "Just in case there's any problems."

Deirdre scowled.

"And what do you expect me to do if *you* have a problem?"

"I want you to climb back through that window and get back in your bed." He pointed towards the dormer that led down into the girls' half of the dormitory. "I don't see a point in both of us getting in trouble."

"But I couldn't do that!"

That was Deidre's problem: She was the most caring and compassionate person he had ever met. More than the priests who visited the home regularly and disregarded the stories the children whispered to them. Certainly, more than the attendants. Algie believed she was more compassionate than his own late mother. Definitely more caring than Mrs. Billew.

So, she was always coming up on the short end of the deal, cutting her portion at the table in half to give seconds to another. There were other things that happened in the girls' half after lights out that Deirdre wouldn't even whisper about. Algie only knew it wasn't reading bedtime stories and braiding each other's hair. He couldn't allow her to be hurt any more.

He hung his half of their bundled provisions over his shoulders like saddlebags and slipped the leather harness under his arms. He cinched it as tight as was comfortable. He then grasped the hand holds and, with a smile over his shoulder, said:

"Wish me luck!" He tossed her the spool of kite string that would let her pull the carriage back to her side when he was done.

"Good luck!"

He kicked off and was sliding downhill into open space. He started picking up speed almost immediately. With a fifteen to twenty foot difference between the two anchor points, the incline was fairly steep. As he crossed the midway point, at a pace that could outrun any dray horse, he realized the one safety feature he had not installed.

Brakes.

He sped down the rope towards the other building. Not the other roof or chimney, as planned, but an oncoming brick wall just above a third story window. Extra weight and the moisture of the snow allowed the rope to stretch significantly.

He slammed face-first into the brick wall at the speed of a postal express locomotive. There was a moment of exquisite pain and a display of pyrotechnics across the dark red bricks. He seemed to bounce backwards right after that.

He lost his grip at the same time. He fell free until he hit the end of the leather safety harness. His weight and the sudden jolt tightened the leather loop around his chest even more. Algie's eyes went wide as he realized another major design flaw. With the harness constricting his ribs, there would be no way he could take in another breath.

He franticly worked his fingers under the belting to loosen it. His mass and momentum, unconcerned over little things like breathing, slammed him back into the building again. This time the back of his head struck first.

Algie danced in the air like a murderer on a gibbet, unmindful of everything but his next breath of air. He heard the crashing of glass and realized he'd kicked in the window below him. There was a screech and he felt a hand grasp his ankle after the window flew open.

An angular, hatchet sharp face in a cloud of salt and pepper hair looked up at him and screamed his name. He didn't recognize her at first in her nightgown and green and black dressing gown. She looked like something that would descend from a thunderstorm in a divine fury to avenge some crime against God and society.

It was Mrs. Billew.

Miss Robicheaux, the school's French teacher, appeared beside her, also in her *dishabille*. She would have been so proud that he retained that bit of French even as the oxygen was cut off to his brain.

Somebody on the other end must have cut the rope. Without warning, the leather loosened around his chest and he fell into the less-than-loving arms of Mrs. Billew.

*

Deirdre sat in the stiff wooden chair before Mrs. Billew's desk. She sniffled into her plain white handkerchief prodigiously, weeping even though she was the one that had turned herself in to the home's authorities. She had also caught cold standing on the roof with Algie.

Algie opted to stand beside her, his one hand on the wooden back of the chair for support, and to take off some of his weight. Mr. Thackeray, the handyman, had already applied twenty strokes to his nethers with a wire rug beater. It stung, but a daily beating of some sort seemed to be the price of admission to the Friends of Children home. That was why he and Deidre had been off looking for a better class of friends.

"You, Mr. Piggrem," Mrs. Billew declared, "are incorrigible."

She was understandably upset about the escape attempt and the pilferage it took to prepare for it. Breaking a third story window was also a whole new level of deviltry, but Eustace implied that interrupting the headmistress and Mlle. Robicheaux was what really got Algie in trouble. He had no idea what the two women were talking about at midnight in Mrs. Billew's chambers, but it must have been horribly important.

"In the four weeks that you have been here," Mrs. Billew continued, "you have come before my desk several times."

She looked over the papers in his permanent record with her face contorted in an expression of resolute contempt.

"First, you and young Derrell Walters were caught beating each other over the head with mop handles."

"We were playing Robin Hood and Little John on the bridge. With quarter staves. It was in our reading that week."

Algie grimaced and tried to discretely rearrange his trousers' seat. Standing like this was hardly any more comfortable than sitting.

"Of course you were." Mrs. Billew looked up another entry. "And what were you thinking when you and Kermit Hermes decided to scale the walls of the boys' dormitories with the aid of the heavy winter drapes."

"Well, I thought they were attached to the walls much more firmly." Algie tried a smile with the quip, but Mrs. Billew wasn't being charmed. "We were the Three Musketeers storming Cardinal Richelieu's fortress."

Mrs. Billew looked over the top of her half-moon glasses.

"As per usual, you were a day late and two Musketeers short. Mr. Thackeray went to a great deal of trouble and expense re-mounting those drapes."

"I'm sorry," Algie said.

"Just because we're a charitable organization, it doesn't

mean our books have to go that deeply into the red."

"Pardon me, ma'am?" He had no idea what colors had to do with him being in trouble.

"'In the red' means that your shenanigans are disruptive, disrespectful, and very, very expensive."

She leafed through more pages in the file folder. Bills, they looked like. Algie risked a glance over at Deirdre, who flashed a brave, but moist, smile back at him.

"Then there was your Dick Daring misadventure on my rose trellis," the headmistress added. She picked up her fountain pen to make some notes.

"Dale," said Algie.

"Pardon?"

"Dale Daring… Boy Airship… Pilot…" Algie regretted opening his mouth as soon as he did.

"Of course."

She pursed and relaxed her lips several times, as if she had a bad bit of *moulage* in her mouth, but she was too lady-like to spit it out.

"And then there was last night," she said. She paused to frown at the two children. "Last night…"

"We are really terribly sorry," Deirdre blurted out.

Algie nodded in agreement, but stopped abruptly when he felt it in his rear-end.

"You vandalized our home," Mrs. Billew said, "you risked your life, *and* hers. You literally dropped into my bedchamber through a broken window."

She tapped the tip of her fountain pen nervously on the papers before her. She was leaving dark marks on his permanent record with each tap.

"The other children here, they have already started to whisper about you as if you were some kind of mythical figure. There is no room for a hero in a home like this."

Algie felt his stomach tying up in knots. He had made a terrible mistake, and now Deirdre and he were going to pay for it. He had no idea how horrible it would be.

"Ma'am, we just wanted to go home," he finally said with great difficulty. His voice cracked as he thought of his mother now gone just like his father.

"But Algernon," Mrs. Billew said, her voice suddenly sweet, "you know that you don't have a home any more, don't you?"

"I know!" Algie's eyes stung from tears about to break free. He wanted to be strong and heroic, but he was just an eleven-year-old boy. He looked over at Deirdre who was starting to cry harder herself.

"You can't just go live on the street," Mrs. Billew continued. "You would starve, or you might be stolen by terrible people who would do horrible things to you."

He was pretty sure that had happened to him already. This time, he was wise enough to say nothing, just stare straight ahead and try to control his ragged breathing. Deirdre was sobbing beside him.

"You've been wanting an adventure, young Master Piggrem, and we will happily provide one for you."

Mrs. Billew smiled at them both like a crocodile about to attack. "How do you feel about a trip to Australia?

THREE

16th of August 1889
The High Silk Road,
west of Hami, China

Much of the rest of the airship battle was a blur for Algie. He was still on his tether, swinging every which way as the *Wu Zetian* levelled out and banked port wise away from the cruiser behind them. The armored airship was not prepared for their sudden maneuver. It pursued, but still at a level with the *muhafez* cutter. The pilot was clever enough to bear hard starboard to pass behind the smaller craft.

The two *picaroon* vessels were little more than ten meters apart when the Mermaid's Purse detonated. Algie hung perhaps two hundred meters away, but completely exposed on the end of his rope. Chinese fireworks were never meant to be viewed at the same altitude.

The first explosion sounded like the sky had cracked open. A ball of yellow and orange flames spread across the top of the cutter's gas envelope. The *picaroon* who had scaled the rigging to dislodge the Mermaid's Purse had been set on fire and thrown clear of the ship. He descended like a shooting star to the desert below.

The afterimage of that blast hung before Algie's eyes for several seconds until he finally blinked it away.

The jellied spirits Feng Po had mentioned before burned in discrete puddles across the oiled silk of the envelope with blue-white flames. More of the flaming goo had splashed across the hull of the German cruiser and the gunmen on the exterior catwalks. In one swing by, Algie saw a man with his clothes set alight. He and his friends franticly tried to slap out the fire with their bare hands.

As Algie swung the other way, the phlogiston, the pure essence of fire in gaseous form that held airships in the sky, ignited. Algie felt as if he'd been swatted by a red-hot iron rug beater. He swung forward and spun on the line like a top. Every few seconds, he came back around to see the disabled cutter.

What had once been an airship with two dozen souls on board was now a rowboat dropped from a great height with a burning sail.

He spun faster until he squeezed his eyes shut to avoid puking his breakfast out over the Chinese landscape. He could still hear shouts in Ships' Cant, gunfire, and distant explosions. His leg and side felt like they were on fire. Everything worthwhile seemed to be draining out of his head. After several long minutes, he felt himself being reeled in by his climbing harness. Multiple hands grasped him and pulled him over the railing and set him on the bamboo deck. His head still swam, feeling like he was swinging back and forth, even though he was now set in one place.

A distant voice called out:

"This is a first! I've never seen a fish reel in a boy like this before!"

The joke was repeated in Chinese and the boys around him all laughed. It was easier, for the moment, for Algie to simply listen.

"So, are you alive?" he heard Feng Po say.

He opened his eyes with some difficulty.

"You tell me."

Feng Po produced a damascene blade with a flourish. Algie felt drawn to the waves of dark and bright steel on the knife and the sun gleaming off of it, as he was pulled into that iron pool eyes first. He lost track of it as Feng Po cut away Algie's shirt and trousers from his wounds.

"Aw, this is just a scratch," he told Algie as he exposed the injury on the boy's chest. "It barely broke the skin here."

Feng Po tore off a strip of the shirt to blot at the bullet wound just below Algie's right hip.

"Now, this one," his mentor observed, "took out a bit more of a bite. But there's a hole going in, and another hole going out. That's the best way of getting shot if you're going to be doing that sort of thing."

"I tried my best," Algie murmured.

Feng Po both shook his head and shuddered at once. He looked like a dog shaking itself off after a bath.

"That you did." Feng Po laid a parental hand on his shoulder, a gentle but firm grasp. "If you ever do anything so boneheaded again, *chong wu*, I will cut your tether myself and leave you to the *picaroons*."

Algie tried to laugh, but it came out as just a change of his breathing. Peng, his best friend of all the *Lǎoshǔ*, appeared at his right side. He babbled at him in a mix of Chinese, French, and many Ships' Cant words he hadn't learned yet. They clasped hands even as Algie's eyes started to close all by themselves. Somehow, he mustered the strength to fumble through the remains of his clothes and give Peng the red rubber ball and his last tin of *moulage*.

Feng Po opened one of Algie's eyelids with his thumb and peered in at him. With his hand pressed to Algie's forehead, the first mate scowled and began barking Ships' Cant orders.

"What about the *muhafez*?" Algie muttered. "The *picaroons*?"

"Don't worry about them, Pig. You have a table reserved for you in the sick bay."

Feng Po McLaren lifted him up as the other *Lǎoshǔ* laid out a jute and linen hammock beneath him. They placed him on it and crossed his arms across his chest. Then his friends wrapped him up, too much like a burial shroud, and began to lower him down the rigging to the ship below. He could see through the mesh well enough to make out two fires and columns of smoke where he and the *Wu Zetian* met their first air pirates.

*

Algie woke on one of the padded surgery tables deep below

decks. The interior walls, like the outer hull, were red-lacquered silk festooned with yellow and black Chinese script. The equivalent signage in French announced he was in the medical bay. The anatomical charts over the apothecary's workbench clearly reinforced that.

He smacked his lips. They were dry, and he had the bitter aftertaste of laudanum in his mouth. He could feel pain in several parts of his body, but he really didn't care. After all the pain, rage, and terror of the battle, Algie was amazingly unemotional. He simply had a mild curiosity about what would happen next.

The doctor had his back to him, and ground away earnestly with a mortar pestle at the work station against the bulkhead. He was dressed in the green and black tunic that was part of the crew uniform, not the white shirtsleeves and dark waistcoat Algie remembered as the doctor's uniform. As he pulled ingredients from the many small drawers in the cabinet above the table, he maintained a rapid sing-song monologue in Chinese. The stranger also had a long black braid that hung down his back, just like Feng Po's.

That seemed wrong.

Dr. Koslowski was a proud Pole, a graduate of some ancient university in Prague. The three or four times Algie had been in sick bay before, the doctor had come just short of pulling his diploma out for proof. Algie didn't think the gnarled old doctor knew more than a few words of Chinese.

"So, our boy adventurer still lives," someone said with a pleased tone to their voice. A pleased Scottish tone. "I was beginning to worry about you, Pig."

If what he remembered was real, Algie himself would be worried once the laudanum wore off.

"They shot me," Algie said.

Feng Po pulled up a stool so that he could squat down pretty much face to face with Algie on the table.

"If it makes you feel any better," he said, "I'm quite sure that you killed them all."

Algie scowled, most likely in a lopsided fashion because it felt like there were more drugs in one side of his face than the other. He had never thought he would end up killing somebody today. Dale Daring and August Vogel fought air pirates and anarchists all the time, but somehow it always seemed that the bad guys leapt to safety just at the last moment.

Those that did wind up dead usually did so from their own evil actions. Algie remembered the *muhafez* that was grabbing for the Mermaid's Purse as it went off. He came apart in the blast and the pieces caught fire. There is no way to pretend he made a safe landing in the rocks and brush below.

The old man at the work station finally turned around, and Algie could see it was Huang Yu Tu, the man who had shouted out his devotion to the Silk Empress just before the battle. He held a wooden bowl in one hand and a roll of bandages in the other.

"*Nǐ hǎo, Xiǎo Zhū*," Huang beamed. He burbled out a long string of Chinese afterwards that had no meaning to him.

"I got the first part," Algie murmured. "What did he say after 'hello, little pig'?"

"He says he's heard of your exploits," Feng Po translated. "He is sure your parents look down from the heavens with pride."

"*Xiè xiè.*" Algie smiled and nodded at Huang, but he wasn't entirely sure that his mother would approve of his violent actions. His father, as a combat engineer for Her Majesty's Marines, would have understood, though he might have thought twelve was a bit young to be starting a soldier's profession. Algie shifted to find a comfortable position and twisted his upper thigh, the one with two holes in it. He screeched in a very non-heroic fashion.

Master Huang's round face turned from all smiles to a scowl of concern. He spat out a line of very-angry-sounding Chinese.

Feng Po translated again:

"He says the opium is wearing off already, that he told the Western doctor that poison was no good!"

The old man put down the bowl and bandages and retrieved a small black lacquered box from a cubby on his work table. He opened the red and gold lid and held up perhaps a dozen silver needles for Algie to inspect.

"This is for pain," Feng Po translated.

"Yes, it is," Algie protested. "That's going to hurt!"

Algie had heard the other *Lǎoshǔ* tell of the needle medicine that the old man practiced. He didn't see where puncturing people with pins over and over to let the sickness out could ever work. It certainly wasn't something Algie could stand. He had almost fainted when Koslowski gave him the Jenner vaccine a few weeks back.

"You jumped into empty air with five kilos of explosives in your mitts," Feng Po scoffed. "Are you trying to tell me that you're frightened of a little pin prick?"

"Wellll…"

"Would you like me to tell all of the other boys that you're frightened of a little pin prick?"

Algie took a deep breath. What would Dale Daring do if faced with multiple needles like this? Then again, considering what the boy airship pilot had done for him so far today, maybe Algie should do some of his own thinking.

"Those will really make my leg stop hurting?"

"*Zhēn cì*[5] medicine has been practiced in the Middle Kingdom for centuries," his mentor said. "It must have worked on somebody."

Algie took a deep breath and steeled himself for the pain.

"All right, let's get on with it."

Feng Po gestured to Huang and the old man came up to the surgery table with his box of needles. With his fingertips, Huang traced out lines on Algie's leg as if he were plotting a course on a chart. All the while, he kept up a pleasant-sounding babble in Chinese.

"What's he saying?" Algie asked.

"He's trying to explain *zhēn cì*," Feng Po said. "He says all pain and sickness comes from an imbalance of *chi*. By placing the needles in the passageways of the body, he can unblock the *chi*, or get it to flow to places it's needed."

"So, this *chi* is like my blood or something?"

Feng Po's mustache twitched from side to side as he came up with a response.

"It's supposed to be some sort of invisible energy, like your soul, I guess."

"He's manipulating my soul?" Algie tensed up, which caused his leg to pain him like a red-hot poker. Huang scowled up at him and then had a short angry exchange with Feng Po in Chinese.

The old man slapped Algie's leg and went back to plotting while muttering some very irritated remarks, at least from the tone of them.

"What did he say?"

"He said," Feng Po replied, "quit thinking like a stupid missionary and sit still. Then he said something about your head. And a melon. And an over-amorous raccoon dog. It's hard to translate into English."

"Fine," Algie said. "Let's get it done with."

After his mentor translated, Huang picked up the first needle and pierced Algie's leg. It was a swift throwing gesture, like lancing his leg with a tiny harpoon. Algie was amazed that, with the thickness of the needle, it barely hurt. Huang looked up and Algie responded with the best smile he could muster. In quick succession, the old man stuck maybe two dozen more needles into his thigh.

Huang twisted each needle back and forth rapidly, like spinning the tiniest bow drill to start a fire. Algie started to feel a funny tingling in his leg.

With a comic glean in his eye, Huang leaned over and delivered a single poke with his finger to the meaty part of Algie's leg between the two wounds. If he had not been watching, Algie would never have known it had happened. Algie was shocked.

"Nothing," he said with a shrug.

With a laugh, Huang Yu Tu removed the needles and dressed Algie's wounds with what Fang Po said to be Four Herb Chinese Medicine. The wound on his side was simple, nothing more than a long deep scratch across his ribs. The bandages had to go all the way around his chest, but they stayed where they were put. The in and out wounds had to be packed with the greenish-brown herbal paste and then wrapped with more clean linen. Huang wrapped the dressings around the leg several times and across the waist to hold everything in place.

Algie stood on his good leg for this with the First Mate holding up his right arm for balance. There stood Algie, with one pants leg and a bit of the middle left to him, and no shirt at all when he heard a sharp report in the doorway.

Everyone in the sick bay turned their head in that direction. Jakinda, Mme. Streif's chief Conversor, had just snapped open her iron fan and was now waving it serenely at her face. She wore a red day dress, not much different from what his mother would have worn before her suffragette days, but made of flame red silk and jet beads. It matched her red lips and black hair. She was a beauty, but of a form the Devil himself would take if he were up to mischief, as his mother often said of her actress friends. Algie felt painfully aware of how small and battered he looked.

"So, is our daring young hero going to recover?" she asked. Her voice was sweet and she half-smiled as she spoke.

Among the *Lǎoshǔ*, the Conversors were believed to be something like witches, more cunning than real women and totally without human feeling. That might be true, but it was far more likely that his friends knew nothing of real women.

"No doubt about that," Feng Po said. "He has been properly patched together by good Master Huang. A much better job than that over-stuffed Prussian sausage could have done."

Jakinda smiled in the way women often did when speaking to First Mate McLaren: mildly charmed, but not at all convinced.

"I'll be sure not to tell him that," she replied.

Huang and Feng Po had a quick conversation. When they finished, Huang turned to the Conversor and bowed. She returned the bow, but just a hair or two deeper than his.

"*Xiè xiè, Shīfù Huang*," she said. Then she turned back to Algie. "Mme. Streif would be pleased to have the honor of your presence at her next Salon, provided you are feeling up to the exertion."

His mother, as a writer of philosophical science essays, frequently attended Salons in Portsmouth or even as far away as

London. She often said they were a great honor and a dreadful tribulation, but she was always happy when she returned. He would love to see what a real Salon would be like.

"I would be honored," he replied and bowed as deeply as he dared in his precarious position.

"Just avoid Mr. Liu at that party," Feng Po warned Algie. "I'm sure he's upset that you broke his ship."

She curtsied to him with the slightest inclination of her head with her fan set lightly over her heart.

"I will inform Mme. Streif." She held up a finger, signaling a pause for thought. "You might want to consider a new pair of pants."

"That might be difficult," Feng Po said, "considering the bandages and the extra holes in his legs."

"Then, we will secure something a little less restrictive," she said. "Chabi will deliver it to the First Mate's cabin. We will set a date once we have moored at the Turfan caravanserai for repairs, Master Piggrem."

She withdrew down the hall in swish of silk and underskirts. Algie felt a little breathless.

Feng Po guffawed and gently mussed Algie's hair.

"You're moving up in the world," he said, "and all you had to do was jump off the ship. There's so many others here that I'd like to recommend that strategy for advancement."

5 "Acupuncture", Mandarin

FOUR

18th of August 1889
The High Silk Road,
the Turfan Depression

The *Wu Zetian* limped through the sky like a wounded albatross on her way to the nearest stop that held a dock for extensive repairs. Algie was allowed to spend most of that time in the gardens of silk flowers and bamboo pagodas on the foc'sle deck. He and Dieter Euler were the two most badly injured of the crew. The spirit engine tech had put out a fire with a rock wool blanket and his bare hands in the engine room, making him almost as much of a hero as "*Xiǎo Zhū*, young Master Pig".

They were guests of Mme. Streif and her Conversors. The two young men were all of the ordinary crew ever welcomed into Women's Territory.

Algie sat in the shade of the flying jib sail and a forest of twining man-made flowers and watched the landscape below. Low scrub and hills melted away into red sandstone desert as the airship crept along for three days. Algie ate biscuits, drank tea and chicken broth, and was tutored on his French.

Dieter took lessons, too. It seemed the Germans were no more likely to learn the language of the European courts than the Americans. If they were lucky, Jakinda handled their lessons. She spoke English and German, along with a half-dozen other languages it seemed, so both Algie and Dieter could be prompted in their native tongues. The three of them could spend a lazy afternoon engaged in polite social conversation or repeating back and forth the parts of the ship and the objects around them.

Lessons with Ayotunde were quite different. Her people were the Yoruba of Nigeria and, though she spoke nearly as many languages as Jakinda, he had been told that none of those included English. She was familiar with both German and the physical sciences, so many of her lessons included words like sublimation, convection, and thermodynamics. Algie would blunder through lessons, occasionally getting caught up through Dieter's halting English.

It made him feel like an idiot.

Sometimes, his mind would drift away and he would fixate on some unusual detail of the Conversors' Garden, like the ornate carvings of the pergolas or thousands of silk flowers that sprouted amidst leaves and vines. A few times, he gazed unthinking at Ayotunde. He couldn't help himself; there was no one he ever seen like her in Portsmouth. Her skin was brown as a nut, her hair looked like a tight cap of lamb's wool, though she usually kept it covered in a brightly colored scarf. She always wore elegant dresses of finest silk in colors of orange or gold. In a way he would have never thought before meeting her, she was fascinating. When she caught him staring, she gazed back at him with half-lidded eyes and a mysterious half-smile.

Lessons then shifted to two important phrases in French: "It is impolite to stare" and "I am sure your mother raised you better than that." The latter phrase always caught Algie with a twinge of guilt.

Airships of multiple nationalities passed them in both directions during those days, many as badly damaged as the *Wu Zetian* in encounters with *picaroons*. The Conversors demonstrated their value calling across to other ships in the crews' native tongues with voices as loud as foghorns. Nelinha spoke Portuguese to the Brazilian craft. Ayotunde communicated with a crippled Egyptian merchant in Arabic.

Others called out in French, and Japanese, and Russian.

The youngest of the Conversors joined Algie, Dieter, and Jakinda on the last day. Her name was Chabi, and she was a Mongol. Algie had read about the Mongols in one of the August Vogel books, "Hunt for the Death Worm," and some of his histories. He always imagined them as slant-eyed, screeching warriors on horseback, all long hair, bows, and mustaches. For some reason, he never thought there were any Mongol women.

Chabi had no mustache, and she showed no signed sweeping across the steppes on horseback. He had no idea how old she was, but she was the only one of the Conversors that was actually shorter than Algie. Her skin was paler than his, but her hair was as black and shiny as fresh tar. She favored sky-blue dresses, but in the same style as the upper crust women in England. Again, he didn't know what to think of this one.

She drifted towards the bowsprit like a cloud and rested her arms on the forward railing. She stared ahead at the Turfan caravanserai the *Wu Zetian* approached, and the red and orange mountains beyond that. Even at a height of three hundred meters above, the broken back ridge looked like it was capped with flames when hit by the afternoon sun. Chabi spoke after a while, in French, quietly relating a story Algie couldn't follow. Jakinda was kind enough to translate.

"These are the Flaming Mountains," the Basque woman said, "They are the boundary between Xingjiang and the Taklamakan desert. The Uyghur people who live here tell the story of a brave young man who killed a dragon that threatened their people. The Uyghur warrior knocked the beast out of the sky, and it burst into flames as it fell. It broke into pieces that still burn today. That's what we see now."

She looked over her shoulder and smiled, blurting out something that must have been very clever. Jakinda chuckled and nodded, but said nothing.

"Excuse me," Algie said. "I didn't catch that."

"Oh sorry, I forgot." Jakinda seemed mildly irritated that Algie's French hadn't improved enough to understand. "She said that it is a much more interesting world filled with heroes and dragon bones than just sandstone and dust."

Algie looked out past her at the long vistas of reddish stone and dust that spread out before the prow. The tiny green miracle of the Turfan caravanserai perched on the horizon. He could just barely make out the line of *qanats*, round wells connected to an underground aqueduct every hundred meters or so, which led down from the mountains to the north. They looked to be punched in the desert floor by a gigantic sewing machine.

"That's nonsense," a familiar voice said above them all. "They're flaming bricks, don't you know anything?"

Everyone in the silk garden craned their necks to look up at the same time. Feng Po dangled from a rope slung under his buttocks like a seat, the hemp above and below him clutched in both hands to hold him in place. He loosened his grip enough to descend to about three meters above the deck.

"In *The Journey to the West*, the Monkey King was thrown into a heavenly furnace to teach him some manners. He was quite irate with the treatment and kicked the furnace into a million pieces. That's what you're looking at, burning bricks, not some dead dragon."

Jakinda scowled at the First Mate. That fan of hers cracked open like a gunshot.

"And speaking of bad manners," she said, "you know that no man is to set foot in Mme. Streif's garden without an invitation."

"Do my feet look like they're anywhere near your bloody deck?"

Jakinda took in a breath to respond, but Feng Po beat her to it.

"I'm not here to argue with you, as entertaining as that might be, but to invite Pig to watch us dock from Fish's Mouth, if he would like."

Algie looked at the rigging that ran up from the gunwales to the observation deck and calculated his chances.

"That looks like a long way up," he said.

"Oh, don't worry about that."

Feng Po whistled and the *Lǎoshǔ* flung down a rope. A padded rescue yoke dangled from the end about a meter above the bamboo deck.

Feng Po cocked his head at the grim expression on Jakinda's face.

"We promise we'll be gentle." Feng Po turned a broad grin at Algie that curled the ends of his mustache practically into his eyes. "It's the best view in the ship… as long as you promise not to jump off again."

Algie shook his head.

"I promise I'll never do that again."

"What does the doctor say?" Jakinda asked.

"*Sifu* Huang says the leg is healing well and should be fine as long as we don't jostle it around too much. Dr. Koslowski is still considering amputation." Feng Po shrugged as he dangled. "I say we split it down the middle."

"May I please, ma'am?" Algie pleaded.

Jakinda relented and her frown turned into a funny up-and-down curl like waves on the sea.

"Very well," she said, "but if you are well enough to do this, you are well enough to start taking exercise once we touch ground."

"Whatever you say, ma'am!" Algie stood up from his chair and hopped over to the line.

As Algie slipped the yoke under his arms, Dieter took more tea and a date from the tray. The tech still needed to use his less-burned left hand.

"You go up," the German said. "I look the sights from here."

He waggled his eyebrows towards Jakinda and Chabi and then winked as he popped the date into his mouth. He looked quite happy where he was.

"Thank you very much, Mistress Jakinda," Algie said.

"Just don't hurt yourself," she replied.

Feng Po gave out a little whistle and shouted at the hands above:

"*Corda lah, Lǎoshǔ!*"

The line went taut and Algie's feet lifted off the deck as Feng Po shimmied up his own rope ahead of him. Chabi gave a gentile little wave.

"*Au revoir, Mssr. Cochon!*[6]" she called out.

Algie waved back and then rose up above the silk garden and the carved wooden pagodas like an angel in an over-ambitious Christmas pantomime.

*

Due to the desert crosswinds, the airship had to circle around the entire settlement to approach the docking tower in the right direction. It wasn't an easy task with one wing and an engine gone, and no ballast besides, but the *Lǎoshǔ* laid into the task with enthusiasm. Three of the boys hung from the free end of the jib's boom and swung it from one side of the ship to the other like a faire ground ride. The wind filled the triangular sail and allowed the *Wu Zetian* to tack against it until the order came time to switch the other way.

Algie saw Turfan laid out below as a green rectangle in a sea of tan and red, with a small clot of orchards and fields surrounding the *qanat* canals. Dale Daring and August Vogel had many of their adventures in caravanserai, rest stops for ancient trade caravans that became way stations for the airship traffic between East and West. In the center of the complex, camels and horses gathered around an open fountain. Stables and other mud brick buildings circled around that central plaza. Stately manor houses and gardens lined the edges just inside the walls. Something that looked like a church occupied the rise to the north of the town. An odd-looking golden tower, a squat rounded cone almost like a teardrop, sat next to it. As the sun set behind it, Algie heard a man's voice, a high plaintive wail, ring out from the top of that tower.

"A call to prayer," Feng Po explained. "Folks in these parts are Moslems, instead of proper Buddhists."

"How could that happen?" Algie asked. "Here in China?"

"That's the way of the world in these parts. People wind up where the Silk Road drops them. An English piglet on a Chinese airship crammed with Americans and Europeans should be able to appreciate that."

Feng Po excused himself to shout more orders into the voice pipe. The ship took a wobbling pass at the golden tower and made way against easterly headwinds towards the airship works to the west of the caravanserai walls.

Their target gleamed in the low-angled sun. The repair tower was a futuristic nineteenth-century construction of riveted steel that straddled a medieval world of brick and wood below it. At thirty-five meters tall, it held the docking cradle at a height set for the *Wu Zetian* to simply drop in. As damaged as she was, of course, there was no "simple" to it.

The airship chugged west of the tower under the First Mate's direction and slowly slid over the generators and metal tanks that filled much of the space around the tower's base. Workman looked up with expressions of surprise and wonder as the ungainly combination of winged fish and imperial junk flew overhead. Algie couldn't help himself again and waved to the people below. Some waved back with smiles on their faces. Some looked shocked at the airship's damage. Algie was having the time of his life.

The engines cut off and the starboard propeller wound down to silence. Now, Algie could hear the sounds of tools on metal and machinery below, along with shouts in languages he couldn't decipher. The wind caught the *Wu Zetian* and she drifted towards the tower and its cradle at what felt to be a snail's pace. As she was slowly pushed into the right position, the crew and *Lǎoshǔ* swarmed the rigging to stow the fins and sails for docking. Three of the crew pulled the starboard wing shut and lashed it against the control ring so it wouldn't strike the tower when they came into position. More of the crew struggled to furl the keel fin, as it had been damaged in the battle and still had the broken port motor strut lashed to it. Algie heard much swearing and straining coming from the underside of the ship.

A crew of dock men in dirty blue work uniforms lined the far side of the cradle. They looked to be about half locals, burly tanned men with thick beards. One of them was even a ginger. The rest seemed to be from anywhere an airship had touched down on Earth. Each of the crew had a coil of rope at their feet. As the *Wu Zetian* drifted within range, the dock men let fly, their hawsers arcing across to the ship like snakes striking out at prey. The *Wu Zetian*'s crew swarmed the starboard rails and secured the lines around stanchions from bow to stern. Algie marveled at the organization in the action without any previous planning. This was their job and they did it without any waste of time or energy.

The dock boss, the one with the yellow tabard over his blue tunic and steeplejack pants, shouted out orders in Ships' Cant. The dock men took up the slack on their end and pulled in unison, shouting as they did:

"CORDA LAH!"

The men and boys aboard the *Wu Zetian* loosed the lines on the stanchions, pulled a few inches, and snugged them down again. They shouted back as one:

"LAH!"

Six inches at a time they nudged the airship into her berth. Workers below the cradle and on the tower above the gas envelope called out directions.

"CORDA LAH!"

Though airships could be as big as a house, many of them were as delicate as a dragonfly's wings. These men were going to place the *Wu Zetian* in her berth like a sleeping babe.

"LAH!"

After a few minutes of crawling sideways like an inchworm, the *Wu Zetian* floated square above the cradle. The dock boss shouted more orders and a boom and hose swung over to stop over the ballast port amidships. As they refilled the ballast tanks with water, Feng Po gave the order to vent gas. The damaged airship settled into the repair cradle at the pace of a slug on the sidewalk. The dock men swarmed over the hull and secured the long strips of batten cloth and wood around it. Another team locked in place metal supports for the control ring as the gas envelope started to deflate.

A loud steam whistle went off down below. The dock men returned to their places on the tower. Workers down below cleared out of the repair bay. The *Wu Zetian*, wrapped in a shroud of cloth and wood and iron, vented her highly flammable phlogiston.

Feng Po ambled down to the end of the catwalk and clapped Algie on the shoulder.

"Quite a show, aye Pig? Who needs the opera when you can watch this for the rest of your life?"

6 "Goodbye, Mr. Pork!", French

FIVE

Sometime in February
1889
South Atlantic

The crew of the *Roscommon Venture* gave up lying to the children two days out of Portsmouth. Not that Algie was fooled at all. A drooling idiot could tell with a single glance that this was a livestock transport, most likely bringing sheep and cattle from Australia and in need of some cargo to avoid the waste of traveling halfway around the world with empty holds.

The main hold was split into two large cages, boys on one side, and girls on the other. Straw covered the wooden decks as bedding and a half-hearted attempt to cover the layer of effluents ground in over years. Nothing could disguise the smell. It was almost always dark, lit only by an oil lamp near the door and the row of green glass deck prisms in the ceiling. The prisms were like pyramidal Swords of Damocles that dangled above the children's heads as they scattered sunlight through the deck above.

Each of the passengers was given a ratty blanket and a straw-filled pillow. That was about the only luxury the children received over the livestock. Meals were a shared platter of hard rolls, salt pork, and boiled greens. The sanitary facilities were a tin bucket in the back corner and a cooler with a tin cup on a chain.

As the mute cook's boy served up their second dinner at sea, the bosun's mate stood outside the cages to taunt them. He was an Irishman named Dolan, and an absolute villain, the type at Mrs. Billew's that took real pleasure in telling the younger ones that Father Christmas was a lie.

"Ah, ye' poor babes," Dolan mewled at them, "you still believe you're off to see your new mummies and daddies. You won't being seeing much more than each other's elbows and dirty backsides."

Just in case all the children didn't remember he was an absolute bastard, he cuffed the cook's boy hard across the back of the head as he backed out of the boys' cage. The nameless boy wound up spilling a good deal of the girls' horrid supper across the deck and Dolan's boots. The mate struck him twice as hard for discipline's sake.

"You clumsy ass, watch where you're throwing that slop!" Dolan paused for a second, as if he couldn't remember which vial of venom he had open, then laid into the children again. "You idiots aren't being adopted. You've been sold! You'll be seeing the gold mines and the sheep stations long before you see a nursery. You snot-nosed brats will have to work hard to get a repast as fine as the one we're giving you now for free. Your limbs will ache and your backs will crack, and you'll be wishing you had the luxuries that we're providing."

He turned to leer at the girls in their cage.

"The girls will go to the laundries and plantations, too, but if they use their heads, they'll get jobs where they can lay down on their backs without bearing too much weight."

Dolan focused an unpleasant grin on the older girls. Though Algie didn't work out all the bosun's mate had said, the tone and that sticky smile made him feel sick inside. Heather, one of the older girls who'd grown into her womanly figure faster than the rest, must have fallen upon the hidden meaning right away.

With a cry like a wildcat, she picked up the girls' communal bucket and pitched it at Dolan through the steel bars. He side-stepped it easily, except for a bit of the splash, but the cook's boy was not so lucky. Half a gallon of filth caught him on the back of his head, dowsing his clothes and dripping into the big double-handled pot that carried the boiled greens.

The boy spun around, wide-eyed but wordless. He let out strangled wails to express the anguish and confusion that was plain on his face.

Dolan took a step back and laughed.

"God, they caught you again," he coughed out. "I don't know what special kind of idiot you have to be to let them do this to you three times."

The cook's boy moaned and dripped, but did little else. Dolan kicked at him with the tip of his shoe.

"Come on with ye, collect up all your pots and pans and we'll rinse you off with a couple of buckets of sea water," Dolan said. "Unless you'd like us to drag behind the ship for a league or two to rinse off the stink?"

The boy shook his head vigorously and gathered the nesting pans. As he stumbled out through the main hatch, the bosun's mate pointed at Heather and grinned.

"And as for you my little Hellcat, I'll be back some other time to teach you some manners."

He shut the hatch behind them. The children stood silent for several moments. Finally, Algie spoke up.

"Well, that crimps it. We have to get off this boat before we reach Australia."

"You have any idea how to do that?" Heather asked.

"Don't worry," Deirdre replied. "Algie always has a plan."

*

With Keogh standing on Algie's shoulders and Alistair on all fours supporting them both, the smallest boy on the ship could press his ear to the crack where the deck prism came through the top deck. Along with a lot of language that curled his nose hairs, Keogh heard that the ship would be putting in to port at Capetown tomorrow.

"Then that's it, then," Algie muttered as he lowered Keogh

to the bed of straw below. "We put the plan into action to-night."

He stepped down from Declan's back to squish his stocking feet in whatever fluids congealed on the deck below yesterday's layer of fresh straw. He would have preferred to keep his shoes on, but Declan was having none of that if he had to put his own hands and knees in that muck.

"Do you think he can finish the job in just a few hours?" Declan asked as he stood, wiping his hands on his shirt tails. Like everyone else in the cage, he was covered in offset layers of piss, shit, and vomit. It had been a rough passage from England.

"Keogh's tough," Algie replied. "If I could lift him high enough, he would chew through the last bits of wood with his teeth."

The deck prism, unusually large at twelve inches across, sat flush with the deck on top and scattered light throughout the hold with its facets below. It was held in place with some caulk around the edges and a thin ridge of wood below it. The boys had been taking turns the last few days holding up Keogh as he scraped away the wood with a sharpened belt buckle. It had been, up until now, a careful balance between taking until after they left port to remove it safely or having the prism give way under a sailor's weight. Tonight, it was a race to the complete the job before midnight.

When the cook's boy and bosun's mate arrived that evening, the children did their best to act as calm and cowed as they had been the night before. Any agitation, and the boys' hesitation to eat their salt pork, was covered by a confession of sea sickness. Dolan made his usual taunts as the boy smiled meekly and stole anxious glances at the cage full of girls. He packed up his pots and backed out of the hold, also cautious and watching for the contents of a flying chamber pot. The mate cuffed him behind the ear and they both left the hold for their own dinners.

Algie quietly counted off the seconds after he heard the sound of the hold's latch being thrown:

"One Piccadilly. Two Piccadilly. Three Piccadilly…"

When he got to a hundred seconds, he nodded, and the boys went to work. For days the children had been saving the fat from their salt pork rations. The boys took to warming it in their hands and mashing it into a paste as he counted. When he was done, they fell to their knees and cleared the straw from the floor. The dark residue from years of livestock oozed out of the fetid wood planks. This got mixed with the fat until they had a compound that was slippery as politics, black as night, and smelled like original sin.

Standing on Declan's shoulders, Algie worked on removing the prism. It only hung on a few bits of wood and four belt buckles. That took only a minute or two of work. Once the twelve pound chunk of glass was free, he dropped it into the pile of straw at Declan's feet.

Now came the tricky part.

While Algie had been removing the deck prism, the others had stripped Keogh down to his skivvies and thoroughly coated him the black grease they had concocted. Everything but his eyes, palms, and soles was pitch black. He smelled like the back end of a sheep that had glutted itself on too much spring grass.

Algie didn't savor this next step any more than Keogh.

"Come on," he said. "We don't have all night."

While it would have been difficult to lubricate him at a height, it was proving damn near impossible to lift him up once he was covered with pork fat and excrement. After several painful grips on Keogh's anatomy, and many unfortunate footholds on Algie, he was finally up on Algie's shoulders and gripping the edge of the deck.

"Now, remember," Algie whispered, "stick to the shadows and circle around to open up the hatch. Move slow, so nobody sees you."

Keogh nodded silently, though everything shook from cold and the misery of having to smell himself. He slid through the gap in the deck a bit at a time, first an arm, then that shoulder and his head, and then with a bit of squirming, his other arm. With the thickest parts of him through, the rest slipped out like smoke out of a bottle. With a tap of knuckles to the deck to signal he was clear, Keogh was gone.

"Quick now," Algie told the other boys, "before somebody

steps in the hole and breaks a leg."

The others handed up the prism and the loose belt buckles and he made quick work of it. It probably couldn't hold a grown man's weight, but hopefully they would be long gone before any of the sailors could put their weight on it.

Algie dropped to the straw below. Like the rest of the boys, he used the straw to wipe the black grease from his hands and clothes. When he felt cleaner, there was no way he could ever feel *clean* in the hold of this livestock steamer, he looked across the way to Deirdre and the other girls who stood at the bars of their cage. He signaled a thumbs up and she smiled in return.

The children all settled into the straw and waited.

After what felt like hours, Algie heard the latch turn and the main hatch creak open. He felt a moment of exultation when he saw Keogh come through, until realized that the black-painted greasy boy held his one arm back and up in a peculiar way. Then Algie saw a larger hand wrapped around that arm and the glint of a steel blade near Keogh's ear.

✳

Algie could tell who had caught Keogh before he could see his face. The inarticulate grunt was nothing like a word and never would be. The cook's boy moved the knife away from the smaller boy's throat and pushed him through the hatch. He then turned on his heel and barred the door behind him. There was a gnawing silence as the mute boy turned back to the caged children and put the tip of his knife between Keogh's shoulder blades. Keogh shivered like a rat caught out in the light, unsure whether to freeze or run.

Deirdre was the one to speak up first:

"Oh how very clever of you, Keogh! You've brought help."

The cook's boy made a sound of distress that rivaled his response to being dowsed with the girls' chamber pot. Algie might have made a similar noise if he were capable of making any sound. Deirdre pressed on fearlessly, smiling as she stepped up to the very front of the cage.

"You did come here to help us, didn't you?"

The cook's boy screwed up his face. He looked over to the

boy's cage, maybe expecting an answer. Algie tried to respond with a happy face, but it felt awkward and twitchy. The cook's boy scowled and went back to Deirdre.

"We really need your help," she said. "And if you help us, we could help you."

The boy looked wary, but intrigued. Algie decided to join in with his persuasion.

"Sure, if you help us get off the ship, we could take you with us."

The doubt and distrust on the boy's face was actually quite hurtful to Algie personally.

"He is quite clever," Deirdre said. "He's the one who came up with our escape plan."

The cook's boy scoffed and gripped Keogh tightly by the back of the neck just below the skull. He lifted the smaller boy to stand up on tiptoe and shook him vigorously as if he were bell, just to show how truly clever the escape plan had turned out to be.

Deirdre made no quick response to that, but instead looked to the other girls for some helpful suggestion.

"I'm terribly sorry about dowsing you the way I did," Heather said with a wan smile. "Perhaps, if we were to become friends, I could make it up to you.

The cook's boy smiled, but showed that he was unpracticed at the gesture. His eyes flashed up to the ceiling at the sound of footsteps on the deck up above. Algie tried to calculate how close to the missing deck prism they might be. Whatever crewman was up there, he did not put his foot through the gap as he walked towards the stern. As the sound faded away, Algie returned his attention to the boy who held Keogh by the neck with one hand and pressed a knife to his ribs with the other. Algie hoped he looked calm and controlled, but he could feel his eyebrows at the top of his forehead.

The boy made an irritable snuffling sound and released his grip on the smaller, smelly boy. With both hands free, he folded the knife shut and put it in his pocket. He walked over to the center pole where the ring of keys hung from a hook. A quick stretch proved that they were too high up even for him to reach.

He whistled and gestured for Keogh to come to him.

Keogh's eyes got even wider. They flashed bright white in his darkened face. He silently begged for help from Algie. Algie nodded yes and inclined his head towards the cook's boy and the keys. With a look just short of terror on his face, the greased child did as he was asked.

As Keogh came over, the cook's boy hunkered down and made a stirrup of the interlaced fingers of his hands. Keogh put one foot there and his opposite hand on the larger boy's shoulder. As he reached up for the ring, the cook's boy stood beneath him and practically threw him up to the height of the hook. Algie felt his breath catch in his lungs when he saw that happen without warning.

Keogh snagged the ring of keys as he went up and arced away from the post as he came down. The cook's boy did try to catch him, but unfortunately, the smaller boy had been thoroughly lubricated. He slipped out of his grasp and slid a short way across the decking. In the end, he still had a firm grip on the key ring and his head attached to his shoulders. Some of the black had been scuffed off on the wooden decking, but besides that, he was fine.

The cook's boy reached down and took the keys from him and went immediately to door of the girls' cage. It took him a moment or two to find the right key, but after that it was the work of seconds to open the latch.

Deirdre opened the door very slowly, gritting her teeth as it squealed a complaint. The girls padded out quickly once it was pushed all the way. They all had their skirts bound around their thighs and their shoes in bundles tied up from their blankets in preparation for a stealthy escape.

Heather came up to their rescuer. With a whispered thank you, she gave him a gentle kiss on the cheek. The cook's boy looked befuddled and petrified.

Keogh reacted quickly enough. He snatched the keys from the lock and undid the boys' cage. He slipped into the cage before anyone had a chance to come out.

"Give me my clothes for Christ's sake! It's bloody cold in here."

The boys filed out until the center of the hold was full and the livestock pens held only the one boy getting dressed. The cook's boy gave a sharp low whistle to get Algie's attention. As Algie turned his way the other boy folded his arms across his chest and gave him a questioning look.

"I suppose you're wondering what's the next step in our escape plan?" Algie said.

The cook's boy nodded.

Algie himself was wondering what the next step was to be. It was time to gather some intelligence.

"Keogh!" Algie called out. "Is the ship moored in the harbor?"

"How the bloody Hell should I know? I popped out of the hole in the deck and all I saw right away was a knife pointed at my face."

Even Deirdre's supportive smile slipped a little bit loose at that point. The cook's boy tapped Algie on the shoulder. He shook his head until Algie got the gist.

"We're anchored outside the harbor then?"

The cook's boy nodded slowly enough for even an idiot to understand.

"Why the Hell would they do that?" one of the boys exclaimed.

The boy held one arm out flat like a ship and mimed with the fingers of his other hand people running along and leaping off.

"So the children won't jump ship at the dock and run away," Deirdre said. She always was the best at charades.

"Of course they'd do that," Algie muttered. "And they'd want to be far enough away that no one would hear us screaming for help. How far is that?"

The cook's boy waved the milling children away from the center of the hold. He went back to the door and stood with his back to it. Holding up fingers in sequence, he silently asked for someone to count off his steps. He paced off yard-long steps from one end of the hold to the other and back again until he came to twenty. The cook's boy stopped with a shrug.

"Sixty feet?" Algie said. "That's not so bad."

The boy shook his head. He held up two fingers and waggled them in Algie's direction.

"One hundred and twenty feet?"

He shook his head again. Then, he slapped his two fingers against his forearm a total of ten times.

"Well, that's…"

"Nearly a quarter of a mile," Deirdre said. Unfortunately, she was always the best at figures, too.

"Bugger that," exclaimed Keogh. "None of us can swim that far!"

Algie checked the others. No one seemed to disagree with that fact.

"Is it possible we could lower one of the lifeboats and row it ashore?" Algie asked.

It was amazing the number of scathing insults the cook's boy was able to convey without saying a single word. Then again, he'd had all of his life to perfect the skill.

Algie looked away, embarrassed at how far from his heroic ideals his actual escape skills had fallen. As he tried not to look any of his disappointed comrades in the eye, his attention fell on a stack of wooden barrels in the corner. He went straight over to them and waved for the cook's boy to follow.

The first one he came to was filled with salt and rigid dead fish. He pulled one out and thoughtfully tapped it against the rim of barrel. It made a flat sound like wood on wood. The outlines of yet another plan began bouncing around in Algie's brain.

"Everything for the galley," Algie said, "it comes in barrels like these, right?"

The cook's boy nodded, though he didn't seem to be following Algie's train of thought.

"What do you do with all the empty ones?" Algie asked.

A little bit of light caught in the other boy's eyes, then. Algie thought he saw understanding and maybe just a little bit of hope.

SIX

18th of August 1889
Turfan Caravanserai

Algie had to be lowered back down from the Fish's Mouth with the rescue yoke, as he still couldn't climb with his game leg. Since he was already dangling from a string, it seemed perfectly logical to have him help inspect the damage to the lower hull. The periscopic camera was a bit unwieldy, but he had no idea how to load the  glass plates into the mechanism above, and Liu Jean-Pierre was deathly afraid of heights. Algie wrestled the accordion-pleated tube of fabric and metal as Fang made distressed noises up on the main deck.

"Don't worry about him," Feng Po called out loudly enough to heard almost anywhere on the ship. "Pig is good with his hands, even if he doesn't have the brains it takes to be frightened."

Algie guessed that would be as close as he was going to get to a compliment from his mentor. With final twist, anchoring his good leg against the hull, he got the lens head aimed at the first of the grape-shot breaches. Most of the five holes were as round and smooth as if they had been cut in with a drill bit. Only where three of the slugs had hit the lacquered silk too closely together was there any sign of splintering like there would have been on a wooden hull.

Algie was fascinated. He had never had a chance to make an

up-close inspection of a *Qī Fēngzhēng*[7] hull. This allowed him to see a cross section of the many layers of the construction. The outer layers were cinnabar red and sanded smooth. Beneath that were alternating layers of honey amber resin and pale silk laid over a foundation of rough batten cloth. Algie could even make out a bit of the bamboo framework that gave the whole vessel its shape.

"A little bit to the right, please, Pig!" Liu shouted as he waved a white scarf in the desired direction.

Algie focused the camera on the most interesting damage and did his best to hold stock still. He had never had a chance to see the ship from this angled before, but she was still a beauty. The *Wu Zetian* was the first of her kind, Liu had said, the largest *Qī Fēngzhēng* ever attempted, the big sister of the three-man and five-man fliers which had torn the European Fleet to shreds. She was assembled by Liu Zhao Su and his family with love and pride, more like a musical instrument than a merchant ship.

"Good!" Feng Po shouted. "Let's move another three meters towards the stern."

"*Shì de, lǎoshī.*"

He began sliding the ungainly rig along the rail as Feng Po and the *Lǎoshǔ* swung the rope to his new position.

*

After what felt like an hour of dangling and assessing damage, Algie was reeled up to the main deck like a trophy fish. He saw nearly everyone of any importance on the ship gathered there in deep discussion.

"What's all this then?" Algie asked as Feng Po helped him out of the rescue yoke.

The first mate snorted derisively.

"While we were a wounded beast in the air," he said, "there was only one thing to do and one place to do it. Now that we're here in Turfan, our options have opened up significantly. So, of course, they have to argue about that. The cat's let loose amongst the pigeons."

Liu made a sad little grimace of frustration as he put the last of the glass photographic plates into his light-tight case. Once he sealed it up and stood again, he stiffened. The captain, the owner of the ship, and all her entourage were on their way to speak to him. Even Zhao Guanting, the Dowager Empress' personal representative, in his court robes jockeyed for a position of significance.

"*Shî*," Liu muttered under his breath. In an instant, Algie saw him change from a confident technician into a boy only a few years older than himself. He was already starting to hurt for Liu as Mme. Streif spoke first.

"So, Jean-Pierre, how have we fared? Will you be able to repair our floating palace?"

She spoke English clearly, with only a trace of an Eastern European accent, and with her head tilted to one side as if the question and Mr. Liu were both slightly amusing. Though she was three or four inches shorter than the young man, she kept her eyes level and her expression placid.

"The damage from the *picaroon's* guns is minimal. I will be able to effect repairs from our supplies in only a few days. But the damage from that explosive mine..." Liu gestured at shards of the port wing wrapped up above them. "I- I don't see how that can be repaired outside of our factory."

"See, it's just like I said," snapped Captain Strausser. "We have to turn back." He was in his full green and black braid livery and peaked cap. It set off his reddening face and white hair. With his round face and white sideburns, the captain always impressed Algie as an enraged sheep.

"The Divine Empress Cixi's investment must be protected," Zhao declared. As the ship's Purser and a personal favorite of court, so he said, he was accustomed to his words bearing great weight in discussion.

"We are not turning back on our maiden voyage," Mme. Streif declared. She pulled herself as rigid as an iron rod. In her purple and black silk gown, she looked like a queen. Not those doughy pictures of Queen Victoria, but a woman who was used to people backing out of her presence and saying "As you wish" a lot.

"Our holds are half-filled with cloth, bamboo, and raw

lacquer," she continued. "I would think you could build us a second airship with the damage control supplies your father put back for us."

"It's not just the damage from the attack," Liu sputtered. "That turn maneuver we executed uncovered some severe design flaws. This ship is a folly, a pleasure cruiser, not a battle ship. My father will need to re-work the entire control and suspension system."

"That maneuver saved your life," Mme. Streif declared. "Mr. McLaren saved all our lives."

Feng Po ducked his head to acknowledge her kind words and tipped his hat, but said nothing to interrupt her. Algie hoped that Mme. Streif might have some word of praise for him too, but all eyes were on the shipwright's son.

"Not that I'm not grateful," Liu blurted. He turned to Feng Po and bowed his head quickly. "*Xiè xiè, Shīfù* McLaren!"

Liu wheeled back to his argument: "Since the main hull is suspended from the gas envelope with no rigid supports, sudden banking or rising maneuvers could cause erratic stresses. The two could possibly just… separate in midair."

"Certainly, someone as clever as you, Liu Jean-Pierre, could come up with at least a temporary solution."

Liu Jean-Pierre goggled at Mme. Streif. He started to speak his piece once, perhaps twice, until he spoke out at last. Algie saw that he was on the edge of tears.

"You have the wrong Liu. I am not the smartest son, or the best at business. Certainly not the best with a sword or the empty hand. I'm just the one Father could do without for several months."

Mme. Streif sighed, looking saddened by Liu's confession as much as Algie was.

"You should know that I requested you specifically, had to negotiate with your father to get you. Though I occasionally hire lunatics…" She looked over Liu's shoulder to fix Feng Po with a significant look. "I do not accept someone who is not at the top of her or his field."

She craned her neck to take in the whole web of hemp and bamboo rigging and the slowly deflating gas envelope above them all.

"Let us pretend for a moment that I were speaking to a brilliant man with no fear of failure or ridicule. What would he suggest with the materials at hand?"

Liu Jean-Pierre mumbled and dithered, making engineering calculations under his breath, then coming up to the edge of an idea but not having the courage to speak. He went on like that for several long painful moments.

Jakinda came up on Mme. Streif's right shoulder. With the raising of her eyebrow and the tip of her closed fan on her lips, she seemed to be asking the older woman a question. Algie himself had no idea what the code might be. Mme. Streif nodded regally, though, and Jakinda advanced upon Liu in a slow but steady pace.

She lowered her eyes when Liu saw her and froze in panic. As she came to stand toe to toe with him, she laid her fan on his left shoulder. It caught Liu's full attention. She opened it slowly to reveal the painted Chinese garden on its silk. Jakinda leaned in on his right side, whether to kiss his cheek or whisper in his ear Algie couldn't say. The fan hid all.

The pair stood like that for twenty-eight Picadillies. Then, she straightened, quietly shut her fan, and returned to her place at the right hand of Mme. Streif. Liu blinked in the ruddy light of a desert sunset.

"Why, yes," he murmured. "I believe you're right. *Xiè xiè,* Miss Jakinda."

He pointed to the rigging above them as he started to speak clearly and plainly.

"The problem can be resolved with a combination of lateral cross-rigging with standard hawsers and an improvised rigid pylon system made of bamboo and stiffened silk cord. We could connect it to the control ring around the gas envelope and then connect into the gunwales of the hull just behind the bridge and then here in the area just behind the flying jib mast arm."

"Do you think it will work?" Mme. Streif asked with a half-hidden smile.

Liu Jean-Pierre worked his mouth from side to side as he

worked out more calculations in his head.

"I can definitely make this work," he declared. "Though it won't be pretty."

"If I have any compulsion to 'make it pretty'," the older woman said, "I'll have the *Lǎoshǔ* wrap it in silk flowers."

Liu, a bit excited now, led the entourage aft, pointing out points of stress and connection points as he lectured. Algie and Feng Po stayed behind to stow away the equipment.

"What did that Conversor do to him?" Algie asked his mentor. "Was that some kind of spell?"

"I'm sure it was, but of a more domestic and commonplace kind of magic than what you might be imagining."

Algie frowned.

"That means you'll tell me when I'm older?"

"I do hope you're keeping a running list of these topics," Feng Po said. "And you are storing it somewhere we might find it in the future."

Algie sniffed and looked out over the rail, across the caravanserai and the desert. The sun was a half-circle resting on the jagged horizon. The sky took on all the colors from deep violet to fiery pink on the undersides of a few clouds. Just where the sky turned from leaf green to dark blue, Algie saw two tiny black objects.

They moved slowly from north to south, though no doubt moving fast as bullets at a great distance. Algie caught bright flashes, either the reflection of sun off of metal or tongues of fire.

"*Lǎoshī*," he called out, "are those more *picaroons* to the west?"

First Mate McLaren unhitched his altitude mask from the hook on his belt to peer through the magnifier. He chuckled once he was able to focus in on little dots.

"You have God's own eyes. You keep this up and you'll have yourself a permanent lookout berth in the Fish's Mouth."

The second compliment of the day had Algie's head swimming.

"*Wáng bā dàn!*" Feng Po exclaimed.

Algie squinted to make out the two distant objects. One of

them flared bright like a candle and dropped below the horizon. The other dark object twisted in the sky like no airship Algie had ever seen.

"What is that?" he asked.

Feng Po, who looked thoroughly gob-smacked, handed over the mask.

"Here look for yourself and tell me what it is."

Algie had just a short time before the object disappeared into the gloom. He saw something with a long wriggling body like a serpent's, two wings nearly as wide as the thin torso was long and a bright flare like a flame on the thickest end.

"If I was crazy, I'd say that was a dragon." Algie had no idea what it could really be.

"I thought it was a dragon, too," Feng Po muttered, "so you must be crazy. We'd better be telling what passes for authorities here about it. Though, I'd leave out the dragon part."

7 "lacquered kite", Mandarin

SEVEN

18th of August 1889
Turfan Caravanserai

In less than an hour, all of the crew and passengers of the *Wu Zetian* had their bags packed and were trouping across the gang plank. Feng Po held Algie and the other *Lǎoshǔ* back to let the adults and important personages cross over and gather on the open lift platform of the repair cradle. His young friends were not satisfied with waiting in line. Instead, the boys climbed the amidships rigging and entertained themselves with throwing about the red Indian rubber ball.

That left Algie at the head of the gang plank with the first mate and Mssr. Patrouille, the last of Mme. Streif's entourage. As was often the case, Mme. Streif's literary pet was decked out like a peacock in a bright blue cutaway coat, matching high hat, and a waistcoat covered in squirming paisleys of every color. His cravat was a fire-bright orange just to set things off like a fuse. He stood at the very edge of the gangplank and clutched his carpet bag to his chest as if it were a life preserver. He might have gone pale, but Algie couldn't properly tell. He didn't know there was such a thing as a black Frenchman until he'd come aboard the *Wu Zetian*, but then again, he was only beginning to understand the number of things he hadn't even dreamed of before.

"How do you do it?" Patrouille murmured. His English, like his pomaded hair and mustache, was nearly perfect. "How do you just walk out over space without a care?"

Up until this moment, Algie had never had the chance to speak with Mssr. Etienne Patrouille, accomplished author and playwright and a pampered passenger of the *Wu Zetian*. He was pleased to get such a celebrity's attention. Algie assessed the gang plank provided by Turfan. It was heavy wood, twice as wide as the observation deck out of the Fish's Mouth, with three heavy rope railings on each side. It would take a dedicated act of will to fall off of it.

"I dunno," Algie said. "You just have to keep your mind on what you're doing instead of what awful thing could happen while you're doing it."

Mssr. Patrouille grimaced as he edged forward to get a peek of the repair shop some hundred meters down.

"And that is how you came to leap off of a perfectly good airship with a barbed satchel of explosives in your hands?"

"Well, I saw how chancy it was all getting, and I said to myself, 'What would Dale Daring do?'"

Mssr. Patrouille reacted as if he'd been slapped. Algie saw the whites all the way around the Frenchman's eyes. Algie remembered a Strand cartoon of a rat terrier with that expression, immediately after it was introduced to a kangaroo.

"You--WHAT?"

"Dale Daring," Algie said quietly, "boy airship pilot. He has adventures all over the world. I've read all his books."

Algie knew that the author was as cultured as he was fashionable, but he didn't think he would have had such a negative response to Algie's fascination with penny dreadfuls.

"And you risked your life, based on what that imbecile guttersnipe did in a trash paperback?" Mssr. Patrouille's eyes seemed to be settling back into their sockets, but he still seemed very upset.

"I know he's made up," Algie said, "but the science is basically sound."

"Sound? There is no science in a Dale Daring story. It is all sensationalist claptrap and the so-called author doesn't know an airship from an enema bag." Patrouille dropped the carpet bag and clasped Algie by the shoulders, leaning down to look him directly in the eye. "For God's sake, my young friend, don't ever, *ever* again do what you think Dale Daring would do. On your mother's grave, promise me?"

Algie stood there for several long seconds, mulling over what the Frenchman had said, which pulled his thoughts in several directions at once.

"So, do you know the man who writes Dale Daring?" was the first thing to come out of Algie's mouth.

Patrouille closed his eyes and shook his head as if he'd been hit by something hard square in his forehead. He shook it off.

"I do know the man who writes under the *nom de plume*[8] Timothy Freemarch," he admitted. "Up until now, I had not realized what an irresponsible idiot he had been."

"What do you mean, Mssr. Patrouille?"

"I mean," said the Frenchman with a sigh, "that we might cross that bridge when we come to it, but I need your assistance crossing this one first."

"Of course, sir, what do you need?"

Patrouille took up his carpet bag again, along with the little bundle of Algie's clothes and possessions.

"I would like you to escort me across this rickety footbridge and help me keep up my courage."

Algie nodded and moved over to Patrouille's left so he could walk beside him without tripping the man up with his crutch. The author put out his left elbow and Algie slipped his right arm through the crook. The two of them took the first halting steps onto the wood way.

"And if I look to be about to succumb to melancholy or humiliation," Patrouille muttered, "please keep me from throwing myself over the rails."

*

The two of them made it across alive and uninjured, though there was one moment of misadventure. A sudden gust of wind caught Mssr. Patrouille's hat and snatched it off his head. He dropped their baggage and caught it by the brim. In doing that, he threw both of them off balance and against the rope railing.

Patrouille squeaked like a frightened kitten as his gold-rimmed *pince nez* slipped off his nose and fell to the repair floor some thirty or forty meters below. His breathing stopped for a moment as he stood frozen and watched their descent. Algie kept a hold on him with a fistful of paisley waistcoat.

"Is this an attack of melancholy?" Algie asked after a tense moment. "I've never seen one before."

"*Mon dieu*, no," the older man rasped. "That was just me risking our lives to save a ten-franc toque."

He jammed his hat back on his head, almost down to the bridge of his nose so it would stick, and took up the carpet bag and Algie's bundle.

"Let us be gone before the wind picks up again." He pulled Algie off of the railing and made for the far end of the gangplank. Algie hopped along to keep up with his hurried walk. The boys in the rigging let out a cheer when they reached safety on the platform.

"See, that wasn't so bad, now was it?" Algie said as he took back the bundle of his possessions.

Patrouille's responding look was sour. He set his hat back on his head where it belonged and shrugged the shoulders of his coat into place.

"Her Highness said this would be a tonic for me, an inspiration for my work. A leisurely airship cruise across Asia." The Frenchman laughed loudly and without humor. "This has been nothing but weeks of privation, punctuated with encounters with *picaroons*, barbarians, and the socially deplorable."

Feng Po brushed past them as he crossed the gangway and made for the elevator platform.

"If you just stand there jawing like that, Pig, you'll miss our ride." The first mate tipped his coachman's hat to Patrouille. "Come along! Hot baths and cold beer for everybody."

The *Lǎoshǔ* came over next. They swung on ropes over the gap and dropped to the repair deck like monkeys. Algie felt jealous of the fun they were having. He nudged the writer towards the open elevator.

"Come on. Like the First Mate said, we'll miss our ride."

"Oh yes," Patrouille muttered. "It looks like as much fun as a cruise on the High Silk Road."

Algie hooked a finger through the handle of the carpet bag and led Mssr. Patrouille forward by his grip on the bag, something that would not seem as embarrassing as taking his hand. The boy hobbled along with the man following along behind like a large surly dog on a lead. In a minute or two, they joined the rest of the passengers and crew.

Liu Jean-Pierre had told him that the airship would not be lowered to ground level until the gas envelope had been completely vented of flammable gas. Then the caravanserai's porters would retrieve everyone's luggage. Only the most precious or necessary items were carried by each person on the platform.

Patrouille had said he carried his toiletries and his most recent manuscript in his carpet bag. Chabi the Conversor carried a paddle-like fiddle with a carved horse's head at the end of its neck. A recurve bow and quiver were slung over one shoulder. Another Conversor Algie had not met yet carried leather tubes of maps and bright brass navigation instruments. She was a swarthy, dark-haired woman with two dark lines etched into the skin from her mouth to her chin. Mme. Streif stood in the center of the circle of Conversors and crew. Though she owned practically everything on the ship, the only item she considered vital enough to bring with her was a small black and white dog with large furry ears like a butterfly's wings. She called him "Kosciusko" or "Kozzie", and he seemed to be the only thing in the world that made the old woman truly happy.

Zhao Guanting, in his red and gold silks and high Imperial headdress, stood close to the Conversors with three of the largest Chinese crewman at his back. They carried three enameled caskets that probably held the silver *taels* and Austrian gold coins that made up the ship's treasury.

All Algie had with him was his bundle of British clothes, a pen knife, and a single Dale Daring book he had been able to find in Macao. His mother would have approved of his lack of possessions, a sign of spiritual freedom. He tried to feel in his heart the way she did, but he would have still have preferred to have had a few more books.

Or her.

A loud buzzing noise from overhead caught everyone's attention. Three Magnus chiropters buzzed by, heading for the sunset. Their spherical gas envelopes, bracketed by canvas bat wings, spun slowly as they soared into the west. Each had a single pilot in a BC&I redcoat dangling beneath and a noisome spirit engine and propeller mounted behind.

Feng Po nudged Algie and pointed at the receding craft.

"Say what you like about those murderous, avaricious Brits, Pig," he said, "but they don't let the grass grow under their feet."

Algie grimaced. He was used to insults as part of his tutelage, but this was a bit much.

"You do realize that I'm British, don't you?"

Feng Po looked at him sideways with a sly grin.

"Nothing that can't be beaten out of you."

*

Jakinda invited Algie to sit with her and Mme. Streif's entourage on the passenger tram. He had wanted to sit in the cab of the steam lorry that pulled the four open cars and see the working of the controls and boilers, but the black-bearded Uyghur fireman was having none of it. He had brandished his coal shovel and grunted out something that Chabi had translated into French as "No children."

From the smirk on her face, Algie guessed there were several words untranslated as they were unfit for his ears.

So, instead he sat on the cushioned seats of the tram between Jakinda and Chabi with his packet of possessions beneath his seat. Across the aisle sat Ayotunde, Mssr. Patrouille, and the one Conversor he had seen earlier with the maps. She had introduced herself as Keijín. She was barely taller than Algie and had coal-black hair, nearly black eyes, and those lines tattooed on her chin. Algie found it hard not to stare. He'd heard rumors amongst the bridge crew that she was an American savage prone to scalping and massacres when provoked or drunk. She had her hair done up on the top of her head and wore a brown and black check dress just like any fashionable woman of Portsmouth.

Algie kept his eyes moving, for as Ayotunde had taught him, "*Il est impoli de regarder*[9]," and she was close enough still to kick him in the shins. He saw that Jakinda had a thick bundle of books wrapped around with a leather strap on her lap.

"*Isilmandatu*," he read out loud from cover of the topmost. "What does that mean?"

Jakinda smiled minutely, exchanging quick glances with the other Conversors.

"It's a secret."

"Can't you tell me?"

Mssr. Patrouille guffawed.

"She just did!" He leaned across the aisle and tapped the book. "That is the word for 'secret' in her mother tongue."

Jakinda made a face at the writer as if he had just spoiled all her fun. He smirked back at her.

"It is said that the Basque women, besides being the most beautiful on the Iberian Peninsula, are the most virtuous, that they cannot be tempted because their language is too difficult for the Devil to learn."

"So it is said," she replied.

"But Mam'selle Jakinda, like all of the ladies present, comprehends enough other languages that some arrangement can be made."

"*Vous êtes le diable*[10]," Jakinda said with a smile.

"*Merci*." Patrouille acknowledged what Algie assumed to be a compliment with a bow of his head.

Algie realized that he was going to have to work doubly hard on his French if he were to have any idea what the adults were talking about.

Ayotunde swatted Patrouille's knuckles with her fan and scolded him. It was a string of French spoken too quickly for him to even catch the breaks between words. His eyes widened with outrage, but she gave him no space to wedge in an angry word. After another quick barrage of words, he apologized and turned himself to look out the open side of the tram. She fired off something else at Jakinda, and then turned herself the opposite way, fanning herself frantically.

Jakinda must have seen the bafflement on Algie's face, as she immediately began to translate:

"She is irritated by Mssr. Patrouille and I. Almost any time we exchange more than a few words, it ends up in devils and temptations, or even more carnal subjects. She didn't want any unseemly conversation in front of the child."

"He's not a child for God's sake," Patrouille snapped without looking back at them. "He's twelve years old. There have been kings younger than that."

Ayotunde muttered something over her shoulder. If Algie was right, she was telling the writer not to blaspheme.

"Well, he's right. I'm not a child. I was old enough to kill a whole ship full of air pirates this week!"

Algie still wasn't entirely sure that was really a good thing, but it was certainly the most adult thing he had done on this voyage.

"Madame Streif has noticed your accomplishments," Jakinda said, "which is why she has asked me to include you in our morning exercises. You will be the first man to have been taught in the Secret School for a very long time."

Jakinda opened the book and read the first few lines. They were in Basque, but when she reached the end she translated for Algie's sake into English:

"Long before men blackened the skies and trees with their inventions, there was a little girl called Opari who remembered the times between her incarnations. When she was old enough to speak, she told of the place where one's heart was always connected to all others and all Five Veils of Godhead were revealed."

Ayotunde made another angry exclamation, most likely in French. From Mssr. Patrouille's expression, Algie guessed it was both extremely offensive and highly creative in word choice and construction. Jakinda screwed up her pretty face in response.

"Would you mind if I moved over here for a few moments?" she said. "Mam'selle Ayotunde and I must have a little *tete a tete.*"

The elder Conversor stood then and went to take Chabi's place opposite Ayotunde. Algie slid into her vacated spot. Mssr. Patrouille looked on with a bemused expression. Rather than watch the two women argue in hushed tones behind open fans, Algie settled his arms on the window sill and took in the spectacle of his first caravanserai.

The steam lorry was still weaving its way through the repair bays. It was a wonderland for a boy fed for years on the adventures of airship pilots and inventors. Woodworkers in one shop repaired the struts and members of a bat-like wing. The rest of the disabled Magnus chiropter leaned up against their back wall like a trophy fish on the docks. Sparks rained down from another shop's upper level as intricate pierced strut work for a rigid airship got ground and welded into shape. The workers in masks and heavy leather looked like devils enshrouded in smoke and fire.

A stream of traffic going the opposite way—a clot of carts and merchants on foot—blocked his view for a few moments. As they cleared away, a marvelous sight appeared to Algie: a repair hangar twice as big as a soccer pitch with the entire fabric skin of an airship spread out across its concrete floor. Cloth rolls the size of locomotives lined the walls. Shirtless men with glue pots and mops tended to a rip in the envelope. As others laid silk over the adhesive, burly men with handheld industrial sewing machines stitched down the edges of the patches in clouds of steam and noise.

Too soon, the passenger tram moved around a corner and left the hangar behind. They moved out of the repair works to the docks where dozens of airships rested in their paddocks or floated alongside landing towers. Algie recognized craft from China, Brazil, France, and Tunisia by their silhouettes and flags. He guessed at the homeports of many others from their insignia and lettering he saw on their hulls or envelopes. He had a sudden urge to take pen to paper to fill a journal like a birder with all the shapes and sizes of aircraft he had seen.

The cobblestone road turned towards the gates that pierced the massive mud-brick walls of the caravanserai's central compound. The cargo from all these ships fed onto the road on the backs of merchants, in ox carts, or steam lorries. The fabric bundles and labeled crates displayed every color of the rainbow. The men and women transporting them came in every color God had made, including several Algie had never seen before.

As the crowd funneled into narrow gate, the passenger tram slowed to a crawl. Algie heard the babble grow louder as they began to press cheek to jowl. A wizened woman with a wicker basket full of shrieking birds stood just outside Algie's seat. To see any more of the sights, he would have to look over the top of her grizzled brown and gray hair. She stole sideways glances at him with an exhausted expression on her face.

Algie twisted back around to face Mssr. Patrouille and avoid the bird woman. The Frenchman raised an eyebrow and grinned. Algie sighed and turned further to check the Conversors' urgent conversation. It still went on behind colorful landscapes painted on their fans.

Algie was never comfortable when adults spent any time at all discussing him. That's how he found himself on a sheep freighter to Australia. He wound up as the first mate's apprentice and whipping boy the same way. He didn't want to think about where he would find himself tomorrow.

A voice like nothing Algie had ever heard came from the center of the caravanserai. It was high and clear and louder than any human he could remember hearing, save the Conversors. The song rose and fell in pitch like the flight of a bird.

Jakinda and Ayotunde stopped their conversation immediately, folding their fans and leaning back into their seats. The engine at the head of the tram stopped, too. Algie heard more than saw the escaping cloud of steam as it shut down.

"What's happening?"

Algie saw many of the people on the road stop and turn completely around to face the spot where the sun had just set. It was unsettling how many apparent strangers did that all at once. Many bowed their heads or crossed their arms across their chest. Even the bear-like man that attended the lorry's steam boiler stood beside the iron wheels and faced the West.

"Excuse me," Ayotunde said in French as she stood, "it is time for evening prayers."

She stepped down from the tram as she pulled a white silk scarf up over her hair and joined the throng. Algie leaned forward to get a better look at what happened next.

He felt a sudden sting on his left knee and an iron force that pressed him against his seat. Chabi had slapped her fan across his leg just as Keijín pushed hers into his breastbone. She narrowed her eyes and shook her head before she let him go free.

"Though she didn't have the chance for the proper ablutions," Jakinda told him, "or time to reach the mosque, her prayers are a sacred communication between her and her God, not a show for gawking little boys."

His mother had never been much for prayers and church. As a matter of fact, she had been openly hostile to the rank and file of the Anglican Church, but she had always taught Algie to never belittle something that a person held as holy and their own. For just a moment, he felt his cheeks flush at the thought of what his mother might have thought of him.

"I didn't mean any harm," he muttered quietly.

"Behave yourself, and there won't be any," Mssr Patrouille said. "After all, this is their portion of the world. We are only flying through it."

Algie made a sour grimace and nodded his agreement. He had a feeling this is what an adult should do. Being an adult was no fun at all.

He was untying his bundle to fish out his book when he heard the sound of engines. It came from the south, and if they were anything like the *Wu Zetian's* spirit turbines, it was coming in fast and very low. An airship in an airship dock should have been nothing unusual, but Algie's ear plotted it out as crossing the stream of traffic just in front of the gate. He dropped his belongings and leaned back out his window to catch a glimpse of the mystery ship.

The bird peddler didn't like him interfering with her prayers either. Algie quickly moved to stand in the doorway and hung by one hand on the brass grip to get an unobstructed view. Keijín, with a look of mild curiosity on her face, rose to look over his shoulder.

The airship was only a noisy shadow at twilight. It ran

without lights, banners, or insignia, just a paint job of mottled grey and black like a storm cloud. The engines roared loudly enough to drown out the call to prayer. The people in the crowd were no longer looking to the sunset but up at the intruder.

Algie looked over his shoulder once and bolted. This was too good a show to miss. He got his good leg up and planted his foot on the window sill. Before any of the Conversors could reach out to snatch him, he clambered up onto the roof. He had a clear view of the panic on the ground and the airship hovering near the gate. A wooden platform hung close beneath the ship from four cables. Several men crouched low in the space between it and the ship's belly.

Algie could hear Jakinda shouting at him from below:

"Young man! Get down from there this instant!"

With a mechanical sound as loud as a pistol shot, the winches released and the platform ratcheted down to just a few feet above a heavily laden wagon. The invaders, dressed in bright colors and armed to the teeth, leaped off to the wagon and the ground around it. The bystanders on the ground scattered in all directions, including through the gate and over the guards in the bright red BC&I livery. The armed men went down like nine-pins beneath the wave of frightened people before they could bring their rifles to bear.

Algie rushed forward in his eagerness to get a better view. Jakinda may have still been shouting, but not loudly enough to be heard over the pandemonium. He slowed for just a moment to leap the space between the two tram cars. The landing brought a twinge of pain from his leg, but not enough to slow him down.

The men from the airship looked one like the other: dark, bearded men in red embroidered skullcaps. They wore loose gray-green coats bound tight around the waist with sashes that matched their caps. Bandoliers packed with bullets and knives crossed their chests. These were the air pirates he had always been promised in his books.

While two of them held the yoke of the oxen that pulled the cart, another kicked the driver off his seat. Before the old man in Chinese silks could hit the ground, the bandits began unpacking his crates and pitching them up onto the platform. A few men on the ground collected whatever the fleeing merchants had discarded.

Algie leaped down into the coal car just behind the lorry. The fireman and the engineer still cowered in the cab, putting their bodies behind the hundreds of pounds of iron of the fire grate and boiler. From the top of the coal pile, Algie could look over the machine and see the brigands loading the platform no more than twenty meters ahead.

These didn't seem to be the kind of Asian outlaws Algie would have expected. Instead of caskets of gold and jewels, they loaded the platform with sacks of grain, rolls of electrical cable, and crates marked as holding Edison bulbs, nails, and other hardware. Clay jugs that might have held beer or wine went up into the cache along with bundles of vegetables and braces of flapping chickens bound up at the ankles. It looked more like grocery shopping at gunpoint than brazen robbery.

The tall man Algie guessed to be the leader stood back and watched the entire operation. He was older than the rest with bars of gray on either side of his beard and at his temples. A pale scar across the bridge of his nose stood out from the tanned and wrinkled skin of his face. Algie committed as much to memory as possible so he would be able to identify him to the police when they arrived.

The leader whistled sharply and gestured upwards. His men cleared out as the winches reeled in the platform. The airship rose up into the sky without waiting for its passengers. They were running for a small herd of horses left for their escape.

The older bandit made a final inspection of the area. Most of the bandits had already mounted their steeds; the merchants had all fled or hidden. He looked directly at Algie for a moment and the boy felt his chest clench around his heart. The bandit regarded him for just a second, and then gave an amused salute, touching his forehead and then extending his open hand out to Algie.

That was about the time the guards and their reinforcements returned. They hunkered down and opened fire, striking the leader several times in the back. A few stray bullets screamed over Algie's head. The bandits milled around on the backs of horses unaccustomed to gunfire. The older bandit brought his hand up to one of the holes blown through his heavy woolen coat and almost absently rubbed the clear fluid that came from his wounds between his fingers. Distressed cries in an unknown language went up from the bandits, no doubt fear for their leader and rage directed at the redcoats.

The leader raised a hand, a commanding gesture that showed that he was alive and still in control. He unholstered the two pistols on his belt and turned on the guards. The men fell down and stayed down when he shot them. A raucous cheer went up from his comrades at the sight. Without a backwards glance, he ran for an unladen horse and leapt into the saddle. In less than ten seconds, the lot of them disappeared from view.

Algie stood watching them and the airship, for a little while. Then a strong hand grabbed him by the ear as several other hands grasped him and lifted him from the coal car. The women attached to those hands pinwheeled Algie through the air and placed him gently, but firmly, on the earth.

"You may believe you are invincible and immortal," Jakinda said in an angry tone, "but you will learn to take orders, or you will find yourself on an airship to the most God-forsaken spot on this planet."

Algie intended to say something, but he thought better of that.

After a quick examination of his wounds, Jakinda led him back to their tram car ear-first and sat him between herself and Ayotunde. Both fanned themselves furiously as they waited for the steam lorry to move once again. The silence went on for what seemed forever as Algie stared straight ahead at Mssr. Patrouille. He spoke up once they had gotten underway.

"So... You saw what transpired out there? I myself got pressed to the floor by these Amazons."

Considering the Conversors' expressions, Algie just nodded in response. The writer's face brightened as he reached into his bag and withdrew a pencil and a notebook.

"Fabulous! Tell me everything."

8 "pen name", French
9 "It is rude to stare." French
10 "You are the Devil" French

EIGHT

19th of August 1889
Turfan Caravanserai

Algie expected to be paddled for his crimes, or at least sent to bed without supper. After they had finally been settled into their quarters, a rented villa just inside the verdant northern section of the walled city, he was brought into the presence of Mme. Streif.

She had no more time than he and First Mate McLaren had been given to settle into her quarters, but somehow her sitting room was prepared as a throne room for traveling royalty. A life-sized portrait of her deceased husband Jean-Pierre Streif already hung on the whitewashed wall, though Algie did not remember seeing anyone carry it off the ship. A single red-and-gold brocade wingback chair had been placed beneath it like a throne. A brass-bound leather box sat on the marble table at her right hand. Algie guessed that it could contain anything from an engagement book and some of her favorite sweets to a woman's derringer.

As he stood before her, propped up like a soldier on inspection between Jakinda and Feng Po, Algie longed for the relatively pleasant meetings with Mrs. Billew. With all five Conversors and Mssr. Patrouille seated along the sides of the room, it felt like a court of inquiry with its own firing squad installed.

Mme. Streif was still dressed in the purple and black gown in which she had started the day, but Algie could see she had re-done her hair and make-up. Kosciusko was curled up in her lap as she scratched behind its over-sized ears. The old woman looked at Algie with heavy-lidded eyes and then made a sound of great exhaustion.

"Firstly, Master Piggrem," she said, "I must acknowledge the debt every person on the ship owes you for your heroic actions in the *picaroon* attack."

Feng Po sharply nudged Algie in the back with the tip of his baton. That meant he should say something.

"Thank you, ma'am."

"But that debt is not an account you can draw on any time you choose."

Algie was honestly confused.

"Pardon me?"

"You were told to not climb up on the roof of our passenger tram in the midst of a bandit attack, is that not so?"

"I was excited," Algie said. "I just wanted to see."

"And it never occurred to you that you might have been hit by a stray bullet?"

He had been partially aware of the bullets flying when the guards opened fire. It only had some reality to him when afterwards, when Ayotunde pointed out the perfectly round hole in the tram's woodwork just above their eye level.

"No, ma'am. Not really."

Mme. Streif raised an eyebrow in polite amazement.

"Young man," she said, "you've already been shot twice this month. For anyone else, not getting shot until at least September would have been topmost in their mind."

Algie was silent until he got another sharp poke in the buttocks.

"I guess I didn't think."

"Did it even occur to you that one of my Conversors might have been injured, perhaps even killed, as they were pulling you to safety?"

Algie shook his head without making a sound. The thought of another woman paying the price for his stupidity or inaction was almost too much for him to bear. That was probably why he avoided thinking about it. As his mind wrestled with that, Mme. Streif fixed him with an assessing eye until he felt like a wriggling butterfly on a pin. Jakinda and Feng Po grasped him to be sure he didn't wriggle away too far.

"You did not think because you do not know," Mme. Streif said. "The French have a saying: *Mieux vaut prévenir que guérir.* Could you translate that for me?"

Algie chewed at the problem for a moment, trying to break the phrase into words in the right places and to match the sounds with the few words he knew. He thought he recognized the word *guerre* as in *c'est la guerre*, but he wasn't sure.

"I don't know. Something about war?"

Mme. Streif and Feng Po chuckled humorlessly as Jakinda sighed.

"Well, it could be applied to war, as with many other things," Mme. Streif said. "It actually means 'It is better to prevent than to heal.'"

"Oh, I see." Algie had started the evening being seen as an idiot and just provided more evidence every time he opened his mouth. He shut it.

"We have already made arrangements for you to start taking exercise with the ladies each morning," Mme. Streif said. "After that, you will improve your French with Mssr. Patrouille."

Patrouille sniffed and waggled his mustache as if a bug were hanging from the curlicue tip.

"I would like to see if you have a proficiency at languages equal to your knack for getting into trouble. Mlle. Ayotunde and you will be taking lessons with some of the caravanserai staff on the local Uyghur dialect after lunch each day."

Ayotunde said something in French. Algie caught words he thought meant "language" or "dialect," very common words when you converse with Conversors. Mme. Streif replied politely in French, then returned to him.

"She said it should be easy since the Uyghur tongue is a Turkmenic dialect. Do you speak Turkish, Master Piggrem?"

Feng Po didn't need to prod Algie's buttocks for a response. He blurted out "No!" on his own initiative. Mme. Streif softened a bit around her scowling edges and murmured something Algie couldn't make out.

"Well, that can be a goal for later, I suppose. Finally, I would like you to be prepared to attend my salons without embarrassment for anyone. That is why your last lessons before dinner will be etiquette and deportment with Mam'selle Nilenha."

Algie glanced over at the Conversor, a red-headed woman from South America, who seemed neither happy nor displeased to be giving him lessons. All he knew about her was that she came from a house of entertainment somewhere in the wilds of Brazil.

"Excuse me," he said without thinking, "but is that such a good idea? I mean, what kind of etiquette does she know?"

The old woman chuckled politely in response.

"Mlle. Nilenha is highly trained in all forms of social concourse, both of the European Courts and her native lands. What was that charming little tip you gave about etiquette in the Amazon basin?"

The Conversor smiled like a hungry wolf as she spoke:

"Always hold out your little finger when consuming the entrails of your enemies."

Mme. Streif nodded agreeably and turned to Algie:

"Any other questions?"

"Yes, ma'am. How long shall I be taking these lessons?"

Once he had jumped ship in South Africa, Algie had thought he was clear of school work for the rest of his life. Mme. Streif's expression showed that she was quite amused with his question.

"Why, when you have mastered movement, French, Uyghur, and etiquette, of course."

"Oh, I see."

"Then I shall come up with a new course of study for you." She blinked at him amiably. "Do you have any other questions, young Master Piggrem?"

Feng Po didn't really need to poke him in the kidney to make him respond, but the first mate did anyway.

"No, ma'am," Algie murmured. "None at all."

"Good, then go to the kitchen for something to eat before

bed. You look like we don't feed you.

*

Algie awoke in an actual bed the next morning. It was only a bag of rushes on a web of ropes, but it didn't sway as he moved or threaten to topple him headfirst onto the deck if he came too quickly out of a nightmare. Feng Po preferred a hammock like most airmen; he was in one even now, suspended between two hooks in a corner of the room. He swayed and softly snored as someone tapped on the door for a second time.

Algie threw off the wool blanket and swung his feet down onto the floor. He was still somewhat shaken by his dreams of his hunted days in Capetown. The stone and the air were ice cold, encouraging its own type of shaking. He checked the geometric gaps cut in the window's shutters and saw only darkness. He wasn't sure if he had made it to morning or if he was still stuck in very late last night.

"Just a moment," he called out as he stood and made for the door.

He ducked to the left as an India rubber ball flew through the space where his head had been a second before. Hurling balls was how the first mate woke Algie from nightmares, or shushed him if he made too much noise after lights out.

"Still sleeping, *chong wu*," he muttered without opening his eyes. A second ball sat ready in his hand.

Algie padded to the door, holding up the hem of the nightshirt Feng Po had loaned him to avoid tripping. He undid the latch as quietly as he could and opened the door enough to peer out through the crack. Chabi in bright blue silk pajamas beamed back at him.

"*Bonjour, Monsieur Chopon!*"

"Good Morning, Miss Chabi. I mean, *bonjour*."

Another ball bounced off the door only a few centimeters from Algie's face. A plaintive moan came from the man in the hammock:

"Sleeping!"

Algie opened the door wide enough to slip out and put the heavy slab of wood between him and Feng Po's balls.

"What time?" Algie hoped he asked in French.

The young woman responded with a very long phrase in Chinese and then two words in French:

"*Trois cloches.*" Three bells.

Algie did some quick calculations. Since it was still dark, it was probably still in the middle of third watch. That would make it five-thirty in the morning. Far too early for anything decent to be happening.

"What are you doing here so early?" he attempted in French.

He was sure he got the articles and declensions all wrong, but Chabi seemed to get the drift. Without putting down the brown paper package, she stuck one leg straight out in front of her and slowly bent the other leg until she was only a dozen centimeters from the ground. Then she reversed the process and returned to standing, moving as steadily as a piece of hydraulic machinery. All the while her free hand executed graceful arcs and curves like a bird in flight. There would be no way Algie could keep up if this was the Conversors' idea of morning exercise.

With both feet on the ground, Chabi smiled and presented the package to Algie. He peeled away a bit of brown paper to reveal blue silk.

"I am not wearing this!" he said loudly, in English, and without thinking. The outfit was gaudy and scandalous enough on a woman. If Algie were caught outside in blue silk pajamas, he would look like… like…

He wasn't sure what it would be like, but it couldn't be good.

He went rigid as two more of Feng Po's balls slapped against the other side of the door. He looked over his shoulder out of pure reflex.

Chabi had that disappointed but determined expression that mothers and teachers put on just before going to war with their charges. Algie knew he could do things Mme. Streif's way, or find himself forwarded on to whatever fate Mrs. Billew had arranged for him in Australia.

"I'm sorry," Algie muttered. "I'll be changed in just a minute.

*

As he and Chabi had just stepped into the arcade around the inner courtyard, Algie heard the music start. String instruments and flute, played by three of the *Wu Zetian's* Chinese crewman, kept up a slow steady rhythm as the other Conversors in blue gathered on straw mats over the flagstones. It was a cool refuge from the high summer's heat, surrounded by two floors of marble arches. Carefully tended plants and lawns denied the fact this city was in the heart of one of the largest deserts on earth. A tall statuary fountain babbled away in the middle of a tiled lined pool in the center of the courtyard.

Seeing the four Conversors in form-fitting blue pajamas like the set he wore, without any skirts or corsets to be seen, gave him pause. Mssr. Patrouille had taken him aside the night before and warned him to be neither a prig nor a lech when confronted with such a sight, reminding Algie of the time Dale Daring had to hide in the harem of the Sultan.

As he joined them, Jakinda herded him into his spot in the center of the line of women. She didn't wait for him to say yea or nay as far as his being ready, but just called out commands, first in French, then in English for Algie's benefits.

"We will start out with some simple stretches. To the right!"

With his left arm over his head, Algie tried to bend over to one side without hurting himself. The wound across his ribs burned like hot iron again as the scar stretched centimeter by centimeter. He grimaced and Jakinda noticed straight away.

"Are you hurt?" she asked. "Should *Sifu* Huang take a look at you?"

"I'm fine," Algie lied. "It's just a little twinge."

The Conversors kept up their stretches, moving steadily and slowly like trees bending in the wind. Grace was not one of Algie's strengths. He kept up with the women, but he felt like an overfat badger trying to keep up with swans.

They started bending forward with feet spread wide. First, they touched their fingertips to the mats, then their elbows, and then their foreheads. Algie nearly got his elbows down to the mats when he hurt himself. The bullet holes in the meaty part of his right leg screamed with pain. It felt like a crocodile sinking its teeth into his buttock and twisting to rip off a piece. He braced his hands on his knees and breathed hard and heavy to stop from screaming. If he was man enough to get shot, he was man enough not to winge about it.

"I think that you are no longer fine," Jakinda said. "Ladies, take him over to that bench.'

The Conversors gathered around him, nearly a half dozen concerned older sisters, muttering and cooing in just as many languages. They lifted him and carried him lightly to a stone bench made up with comforters and pillows as a sick bed. Chabi rushed off to bring Master Huang.

As they waited for her returned, the other Conversors settled down in the shady verge of the courtyard around Algie and fell to their own occupations. Keijín got out her sketchbook and pencils and went to work on a drawing of the fountain. Jakinda, with a spool of heavy cotton thread and a shuttle fell to tatting lace.

"Is this the Arts and Crafts hour, then?" Algie asked.

Ayotunde scowled for a moment, and then returned to carving away at a piece of yellow jade with a steel scribe.

"This is *opari*," Jakinda said without losing a beat on her handiwork. "A task of Heart and Hands which heals the Heart. It is another part of the Secret School beyond movement and defense of oneself."

"We all have something that calms us and allows us to focus on creating beauty." Nilenha halted her intricate passes and shuffles with playing cards. "You're are so fond of your little pocket knife. You should take up wood carving."

Algie felt immediately doubtful about this.

"Oh, I don't think I could ever be any good," he said.

"It is not how well you do it," Jakinda said, "but that you dedicate yourself to doing it."

"All right, I'll think about it."

Master Huang and Chabi arrived then and, before Algie could squeak out a complaint, his blue silk pants were pulled down and his dressings removed. The Chinese doctor muttered to himself as he examined Algie's wounds. Algie gritted his teeth with each poke or prod. As the old man collected his jars of salves and his needles, Jakinda translated his remarks.

"Master Huang says you haven't torn out any of your stitches and there is no sign of infection," she said. "So, the pain is just a part of the natural healing process." The other Conversors still gathered around with expressions of concern on their faces, five young women in scandalous outfits staring at the bullet hole in his naked bum. It did not help his state of mind.

"I'm so glad this is going well," Algie said. "I would hate to learn what bad healing would feel like."

"You have been shot after all. It's the sort of thing that kills quite a few people," Jakinda said.

Algie simply grunted as Master Huang applied his herbal concoctions on the wounds and plotted out the best place to stick his needles.

"I think you should rest for the duration of this morning's exercises," Jakinda said. "We can start again tomorrow."

Algie nodded as the Chinese doctor twiddled the needles stuck into several meaty parts of his leg.

Nilenha, his new etiquette teacher, laid a hand on Jakinda's elbow.

"Perhaps," she said with a playful half-smile, "the young man needs some motivation to continue his studies. A hint of the potential of Isilmandatu, when one applies themselves?"

"Normally, I would say 'no'," Jakinda replied, "but young master Piggrem *is* a special case."

She inclined her head towards Chabi and murmured a few words. The Mongol woman flashed a quick smile at Algie, an expression both fierce and gleeful. She picked up one of the fans on the nearest bench and fluttered with it to the center of the rice straw mats. Chabi stood motionless and demure, waiting for whatever Jakinda had planned next.

"You do understand," Jakinda told Algie, "that you cannot tell anyone what you see here?"

"Why not?"

"Isilmandatu is a secret that has been handed down for generations, from mother to daughter. It could be dangerous for the outside world to even know we exist."

"I don't understand."

"Understanding will come with time. For now, I need you to promise." She examined him closely, as if she were looking for defects beyond the bullet wounds. "Promise on your mother's grave."

Algie took in a sharp breath at that, surprised that Jakinda would mention her. Whatever he was about to learn, it must be deathly important.

"I promise."

Jakinda called out in Chinese and Chen Bolin stood up ponderously from his kneeling position behind the stringed *guzheng* he played. He was a favorite of the Germans in the engineering division, mainly because he could do much of the heavy lifting in the engine room without their having to assemble a hydraulic jack in tight quarters. He cracked and stretched his joints as he ambled over to the mats. Chen bowed to Jakinda, and she to him, as she took over his place at his instrument.

She ran her fingers across the multiple strings in a run of rapid notes that rang out like rain on a tile roof. She picked back up the strange Chinese tune Chen had been playing. Two other crewmen, playing a flute and an *erhu* fiddle, accompanied her.

Chabi flipped her fan to and fro in time with the tune. Its movements became faster and more extreme, cutting great arcs through the air like a bird fighting to pull free of the tiny Conversor. The other women clapped along to that tune, encouraging her to dance. She began to spin like a top and leap higher in the air than Algie would have imagined possible. She twisted in the air like a pinwheel.

Chen stepped up to the weapon rack at the edge of the straw mats. He removed his artificial left hand with a twist and replaced it with a wicked curved blade that fit into the socket.

Chabi dropped to the ground and stuck there like an ax in a stump. The clapping stopped, though the musicians played on. The opponents came within a few paces, faced each other, and then bowed.

Then, they began to circle each other.

Chabi smiled up at Chen and fluttered her fan before her like a courtesan. Chen took great sideways strides to sidle around her. He executed many fine flourishes with his blade to show he was no novice with the weapon. Algie was beginning to worry for Chabi's safety; as nimble as she was, it would only take one blow to do grievous damage.

Chen lunged forward with a shout, driving the point of the sword straight for her heart. Algie jumped in spite of himself.

Chabi was not there at the end of Chen's thrust. Somehow, she flowed beneath his extended arm and rose up behind him. She folded her fan closed with a sound like a steel trap and swatted his backside. Chen swung around behind him, but she was already gone.

Chabi danced around the big man, avoiding his attacks and goading him with the fan until he finally seemed to go mad. With an inhuman stillness, Chabi waited for his attack then. He charged at her like an angry bull as he shouted at the top of his lungs.

Then, something happened.

Algie couldn't really see what. Chabi became a blur of blue motion. He did know that the metal blade detached and flew one way, and Chen Bolin somehow flew another. He landed on his back and bounced just a little bit before coming to rest. Chabi drew back, looking prepared for murder.

Jakinda stopped the music and shouted out something. Algie didn't even guess the language it was in, but he recognized the tone:

"Stop! Enough!"

Chabi went back to her resting position, placidly fanning herself as she watched three of the other Conversors rush over to lever Chen to his feet. He moved slowly, sounding like he had the wind trounced out of him, but he showed no ill will. He bowed courteously to Chabi with a wary grin on his great round face as he retrieved his hand. She returned the bow just as politely.

Nelinha was suddenly at Algie's side, a devilish smile on her lips.

"So," she said, "do you think you'll be up for exercises tomorrow?"

Algie was unable to say anything that could describe just how much he wanted to learn this, but he was able to nod his head 'yes' until he felt like it might fall off.

NINE

15th of February 1889
Capetown Harbor

Keogh, Algie, and the cook's boy crept down the hallways that led down to the storage hold beneath the galley. The rest of the live-stock of the *Roscommon Venture* were left behind. Even when their futures and free-dom were at stake, the chil-dren could not keep silent for more than a few seconds at a stretch. The excitement of escape was too much for most of them and they frequently broke out in squeals, tears, or scuffles.

Dale Daring or August Vogel never had problems like this with hostages. Maybe foreign women and children had better control of themselves.

Algie scratched an arrow in the floor with his sharpened belt buckle. If they could make their way down to the hold without being caught, the others should be able to follow their path from the signs. If they did get caught, Algie didn't want to think about it. He wondered if sea captains still ordered keel-hauling for discipline.

They made it down to the stairway that led to the right level in the hold before Algie confirmed what he had been guessing: there was practically no one on the ship. No sound of footsteps or talk. No lights in any of the cabins they passed.

Algie tapped the cook's boy on the shoulder to catch his attention.

"Has everybody left the ship for shore leave tonight?"

The boy shrugged expansively, but kept walking down the stairs. If Algie and Keogh wanted to find a way off this ship, they had better stick with him. The three crept like shadows along the wall and into the hold.

The place smelled horrid, a combination of rotted cabbage, rancid fat, and dead fish. All the loose wood and chains rhythmically rattled and groaned with the gentle rocking of the ship. Empty barrels from the galley laid on their sides between two rails. Those would guide the barrels as they rolled towards the large hatch at the far end of the room. Algie had seen ships at Portsmouth harbor off-loading their depleted barrels into the harbor to be fished out by the chandler's mates and local merchants later.

Algie jangled the chains that held the barrels in place at the end of their run. They were secured with a simple bolt and nut that Algie could loosen with his bare hands. He went to the hatches to inspect them. He could open the bar and bracket easily; the double doors swung open of their own accord on squealing hinges. The one on the right swung all the way to bang against the hull as the ship dipped with a wave. All three cringed with terror at the noise, but Algie was the first to anchor one hand on the top of open doorway and reach out to grab the swaying door.

The ship moved and the door pulled at him as it moved to strike the hull again. Algie felt both Keogh and the cook's boy grab him by his belt to keep him from going over the edge. For several long seconds he dangled over the dark water and calculated how far the drop to the ocean was and how likely the barrels were going to actually land open-side up. The hinges squealed with every movement like a hungry cat begging for fish. That noise ran right up Algie's spine.

He was about to ask to be pulled in when Algie heard the hatch directly above them unlocking. He looked over his shoulder and the cook's boy waved for him to hold the door all the way open. Algie saw the logic in that. Anyone looking down would see the half-open door below, but not if it were pressed against the outer hull. The squealing of hinges when he pulled it all the way closed would encourage them to look down.

He dangled there, with Keogh and the boy acting as his anchors, and muttered over and over in his mind: *Please, don't look down. Please, don't look down.*

The sound of metal pail being jostled through the hatchway came from above. A pair of hands held it out the back of the ship and up-ended it. A rain of fish heads, meat scraps, and moldy biscuits fell past Algie into the sea. Only a little bit of it got blown into his face by the wind, the rest formed a chum slick on the surface. The galley worker banged the bucket against the ledge to dislodge the very worst bits from the bottom.

Most of that hit Algie, but he was trying to hold off vomiting until the hatch above was sealed again. He breathed through his mouth raggedly and counted off fourteen Picadillies in his head as he dangled above the water. He looked down when he heard the splashing.

Long dark forms swarmed through the garbage slick, twisting and snapping at each other. Dark gray backs and pale white bellies flashed just beneath the surface. Bright white teeth in multiple rows lined the creatures' mouths.

Algie had never seen anything like this before, but he identified them as soon as he saw them swimming away from their feeding. The triangular fins meant only one thing.

"Sharks," he whispered to himself.

The hatch above closed and latched from the sound of it. Algie waited just a few seconds to pull himself in and closed the doors behind himself.

"That was close," he said.

He caught his breath for a moment before getting on with their escape plans.

"We need to take a look at the boats up on the deck before we try this," Algie said.

"Is there something wrong?" Keogh asked. The cook's boy's expression asked the same thing.

Algie wasn't sure if he wanted to tell anyone about the

sharks, but he didn't necessarily want to go into that water in a barrel smelling of salted fish.

"No. I just want to check out every chance we might have," Algie said. "If there really is only a handful of crewman left on board, maybe we could lower a lifeboat and row ashore."

The cook's boy scowled and shook his head. When Algie pressed the question, he pantomimed an answer. He pointed at Algie, then pointed at his own head, tapping the temple with his fingertip. Algie recognized the next actions as pulling ropes with both hands through a pulley and then pulling on a set of oars. Then a questioning look with hands spread wide.

If there were any boats, would you know how to launch and row one?

"I'm good at mechanical things," Algie protested. That time he nearly strangled himself outside Mrs. Billew's window didn't really count.

The cook's boy did not look convinced. It took several minutes of coordinated wheedling to finally force him to lead them upstairs to the main deck.

*

There was just one boat left, a dinghy about twenty foot long. It hung from davits at the rear of the ship, just on the outside of the rails. Algie saw three empty brackets where the other boats had been lowered and rowed away. Beyond them, the lights of Capetown glittered in the night. Houses, ships running lights, search lights and airships in the aerodrome, they all pointed the way to a life better and longer than the children could expect in Australia.

Between the *Roscommon Venture* and that city were a quarter mile of dark water, cold as ice and running in unknown currents. Monsters with great, pointy teeth lurked beneath the surface.

Algie definitely wanted a boat to make that crossing.

The three boys skulked up to the last boat, hiding in the shadows as best as they could. They froze as a flock of sleepy seagulls atop the wheelhouse argued among themselves.

With no sign of crew, they went to work on the mechanisms

of the lifeboat davit. Algie grasped the end of an upright lever taller than himself.

"It looks like this is the lock on the winch ratchet. We would have to pop this out to be able to swing the boat away from the railing and then crank it down to the water." Algie pointed out the different mechanisms as he spoke. "Once we're down, we just disconnect the hooks under the block and tackles and we're off."

Algie looked expectantly to the cook's boy for his reaction. He seemed convinced but not exuberant. Keogh might have looked scared pale if he weren't painted pitch black.

"Can we even pop that lever out?" Keogh asked.

The cook's boy shrugged.

"There's only one way to find out," Algie muttered.

He pulled on the lever. It didn't move.

He lifted his feet up and braced them on the davit arm so he could put all of his weight into the effort.

It did no good.

First the cook's boy, and then Keogh, joined in pulling on the lever. They tugged and grunted, but the lever did not budge. The three hung from the steel arm like the monkey on a stick toy his mother had bought him at the circus.

"Is there any way we can lower the boat without pulling this lever?" Keogh asked between heavy breaths.

The cook's boy, who was hanging upside down, shook his head in a cloud of dark brown hair that obscured his face.

As Algie calculated what their next step could be, a loud noise came out of the night, down near the water. Algie and Keogh shrieked in surprise and dropped to the deck. The cook's boy merely fell. They scrambled to their feet and saw a steamship passing close to their own. It was less than a hundred yards away at its closest. It blew off another powerful blast of its foghorn and steamed into the harbor.

A hatch on the upper deck popped and someone shouted at them from inside.

"Who the Bloody Hell is making that ruckus out there?"

Algie stiffened and then quickly pressed himself into the shadow of the boat. Keogh froze in plain sight, but painted as he was, he looked to be a shadow himself. The boy did not hesitate. He slapped each of them on the back and pointed them towards cover. As Algie and Keogh ran, he pulled a crust of dark bread from his pocket. He shredded the bread as he gave out a high whistle. That caught the seagulls' attention. They descended on the deck like a summer storm of feathers, beaks, and appetite.

As the boys took cover, the door of the wheelhouse creaked open. Whoever had yelled first was hanging out that door and throwing things at the seagulls.

"Get your bloody asses off my boat, you bunch of sea rats!"

A pewter tankard landed amongst the birds, but that lofted them for just a second until the bread was all gone. Algie and company took the opportunity to slip below decks.

"All right, barrels it is," Algie told the cook's boy. "Bring all of our lot down to the hold while I try to get this ready to go."

As the cook's boy slipped down the passageway with Keogh, Algie wondered what would be the best way of dealing with sharks without guns, knives, or August Vogel's Electrical Stun Rod.

*

With a short frenzy of work with ropes and barrels, the children executed Algie's escape plan. The cook's boy didn't seem to think was it entirely brilliant, but he never brought forward a better alternative. There were twenty-eight children, boys and girls, and fifteen empty barrels in the hold. That meant only two a piece with single berths for the eldest and largest of them like Hanna and the nameless boy.

As they started wedging the smallest children in the first barrels, two by two, Deirdre caught his eye. She looked very concerned as they hammered down the lid of Keogh and Mary's wooden vessel.

"Are you entirely sure this will work?"

"Of course," Algie answered. "The mechanics are all basically sound."

"The mechanics of that cable slide you made were sound," she replied, "but it still nearly killed you."

Algie saw some of the others looking over at them at the word 'killed.' He stepped closer to his friend so their conversation could be carried on at a more private level.

"I simply didn't have enough time to work through the design flaws on that."

"How long have you had to work on this?" Deirdre gestured at the barrels on the ramp. "No more than an hour, I'm sure."

"Do you think we are going to get any more time?"

"I think," she hissed through clenched teeth, "that you are going to drown some of us if you aren't careful!"

Algie had no response for that. The rest of the children in the hold fell silent. It made things quiet enough to hear the uproar coming from the forward part of the ship. Algie listened for a few moments to convince himself that this was just another drunken brawl amongst the crew, a common enough occurrence on this ship.

Deirdre looked at him wide-eyed in terror.

"They know that we're gone," Algie said. "We have to leave now."

The boys and girls stood around the barrels, doing little more than watching him and Deirdre. He looked back at them stupefied.

"That means we have to leave NOW!" Algie waved his hands at them as if he were herding chickens. "Everybody to their places unless they want to spend their lives in those cages."

Deirdre waded in and forcibly thrust the children into whatever empty barrels were at hand. He and the cook's boy unlatched the doors and hooked them out of the way. A quick glance over his shoulder showed that almost all of the children were in place, though only a few of the barrels laying sideways in the ramps had their covers hammered tight. The sound of angry voices from the decks above indicated they weren't going to have time for such luxuries.

Algie pointed and half-shoved the cook's boy towards his barrel on the uppermost ramp. As the boy climbed the exterior of the framework and then slid into his barrel feet first, Algie picked up a damage control cone and a mallet and made for the door.

The wooden cones were supposed to block a hole punched in the hull by a cannon ball, but it would do just as well to wedge shut a wooden door. Algie put the point of the cone in the gap under the door and hammered it home.

Algie sprinted over to the release and put his whole weight into it. With a pained groan of wood and metal, the first barrels rolled down the ramp towards the door. The lengths of manila rope that the children had twisted in the direction opposite the rotation of the barrels untwisted and stretched out taut and straight. As they flipped over and over and again, the children inside them squealed in pained surprise, making sounds like kittens rattled around in a wooden pail.

The first barrel made it clear of the framework and rolled towards the door. The second and third followed close behind it. Just as the fifth barrel came down the track, it jammed. The first barrel was pulled up short as it was flying out the hatches. It collided loudly with the outside hull just beneath. The noises escalated to terror and blazing obscenities since that was Keogh's barrel.

The barrels behind the fifth crashed into it one on top of another with a sound of wooden pins knocked down in a bowling alley. Deirdre popped her head out of her barrel. On her face she bore a grimace of knowing disapproval.

"So what is wrong now?" she shouted down at him.

Her head stuck out far enough to leave her neck at a level with the wooden framework that boxed in the ramps. Once everything got moving again, it could take off her head like a headsman's axe.

"Bloody Hell!" Algie pointed at her with the plank he intended to use as an oar. "Get your head back inside before you lose it!"

The collisions eventually were enough to loosen the jam and the barrels once again rolled out the hatchway. Deirdre felt the movement and, with a shriek, withdrew like a terrified tortoise. The topmost barrels started their descent with a loud crash where each dropped to the top of the next ramp. The battered children inside cried out with each sudden movement, making smaller, fleshy impact sounds of their own.

By the end of this night, Algie told himself, the children would be free, but not happy.

He had lost count of the number of splashes he heard since the makeshift train had gotten on the move again, but it seemed to tally with the number of barrels remaining. He didn't have the time to do a careful count since they were coming up on the point where the original plan had collapsed completely.

At first inception, he wanted to get everyone into their assigned barrels and pull the lever with a bit of cord. Since that plan had gone paws to Jesus, he had two options. He could either dive headfirst into a rolling barrel in the twelve feet between the ramp and the hatch, or let all the barrels go out the hatch and leap down into his berth. The latter gave him opportunities to land with legs astraddle the wooden wall, land in shark-infested water, or spike the barrel and possibly punch clean through the bottom. All of those scenarios pressured him to choose Plan A. He had heard variations of "a flying leap at a rolling doughnut" many times on the streets of Portsmouth. They had never sounded like any fun.

Four barrels still rolled down the ramps; three more spun out through the deck space between the ramp and the hatch. He was running out of time.

He could see Deirdre's head bouncing about inside her barrel as it spun down the last few feet. The cook's boy had the sense to brace his arms inside the mouth of his barrel. He glared out at Algie with an expression of fierce determination.

The last empty barrel was his and it was on the bottom ramp. He pitched his piece of oar wood into it and dashed to the end of the framework. It seemed like forever as he watched Deirdre and the nameless boy come clear of it. Then, it was his turn and Algie made a mad dash for the open mouth of his wooden doughnut.

He leaped at the last moment, covering his head with his arms in midair. A second later, he crashed into the bottom of the barrel and a few stray gobbets of salt pork. He started tumbling about inside like a handful of ingredients in a chemist's mortar. His makeshift paddle pummeled him about the back and shoulders like the pestle.

After a blessedly short period of beating, he felt himself fly out of the back of the ship and splash into the ocean. He still felt like he was spinning about. The actual up-and-down motion of the waves added to complicated figures his stomach made in space.

He pushed his face up out of the residual salt and fat, but it was too late. After a few painful constrictions of the back of his throat, he heaved up his last evening's dinner of gruel and salt pork all over the wooden walls and himself.

Drained and battered, Algie twisted his body right side up. Popping his head up, he was able to see the others spread out across the water. Deirdre, the cook's boy, and a few others were leaning out of their barrels. Most looked the way he felt: bruised and spattered with yesterday's lunch. The cook's boy was tugging on the rope between his tub and Deirdre's, pulling them closer. When he caught Algie's attention, he made a circular gesture over his head, making the sensible suggestion that they circle up and bind together their wagons just like in the cowboy adventures.

Algie reached into the water with his bit of wood and took of the slack of his rope. A glance to the left told him that they had caught the right current and were floating away from the *Roscommon Venture* and in towards the harbor.

They were free, but definitely not clear. That would take a lot more work.

The cook's boy loudly slapped the side of his barrel and pointed at the ones at the front of the chain. Most were still covered. One was riding low in the ocean, probably taking on water. Algie could hear the children inside shrieking in terror.

Bloody Hell, thought Algie. *A HELL of a lot more work.*

A large fish splashed around in the water, rubbing against the outside of Algie's barrel. Its mouth gaped open and shut, looking for any stray garbage that might be attached. He couldn't tell if it was a shark in the dark, but Algie wasn't taking any chances. He whacked it in the head with his stick sharply. When it swam away, Algie went back to pulling his barrel closer to the other escapees.

TEN

20th of August 1889
Turfan Caravanserai

Algie limped over to Mssr. Patrouille's rooms after morning exercises. They were just a short distance down the arcades from the central courtyard. He wasn't quite sure what he was expecting of French lessons with the author, but it proved to be even less practical than he had guessed.

Patrouille invited Algie into his sitting room for tea and biscuits among the piles of books and racks of colorful clothing. They discussed the weather and furniture and clothing in French, with only the most oblique references to comely young women in blue silk pajamas. Algie at the best of times was not the most focused student. This afternoon his mind whirled from what he had seen in courtyard. Mssr. Patrouille must have seen that chaos playing out on his face.

The lesson finished after only two cups of tea and seven biscuits. As Patrouille nudged him towards door, he stacked evening reading books into Algie's arms to just below his chin. He felt their crushing weight on his spirit until he realized most of them were Dale Daring novels in the original French. A few works of Alexandre Dumas and Victor Hugo rounded out the collection. A French-English dictionary larger than a Mermaid's Purse acted as a foundation for his tower of books.

Algie tottered down to his own quarters with the books, only to deposit them on the table at the side of his bed and leave. A fist-sized block of wood had already materialized on his table next to the jackknife. Jakinda had told him earlier he had an hour for lunch at the common dining hall. Immediately after that, and she put a great deal of emphasis on the word *immediately*, he was to meet Ayotunde at the staff quarters just east of the Governor's residence. Considering the fact that she was twice the size of Chabi and no doubt trained just as well in the Secret School, Algie did not want to offend her by being late.

Crossing the main thoroughfare of the caravanserai was no simple feat. People were flooding into the walled city just as quickly as there were folk returning to the Silk Road. Every steed and conveyance Algie had ever read of was on the high street—and quite a few he had never imagined. He saw glistening horses from Araby dressed as fancily as their robed riders. He saw red elk from Japan bearing bowmen that kept their faces hidden behind rough wool. Shadow figures rode in curtained palanquins carried on the shoulders of men muscled like oxen. Many of those bearers carried curved swords to protect their hidden masters.

Oxen, horses, and strange metallic beasts pulled caravan wagons, ornately carved and brightly painted cottages on wheels that were both home and place of business for solitary merchants. Their stock in trade was painted on the caravans' sides. In just a few moments he saw jewelers and armorers and tinkers and cobblers and purveyors of fine spices. Others streamed by in languages he couldn't read or recognize.

Algie pulled himself up short. He had no time to be gawking. He had only a little time to get food and then meet with Ayotunde.

Or die.

It was easy enough to push into the crowd of foot traffic on the outside. The slowest walkers were pushed to the right while the larger and more dangerous vehicles stuck to the center going either way. He felt the fear tighten within him, from gut to throat, when the dray wagons rumbled past. That reminded him too much of the last time he saw his mother.

Fear never stopped Dale Daring in his adventures, and Algie had done well enough to put it aside when faced with danger. But he was still a living creature on his most basic level, and an animal never wanted to die under crushing iron wheels. He pushed his way across the stream of traffic between the slow sputtering steam rickshaws and two-wheeled carts drawn by donkeys. He had just dodged around a heavy wagon pulled by a team of four when he saw the pedestrian bridge four meters above.

Algie felt himself a proper idiot dodging around like a scared rabbit with a game leg when he could have simply strolled across the wooden span. He stood still for just a moment as he called himself every name he could remember in English and then started all over in French. That is how the bronze palanquin-bearers nearly ran him down.

The headless humanoid figures wore bell-like rangles on their hips, but the warning noise was lost in the sound of the crowd. Algie only knew they were bearing down on him when they were on either side of him. He spun and ducked between them and then beneath the ornate red and gold car of the palanquin.

As he walked between the automatons, Algie could hear the delicate sounds of the machinery otherwise drowned out by the rangles and the noise of the crowd. Each time a limb moved, metal plate rubbed against metal with tones like a cymbal. The inner workings ticked like a dozen clocks with occasional twangs like piano strings.

It took only a few paces for him to clear the palanquin and the headless bronze men. Then, he was almost underneath the team of six iron bulls that followed.

This was something he was ready for. He rushed up between the two lead machines and got a foot up on the harness tree between them. Like any of the other *Lǎoshǔ*, he turned and climbed up to seat himself on the back of one of the metallic beasts. He wasn't sure where he would go from there, but at least he wouldn't be trampled.

It was rather fun just riding along and looking down on the masses, once he got up there, like he was a young maharajah on the back of a clockwork elephant. He laughed out loud at the thought. He wondered if Mssr. Patrouille's friend might write that into the next Dale Daring adventure.

A panel swung open on the back of the palanquin and an old man leaned out through the opening. His skin was tanned and deeply wrinkled, like one of those faces carved from an apple and left to dry in the sun. His beard, which grew only from the point of his chin, was yellow-white. He wore a black turban held in place by a woven golden band and jewels. His eyes were a most unusual bright green.

The man in the palanquin fired off a long string of words in an unidentifiable language. They came out the way Feng Po spoke French to torment Captain Strausser. The old man did not seem to be angry, but he was waiting for an answer.

Algie shrugged and held out his open hands. It was a terrible answer, but it was all that he had.

The old man continued to speak. He gesticulated with great energy at the bulls and the carriage that they drew. Algie turned and saw that it was a flatbed that carried ornamented wrought-iron cages. In the cages closest to him he saw dovecotes holding dozens of birds of many colors.

The old man began shouting again and Algie turned back to face him. He placed his cupped hands behind his ears and shouted back:

"I'm terribly sorry, but I don't understand what you are saying!"

An expression of absolute delight spread across the old man that made his beard swing back and forth.

"You are sorry?" The man laughed out a clear rising note like a trumpet. "Are you an English boy?"

"Yes, sir. I am."

"I am Tuareg!" The man gave a greeting that sounded like one of Ayotunde's languages and gave a salute by touching his fingertips to his forehead. "So, why are you getting underfoot and throwing my *karakuri* out of their balance?"

"I didn't mean to be any trouble," Algie replied. "I'm just trying to get across to the dining hall!"

Tuareg looked at Algie as if he had said the most

extraordinary thing. He then gestured with his arms at the bridge, taking in the entire span as if pointing out all the people in the caravanserai that were smarter than Algie.

"I didn't see that when I started."

"A caravan without a map," the old man said, "seldom arrives at its destination."

Algie was sure that meant something like "look before you leap," or at least, "look at a map before you throw yourself under a dray wagon." Adults had told him enough variations of that aphorism that he considered using it as an extra middle name. Before he had a chance to respond, Algie heard the most terrifying thing imaginable: an adult shouting his name.

"Algernon Piggrem," Ayotunde shouted from somewhere above, "*Vous avez beaucoup de peine!*[11]"

He didn't need his improved French to know he was in a great deal of trouble. The Conversor's tone of voice translated for him quite well. He stole a glance up at the bridge to confirm that Ayotunde was indeed passing judgement on him from on high. She stood leaning over the guardrail with her hands clenched on the outer edge. A small woman, slight, nervous, and dressed in bright colors, looked anxiously between the angry woman on the bridge and the frightened boy on the iron bull. Algie guessed she was their language tutor.

He had been told he could no longer use what Dale Daring would do as a guide for his life, so he fell back upon his only other male role model: Feng Po McLaren.

He smiled broadly, looked the Conversor right in the eye, and used one of the first mate's common gambits.

"Bon jour, Mademoiselle Ayotunde. J'espère que vous vous sentez bien aujourd'hui.[12]"

She was not feeling well today and she was not susceptible to Algie's charm. She crossed over to the other side of the bridge as he and Tuareg's clockwork caravan passed beneath it. She blocked her way through foot traffic like a rugby forward. Algie tried again.

"We will be right over in a moment to join you for lunch." He didn't know how to say that in French, so he said it loudly and slowly in English with all the proper gestures for a game of Charades.

Tuareg spoke up and took over the conversation. It started in French, then drifted into Arabic, Algie guessed, with the appropriate *salaams*. Where they ended linguistically, he had no idea, but Tuareg once again laughed, Ayotunde displayed a hint of a smile, and Algie fostered the faint hope that he might not be skinned alive. The old man in the palanquin translated when all was through.

"I explained to your lovely friend," Tuareg said, "that I saw you in the crowd and I was quite concerned that you might be crushed by some careless driver. So, I gladly invited you to ride on my Iron Auroch, as my guest."

"You lied to her."

"Most convincingly, I am told."

Algie didn't doubt that at all. It was obvious that Tuareg was a traveling peddler and a master of that subtle deceit called Salesmanship.

"What are we to do now?" Algie asked.

"I told her that I would bring you to the eastern door of the Governor's Compound." Tuareg chuckled as he pulled an ornate cross from some fold of his robes. "Hold on tightly as I make good on my word!"

He blew a melody on the brass cross like a bosun's pipe and settled himself into the cushions of his conveyance. The headless automatons lurched to the left to cross the fastest stream of oncoming traffic. They were heedless to the approaching steam lorry or the line of passenger carriages that folded up like the curves of a snake as it braked to avoid them. The Auroch beneath Algie gave out a metallic lowing sound and followed the palanquin through the chaos. Shouts, curses, and overripe fruit were hurled their way as they cut through the mass of humans and their machines.

Algie held on for dear life, not knowing whether he should scream or laugh at the spectacle around him. Hay carts upended and wooden cages of birds and animals spilled out their prisoners. Algie tried to isolate the specific words that sounded like obscenities, so that he could submit them to Feng Po for translation. That was a daunting task. All the while,

Tuareg waved and apologized to those he crossed, each in their own language, it seemed.

Eventually their trail of destruction broke free of the line of foot traffic. Tuareg used his whistle to order a double time march though the alleys that led to the dining hall and the Governor's Compound. Algie bounced on the back of the bull. His teeth clicked together with each landing. The ride was the best time he had had in a long time, and he wondered how many more strange amusements he would find like this along the High Silk Road.

11"You are in big trouble!" French
12 "I hope you are feeling well today." French

ELEVEN

20th of August 1889
Turfan Caravanserai

Their Uyghur tutor, Meryem, awaited them beside a table in the garden. Like many of the locals, she wore a brightly colored dress and headscarf made of the regional cotton & Atlas silk. Her skin was dark and her features were strong like a Greek statue. Her hair was strawberry blonde and her eyes a luminous green. Algie thought she could easily fit in the company of Conversors.

She greeted them quietly, in words that made no sense to Algie.

It would have been much easier to learn the Uyghur dialect if there were any one language that all three of them shared. Ayotunde spoke Arabic, Chinese, and of course French. Meryem spoke Uyghur and enough Chinese to carry out business with the traveling merchants, but only a little English. Algie was left with a smattering of French and his native English, which he was beginning to lose faith in.

He had always assumed that everyone around the world learned English as the common tongue of the greatest military and financial empire in the world. One so broad, his father had once told him, that the sun never set on the commonwealth. Here, on the edge of the Taklamakan Desert, the British Empire was not the foremost topic on everyone's mind. In the little sitting room in a corner of the Governor's mansion, with these two foreign women chatting over tea and books, it didn't seem to exist at all.

Meryem started with must have been a standard greeting in her language

"Assalaamu alaikum."

Ayotunde repeated that perfectly, as far as Algie could tell. Algie made his own attempt. Meryem smiled at both of them and made a great show of being pleased.

At Ayotunde's urging, he tried again.

The Conversor still was dissatisfied. He tried one more time. Meryem went on to other things, either because he had gotten close enough or that they had limited time for lessons. The Uyghur woman invited the two of them to sit down and have tea.

He'd had tea earlier that day, but in French. The cups and saucers were the same, just as were the tea and the biscuits. Only the language differed. Tea in French was fussier, requiring declensions, conjugations, and articles. Patrouille had demanded grammatical perfection. Uyghur seemed to be simpler, at least in how the words were put together. The words usually were at least three syllables long and filled with slippery lilts and diphthongs. Spoken at its natural pace, it flowed together like a long stream of honey with no discernible points to break up the words. As he learned new words, Algie would be able to find those points.

The afternoon was mostly pleasant, learning the fundamentals of Uyghur as Ayotunde laid into the heavy work of dissecting a living language. Meryem was not a trained linguist. She spent her time with them giving the names of simple objects and letting them parrot the words back to her. She wrote down many of words for him, but it did no good. Her people used the same alphabets as the Arabs. The left-to-right strings of snakes and specks made no sense to him, so Ayotunde took possession of those notes when they finished.

They said their goodbyes in multiple languages. Then, Ayotunde and Algie walked back to their quarters along the far less strenuous pedestrian bridge. He carried the books Meryem had loaned them. Ayotunde walked beside him, perhaps a good sign. She didn't throw him off the bridge to be trampled under the wheels and feet of the merchant traffic, which was an even better sign.

They didn't speak. All the times Algie glanced up at her for a clue to her mood, she looked straight ahead as a model of poise and independence. Algie didn't want to say anything that might remind her that she had caught him on the back of an automaton bull.

She took the books from him when they arrived at their quarters. She gave the slightest inclination of her head as she took them and murmured "*Merci*".

Algie assumed he would live through the night.

Nilenha waited for him in Mme. Streif's sitting room. From the table setting, Algie knew his first lesson on etiquette would be tea. Everything for a full and proper high tea crammed the cart: tea pot, sugar, cream, lemon, biscuits, scones, jam, nuts, and clotted cream. Under normal circumstances, it would have looked like paradise, but he had had tea twice already today.

Algie was full up and sick of tea and lessons.

He stepped further into the room with the utmost caution and respect. He had been warned by both Conversor and *Lǎoshǔ* that Nilenha didn't like children. After the morning's exercises, he fully knew what a Conversor could do to a person she didn't like.

She sat in a most provocative pose on the settee: half-reclined with her back against one arm and one leg crooked up with her foot on the upholstery. The hem of her red and black day dress was hiked up to above her knee there, exposing her stockinged foot and leg. Though he had seen all the Conversors earlier that day in form-fitting pajamas, this seemed more scandalous since only that limb and her expansive cleavage were exposed under a relatively modest dress.

Algie felt transfixed.

Like Ayotunde, Nilenha was not what Algie would have called pretty before his days on the *Wu Zetian*, but she was engaging. Her skin, not nearly as dark as Keijín's, fading to almost a yellow hue along her hairline. Brick red freckles marked the bridge of her nose and her cheekbones and her hair was the color of a terra cotta pot. Several jet bead combs held up her elaborate hair-do of braids and curls.

The Conversor occupied herself shuffling and fanning a

pack of cards. She only glanced at him for a moment. Her eyes were a deep, clear blue that looked more in place in a Prussian uniform than in a human face.

"When a gentleman enters a room, he should greet a lady," she said. Thankfully, she said it in English.

"*Bonne après-midi*,"[13] he said in French. He hoped she would appreciate his scholarship.

"*Boa tarde e bem vindos*[14]," she replied coolly. He guessed that she was speaking Portuguese as she hailed from Sao Paolo. She did not act impressed by his very minor display of worldliness.

She folded her cards back into a compact deck and placed it beside her place setting on the table. She gave the deck a sharp rap with her fingertips. As she turned herself about to sit at the table properly, she said:

"A gentleman always asks for permission before he sits in the presence of a lady."

Algie gestured towards the seat opposite her at the table.

"May I?"

"Please."

Algie pulled out the velvet-cushioned chair and placed his buttocks upon it. He tried to slide up to the table in a single smooth and stylish motion, but it still took two or three times before his belly was up against the edge. Nilenha indicated the assortment of china and cutlery in front of him. Out of reflex, his brain went through the name for each item in three languages.

"High tea in the European courts is very complicated," she said. "Especially for the English. There a few simple, hard-and-fast rules. Beyond that, you may do what you like."

"I'm all ears, ma'am."

The Conversor twisted her mouth to one side.

"I'm not sure how I feel about 'ma'am,' but you are still a bit young for *xodó*[15]. Let's just not tack anything on the end of our sentences. Agreed?"

Algie nodded. That would prevent her from calling him 'Pig' or '*chong wu*' also.

"Fine then. Never tuck your napkin into your collar. Never make a noise when drinking your tea."

She looked him in the eye with an odd smile on her heart-shaped face.

"A gentleman is always sure that a lady is serviced first, especially at tea."

"I understand," Algie said, even though he had the feeling she was saying something else.

"Don't put your spoon down on the tablecloth after stirring and, for God's sake, don't hold out your pinky. That just makes you look like an effete imbecile."

"But you said last night about the entrails of your enemies—"

"One never serves entrails at high tea." Her expression made Algie think she was joking, but he couldn't be sure. "And most importantly, never break wind in front of company if you can avoid it."

"I will do the best I can."

"Good," Nilenha said brightly. "Let's forget all about that nonsense, then."

She stood and grasped the tablecloth in each hand. In one smooth, even motion she pulled the tea settings to one side and left the bare wooden tabletop before them. She picked up the deck of cards and sat down to dealing them out to Algie and herself.

"We will spend the rest of our time together learning something truly important. This is how you play whist. When you've mastered that, we'll try faro."

13 "Good afternoon", French
14 "Good afternoon and welcome". Portuguese
15 "Darling", Portuguese

TWELVE

27th of August 1889
Turfan Caravanserai

Though Algie's wounds had healed enough to wear them, Mme. Streif's household did not have anything like boy's trousers that would be refined enough for a dinner at the governor's mansion. Once again, he had to wear red silk robes of some young Indian potentate. The gold bullion embroidery was scratchy and the cut at the bottom let in a sudden draft to his drawers. At least he was allowed to wear good English lace-up shoes instead of some ridiculous pointed-toe slippers.

Mme. Streif and her Conversors wore their best for the evening, all bows and buttons and bright jewels. Every color of the rainbow was represented, especially with First Mate McLaren. He had thrown his green and black ship's uniform tunic over his most garish brocade waistcoat. Knotted cords and carved cinnabar amulets in blue and red hung from the black braid and frogs of his jacket front.

"For luck and protection," Feng Po had explained while they were dressing, but Algie suspected it was also to provoke Captain Strausser and the more straightlaced members of the bridge crew. Feng Po kept his wood and ivory baton tucked in his belt front and center to "Let the Governor know what he had," as he put it.

Mme. Streif lead the parade into the banquet hall of the Governor's Mansion with her head held high. Her attitude was serene but unyielding. She looked from side to side with that dangerous smile of hers, no doubt checking to see if anyone in the hall did not agree that she was the most important personage in the caravanserai. Though only he and Chabi were shorter than her, she moved as if she stood three meters tall.

Algie watched the procession from the door, waiting for his place to come up in line. Since the Governor was hosting, this was practically a state dinner. The passengers and crew of the *Wu Zetian* were arranged in order of importance as they passed through the receiving line. Mme. Streif came first, followed by Zhao Guanting, Liu Jean-Pierre, Capt. Strausser, and Feng Po McLaren. The esteemed author Mssr. Patrouille, dressed in lime green and ochres tonight, came next in order.

A handful of the bridge crew lounged along after the truly important people. They were not at all bothered being put in the middle of the line, as far as anyone could see. Free food and wine were far more important than position and prestige.

The five Conversors followed close on their heels. The women all had smiles on their faces and silk fans fluttering in their hands. Algie would have thought they looked sweet, but he knew better from exercising with them this week. They arranged themselves in their own hierarchy, with Jakinda up front and Chabi at the end. Algie came into the hall after all of them. If the ship had a cat, it would have probably come in ahead of Algie.

The governor, his wife, and the local BC&I representative stood just inside the great double doors. A servant in a powdered wig, velvet cutaway coat and knee breeches announced the name of each guest as they stepped up. Everyone exchanged a polite handshake, a few quiet words, and then the guest would be seated at a banquet table nearly as long as the *Wu Zetian's* foc'sle deck.

Mrs. St. George beamed as she saw Mme. Streif and her entourage.

"Oh, look at this," she said while waving her silk fan to take in the cadre of young woman in brightly colored silk. "It's like a menagerie, with women from every corner of the world. How on earth did you collect them all?"

Mme. Streif said nothing, as did the Conversors, but Algie could feel a sudden tension in the room. The governor's wife retained her vapid expression.

"The most entertaining thing about menageries," Jakinda said after a few moments of awkward silence, "is that if one finds oneself on the same side of the fence as the animals, one might be devoured."

Mrs. St. George's eyes flicked from side to side, as if she were re-reading the text of the Conversor's remark. She giggled politely and shook Jakinda's hand.

The greeting line moved forward without further incident.

As Algie stepped up to the dignitaries, they seemed fairly relieved that there was no one else left to treat politely. Governor Tristan St. George stood nearly a meter taller than Algie, with a physique like a side of beef wrapped in blue velvet and gold braid. A gold sash of office and numerous medals of the Empire decorated his broad chest. He looked down through dark blue tinted spectacles and extended a massive hand.

"So, Algernon, what are you? The ship's mascot?"

Algie really didn't know how to answer that. To say that he killed air pirates might be considered a bit presumptuous, as well as something you shouldn't admit in polite company. Besides, that wasn't what he was being trained to do.

"I am the first mate's apprentice, sir."

The Governor's wife, announced as Hannah Hedsbury Wilmington St. George, billowed up before him, a mass of silver ribbons and bangles topped with golden curls. She laid one hand on Algie's shoulder and drew close with red grinning lips and bright blue eyes.

"Oh, he is so adorable," she cooed.

Algie bobbled his head, not being sure how low he should bow to English nobility.

"Thank you, ma'am."

She beamed up at her husband giddily. Algie had yet to see anything actually move on the Governor's face.

"And he speaks English so well!" she said.

Algie caught on quickly that his exotic clothes and his tan from working the rigging had convinced Mrs. St. George that he was yet another one of the fascinating foreigners invited to table, his blonde hair and blue eyes notwithstanding. He recalled something Jakinda had said about him when he first came aboard the *Wu Zetian*.

"The Conversors have been coaching me on elocution since they learned that I was born in Portsmouth," Algie said. "They say I've overcome my initial shortcomings."

The Governor tilted his head minutely.

"So, you are a subject of the Queen?" he asked.

Algie had no idea how to answer that. He had been born in England, and his father had served in her royal marines. But then, Mme. Billew had him transported to Australia like a common criminal. Or sold like a prize sheep. It put his citizenship in an amorphous position, especially after he jumped that transport ship. He realized, with uncharacteristic foresight, that sharing his doubts with the Governor would not be good.

"I was born very close to Portsmouth harbor, sir."

The BC&I representative, a Mr. Aramis Boycott, the herald had said, squinted his eyes and peered at him sideways. Algie didn't want to look at him too closely, as there was something about the dark beetle of a man that reminded him of every single member of the Roscommon Venture crew.

"How did so young a boy wind up so far away from home?" Boycott asked. There was a plaintive squeak to his voice that made it sound like there was a hinge somewhere deep inside him that needed oiling. "Why are you aboard a Chinese ship under the flag of such a faithless individual as Streif? I mean she is the traitor that financed the Europeans' defeat at Palikao."

Mme. Streif made no secret of the hatred that British China and India Company had for her. He was surprised that one of their hosts made no effort to hide it either. It made it very difficult to come up with a convincing lie.

"Welllll," Algie said. "It's a very long story. Very, very long. And a very involved one, too."

He looked up at Mrs. St. George who was hanging on

tenterhooks to hear the story of his adventures. Though he had promised Mssr Patrouille he wouldn't do this anymore, Algie thought to himself: *What would Dale Daring do?*

"I was a penniless orphan fighting for survival on the cruel streets of Portsmouth harbor," Algie started.

He stopped just as quickly as someone placed two hands on his shoulders from behind.

"That'll be quite enough of that for tonight," Mssr. Patrouille said quite loudly.

"Excuse me?" said Mrs. St. George, with a befuddled expression.

"The life's story of Algernon Piggrem, boy adventurer, is not something to be told in a noisy hall where only a few can appreciate it," Patrouille replied. "It is much better suited for a more *intimate* space."

Algie couldn't tell if it was disappointment at a good story interrupted, or something about the way Patrouille addressed her, but the Governor's wife swiftly and silently progressed into self-righteous offense. Jakinda appeared in the void between her and the writer to intercede.

"You must forgive Mssr. Patrouille," the Conversor cooed. She waggled her fan in her left hand as she spoke. "He meant no offense, but was merely suggesting that such a tale would be better heard at one of Mme. Streif's salons. Don't you agree, *Madame Governor?*"

Mrs. St. George lost her head of steam quickly and drifted into a girlish state of reverie.

"I have heard of the Madame's salons for *years*," she whispered. "Always the best people, always the most… stimulating conversation."

"Perhaps you and your husband would like to join us when we convene next Wednesday evening?" Jakinda asked helpfully.

Mrs. St. George looked up at her husband, who looked as impassive as if he had been cast in bronze. Her eyes gleamed as she turned back to the Conversor.

"Well, I can't say, at least, right away without consulting our social calendars," she burbled. "But we would both love to come."

Patrouille bowed his head low enough that his nose almost came down to Algie's shoulder.

"I will see that you will receive a proper invitation." Jakinda turned her eye on Boycott, who had been silently fuming during the little *tete a tete*. "And you are invited too, if you would like, Mr. Boycott."

He stole a quick glance over at Mme. Streif with an expression on his face as if he had been served up a steaming portion of road apples and mountain oysters. Still, he smiled tightly and replied:

"I would be honored."

He and the St. Georges turned their attention elsewhere, allowing Mssr. Patrouille and Algie to effect their escapes. The author murmured something to Jakinda and then dragged Algie over to sit beside him.

"You would think people in their position would better hide their bigotry," Patrouille whispered, "I believe, this sets us even for saving me on that catwalk last week."

"I don't understand," said Algie.

"Next time, pick a better book to plagiarize for your biography. *Dale Daring and the Moroccan Mummies*? That was the worst of the Freemarch manuscripts."

*

Algie spent the rest of the evening studiously avoiding breaches of protocol. He spread his linen napkin on his lap instead of tucking it into his collar. He used his utensils from the inside out as they worked through the courses, even though he had become accustomed to the Chinese way of eating food chopped small and grasped with two sticks. For the most part, he smiled and nodded at dinner conversation to avoid speaking with his mouth full.

He guessed that the governor had brought his cook along from England. Everything served had a definite British taste to it: Roasted, boiled, or simply bound up in aspic like the trifle. Patrouille, who was seated across from Algie, did not approve. He was not so rude as to say that out loud, but the twitches of his handlebar mustache were like telegraphy for anyone familiar with the author. Also, he overindulged in the red wine, using it to wash down every bite of his roast and potatoes.

The Social Repeater trundled down the tracks that ran along the center of the table just as Algie was cleaning his plate. He had read of these devices before, but he had never been at a dinner so drawn out over distance to need one before. Mainly, it was a brass head resembling the Governor's on an electric traction platform. Using the same technology as the electric voicepipe, it relayed the Governor's words at the head of the table, with some added motions of the eyes, brows, and mouth. To be honest, it was slightly more animated than the original article.

The head spoke to Mssr. Patrouille first.

"My wife and I discussed your gracious invitation." The Repeater said. The voice was a fair simulation of the Governor's, though it tended to vibrate some of the metallic parts and give it an unhuman rattle and buzz. "We would be honored to come to your next salon."

Patrouille dabbed his lips with his napkin and set it across his plate.

"It would be an honor to allow us to show you our hospitality, meager as it might be."

The author made a drunken attempt to smile politely at the automaton, his eyes going every which way to avoid looking the Repeater in its glass eyes. Algie snickered in spite of himself at the performance.

The Social Repeater spun around on its platform to direct its dead-eyed gaze at Algie. He leaned back in his seat as it did and clutched the edge of the table in his hands. He didn't know why, but the thing horrified him. He wondered for a fleeting second how much those eyes could actually see.

"Young man," the Social Repeater buzzed. "I would like you to join us in the library for brandy and cigars."

Algie stretched up and over to get a look at the head of the table, maybe to see if the Governor thought he was talking to someone else.

"But... I'm twelve, sir."

"Milk and biscuits for you, then. Madame Streif and First Mate McLaren believe you should be a part of the discussion."

The traction platform jerked a bit, rammed a bowl of capers that Mssr. Patrouille had placed too near the track, and buzzed down to where the bridge crew sat. Algie heard it strike up a conversation with them. Whatever was going on in the library, it sounded like it included Ensign Bigsby and his lot.

"A private meeting with the Governor," the author murmured in French. "I am so envious."

The sarcasm translated easily, but Algie wasn't laughing. He could, in the space of a few minutes, imagine a hundred topics of the upcoming meeting. At least half of them would have been bad for Algie. It was like being called up before Mrs. Billew.

Patrouille continued to smirk across the table at him. Algie savaged his trifle with a spoon.

*

Algie expected a library to be simply rows of bookshelves with some reading tables and lamps. A British gentleman's library in Turfan contained so much more than that. The walls not covered in dark wood bookshelves held captured weapons from other lands, the mounted heads of game animals, and assorted gold-leaf frames. Some frames held paintings and photographs. Others displayed certificates of Governor St. George's achievements. A state portrait of the Queen hung over the bar. A slightly larger painting of the Governor and his wife stood over the mantelpiece. Enormous firearms, looking like they could take down an elephant or an airship in a single shot, supported it on either side.

Servants with trays of with trays of wine and spirits in crystal glasses came and went through a secret door behind a bookcase. Algie found that fascinating.

He had come in shortly after Mme. Streif made her entrance. There was a throne-like red leather wingback chair to one side of the fire. Evidently, that was the Governor's seat. On the other side was a fancy chaise, what his mother had always called a "fainting couch." One of the liveried servants directed Mme.

Streif to recline there.

She opened her fan with a snap and examined the Uyghur man in European uniform from head to toe. Dismissing him, she turned back to their host. Her eyes narrowed as she looked up at St. George.

"I cannot sit there," she said. "My spine, it does not easily bend in certain circumstances."

The five Conversors lined up behind her as they often did. Through some unspoken signal, they all snapped open their fans at once. The sound was like a firing squad.

The servants scattered like startled pigeons. The offending couch was removed and a stiff-backed chair like the Governor's was put in its place. Mme. Streif settled herself in it, her neck rigid, her chin high. Four of the Conversors alighted on the couches and chairs to her right. Nilenha curled up on the velvet chaise like a cat and patted the vacant spot at the end for Algie to join her.

The servants circulated the room offering drinks and cigars. Meryem, in her kitchen uniform, appeared on Algie's left elbow to give him a glass of cold milk and a small plate of tamarind cookies.

The men of the *Wu Zetian* crew assembled on the other side of the library. They spoke in low voices in their little knot, already creating clouds of cigar smoke while sipping brandy from over-large snifters. The Americans and Germans seemed quite comfortable in this kind of library, though not one with women in it. Feng Po's jibes and raucous laughter just added to their discomfort. As Governor St. George took his position at his chair, Patrouille took his brandy and stationed himself behind Mme. Streif. With his sly smile and darting eyes, it looked to Algie as if the Frenchman was an eager fan at the start of a football match.

The Governor held his brandy high and waited for the chatter to subside.

"First off," he said in a clear, loud tone, "I would like to welcome you, the crew of the *Wu Zetian*, to the Turfan caravanserai. We receive airships and travelers from every corner of the world, but seldom do we see such exotic craft or beautiful guests."

"Thank you, Your Majesty!" First Mate McLaren called out as his glass was being refilled by a servant. "It is so nice to be appreciated for something besides our skills and character."

Captain Strausser and the bridge crew were mortified, Governor St. George, momentarily befuddled. The Conversors, who might have all been thinking something like what Feng Po had just said, sat smiling meekly and fanning themselves. They showed no sign of a reaction beyond that. Algie remembered Jakinda telling him after lessons earlier this week that men call women "pretty" when they couldn't think of any complement relating to their value as human beings.

Mme. Streif raised her ridiculously small aperitif glass.

"We thank you for your welcome."

"Yes, welcome," the Governor continued. "To the *Wu Zetian*, and to the Queen."

"To the Queen!" several people replied.

"And to the glorious Guangxu Emperor," Feng Po added. "Long may his minority last!"

Algie didn't understand what that meant. Only Masters Zhao and Sun, personal representatives of the regent Empress, seemed to comprehend. Governor St. George acted as if it never happened.

"And you have brought quite a bit of excitement under your wings," the Governor continued. "First, was that astounding report of your encounter with Afghan air pirates. Was it really you, son, that leaped off your ship on a tether to set fire to theirs?"

Algie took a moment to appreciate that he was the center of attention and was expected to make an answer. He washed down his mouthful of cookie.

"Yes, sir."

"And how on Earth did you have the wit and courage to come up with such a plan on the spur of the moment?"

Algie saw Mssr. Patrouille waving his hand in such a way as to say: *For the love of God and all that is good in the world, do NOT say anything about Dale Daring.* He was trying to be subtle, but it looked like an attack of St. Vitus' dance.

"I am an apprentice to my *lǎoshī*, Feng Po McLaren," Algie said. "He has taught me everything I know about shipcraft and the ways of *picaroons*."

The Governor took the response with little change of expression, but Feng Po puffed up with pride.

"So, you ordered the boy to leap off the observation platform?"

"No, no, no," Feng Po quickly replied. "I instructed the young lad to drop the Mermaid's Purse off the ship, but, for some reason, he refused to let go when he did. He went over the side with the munition. It all turned out for the best, though."

"So it did. We have found it is vital to crush *picaroons* and anarchists whenever they raise their heads. It is the only way to defend the Empire." He turned his attention to Mme. Streif. "Did you know that we are actually on British soil?"

She looked at him quizzically.

"Is it something you had shipped in crates on the backs of camels and oxen?"

That got a laugh from most around the room, except the Conversors and St. George himself.

"No. It is a treaty agreement that makes this small patch of desert part of the commonwealth," he said. "And so I am a legal representative of the Queen."

"Queen Victoria?"

"Why yes, THE Queen," snapped Mr. Boycott.

"There is nothing so obvious about that. There are dozens of sovereign countries from Sweden to the Hawaiian Islands that have queens. China has two female regents that are effectively queens, and one of them gifted me my ship. It is perhaps rude to think that your Queen is the only one that matters."

Governor St. George sat there motionless. Algie assumed he blinked like an owl in the daylight, but the colored spectacles still hid the man's eyes. After a few long moments, he started up again.

"My apologies, Madame Streif. We did not mean to sound… *provincial*."

Aramis Boycott grunted something like an agreement.

"I have business interests in the Americas, Africa, and all along the High Silk Road," Mme. Streif said. "I cannot afford such restrictive attitudes."

"I understand." The Governor nodded minutely. "What I was trying to lead up to in a delicate fashion is that we have quite a problem with *picaroons* in this province."

"And dragons," Feng Po added.

"That was not a dragon," the Governor said. "That was just a Uyghur airship done up to look like a dragon."

The first mate set his brandy snifter on the edge of a table. A servant caught it before it toppled on to the floor, but McLaren went on without notice.

"That's the first place where you're wrong, Your Highness. No airship ever built moved like that thing. It had wings that stretched from one end of your dock yard to the other without the slightest sign of a gas bag and a spine as supple as a Mongolian acrobat's. That says 'dragon' to me until I have a chance to check its mouth to number its teeth."

The Governor turned in his seat to face Feng Po directly.

"Excuse me, who are you again?"

"And the second place where you're wrong is to think that your local folk are the ones that at the helm of this airship that-is-definitely-not-a-dragon. The Uyghurs have been taxed and swindled by the Brits and the Chinese to the point they couldn't collect enough cash to finance a two-man Von Siegling chiropter."

"We believe," Governor St. George said through his clenched but perfect teeth, "that there are outside agitators financing these rebel groups…"

"Oh, of course, outside instigators." Feng Po was winding up to a highly entertaining rant, one that could still destroy a career or end with someone dangling from their ankles in chains. "If you want to be discussing that, it's the Afghans you will be talking about. They were true and loyal allies of Queen Victoria fifteen years ago when the airships first started crossing Asia. Set up with their pretty harrier craft and letters of marque, Abu Khan had a fine old time taking down the Germans and the French and the stray Brazilian. But you never learned the prime fact of business in this part of the world: You cannot buy the loyalty of an Afghan, but you can lease it by the month or the quarter. Of course, that little slur was first coined by the Empire that bought them and betrayed them in practically the same fiscal quarter. Now, his son has split off with his *muhafez* brethren and Abu Khan is a toothless tiger that the *Saissaenach*[16] have left for the wolves."

The Americans were accustomed to a certain steady level of insubordination, but they must have felt Feng Po had crossed a line of drawing room etiquette, one that Nilenha had yet to teach Algie. Capt. Strausser chuffed and inflated himself like an angry ram. Ensign Dunsail laid a heavy hand on the mate's shoulder.

"You're forgetting your place, old man," the ensign said.

"You don't seem to know who you are laying hands upon, *wáng bā dàn* " Feng Po peeled the young man's hand free and began the act of twisting it into some painful knot the Chinese had mastered.

"Enough!" Mme. Streif said, her voice no louder than normal, but sharp enough to cut through wool and leather.

Feng Po dropped the Dunsail's hand like a dead rat. The rest of the American crew took hold of the ensign and pulled him back a few steps. The Captain glared at Feng Po as he nearly always did. The Governor took in the spectacle, swirling his brandy in an eternal circle that Algie found hypnotic.

Mme. Streif rose to her feet to stand at the same height as the sitting governor. The Conversors were also all standing behind her, their fans closed and their stances prepared for sudden movement, just as he had been learning in morning exercises. Algie never saw them move, even Nilenha who had been on the chaise beside him.

"You do not remember his position, Ensign… Captain…" The Americans nodded their heads and looked contrite. Mme. Streif addressed the Governor next. "This man flew under the *muhafez* flag for seven years. It is his knowledge and his training that have saved our lives."

"How can you —" the Governor started.

"Trust such a man? Results. I make it more pleasant and

profitable for him to serve me rather than to betray me." She smiled. "Have you had any better luck with the other crews you have offered the right to hunt their fellow man?"

Governor Tristan St. George sat motionless as he assayed Mme. Streif through his dark blue glasses. The swirling liquor in his hand spun down to a golden rippled puddle.

"You have led Mr. Boycott and myself to completely underestimate you, Madame Streif." He actually smiled and displayed strong white teeth that looked like they could crack walnuts.

"I have been doing that with men of power since I was a mere slip of a girl of nineteen." She gave out a delicate little cough. "A decade or two ago."

The Governor sipped his brandy and gallantly said nothing.

"Your airship, crippled by a Hephaestus mine, still managed to take down two heavily armed brigand craft. Under a letter of marque, you would have the blessings of the empire along with bounties and percentages of recoveries."

Algie guessed how Mme. Streif might answer, he wanted to see how the others would react. Mssr. Patrouille had an absent smile on his face as the story possibilities seemed to flicker through his mind. The young Americans looked genuinely excited at the prospect for fame and glory. Captain Strausser and First Mate McLaren were strangely in accord, with grim expressions at the young men in uniform.

"Ours is a merchant craft, Governor St. George," Streif replied. "We will not be going to war for your queen."

"Yours is a Chinese ship flying under a Viennese flag," Mr. Boycott stated. "I would think that your loyalty was a matter of expedience."

Mme. Streif chewed on that remark for several long seconds. Then, she nodded her gratitude to the Governor.

"Thank you, sir, for a most delicious meal and delightful after-dinner conversation. We must be going now."

The Governor stood and gave her a stiff little bow of his head.

"It has been a pleasure having you."

With a gesture, Mme. Streif led her people out of the library.

They fell into the same order as when they had earlier entered the hall. Nilenha fell into step beside Algie. There was a devilish grin on her face.

"And that was your first battle over brandy and cigars," she whispered. "Many more people have foundered here than were ever lost at air or sea."

16 "English", Scots Gaelic

THIRTEEN

30th of August 1889
Turfan Caravanserai

In spite of the breach of etiquette in the library, the crew and passengers of the *Wu Zetian* were still treated as honored guests. The repairs and improvements on the airship progressed at flank speed. In his few free afternoons, Algie watched from the catwalks and scratched away at his woodworking. He was fascinated by the machinery used to apply heat and pressure to the silk and lacquer and the efforts of the local workman to weave bamboo and twine into the rigid supports. Liu Jean-Pierre's supervision turned into exercises in pantomime and parlor games. Much gesticulation and shouting replaced true communication.

The *Lǎoshǔ* ran wild across rooftops of the caravanserai as they had no duties until there was a ship to rig. Algie was still not well enough to keep up with them. The Conversors pressed him hard on his lessons. He had learned how to fall without injury and tumble back to his feet like a rolling ball. The morning of the Great Entertainment, Jakinda had even allowed him to try to throw her over his shoulder. The first attempt was slow and measured and she cooperated completely with his intentions. She fell to the ground just as Chen fell before Chabi that first day of lessons. The second throw was done at full speed and Algie got to feel the flow of force and mass that was the secret of Isilmandatu. The third time his muscles remembered the movement and responded without thought.

Algie would love to see Peng's face the next time he or any of the other larger *Lǎoshǔ* chose to push him around.

The next twelve attempts Jakinda resisted. She at first simply planted her feet or danced around him. Ultimately, Algie ended the exercise dangling from one ankle with his head on the mats.

"It is important to understand how perilous the first months of these lessons can be," Jakinda stated in a calm voice. "A novice might feel that they are invincible, while still not comprehending all the factors of mass, speed, and the natural ferocity of the human animal."

The Conversor released him. Algie did his best to roll to his feet as his tutors did. He did not execute the movement with cat-like grace.

"You will never use Isilmandatu where others may see you. You will not use it in petty squabbles with your friends. The Secret School is a defense for the small and the weak." Jakinda raised her hands to take in all of the other Conversors. "Which we all are, compared to a grown man."

Ayotunde stepped forward and spoke sternly in French. Algie's lessons with Mssr. Patrouille allowed him to translate easily.

"If you break these rules, there will be dire consequences."

The African woman glared at him steadily. Jakinda took up a towel and blotted her face with it.

"Well, that should be enough for today," she said with a smile. "We'll see you tonight at the Great Entertainment."

*

"Most well-off merchants will bring along some form of entertainment on their travels, Pig," Feng Po told Algie. "Though most do not field the full flying circus that Mme. Streif transports along with her five tons of raw silk."

Nilenha who walked beside the first mate gave him a playful swat with her fan.

"No offense," he continued. "But I never saw so many musicians, acrobats, and contortionists under one roof without a trapeze act and a dancing bear."

"Anyway," said Nilenha, "there has been a tradition of Great Entertainments being held weekly at caravanserais. Everyone provides some little performance to brighten each other's lives. I understand tonight we will see musicians, dancers, even a bare-knuckle boxing tournament."

"Oh, and the *karakuri* caracal will be put through its paces tonight," Chabi said in French.

"Tuareg will be presenting tonight?" Algie replied in the same tongue. He inwardly marveled that he could already carry on a rudimentary conversation in two languages.

Ayotunde, who had kept right behind him in the knot of Conversors, sniffed irritably.

"Oh, yes," she said. "I forgot you have met him already."

Algie turned to Jakinda, the person to be asking permission of when Mme. Streif was not on deck.

"May I go to see him before the other events expire, Mam'selle?" The construction was awkward, but most of the Conversors had stopped responding to him when he spoke English.

"I don't know." The Basque Conversor furrowed her brow in exaggerated concern. "Mme. Streif has grown rather fond of you. She would be disturbed if we misplaced you."

"I could go with young master Pig," Ayotunde volunteered. "I have always had a fascination with the *karakuri*."

Algie felt his chances were getting better with her as a chaperone, though she might not be as much fun as Chabi or Nilenha. He had half a thought to try to wheedle and beg Jakinda, the way he might have with his mother, but he knew that was not something the world would allow anymore. Ms. Billew or the *Roscommon* crew might have beaten him for such behavior. The Conversors's punishments, Algie was sure, could be subtle but horrible.

Jakinda gave a prim little nod of her head.

"Very well," she told Ayotunde. "Return him in one piece. We will all be meeting at the Grand Plaza at ten pm. to cheer for Ensign Bigsby. He will be boxing, you know."

"We will be there," she said. There was a broad grin on her face, something Algie seldom saw.

"Thank you!" Algie called out as the Conversor secured him by the scruff of his shirt collar and dragged him into the crowd.

*

Tuareg's bird cage took up a large area in one of the market plazas. The intricately filigreed metal folded out from a tight bundle on the oxen cart to an onion dome eight to ten meters across. Dozens of small wooden boxes were stacked inside it along one side. A smaller cage occupied the center. Inside of that reposed a large brass cat.

Like the headless palanquin-bearers and the broad-horned oxen, its body was made up of interlaced metal plates. Some artisan carefully chased and stained the brass to give it the look of fur and spots. Two enormous pointed ears rose up from the head that rested on its paws.

Released from Ayotunde's grip on his collar, Algie pressed his face between the bird cage's bars as far as he could to examine the cat. It was frustrating being so far away, especially when the creature was completely still. He wanted to see it in action, to hear if its body made faint sounds of strings and bells like Tuareg's other automatons.

"Is that the British boy I see, trying to squeeze into my bird cage?" someone shouted from across the plaza. Algie saw a swirl of blue and black robes, a deep blue turban, and a broad grin on a dark face. Tuareg looked quite happy to see him.

"*Assalaamu alaikum,*" Algie shouted as he waved.

Tuareg pulled a face as if he were both shocked and pleased at Algie's linguistic acuity. He put his fingers to the middle of his forehead and made an intricate salute. For the first time, Algie noticed the dark serpentine lines tattooed on the back of the man's hands.

"*Wa Alykom As-salam,* my friend!"

Algie looked up at Ayotunde, and, for the moment at least, she didn't seem disappointed in him

"Now don't make a nuisance of yourself," she said quietly in French.

"I won't."

"He is a young man full of life and curiosity," Tuareg said, also in French. "That can never be a nuisance."

"Then perhaps you would like to take him on *your* next long journey." Algie couldn't tell if the Conversor was trying to sell him or not. He did know that the two needed to be properly introduced.

"My good friend, this is Ayotunde, Conversor for Mme. Elizabeth Streif," Algie said with utmost formality. "Ayotunde, this is Tuareg."

She chuckled politely just as Tuareg's smile dropped a hitch.

"Tuareg is not his name," the Conversor said. "Tuareg is his tribe."

The man, now unnamed it seemed, gave an apologetic shrug.

"I try to make it easy for the British," he said.

"We never make anything easy for *this* British," Ayotunde replied. "We expect him to be better than his litter mates."

"Then, let me make amends." He bowed to both Algie and Ayotunde. "Allow me to introduce myself. I am called Zdan Ag Ahar."

"*Salaam Alaykum*, Zdan Ag Ahar. I am Ayotunde Balogun. I am pleased to make your acquaintance."

Algie greeted him as properly as he could, though Ayotunde did have to prompt him on the "Ag Ahar" part.

"May we see the caracal now please?" Algie then asked.

"Certainly, my friends. Wait a moment for the good doctor." Zdan waved for a tall African man in evening clothes to catch up with them as he unlocked the gate. He was as tall as any of the Americans on the bridge crew, with pomaded hair, gold-rimmed spectacles, and a close-trimmed beard. He ducked as he came through the gate behind Algie and Ayotunde and walked past them without a word. The doctor's eyes were only for the metallic creature curled in the cage.

"Is there any danger of attack?" he asked as he knelt beside it. He spoke French with an accent similar to Ayotunde's. Algie had not thought until then how other languages can be spoken with a distinctive tinge of the mother tongue just as with English.

Zdan waved his hands and grinned.

"She is perfectly safe. Her cognition is set for rapid movement and small body volume," he said. "Unless you are pigeon, she will take no notice of you."

Zdan undid the latches on the circular cage and spread the folding walls wide like an umbrella turning inside out. This somehow quickened the mechanisms within the *karakuri*. First an ear twitched and then turned towards each of the two men as they spoke. The caracal flexed the toes of one of its front feet. Polished brass claws extended out with a quiet whisper like a sword drawn from its scabbard.

In spite of those warning signs, Algie drew closer, fascinated by the cat. He hunkered over with his hands on his knees to get a closer look.

"May I touch it?" Algie asked.

"Her," Zdan replied. "You may touch *her*. She will not bite."

As Algie reached out a hand, the Tuareg merchant added:

"She likes it best if you stroke her back."

Algie touched the caracal just above the shoulders and ran his hand to the base of her tail. The metal plates were warm. Heated by whatever engine ran her cogs and gears, he guessed. He stroked her back again and felt a rhythmic sound like the plucking of harp strings come from deep inside her chest.

The *karakuri* caracal purred.

He grinned up at Ayotunde, but she was already involved in the men's discussion of mechanics and natural science. It went far beyond his limited grasp of French, though he caught some phrases like moteur d'inference[17] and pile a combustible[18] which he would translate later. Algie tried to soak up the conversation while seeing what he could infer from the evidence of his own eyes.

"May we see the internal mechanisms?" the doctor asked.

"Most certainly," Zdan said. "Let me get this lazy beast on her feet."

The Tuareg merchant stepped back and pulled a feathered lure from his belt. It whistled as he spun it on the end of its cord.

The caracal's ears twitched and tracked the movement of the lure. The cat's eyes flicked open and it was instantly on its feet. In a single leap, the *karakuri* launched itself into the air and swatted down the bundle of feathers. The caracal then took up a stance Algie would have called "proud", with its head and stubby tail held high, and the lure pressed to the ground under one front paw.

Zdan murmured to it gently in some foreign tongue, probably Arabic or Uyghur. He then took up the intricate gold cross that hung around his neck and blew into it. The instrument created a high and wavering note.

The metallic body went rigid. Her head dropped down and away from the neck on a hidden hinge. As it did, the brainpan opened up and the bronze scales split open along the spine. Lit by their own pale fire, minute gears, cogs, and ratchets made of something like amber turned within the hollow of the *karakuri* body. They made a soft sound like the songs of crickets accompanied by the plucking of silver strings. It was like nothing Algie had ever seen or imagined.

The African doctor and Ayotunde barraged Zdan with a rush of questions. Being in the dual foreign languages of French and Science, Algie gave up on understanding. Instead, he examined the inner workings of the automaton and discerned what he could from his personal experience in engineering. He paid careful attention to the latching mechanism in the *karakuri*'s throat, which was the simplest part of the entire creation.

Except for the eyes. Algie quickly realized that glass orbs had no connection to any other part of the caracal.

"Is she blind?" Algie asked.

Zdan looked very pleased at the question. Ayotunde and the doctor looked at each other in surprise and fell to examining the inside of the *karakuri* head.

"Yes, she is," Zdan replied. "Mechanical sight is still a puzzle my patron has yet to decipher. Her hunting is all done by sound."

"Patron?" Ayotunde said. "You do not create these yourself?"

Zdan Ag Ahar opened his mouth as if to answer, but he stopped at the shouts of the crowd that had gathered outside the cage. In the fifteen minutes or so they had spent peering at the caracal's inner mysteries, the crowd had grown three thick with currency and betting chits clutched in their fists.

"We will have to discuss these many questions later. It is time for my beauty here to demonstrate her skills." Zdan pressed the two halves of the head together and then lifted the united piece to its proper place on its neck.

It seated with a loud click. The mechanisms wound up to speed inside the caracal's torso as the metal plates returned to their original positions. The caracal sprang to life again. Zdan jogged over to the quick release cage at the far side of cage while twirling the feathered lure. The *karakuri* bounded after it and into the cage.

"Quickly, now," Zdan called out as he slammed shut the cage. "I need your help to wind my pigeons!"

They hurried over to the stacks of small wooden boxes on the opposite side. The Tuareg merchant picked up and slid open one of the topmost boxes. He removed a lavender-grey bundle of feathers, a perfect simulacrum of a common pigeon complete with black glass eyes. Taking up an ornate brass key, he inserted the male end between the *karakuri's* wings and gave it three sharp twists. Considering his experience with the Mermaids Purse, Algie expected it to explode momentarily.

Instead, it fluttered to the ground once Zdan released it and pecked at the ground like any real pigeon might do. He gave each of them an identical key and gestured towards the boxes.

"Please, the crowd is growing restive. The bars of this cage may not protect us if we force them to wait too long for their sport."

Algie wasted no time. He took a box, removed its automaton, and gave it three sharp key turns almost in a single motion. He released the bird into the air over his head. It fluttered to the ground with a rustle of wings and an authentic sounding "coo." He was on to the next one in seconds.

Ayotunde and the doctor, not accustomed to tying knots and running lines at double time, lagged behind him. In the end he wound up nineteen pigeon automata, more than the two of them had done together. Once the entire flock of synthetic pigeons was loose in the center of the cage, Zdan shooed Algie and his friends out and barred the gate behind them.

The three of them were pressed against gate with a mass of shouting humanity close behind them. The doctor and the Conversor spoke in a language Algie couldn't follow, though some of the words sounded like Uyghur. Ayotunde pointed to herself and said her name, loudly and clearly to be heard over the commotion. She then pointed at Algie and declared him to be "Pig".

The doctor took Algie's hand and grinned.

"Pig? Why did your parents name you after an unclean animal?"

"They didn't," Algie replied. "My real name is Algie."

"So, they named you after pond scum?"

Algie was about to explain how that was short for Algernon, but he saw the suppressed laughter on the doctor's face. It burst out in a good-natured blare of sound.

"My apologies for taking liberties with your good name. Dr. Hakim Esupofo Cookworthy of Fourah Bay College, at your service."

Algie tried to come up with an equally dignified response when Zdan Ag Ahar held up his arms to command their attention. Dr. Cookworthy held a finger up to his lips and pointed to the blue-robed merchant in the center of the cage. The crowd fell silent to the point all Algie could hear was quiet conversation and the soft cooing of the mechanical pigeons.

"Friends, Strangers, Fellow Travellers on the Silk Roads, High and Low," Zdan called out in English and a strong, clear voice. "The Kumari Kandam Company brings, for your viewing and wagering pleasure, the most beautiful work of moving art and the greatest sport of the Afghan courts reinvented: the Caracal!"

He repeated what seemed to be the same short speech in a half-dozen languages. Each time the crowd grew more boisterous, until they were practically frothing.

He strode over to the caracal's cage and laid his hands on the release lever. A roar came up from the crowd that startled the pigeons into the air. Dr. Cookworthy leaned in close to Algie's ear to be heard.

"You British talk about loosing the cat among the pigeons.

This is what that looks like."

Zdan threw the lever and the *karakuri* caracal exploded out of her confinement. She dashed directly for the birds and leaped into the cloud of flapping wings. She rolled, pitched, and yawed in their midst with her spine twisting in impossible ways. Light flashed off of the bronze cat's brass claws. Her movements were not just life-like, but superior to motions of muscle and bone. Feathers scattered in the air and fluttered down around the thrashing bodies on the ground.

Five pigeon simulacrums downed in the first leap.

The grounded bird automata unwound even as the caracal touched earth on the far end of her arc. A roar came up from the crowd and excited chatter continued between bettors and the holders of the chits.

The caracal took up an attentive stance once she had landed. Her ears flicked from side to side to track the artificial pigeons and then she made a quick run around the edge of the cage to build up speed. Another leap with claws and teeth lashing out brought down eight birds.

It took her only two more runs to take down the remaining scattered pigeons.

The crowd of people around the iron cage turned into a churning river flowing in multiple directions. Many moved away, either to the next entertainment or the nearby bars, treading losing chits beneath their feet. A few gathered around the bookmakers and gesturing or waving fists full of bills. Zdan was in the midst of one of those knots.

Algie guessed it would be best to talk to him tomorrow. He and Ayotunde said their goodbyes to Dr. Cookworthy and moved on.

"Did you see those markings on his arms and wrists?" Ayotunde asked in French as she led Algie off to the Grand Plaza.

"His tattoos?" he replied. "They looked like snakes or dragons"

"Draco Caput and Draco Caudus. They are the marks of a Samaritan."

"You mean, like the Good Samaritan in the Bible."

"They share some of the same history." Ayotunde looked

pensive. "There are many secret societies other than the Conversors at large in the world, like the Brotherhood of Lightning Rods that purposely attract the attention of thieves and brigands, or the Tinkers Guild that punishes those troublemakers. They claim their history goes back to the days
of Lemuria, the continent that sank beneath waves of the Indian Ocean."

"Like Atlantis?" Algie had read extensively about the fall of Atlantis is his adventure books.

"Exactly. If you are in dire trouble, a Samaritan often appears at the moment you need them most."

"So, if Zdan is here at the caravanserai, does that mean we're in trouble?"

Ayotunde reached out and mussed his hair, an uncommonly friendly gesture from her.

"No," she chuckled, "because *you* are here, I think we are in dire trouble."

17 "mechanical computer", French
18 "fuel cell", French

FOURTEEN

16th of February 1889
Capetown Harbor

As Algie pulled himself up beside the cook's boy, they exchanged a quick clasp of hands and pulled double-time on the ropes to draw their barrels together. A ruckus rose up from the *Roscommon Venture,* and he guessed that they had a few minutes before the crew would drop the remaining boat and come after the children.

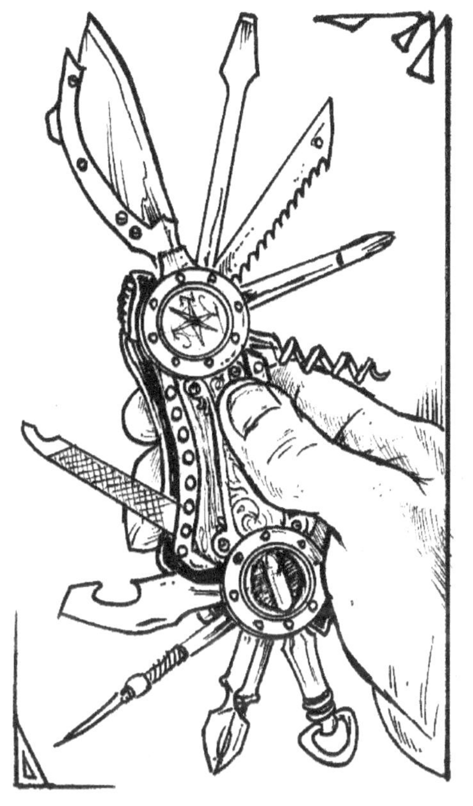

Deirdre said something as the two barrels thumped against hers, but Algie couldn't comprehend the words. He understood the tone, though. She pointed at the sinking barrels at the head of their rope line. They had little more than a hand's width of wood above the water and vibrated with the trapped children's thrashing and their fists pounding against the lids. Algie shouted at the cook's boy to catch his attention:

"Hey! We've got to get them out of those barrels before they drown."

The cook's boy kept pulling for a second, still at his ultimate effort until he stopped and blew out his breath in sound of frustration and exhaustion. He then gestured for Algie to watch him, two fingers in a "v" jabbed at his own eyes. The boy then peeled his suspenders off of his shoulders and shed his trousers and shoes. Popping back up in just his shirttails, the cook's boy flicked open his pocket knife and flopped sideways over the edge of the barrel and into the water.

Algie was watching, but he didn't believe what he saw. The cook's boy, oblivious to the danger, waved for Algie to join him. Deirdre and the few children who were able to breach their barrel lids looked Algie's way with pleading eyes.

"Are you bloody insane?" Algie shouted. "There's sharks in the water. I just had one scraping its teeth on the outside of my barrel. Get out of there before you're eaten!"

The boy in the water just shook his head. He clutched the folding knife between his teeth and swam towards the foundering barrels. He used a calm sculling motion like a frog's to move him through the water without splashing that left only his head above the surface.

"Well, don't just stand there," Deirdre scolded. "Get over there and help them!"

"I'm working on it. Without getting eaten by sharks, if you please!" Algie ran a hand through his hair as he tried to cogitate some brilliant solution to the failure of his last brilliant solution. Nothing came to him but an overwhelming sense of guilt and shame.

He, and especially the kids in the sinking barrels, did not have any time for anything but decisive action. Back to Plan "A" it was.

"Everybody pull! Cinch up the ropes between the barrels so we're all knocked up against each other."

Algie watched for a second at their efforts. Only half of them had punched the lids off their barrels. They were scared witless and, more often than, not pulling against each other. There were too many barrels and too little time to try to direct them himself. The only thing was for him to get his barrel over to the other end right away.

He was already butted up against the mute boy's vacant barrel, with Deirdre's pulled up tight to that one and the one on her other side. Algie started pulling along the line of barrels, tightening the ropes as he went and pulling a loop behind him. It took him only a few moments to pass Deirdre and progress towards the far end of the train.

"It's all going too slowly," Deirdre shouted. "They're going to drown!"

"I'm moving as fast as I can," Algie grunted as he pulled.

"That's not good enough!"

He heard a splash behind him. Before he could turn his head to see what that was about, Deirdre swam past him, still wearing her blouse and pinafore. Her swimming was not as practiced as the boy's. To be honest, she looked like a lapdog thrown into the deep water for the first time. Dozens of the young men's adventures Algie had read told him of the horrors that came out of splashing around in shark-infested waters.

"Bloody Hell, Deirdre! Stop thrashing around like a wounded fish. You're practically inviting the sharks to eat you!"

She may have responded, but her head kept bobbing in and out of the water, so all that came out was a gargling noise. The cook's boy pried at the lid of the barrel with his knife, though every time he leaned over the edge to do that, he pushed the barrel even deeper under water. The kids inside splashed and screamed.

Algie's brilliant escape plan had turned into a debacle and was minutes away from becoming a drowning machine. Even though the mute boy was there with hands on and knife out, he was no use. Deirdre was almost there, but Algie couldn't see what good she would do either. They had to come up with another solution, but quickly.

He looked down the line of barrels. Half of them were still sealed and bobbing in the harbor like a string of stepping stones. Unfortunately, the other half sprouted flailing, screaming bodies out the tops.

An incredibly stupid idea come to Algie then. Considering the situation, it was the only thing that made sense.

He put his left foot on the edge of his barrel and reached out to the teary girl in the nearest one.

"Come on, give us a hand!"

She sobbed and stared at his hand as if it were a venomous snake. He shook it at her and muttered encouragement. Finally, she clasped it and Algie used her as an anchor to pull himself up to standing.

The barrel beneath him leaned heavily against the others beside it. Algie's weight on the one side began to push it away. As he looked down between his legs, he saw something large and dark swimming just below the surface.

With a twist, hop, and a jump, he dropped down next to the girl. It was close quarters, but it was an improvement of his position, by three feet at least.

Deirdre and the cook's boy were still at the top of the other barrel, but all they were managing was to dunk it under the surface repeatedly. No doubt the kids inside were getting agitated like laundry in automatic washing machine.

"Give it a rest for a minute," Algie shouted. "I'll be over there in a second!"

He heaved himself up over the wooden edge, balancing himself on his belly button. Tugging on the rope attached to the next barrel, he drew it close enough for him to slide over onto it like a serpent. The wooden top dipped under his weight, but he held tight to the iron band wrapped near the top. He made bloody sure to keep his fingers out of the water as he snagged the next rope.

Algie was able to repeat the process without dropping headfirst into the harbor. The next barrel had three of the younger boys aboard, already clear of their lid and reeling in the tether from their side. They stopped for a moment as something dark and solid brushed by them just beneath the surface. Two of them let go with a screech and dove for the bottom of their wooden vessel.

The third was having none of that. He took up one of the lid's pieces and thrashed away madly at the dark back and upright fin in the water. The fish disappeared into the ink-black waters.

Algie started pulling again, as did the angry young man with a plank on the other end. Algie dropped feet-first into this next barrel, and then paused to look five links ahead in their train.

Deirdre and the cook's boy were still fighting to pry open the sinking cask without dropping it all the way beneath the low waves.

"You two might want to get out of the water now," Algie shouted. "There's some very big fish out here. Might be sharks."

He tried to keep his tone conversational. Algie didn't want to start a panic, mainly because he was afraid if one started, he'd join in too. The two in the water went about their task with grunts and gritted teeth.

Algie made his way across the next few barrels until he dropped down beside the two girls and a boy in the final one. Keogh was there and still smelled strongly of the bottom of a sheep transport ship. Algie wasted no time snagging the rope connected to the sinking barrel and then getting his feet on the edge of the one he occupied.

"Hold tight on my belt, would you please? I don't want to go headfirst into the harbor."

Secured by all three children, Algie planted his feet wide and reeled in the line hand over hand. The cook's boy finally caught on to the plan and backed away to tread water. Algie sincerely hoped he didn't get eaten in the next few minutes.

The slack in the line was now in the bottom of his barrel and the other one was now pulled up snug. He put his back into the task and pulled it up to the same height as his above the water. That made his level platform lean forward suddenly due to the weight of wood and water. If not for those acting as his anchor, he would have most likely pitched down and broken through the lid with his face.

"Quickly," Algie grunted. "Don't know how long I can hold this!"

The boy swam in and wedged his blade between two of the planks. He was able to pop them off easily and cleared the barrel's mouth in seconds. The boy and girl inside looked like drowned kittens. They were still breathing, though a bit blue around the lips. Deirdre and the cook's boy were able to fish them out and push them over into open barrels nearby.

As those two sputtered and shivered, the cook's boy had swum over and pulled the other sinking barrel over to Algie. He offered up the rope and Algie reeled it in.

Three girls were inside that one. The two largest had held

the smallest up between them. She barely had her hair wet from the dunking. The other two looked mildly drowned, but were able to assist in getting themselves into more seaworthy vessels.

"Deirdre! You, boy!" Algie shouted. "Get into a barrel before you're eaten."

The harbor sharks had been nowhere near as ferocious as Algie expected from the many seafaring stories he had read. It could be that they had already stuffed themselves on garbage and dead fish, or the local predators had yet to develop a taste for escaped child. Whatever it was, he didn't want to risk any more than he had.

Deirdre sculled over to the barrel with her girlfriends and started up an excited conversation. The cook's boy came over to Algie's barrel. He grasped the nameless boy wrist to wrist, the way acrobats and mountaineers do, and hauled him in. The barrel sank and rocked a bit with the extra weight, but the inside stayed watertight. Once the five of them were situated, Algie asked the cook's boy a very personal question:

"Would you mind very much if we gave you a name? 'Boy' is horribly undignified and non-specific."

The boy held his hands out and shrugged, He seemed too cold and wet to be overly concerned one way or another.

"My father's name was Chauncey. He was an engineer and a war hero. You were very heroic tonight. Would you mind if we called you Chauncey?"

The boy made a thoughtful grimace and then nodded his head to the affirmative.

Algie took his hand and shook it vigorously.

"It's a pleasure to meet you, Chauncey."

Chauncey replied with a haggard grin and a shiver. The other passengers aboard their iron-banded dinghy quickly got into the spirit of the moment, calling him by name, shaking his hand, clapping him on the back. Seeing the example of Deirdre's barrel, they huddled around Chauncey to warm him from the cold harbor waters.

Algie raised a hand to all his fellow refugees, thankfully all broken free from their lids now.

"Everybody! This is Chauncey," he shouted. "He saved our

lives tonight!"

The two-dozen or so of the barrel riders shouted out their thanks to Chauncey one or two at a time. Algie heard a low mechanical sound as the raucous cries petered out. It sounded like a steam engine.

A quick scan of the horizon showed a light approaching from the deep-water mooring platform near the *Roscommon Venture*. The spotlight beam swept from side between red and green lights on either side of its prow. The approaching craft let out three precise bursts on its horn.

"Maybe they'll pick us up," somebody said.

A quick debate called out from barrel to barrel ensued. Some of the children waved and shouted as others tried to duck down out of sight.

The boat made the same the three precise "toots" again as it drew closer. It was taking a path clear of the channel other incoming vessels took, one aimed directly at their tiny flotilla of barrels. In less than a minute it came close enough for Algie to see the vessel that it had no wheelhouse and no visible crew.

"I've read about this," Algie said as he picked up one of the planks from the lid. "It's an automatic mail packet that runs from the dock to the shore. Just a dumb machine."

He began paddling even before he spoke:

"We need to get out of its way! Everybody make for shore!"

The children laid into the task with the same coordination and skill as everything else attempted that night. The rope went taut between them as the barrels went every which way. Spread as far as humanly possible across the automaton's path, it caught up with them somewhere between Algie's and Deirdre's positions. It chugged forward as the rope snagged on the bow. The occupied barrels slammed against the hull of the little boat and were held there by the force of rushing water.

Wherever they were hoping to be going at the beginning of their flight, the runaways would be coming into Capetown harbor with the mail.

*

Though it looked slow as it approached, the mail packet's

speed held the barrel train in the bow wave. The seawater washed up over the lips of the barrels and threatened to drown all of the fugitive children.

Deirdre was on the starboard side of the packet's low prow, leaving Algie and Chauncey to rescue the few small and nearly-drowned on his side of the train. It was not going well.

The bow wave lapped over the lip of the foremost barrel. It wobbled and pounded itself against the packet's hull before submerging. The girls inside floundered to keep their heads above water. Getting into another barrel must not have occurred to them.

Algie reached out to the smallest girl, but she only clutched tight to her barrel and screeched. The sea water kept rising up her torso as the other girls splashed their way to the next barrel in the train. The boys there waved them on, even if no one had a plan for the next moments.

"Everybody! Try to climb up on the boat," Algie shouted. He hoped the others on the other side of the boat heard him. He wasn't sure the kids on his side could hear over the screams.

The current was pulling the rope taut as the next barrel slowly dove for the harbor bottom. The girl submerged with it. Chauncey grabbed the hawser and pulled it back toward them. Algie joined in and pulled it and the sputtering child to the surface.

The dunking relaxed the girl's grip enough for Algie's purposes. He let loose the rope and snatched up the girl by the armpits. The barrel sped off towards the stern and slammed into the next one in the chain. They slammed together with the sound of a dray cart accident that chilled Algie's bones. One of the flailing children was catapulted clear. Algie saw them recede into the distance in mere seconds.

Most of Algie's mental and physical energy was bound up in prying loose the young girl and getting her to stay still in the bottom of their barrel. His head whipped around angrily when he felt the series of slaps on his back.

"What now," he snapped.

Chauncey pointed up to packet's rail as he unfolded his pen-knife. The mute boy gestured up and over just in case Algie didn't catch on right away. It was the best idea he didn't hear all morning.

Chauncey jammed the blade into the wood of the hull as high as he could reach. It sunk in with a satisfying sound. The cook's boy wrapped both hands around the handle and pulled himself up to stand on the wobbling lip of their barrel. He danced about a bit to get solid enough footing to reach up to the gunwale until Algie put both hands under his ass and pushed.

Chauncey scrabbled up the hull like a drowning rat and threw himself over the railing. He reappeared shortly. With a clap of his hands to catch Algie's attention, he reached down with both hands for the girl blubbering in the bottom of the barrel. He grabbed her under the armpits, a little too roughly for a young gentleman, but lives were at stake.

"We're going to get you up in the boat," he said as he lifted. "Reach out your hands."

She didn't seem interested in her own rescue and Algie wondered if he had the strength to just throw her up over the rail. The girl finally got control of herself and extended her hands with faint effort. Chauncey snatched her up like a fish on a line.

As soon as she was gone, the cook's boy reached down for him. Algie pulled himself up the same way the girl had. He wobbled back and forth on his unsteady platform and looked over his shoulder to see how far he might have to swim through shark-infested waters if he fell.

The harbor was drawing close enough for Algie to make out the separate ships and buildings on the quay. The lightening sky even let him make out some of the signs on the waterfront warehouses. They were written in some sort of near English that almost seemed to make sense to Algie. He was afraid one of them said "Fresh Children."

Chauncey caught his attention with a sharp whistle even as he grasped Algie's right wrist. His free hand pointed to the knife imbedded in the hull and then made a repeated grasping gesture. Algie caught on right away.

"Sure, I'll get it for you."

He leaned over with his left hand as Chauncey held tight to

his other wrist. The barrel bucked and rocked beneath him. His stomach mimicked the motion in exacting detail. More a moment of panic than confident action, Algie grasped the handle of the penknife. He pulled hard, but all that did was swing him leftwards. The knife didn't budge. He tried to pull the blade straight out, again with no luck.

"I'll buy you a new one," Algie shouted, not really knowing how'd he accomplish that.

He reached up his left hand and Chauncey pulled him up and over the rail. Algie found himself face down on the deck beside a small stack of oilskin mailbags, wallowing in a layer of grit and filth that rivalled the sheep pens of the *Roscommon Venture*. He sprung to his feet, catapulted by panic and disgust.

A cry came from the back of the boat followed by a splash and more children's screams. Algie saw splashing hands and a bobbing head in the water as he dashed back to the rear of the boat.

"Pull them up!" he shouted to Chauncey as he leaned over the rail and grabbed the first pair of waving hands. "Pull them all up! You take that side."

The first little girl flopped onto the deck like a bag of Christmas pudding. The next one weighed considerably more, but she got her feet under and scrabbled up the hull with a bit of effort. The next child came up the same way, and then the next. Algie was faced with an empty barrel.

He leaned further over the rail to grab the rope connecting all the wooden casks. Algie slid a bit at first, but several hands grasping the seat of his pants kept him from falling into the harbor. The barrel drew close to him fast enough. He snatched at the desperate hands that came at him. Others' hands reached down past him and pulled the sodden fugitives into the boat, some of them using him as ladder up to safety.

Algie didn't mind the occasional foot behind his ear. He considered that part of the price of being a hero.

A cheer went up from the other side of the boat and Algie dared to take a moment to look over at the celebration. Chauncey's side had reeled in the last of their little fishes, and they all wrapped their arms around each other for warmth and joy. It looked like there were still a dozen occupied barrels on his side, a very uneven distribution.

The pull they exerted was too much for him to bear at the moment. He let the rope slip from his hands as he laid down on the flat rear deck of the automaton packet.

The vacant barrel on the other side shot forward out of sight as if it had been tied to the tale of a whale. It, and all the other barrels ahead of it in the train, rattled against the hull of the packet with a sound like rolling thunder. The children in the few occupied barrels ahead of it squealed as if they'd just been dropped on a carnival ride.

The line on Algie's side went taut and started drifting out of his reached. He thought he would leap up in reaction, but his body vetoed the motion. Instead, he shouted at the top of his lungs:

"Hey! We're losing them!"

The other children, those still on their feet, were aware of the situation. The godawful racket guaranteed that. Chauncey looked Algie's way and then scanned the little boat for solutions. As Algie levered himself to his feet, the cook's boy went to the closed-in boilerhouse and pulled down a pike pole from the rack on its side.

Before Algie could even track his motion, Chauncey was up on the rear deck and fishing with the hook end of the pike for the rope between the clattering barrels.

Algie couldn't see if the pike snagged the rope, but it jerked forward in the older boy's hands. It pulled him off his feet in the blink of an eye.

Chauncey fell into the water without a sound.

Algie went for a second pike pole, but the last barrel was already out of reach. He watched Chauncey swimming to the nearest barrel and rolling up and over the lip. He and the rest of the barrel train steadily fell away into the night. The children in the far end were still screaming for help.

The last boat from the *Roscommon Venture* rowed toward the sound.

*

Somehow, Deirdre was behind him. Her hand was on his shoulder, gently urging him to turn around. He couldn't bear to see how few of the children were still free.

"Come inside," she said. "It's warmer near the boiler."

Algie turned around then. It seemed that only the smallest of the group had been saved. They were wet, shivering from the cold, and still looking to him to save them.

"Have them pack in first," he said. "They need it more."

"You're freezing, too."

"I'll be all right," he said as he ran his hand forward along the outer wall. He stopped as he found where it was warmed by the boiler, too. "And I can keep an eye out until we reach the docks."

"But..." Deirdre said.

"We only have a few minutes. Dry off while you can."

She slipped inside without further argument. Algie pressed himself against the cabin wall and appreciated the warmth. He thought of wrapping himself up in one of the oilskin tarps stretched over the packet's cargo, but they didn't look very comfy.

The sky was lightening off to his right. A small flotilla of dinghies and longboats made their way off the docks towards the few ships moored outside the harbor. Liberties for those sailors probably ended at dawn. Algie wondered how many of those ships had children or other fractious cargo that might jump ship.

The automaton boat put-putted its way into the harbor, somehow avoiding the outgoing boats. Some of the misses, though, were only a matter of a few yards. One was the longboat from the Roscommon Venture.

Doyle, the first mate, stood hunched over in the front of the little rowboat. He looked sick to death and ready to bite off heads. The other crewmen at the oars kept theirs down, just in case.

Algie froze to the spot, too terrified to move, while hoping that avoiding sudden moves might make him invisible.

The first mate cast a surly glance Algie's way as the two boats passed. Doyle's eyebrows knit and the wrinkles of his forehead collapsed down upon them. No doubt he was trying to decipher why a single child might be riding the packet into the harbor.

Algie, hoping to look normal, smiled and waved.

The whole thought process must have been too painful for the older sailor. He dismissed Algie with a feeble wave of his hand and settled down on his seat.

Algie kept waving as the boat disappeared into the distance. He couldn't help himself.

He rushed to the front of the boat to reconnoiter, just as Dale Daring might do. His brain tried to weigh all the factors at once. The last boat from the transport ship would most likely be pulling in the other children right now. The first mate's boat would catch up to them in a matter of five to ten minutes. That would mean a good chance for pursuit in twice that.

The packet was only a few hundred yards off the docks, literally minutes away at their current speed. Algie could see men standing on the quay, most likely waiting to unload the very boat they had stowed away on.

If Algie trusted his luck and ingenuity, he might have tried to override the boats controls and head for another landing point. He, unfortunately, had learned what his luck and ingenuity were worth in the last few hours. That left only one other feasible plan.

*

The automated mail packet arrived in its berth in a controlled low-speed crash. The multiple rope bumpers along the dock absorbed most of the shock, but Algie was still thrown against the boilerhouse door with the sharp stop.

He could hear dockworkers grumbling amongst themselves and mooring the boat down to deck cleats before he even popped around the corner. They weren't speaking English, but something close to it. It sounded like his drunken uncle at the end of a particularly generous Christmas dinner.

"Good morning, gentleman," he called out cheerily. "I'm sorry I had to catch a ride on your little boat. I hope you don't mind?"

The three poorly-weathered workers in overalls and gloves first stared at Algie, and then each other. As he expected, they had no idea what to do with a stowaway.

He slapped the side of the wheelhouse three times. The door flew open and the remaining child fugitives rushed out. They swarmed over the rail and onto the dock, screaming and flailing their arms all the time. The dockworkers simply spun in place as they tried to track the tiny squealing bodies.

The children went on to the ladders and then every which way. Once Algie was convinced they had all escaped, he leaped off the front of the boat. He missed a cast iron deck cleat by inches, but landed within reach of Chauncey's pen knife.

It was far easier to pull with solid footing. He folded it and thrust it into his pocket before ascending the ladder to join the mad rush of children.

"Good morning, gentleman," he shouted. After all, he didn't want to be rude.

He hoped the other children all remembered to rendezvous beyond the fish market warehouse, but he was not willing to jinx his luck again.

FIFTEEN

30th of August 1889
Turfan Caravanserai

Algie's mother had always detested gambling, stating it was an occupation for degenerates and lay-abouts. The people shouting and jostling Algie in the grand plaza of Turfan fit that description pretty well as they cheered on two half-naked men beating each other senseless with their bare hands. He dodged around flailing fists full of betting chits and the hollowed out wooden ball stuffed with bills that was pitched from bettor to bookie and back. His daily training in Isilmandatu movement served him well.

An inarticulate roar came up from the crowd as a Chinese boxer landed a blow firmly in his opponent's gut. Nilenha and Feng Po gave out groans of disappointment as the pale young man, Ensign Bigsby, stumbled. As he regained his fighting stance, the shouting redoubled as the chits and currency flew. The Conversor and the first mate ramped up their bets with the increased odds against the American.

The Chinese boxer was a stout farm boy with a shaggy black hair and several round bald ringworm patches. He was no legendary warrior of the Open Hand Society, more like a boxing ox, but he looked to have enough muscle to counter Bigsby's skill at Marquis of Queensbury rules.

Bigsby retreated with a little sideways dance, his feet moving far faster than his fists. When the big man lunged forward, Bigsby fended him off with a diffident jab and continued to circle around the outside of the ring.

"This is a fight," Nilenha shouted, "not a Sunday Social dance. Hit him already!"

Feng Po added something in Chinese. Algie wasn't sure what it was supposed to be, but it included a few of the words Algie had been warned not to repeat in front of the Conversors.

The other Conversors with them, Jakinda, Ayotunde, and Chabi, raised their eyebrows and some hid sly smiles behind their fans. None of them seemed scandalized to the point of fainting.

Bigsby's opponent cut across the circle to rush him. He landed a tremendous blow on the American's jaw. Bigsby stopped short as if his feet had just been nailed to the ground.

Another roar went up from the crowd and more bets flew over Algie's head in the wooden apple. The Chinese boxer pummeled Bigsby's midsection time and again until the ensign fell into him and clinched both arms around his neck.

"Enough of the love play," Nilenha jeered. "You are a hairless child, Bigsby!"

The American boxer was too badly beaten to take offense to the reminder that he could not grow a mustache like a proper airman. He simply hung in place until the otherwise disinterested referee separated them. Both men returned to their opposite corners for a short break.

"How long will this go on?" Algie asked Feng Po.

"Until one falls down and doesn't get back up," the first mate replied.

"Knocked out?"

"If they're lucky, *chong wu.*"

Feng Po finished up his bets with the nearest bookies and then gave a conspiratorial nod to Nilenha and the Conversors behind her. The three of them, Chabi, Jakinda, and Nilenha, squeezed their way to the very front of the crowd. Algie saw their fans lash out when some of the men dared to squeeze back. Once at the edge of the ring and behind the beefy Chinese fighter, Nilenha slipped a pair of purple tinted spectacles from her reticule and settled them upon her nose.

Bigsby took a deep breath and drew himself up to his full height. In spite of the welt forming on his forehead and a bloody nose, Bigsby looked to be in fighting form after his break.

The referee shouted out something meaningless and pointed towards the center of the arena. Bigsby danced into the center.

The Chinese farm boy bellowed and rushed at him. With a sweeping blow from his right arm, he looked ready to take off Bigsby's head. The ensign ducked beneath the swing. He jabbed his opponent twice in the gut and was gone before the other even knew he'd been hit.

Bigsby brought his fists up to guard face as the taller man spun on him. Three times he dodged blows to his head as the Chinese boxer grew more and more outraged.

The next blow, aimed at Bigsby's breadbasket, left the Chinaman's face wide open. The American took advantage with a left cross that caught the farm boy completely by surprise and spoiled his attack.

Bigsby danced out of the way again.

Angry shouts came from the crowd as the Chinese boxer shook his head.

Bigsby danced back into range with his fists held high.

The Chinese boxer jabbed at Bigsby's face with his right fist. The American airman deflected the blow and replied with a punch to the nose.

The Chinese tried again with his left, to the same effect. Another attempt with his right was rewarded with a blow that had the farm boy tottering like a half-cut tree.

Bigsby circled around behind his opponent and rained a series of blows onto his kidneys. As the taller man turned to face him, the American delivered a powerful right to the underside of his chin. The Chinese boxer went down like a burning airship.

The crowd turned into a bit of a scrum, then. Angry bettors converged on the bookies. Uyghur, Chinese, Africans, and Afghans, it seemed the whole world was angry at them. One angry European, it sounded like he was swearing in German, brandished a cash-filled wooden ball in Feng Po's face. Algie's mentor was fending the bookie off with the brass tip off his command baton.

A firm, female hand settled on Algie's shoulder and pulled him back into the protective circle of the Conversors. The women kept themselves apart from the fray, fanning themselves in the cool of an August desert evening and the heat of gamblers' passions.

The pandemonium lasted only a few minutes. Then, a cry came up from the tents outside the assembled crowd. Just a handful of people repeated a single word at first. Then it became a chant as a new boxer made his way to ring. From the tone of their voices, Algie guessed he was a crowd favorite.

"I don't recognize the language," Jakinda said. "Darsi?"

"No, that's Kazakh," Chabi replied. "They are calling him The Beast."

The crowd parted behind the Conversors and The Beast sauntered into the ring with his Kazakh handlers. The fighter was a head taller than most of the crowd and half as broad as he was tall. The grizzled dark brown hair of his beard and plaited queue made him look like the wooly ox-like beasts some of the Nepalese merchants used to carry their goods. He sneered at Algie's little group as he passed and Algie saw that all of the huge man's teeth had gone to black. Either they were rotting out of his head or they had been replaced with wrought iron. Either prospect terrified Algie.

The Beast shed his outer garments until he wore only voluminous blue pants, boots, and assorted brass and leather ornaments around his wrists, throat, and hair. With hands held over his head, the fighter circled the ring and roared. The crowd cheered him on.

Ensign Bigsby, still looking a bit battered from his last bout, followed The Beast's circuit with a wary eye. He looked over to Feng Po and Nilenha with a questioning look on his face. Feng Po clenched his fist in the air in front of him and made a resolute face. Nilenha removed her tinted spectacles and handed them to Algie.

"Would you hold these for the duration, please?"

"Certainly."

Ensign Bigsby looked at him as if they had just done something meaningful. He nodded his head and took a drink from the bottle Dr. Koslowski, his coach and second, had handed him.

The Kazakh Beast returned to his opposite corner, still bellowing and slapping his fists against his chest. He looked about ready to bite the head off of a live chicken.

Algie was feeling some definite concern for the ensign. He startled as someone stepped in close behind him and was surprised to see it was Ayotunde.

"I thought you hated boxing," Algie said. As always with her, he had to speak in French.

"I do," she replied. "It is barbaric and ungodly, but I am always willing to cheer for an 'underdog'."

She slipped into English for the last word, as there was probably not a French equivalent that either of them knew. She held up a hand to greet the ensign. He responded with a nod and a weak smile.

"I like Ensign Bigsby, just as I like our ship as we face air pirates." Ayotunde fixed Algie with a placid, but unreadable, expression. "There are times that I even like you."

"But not often?"

"You are not the underdog we need to concern ourselves with just now."

The referee took the center of the ring and beckoned to both fighters. As they took up stances to either side of him, he shouted out announcements in what sounded to be a half-dozen languages. Algie understood none.

Nilenha and Feng Po pressed forward to the very ragged edge of the crowd on either side of Algie. They spoke in English over his head.

"So, do we have decent odds for this bout?" Nilenha muttered.

"Not as long as I would've liked," Feng Po replied. "Topped out at twenty-two to three, those wary *wáng bā dàn*"

"I suppose they have a right after seeing the young ensign

work his magic."

"The Beast is still the favorite. Helmut wanted to offer me odds on Bigsby's decapitation."

The referee threw up both his hands and shouted for the fight to commence. The crowd shouted back and all side conversations abruptly ended.

The Kazakh stood with his feet planted wide and his hands on his hips. With his hairy belly hanging over the top of his pants, he looked like a boar with a beard. He laughed as he looked down at the top of Ensign Bigsby's head.

Bigsby was small for an American, but well-muscled. He put up his fists in a ridiculously formal pose and danced in towards his opponent.

The Kazakh didn't move.

Bigsby took a few steps to the left and then the right, but there was no reaction to the feints. He rushed into to land a quick succession of blows to the gut and rushed out to avoid the Kazakh's reach.

The big man's fists came off of his hips, his fingers splayed out in surprise. He actually took a full step backwards in response to the attack. He just as quickly stepped forward with his arms outstretched, ready to swat the ensign off his feet with either beefy arm, or wrap him in a crushing bear hug.

Most of the crowd cheered The Beast on to murder.

Ensign Bigsby lunged forward for another blow. He connected to a somewhat lesser effect, but was nearly knocked off his feet by the return blow to the side of his head. Bigsby backed away and the Kazakh pursued.

Algie looked to Feng Po for some hope, because things were looking honestly grim for their shipmate. The first mate grimaced as the ensign took two more sledgehammer blows to the head. Nilenha did not yell out any insults this time. The rest of the crowd was savoring the beating Bigsby was taking.

Bigsby set his feet firm beneath him and brought up his fists to completely block his head. The Kazakh jabbed with his full weight, but the American deflected the blow away harmlessly. The next punch skimmed off Bigsby's fists and the top of his head. If that rattled the ensign, he let no sign of that show. He instead took the opportunity to punch his opponent squarely in the nose.

The Beast left himself open for just a moment, long enough to be punched again. He struck back and the two of them stumbled away from each other. Something in the atmosphere changed, a ghastly equilibrium achieved, and the two boxers went about the business of slaughtering each other by centimeters.

"He's going to cheat, you know," a man's voice said in English behind Algie's right ear.

He turned to see Dr. Cookworthy from the *karakuri* cage. His expression was as grim as Ayotunde's.

"He would never!" Algie blurted. "Ensign Bigsby is an officer and a gentleman!"

"Not him, the big fellow." He indicated the Kazakh with a discrete elevation of his chin. "That brass ornament at the top of his plait? The one that happens to be just slightly wider than his palm, with points on either end? It is a *yawara*, a hand-to-hand weapon once used by Buddhist monks."

The Beast punched the ensign in the head three times.

"I wouldn't say that he would need to use it," Ayotunde replied.

The airman attacked the Kazakh's massive gut. Both circled the other, though more slowly and with an increasing wobble to their orbits.

"Your shipmate seems to have the advantage of technique," Cookworthy replied.

Bigsby unleashed a series of blows that brought the bearded man down to one knee. He gave The Beast one more punch to the nose for good measure. The crowd went into an outraged frenzy as he backpedaled to his side of the ring.

"So I see," crooned Feng Po.

"Don't jinx our boy," Nilenha muttered in English.

The Kazakh boxer shook out his head like a great sleepy bear. His long hair fell loose around his shoulders as he laboriously brought himself to standing. Bigsby jogged in place, looking as if he might drop if he were to stop moving.

"And there it is," Cookworthy said.

The American stumbled forward and landed two more blows. The Kazakh absorbed them with little more than a drunken wobble. His supporters in the crowd began to pelt Bigsby with vegetables and small stones.

Feng Po shouted something in Chinese at the crowd. Algie guessed it was something along the lines of "Oy! That's not sporting!" Chabi called out something in what sounded like three or four different languages, no doubt translating. No one seemed to be paying attention.

Ensign Bigsby was distracted by the bedlam around him. He never saw the Kazakh's blow that dropped him like a tree.

The Beast slipped the brass *yawara* beside the American's inert body and paraded slowly around the ring in triumph. The hurried polyglot discussion amongst the Conversors was impossible for Algie to follow, but he did hear every obscenity in any foreign tongue he knew.

The Beast landed a kick in Bigsby's midsection that rolled him over in the dirt. Another kick to the head was enough to decide the issue for Jakinda.

"That is enough of that," Jakinda growled in French. "I'll need a diversion in sixty seconds."

Chabi and Nilenha went left and right as she pushed past Algie and Feng Po. The Basque Conversor gave him some quick instructions in English:

"Consider this part of your lessons. Watch the fan, not the silk. And don't get crushed underfoot."

Feng Po snagged the back of Algie's shirt collar as Jakinda stepped into the ring. She put on a very convincing show of hysterics with her face half-covered by a flowered silk handkerchief. She wailed, sounding quite inconsolable.

The Beast turned his attention from the ensign to her. He spoke, but she gave no sign of understanding. She waved her silk from side to side and sobbed in response.

A commotion rose up from the crowd a moment later. Algie recognized the two other Conversors' voices and a man's hoarse cries of pain.

Most eyes turned in that direction.

A look of grim determination settled on Jakinda's face. She

tossed her silk handkerchief to her left and the Kazakh's eyes followed. She then struck the left side of his throat with her closed fan. It moved almost too quickly to see.

His eyes went unfocused and his knees folded. The Basque Conversor took a step up on one of his bent knees and struck with the iron fan on opposing sides of his neck three times. She alighted completely unmussed as he collapsed at her feet.

"Into the breach, Pig," Feng Po muttered as he rushed Algie into the ring. He picked up the lady's silk as the first mate helped her scoop up the ensign and carry him off to safety. Feng Po also snagged the *yawara* and jammed it into the angry bookie's wooden apple as he passed.

"He and I will have words about this," the mate told Algie in English. "And then I'll let the women have their way with him."

SIXTEEN

30th of August 1889
Turfan Caravanserai

The Grand Entertainment devolved into a general riot within seconds. Dr. Cookworthy joined Algie and the Conversors in carefully considered retreat. He looked sore upset at the way the evening had ended.

"You look like somebody put your pigeon in the pie," Feng Po told him as they stumbled along under each of Bigsby's arms. "Never run from a social engagement in fear for your life?"

"You would be surprised," the tall African replied. "There was a time at the student union in Budapest—"

One of those damnable wooden apples caught the doctor in the back of the head and threw him off his step. Algie picked up the apple and lofted it into the scrum that pursued them. Bricks, bottles and bits of wood flew back at him. He gathered up the ensign's possessions in a tighter bundle and ran to put himself in front of the three men.

"I actually was to give a demonstration after the boxing," Dr. Cookworthy said. "This is all very disappointing."

Some bit of flying debris landed between Feng Po's feet. It caused him to stumble and nearly brought all three of them down.

"What kind of show could you be putting on for this lot?"

"Self-immolation."

"I'm not sure how that would have worked out," Feng Po said with a grin, "but I certainly do admire your sense of spectacle."

Most of the rabble pursuing them had dissipated down the various side channels of the marketplace, but a dedicated few stayed firmly on the trail. Ayotunde, Chabi, and Jakinda stopped dead and turned back as Algie ran past. The three Conversors planted themselves in the path of the crowd.

One after another, the women snapped open their fans. Each one sounded like a cannon shot.

Chabi spoke first in what seemed to be Chinese. Her voice blared as loud as a trumpet. Though he could not see from behind her, he was sure that fire leaped out of her eyes.

Ayotunde's short speech next, in what sounded like their Uyghur lessons, made Chabi sound like a mouse.

Jakinda spoke last. Algie wasn't even sure there were words, just waves of power that he felt in his bones and gristle. With that glorious noise came a deep desire to be as far away from these women as humanly possible.

The rabble slowed to a halt and then slowly backed away. Shaggy men that had moments ago had been shouting and brandishing weapons looked down at their feet and shuffled away. The alleyway was clear in less than a hundred Picadillies.

Algie's emotions were a churning stew of pride, terror, and undirected energy. He was very glad the Conversors were on his side, for the most part.

"What was that?" Algie asked with perhaps too much enthusiasm. "Was it like a magic spell?"

Ayotunde responded in French:

"I told them they were vile and dissipated creatures, and that their mothers would be ashamed to have given birth to them."

"I translated that," Jakinda said. "In a few popular languages."

"Me too, *Monsieur Chopon*," Chabi said. She still called him "Mr. Pork," perhaps because she thought he liked it. He didn't have the physical courage to correct her.

Dr. Cookworthy made an unpleasant sound and Algie

turned to look at him.

The tall man still had a grip on one of the ensign's arms, but little else. His mouth gaped open and he looked somehow damaged from the sound of Conversors in action. Feng Po hitched himself up underneath the unconscious Bigsby and made for their home base, dragging Cookworthy along behind.

"As I said before, leave things to the womenfolk."

*

Dr. Cookworthy received his invitation to the Grand Salon as consolation for his ruined demonstration. Algie would have gladly given the doctor his spot. Chabi was firm, but relentless, in relaying Mme. Streif's wishes. That is how he found himself once more dressed in an Indian prince's silk regalia.

At least this time, he was given a decent pair of trousers.

Mme. Streif's sitting room was laid out for the salon with many new couches, side tables, and ottomans that night. At least four tea trays, stack high with tea, biscuits, and coffee, held strategic places around the chamber. A mirror-bright silver urn filled with ice and a foil-capped bottle and a library cart full of books marked Patrouille's couch just to the right of Streif's.

Algie often imagined the salons his mother attended in Portsmouth. He was pretty sure they never were as opulent and carefully orchestrated as one of the Silk Empress' events.

She settled into her highbacked chair at a few minutes before nine, her voluminous green-striped skirts tucked in between its arms, her black and white dog on her lap. Mssr. Patrouille in his best peacock blue finery made tight circles of the room to assure that every little thing was in its place. Algie and even the Conversors were charged with lifting, carrying, and adjusting all those little things. Feng Po was notably absent from the evening's activities. Jakinda had declared that he was temperamentally incapable of polite conversation for more than a few moments, and thus exempt.

Everyone took their places at the stroke of nine and stood as the guests filed into the room. The few locals hired for that evening, including Meryem, stood quietly against the wall. Hannah St. George, the governor's wife, was the first to enter.

Her dress was huge and white and unruly with so many frills and fluff she seemed to be drowning in it. She beamed at every bit of luxury and European culture on display.

She approached Mme. Streif's little dog Kosciuszko too closely. He nearly leaped off of the Silk Empress' lap as he barked up a storm at the Governor's wife. Chabi took up the little beast to secure it in Mme. Streif's personal quarters.

"Oh my sweet boy," Mrs. St. George exclaimed as she came up to Algie afterwards, "you're attending the *Grand Salon*, too?"

"Yes. This is my first."

"Mine, too." Mrs. St. George giggled as she tousled his hair. "Let me know if you're feeling uncomfortable at all and I will help you right out."

Mssr. Patrouille approached the two of them as smoothly as if her were punting on a quiet lake.

"*Bon soir, Madame St. George*," he said. "Algie."

Mrs. St. George's eyes opened wide with pleasure upon seeing him.

"Oh, thank heavens!" she said. "Do bring me a glass of champagne, young man."

Mssr. Patrouille's face fell. Even the crisp waxed ends of his mustaches looked to wilt.

"I am not the help."

"Oh. You're not?"

"I am Etienne Patrouille. We met at the banquet at your mansion less than a week ago."

"Oh, I forgot you," she responded vaguely. "I am so sorry."

"Forgot?" the Frenchman barked out. She seemed to be having the same effect on him as she had on Kosciuszko. "Did you forget or did you efface my memory, perhaps thinking that someone of my complexion couldn't have any mastery of the arts?"

"I simply forgot. I am very busy you see—"

"France's greatest writer Alexander Dumas was constantly belittled for being of both French & African blood. Like him, I am an internationally acclaimed novelist and essayist under multiple pen names with tens of thousands of sales to my record."

"Is there anything of yours I might have read?" she asked. Her tone sounded vaguely conciliatory.

"I don't know," Patrouille responded sharply, "are you *capable* of reading?"

Jakinda, on the other side of the room, furled and unfurled her fan with a loud report and tapped the folded end against her lips. Whatever message that transmitted, the French writer was instantly chastised.

"Good evening to you both," he said before slinking away.

Mrs. St. George shrugged airily and then settled on her chaise, half-reclining once she gained control over dress, and made exploratory pokes at the dried fruits and pastries on the silver platter nearest her. Though she seemed quite pleased with everything about the salon, she did steal suspicious glances at Ayotunde, Keijín, and Nilenha. Algie wondered what about them disturbed her.

Dr. Hakeem Cookworthy made his entry next.

He still wore his evening clothes from the night before. Traces of dirt and grease from the post-boxing riot clung to his pants legs and elbows. He took in all of the salon with the same studious curiosity he displayed in examining the *karakuri* caracal. A brief flash of calculated terror appeared on his face as he encountered Ayotunde. He quickly replaced it with an endearing smile and a bob of his head as he made his way to the settee beside Mrs. St. George.

The doctor greeted her with a broad smile and perfect English. She responded with a nervous laugh and a quick retreat to her figs.

The last of the evening's special guests was Liu Jean-Pierre. Like Algie, he was dressed for the Emperor's court. He looked as uncomfortable in red silk and gold trim as he did in his indigo laboratory tunic. The poor man was always uncomfortable, but was leaning towards terror for the evening. Chabi offered him a drink and stood at the couch beside his.

Once all the guests were seated, Mme. Streif gestured for Algie and the Conversors to sit. Nilenha curled up on her chaise, pulling her high button boots under her silver-gray striped skirts. She smiled at Algie and patted the cushion beside her.

"You can sit here beside me, *chong wu*."

Knowing better than argue with his etiquette instructor at a salon, he sat. He kept his spine straight, his head erect, and his hands in his lap.

"Such a little gentleman," she murmured into his ear. "I am so proud."

The sitting room buzzed with a dozen such little conversations until Patrouille popped the cork on the champagne. The report was as sudden and loud as one of the Conversors' fans. The doctor tensed at the sound and ducked low as the cork flew over his head.

Algie couldn't track it too easily, but it must have bounced back upon hitting the wall. Mrs. St. George let out a little shriek as it flew through her extravagant hairdo, undoing all the rolls and ringlets on one side of her head. The cork landed at Algie's feet.

He wasn't sure if it was proper protocol to be picking up interesting things at a salon. He let it lay for the time being.

The Governor's wife made little sounds like a disturbed parakeet as she tried to reconstruct her hair. Dr. Cookworthy looked on with an expression of distress and mystification. Everyone else seemed to have the same polite half-smile pasted to their faces. Algie tried his best to emulate.

Patrouille was more concerned with catching the overflow from the bottle in one of the narrow glasses Nilenha called flutes.

"I am so very sorry, Madame St. George," he said. "That was totally unintentional. I can never make those rebound shots when playing billiards."

He handed the first glass of champagne to Mme. Streif, and then gave Mrs. St. George the next. Though she smiled, she was very careful to not touch Patrouille's fingers as she took the flute.

"Perhaps this will assuage your jangled nerves, *mon Cherie*."

"*Merci beuacut, monsieur*," she responded in barely passable French. She smiled to herself as she took her first sip.

As if somebody had opened a throttle valve on a steam engine, the conversation switched from English to French. Algie had hoped they could have stuck with his mother tongue for just a little while, but the governor's wife had just spoiled that.

"Let us begin the Grand Salon," said Mme. Streif. "As is our tradition, we are gathered together to share our knowledge, test theories and eschew assumptions. Tonight, we seek the Truth."

"The truth about what?" Mrs. St George asked as she brushed a loose curl away from her forehead.

"The profound and petty truths that a civilized being might encounter on a day to day basis: Life, Death, the Components for the Perfect Quiche," Patrouille said. "But tonight we will first embark upon a simple topic. What is most excellent in Life?"

A pleased murmur passed through the room. Nilenha leaned closed to Algie and whispered in his ear.

"She's going to do the Genghis Khan quote."

"Who? What?"

"Chabi," she said. "Just watch."

The Mongol Conversor raised her hand for permission to speak.

"Yes, Ma'amselle Chabi," Patrouille said. "What do you have to say?"

She stood and clasped her hands before loudly intoning a few lines in an unidentifiable language. It sounded as if she were giving orders on the field of battle. She bowed her head to Mme. Streif and then Patrouille before returning to her seat. All of the attendees, Algie and Mrs. St. George included, applauded politely.

"A most beautiful presentation," Mme. Streif said. "Don't you agree, Madame. St. George?"

She seemed to go blank for just a moment, then broadened her smile.

"Yes, most beautiful."

"In the spirit of inquiry and discovery," Patrouille asked, "what exactly did it mean to you?"

"Mean?" Mrs. St. George had another one of her blank spells, but then dropped her eyes and fiddled with her petit fours on the tray. "Well, it was both ephemeral... and profound. I found it deeply stirring."

"Which part of it, exactly?" Ayotunde asked in an interrogatory tone.

"Well, I can't say. The Chinese seemed a bit garbled."

"That was Khalkha," Chabi stated flatly. "The noble language of Genghis Khan and the Golden Horde."

"My apologies..."

"Perhaps, if I gave it to you in French?" Ayotunde said. She then recited three or four lines that Algie couldn't quite translate, yet somehow recognized.

For lessons, Patrouille had given Algie the French texts of some of the Dale Daring books, including the Kazakh Tombs. The bad guy in that, a Kurgan mummy brought back to life, had given that as his reason for living. Algie was disappointed to discover that his favorite author had plagiarized Genghis Khan.

"That still isn't quite right, I don't think," Mrs. St. George blathered.

Algie held up his hand and Patrouille acknowledged him with a gesture of his champagne glass.

"Perhaps, if I could give it to her in English?"

"If you could." Jakinda sounded wary.

Algie stood and looked right at Mrs. St. George before he recited:

"What is most excellent in life? To crush your enemies. To drive them before you, and to hear the lamentations of their women."

The room applauded politely, even those he knew did not speak English. He sat down feeling he'd done quite well.

"Well, put that way," Mrs. St. George stammered. "I find it touching because... it reminds me of my husband."

"How is the governor doing?" Jakinda asked sweetly.

"He is suffering one of his sick headaches, tonight. He really did want to attend."

"Our loss, I'm sure," Patrouille replied. "It is your turn next, Jean-Pierre."

Liu Jean-Pierre looked up wide-eyed, his mouth filled with some pastry puff.

"Excuse me?" he asked after a few moments of choking noises.

"What is the most excellent thing in life for you, Jean-Pierre?" Mme. Streif was very gentle and reassuring towards Liu, something Algie was unaccustomed to. "If your life were perfect, what would be the one item central to that?"

"A laboratory, I suppose would be what I would want." He blinked as he seemed to be thinking of more precise wishes. "A full staff and enough space and reagents to work on whatever I thought was important."

"And what about your father?" Jakinda asked.

Jean-Pierre gave out a little nervous cough and sipped his tea.

"My father would not be in my perfect laboratory."

"But wouldn't you want him to acknowledge your achievements?"

Jean-Pierre gave the Conversor a wistful smile.

"You asked for a perfect world, not a total impossibility."

*

As he understood a grand salon to be properly run, Algie felt disappointed in its lack of rigor. He supposed Mme. Streif and Mssr. Patrouille were being somewhat lax with him and, perhaps, Mrs. St. George.

The salon's attendees had a very broad range of phenomena they considered most excellent. Patrouille believed it was Language, how it could be molded and caressed into a myriad of forms to express, to persuade, and to seduce.

Jakinda called him the devil again.

Mme. Streif declared the most miraculous things were Venture Capital harnessed to Compound Interest. She gave a short lecture on how her husband's investment in Liu Chemical Works changed Asia's geopolitical landscape after the first Opium War. Algie had trouble following it, but he could see it rightly disturbed Mrs. St. George. The governor's wife gave her own pretty speech about how all she would really need was a warm bed, a dry roof over her head, a good man, and her garden.

Even Algie, who was verifiably opaque when it came to social occasions, could read the room as completely unimpressed.

Mrs. St. George looked to be crushed as she folded up upon herself.

Algie looked around the room, but saw no silent cue for what the proper action could be. His mother had always told him: "Do something, even if it's wrong. Most of the harm in this world comes from people standing around like hammered sheep." His mother had profoundly hated inaction and inhumane slaughterhouse methods.

"Excuse me for just a moment," he said to Nilenha as he took up her tray of dried fruit.

He stood and crossed over to the governor's wife.

"I thought it was a lovely speech," he said. "Have a fig. They're from Greece."

Hannah St. George looked like she was going to burst into tears at the gesture.

"Oh, you darling boy," she said as she wrapped him up in white lace and the strong smell of bottled roses. "Why don't you sit here with me for a while?"

Algie looked to Nilenha for permission. It felt like he was switching teams. She nodded her head and made the most minute of eye rolls as she slid over to fill the space besides Jakinda.

"It seems that is your turn to speak," said Mssr. Patrouille. "What is the most excellent thing you wish for?"

Algie took no time at all to respond.

"I want to be a hero!"

"You mean like Dale Daring?" Patrouille had the same tone of guilt and terror as whenever the topic came up.

"No, not like him really. He's made up. But I want to be able to do things, to help people, like Feng Po and you Conversors."

"Why would you want that?" asked Mme. Streif. "For the Fame and Adulation? An authentic gold-plated hero would be welcome in any court in Europe or any mansion in the Americas."

"Or maybe the Fortune? There is quite a business in penny dreadfuls," Patrouille cleared his throat and added: "After you split the royalties with your ghost-writer."

"Perhaps, the attention of the Fairer Sex?" suggested Nilenha.

"Those all sound truly excellent," Algie replied. "I can't give you a reason in words, I just feel that it is something I am meant to be."

"Then, you are a very fortunate young man," Mme. Streif said. "Most people go through their entire lives without finding their destiny.

SEVENTEEN

18th of October 1888
Portsmouth, England

There were a few great British ironclads that were designed with the ram as their primary weapon like the Conqueror or the Hero, improvements upon the trireme of Ancient Greece. And, above and beyond all those lesser designs, there was Algie's mother upon a mission. Her last day on Earth, she ran at full stream along the sidewalks of Portsmouth with Algie in tow.

She wore suffragette's white, as she had for the three years since she'd given up widow's black. The dress caught the light of the afternoon sun and attracted every passing eye.

Algie carried the box of pamphlets they had just picked up at the printers as she lectured him on the evils of the patriarchy. He couldn't help but notice the angry expressions of the tradesmen and layabouts as she passed.

"Certainly, this country has a queen, but even she is dominated by her ministers. They denigrate her, dominate her, and treat her as if she were doddering old lady."

A knot of sailors passed close to her and her hand rose up to the back of her broad-brimmed white had where she always kept a fearsome hat pin. Family mythology held that she once pinned a masher's hand to his own thigh with it.

"I hope that if you remember anything else that I've taught you, it's that a woman is just as capable as a man. Treating them like a fragile ornament is just a sinful waste of potential."

"Of course, Mum."

She bent down and kissed Algie on the cheek.

"You are a sweet boy. Let's go have a cuppa tea."

She stepped off the curb but still had her eyes on him. Her mind was on the rest of the afternoon already.

"We'll meet Eliza and hand out those fliers at the park."

She never saw the drayage cart coming up behind her.

Algie saw all of it.

He saw the ice wagon draw up to a sudden halt in the center of the cobblestones. Four enormous chestnut draft horses veered around it to the right at the last moment before colliding with it. Their eyes showed white rings around them as they were stretched too wide in terror.

The driver's eyes looked the same. He already had pulled the reins all the way over in one direction to avoid a crash. There was no play to pull them up to a stop in time.

His mother still smiled, only vaguely aware of the commotion behind her.

Algie's mind didn't have the speed to keep up with what he was seeing. An inner voice told him to drop the box in his arms and snatch his mother out of the way.

He hesitated for a second, thinking that the fliers were valuable, a pound and six pence worth of printing for a women's tea and liberation group that practically sweated blood to raise that money. The streets and gutters were wet, and his mother might be upset.

He hesitated for a second, worrying if he could even reach her in time, then fearful that he might grasp her hand and be pulled under carriage with her.

He hesitated, his brain doing nothing at all for the time it took to say "One Piccadilly." Then he acted.

Algie threw the box behind him, stepped forward, and reached for her hand.

She was already gone by then, run down by the horses, and dragged down the street beneath the cart.

A tremendous noise filled his ears at that moment, a combination of the cries of horror and surprise from the men and women who had stood by disapproving just moments before. The screech of brakes and screams of horses added to that. Algie might have been screaming himself. It rang in his ears as he stood and stared at the place she had been.

A woman in gray skirts and shawls wrapped him up and kept him from going to his mother.

"Come, now, dearie," she murmured. "You don't want to be seeing that."

He didn't know if he did or not. He didn't know what he felt.

He was suddenly empty.

Algie remained wrapped up in that dark pall for days. He kept returning to those lost three seconds, and the myriad life-saving maneuvers he could have fit into that time.

He was sure Dale Daring would have saved his own mother.

EIGHTEEN

7th of September 1889
Turfan Caravanserai

Algie was slow and listless at morning exercises that day after the Grand Salon. The event had kept him up far later than he was accustomed. When he finally did succumb to sleep, he was haunted by dreams of Capetown.

"Keep your head up, Pig," Ayotunde shouted.

Algie snapped to instantly, following the movements of the Conversors on the straw mats to the music of the engineering crew. The minute change of focus awakened his muscle memory. It felt like he was riding his body to the beat through ancient dips and curves.

He also realized that Ayotunde had spoken to him in Uyghur and he had translated it automatically into a simple command.

Things had certainly changed in the last few weeks.

As a treat for Algie, Jakinda began his lessons on leaps and rolls. Chabi demonstrated the intended final result.

She ran at him, her silk pajamas fluttering in the breeze behind her. The Conversor bounced over his head as if he were only two feet tall. She spun like a top and landed just a meter beyond him. Somehow, she leaped again and touched down exactly where she had started.

She bowed deeply to him and sank down to sit, at the same

time twisting her legs in the pretzel configuration all of the Conversors preferred.

The others gave him a series of instructions that should have him hopping about like Springheel Jack if he could keep them all in his mind at the same time.

He walked back to the farthest point on the mats and ran at Jakinda as she instructed. Algie leaped his highest just as he reached her and she used her hands to guide him through a somersault in the air. He landed a bit too hard on the back of his heels and crashed to the mats on his buttocks.

It hurt, but it was a maneuver he had never been able to do before. Jakinda offered him a hand up. He tried it again.

And again.

And again.

Jakinda called an end to the day's lessons when Algie started landing on his head.

As he sat on the edge of the fountain, he looked up into clear blue sky, High above the caravanserai, some kind of craft circled like a buzzard. With each circuit, it drew lower. Whatever the vehicle was, it was long, thin, and seemed to wriggle like a serpent. Two great wings extended from its midsection.

If Algie had not just injured his head, he would have been convinced that it was a dragon.

*

The *Lǎoshǔ* had started up a game on the rooftops as Algie was leaving for his language lessons. He remained in the dark as far as the rules, but he could work out there were two teams with blue and yellow head bands and a rugby ball. They made a complete circuit of the buildings around the courtyard at breakneck speed, sometimes running on all fours like rats.

Somehow, they avoided breaking their necks while tussling for control of the ball. Algie did see a few close calls on the corners. The boys would cheer or snarl as they crossed the goal line, but the scoring scheme was a complete mystery to Algie. It probably didn't matter to them either.

He had no idea how high his friends could count.

He clutched in his left hand the small wooden figure he had

carved. The Conversors had taught him about *opari*, an advanced and perhaps theosophical view of arts and crafts. He had put up some resistance at first, but when he had actually put blade to wood he did feel some sense of inner peace. He even found himself to have some small talent for woodcarving, enough that he wasn't embarrassed in giving his first piece to Zdan.

He was off to visit his new friend that afternoon. Meryem was unavailable for his language lessons. The day before, the local rebels had attacked the caravanserai, leaving seven dead of the guards and civilians of Turfan. No one knew how many of the Uyghurs fell as they carried off all their wounded, but whispers had it that the leader Boway Kashgari had once again proven to be bullet-proof. Any worker at the mansion that had any connection to the rebels found themselves being questioned carefully by Aramis Boycott and his redcoats.

The river of traders and their wares parading into the main plaza looked to be only half of its previous size. Algie had been told it was for fear of another attack from the air. Maybe they believed rumors of dragons outside Turfan's walls, no matter how much Governor St. George and Mr. Boycott strived to quash them.

Algie found the *karakuri* merchant at the site of his demonstration for the Grand Entertainment. The large cage had already been folded up and the smaller automatons crated. The headless palanquin bearers were already loading the crates onto Zdan's flatbed trailer.

"You're leaving Turfan?" was the first thing out Algie's mouth. It came out as more of a whine than he had intended.

"Good Bye and Hello to you, British boy." He latched the metal cagework that bound up the boxes of pigeon simulacra. "I have other stops along the Silk Road to display my wares."

"You're not afraid of the Uyghurs, are you?"

"I am not afraid, but I am feared."

The Tuareg had a quizzical look on his face. He gestured for Algie to sit with him at the nearby folding metal table and chairs in the shade. He poured tea for both of them into little glass cylinders with fancy silver handles.

"The British, and perhaps the court of the Emperor, are not very wise. Because they have a problem with rats, they hunt down mice and squirrels."

Algie thought on that as he took a sip of his tea, strong, sweet, and heavy with lemon and spices.

"Is that a metaphor," he asked Zdan, "or a problem of translation?"

Zdan laughed out, displaying his strong yellow teeth.

"I will miss your visits, British boy!" He pointed at the carving Algie had set on the table. "Is this your work?"

"Yes, I brought it for you."

Zdan picked it up and examined it from all sides. It was one of his headless palanquin *karakuri*, boxy but at least properly proportioned in body and limb. Algie would never admit it to anyone, but the carving had started out as one of the Conversors until he accidentally broke of its head.

"The Conversors, they are helping you to find your *opari*, I see."

Algie leaned across the wrought iron table and whispered:

"You know about that?"

"I know a great many things, including when I am needed elsewhere." Zdan Ag Ahar placed his free hand over his heart. "Thank you, Algernon Piggrem, I shall treasure this always."

*

Algie wandered gardens of the Governor's Mansion and the market for quite some time. He was sad to see his friend go and he wasn't eager to return to the alternating bedlam and intrigue of Mme. Streif's rented villa.

A moment of darkness came over him and the plaza, then, it was gone. Algie, like everyone else it seemed, looked up to the cloudless sky. The thing that couldn't be a dragon had circled even lower to the ground, showing itself to be an amazing simulation of one. It soared on vast golden wings with a tattered British airship clenched in all four of its taloned feet.

There was no way the governor was going to be able to debunk this report.

It dove towards the ground with a strangely musical cry. The sounds of plucked strings and resounding metal filled the air.

The dragon soared low over the heads of the peddlers, over Algie, and then blotted out the sun. The wind in its wake felt like a hurricane. The golden beast made a sharp banking turn like a racing chiropter at the spiral minaret at the far end of Turfan. A tip of a wing tore off the roofed chamber at the top.

The final arc of its turn brought it around to bear down on the market laid out in the Grand Plaza. It let loose the airship. Wreckage and machinery rained down on the brightly colored tents and awnings. The heavier bits of the ship rolled and tumbled towards Algie. Debris cut a path ten meters wide through the stalls and crowds of shoppers.

What must have been the steam power-plant came to rest just after it cut through the stream of merchants, leaving crushed wagons and bodies in its path.

The boiler slowly came apart, rivet by rivet from a wound in the bottom of its metal skin. Steam and smoke leaked out of the collapsing corpse. People and beasts floundered in the cloud.

People were screaming, looked to be bleeding and broken. Fires must have caught in the market, because thick columns of black smoke rose from behind the wreckage. For just a moment, he thought he saw once again the *picaroon* that had been blown apart by the Mermaid's Purse. He vanished in a coil of smoke, but the boy remembered the look in the dying man's eyes.

Algie stood paralyzed. If he were Dale Daring, he would have known exactly what needed done, formed a plan, and leaped into action. He wasn't Dale Daring, though, and neither was the boy airship pilot. Dale was simply the figment of the imagination of Timothy Freemarch, another writer Mssr. Patrouille only described as an *imbecile* and someone that knew even less about aeronautics than Algie did.

A rasping cry drew his attention to a woman pinched nearly in half under a crushed dray wagon. Algie saw her blood and twisted limbs and looked away, even when he could hear her beg for help in Uyghur.

Smoke enveloped him. The woman disappeared from his view. He choked on the smoke and dust and still he didn't move.

His legs and arms seemed to have forgotten what they were

meant to do. His mind was in the same helpless state for far more than three seconds.

A hand grasped Algie by the shoulder and shook him hard. When he didn't move, the strange hand switched its grip to his collar and pulled hard.

"Come along, Master Algie," a voice possibly connected to the hand cried out. "This is no place for a child."

Algie moved, but his attention stuck to the wreckage in front of him. The smells of hot metal in oil and the insides of eviscerated people and animals enveloped him. A few more tugs, perhaps twelve more steps, and he was clear of the miasma. Only then did his eyes trace up the arm to the man who had rescued him.

It was Dr. Cookworthy, wearing the dust-colored tunic and trousers favored by British soldiers and a broad-brimmed straw hat. He looked to be on the edge of tears.

"This is a terrible thing and there is no way we can be of help," the doctor said. "I will take you back to Madame Streif's residence."

The steady, disciplined stream of foot traffic had devolved into what looked like a broken ant hill with the distressed insects running every which way. Dr. Cookworthy pushed into the crowd and Algie had no choice but to follow along like a dog on a leash.

The chaos made navigation practically impossible. After a few minutes, they were turned around and on a different edge of the fire in the marketplace. The doctor drew up short as they came up on the edge of a bucket brigade. Men and women of all types were relaying canvas fire buckets full of water from the troughs at the center of the plaza to the pile of burning debris. The wreckage was piled against the lowest floor of a residence hall. Algie saw frightened people hanging from the upper story windows.

The firefighters were having little success. The wind whipped the flames out in random directions and forced them to throw their water from a distance. Nothing reached the core of the fire that burned like a furnace.

"Perhaps we can be of some use after all," Dr. Cookworthy

said. "Come with me."

He released his grip on Algie's collar to fish through his canvas shoulder bag. They pressed forward through the gawking crowd until Algie felt the skin on his face tightening from the heat of the flames.

"I think that's close enough," Algie shouted.

"It's as close as we dare get, I would say."

The doctor held up a red ball about the size of a pomegranate. It looked hard, as if it were made of plaster.

"You're a boy," Cookworthy said. "Are you any good at throwing things?"

Algie thought back to all his games with the *Lǎoshǔ*, pitching and catching a red rubber ball while dangling from the rigging of the airship. He was not anywhere near the best, but he held his own. He had only lost five balls in the last six months.

"I do all right," he said.

"You need to get this right into the center of the fire."

"What is it?"

"It's a frangible fire-suppressant coating over a fused explosive core," Dr. Cookworthy said. "An invention of mine I was going to demonstrate before the Grand Entertainment turned into a wager riot."

Algie scowled. He knew a request for a translation would do him no good.

"And that will do what?"

Dr. Cookworthy grinned.

"If everything goes right, it will blow that fire out like a candle."

Algie took the ball from the doctor and weighed it in his hands. It was heavier than it looked and the heart of the fire was almost ten meters away. It would be no easy throw.

"I'll do the best I can."

"And I shall pray to Allah and the laws of Sir Isaac Newton."

He shouted out in several languages and waved the people away from the edge of the fire. Algie joined in with what languages he knew, though his Ships' Cant might have been more of a "bugger off."

Algie took a few running steps at the fire like a cricket pitch and then slung the ball underhand to fall into the very center. It bounced once off of a twisted metal strut and then fell into the flames. He backed away as quickly as he could, not knowing how large of an explosive he was dealing with. There was an expectant moment of silence, followed by a somewhat concerned moment of silence. Algie only had time enough to wonder if he'd been handed a dud before it went off like a cannon shell.

A thick white cloud of dust rushed out in directions and swallowed up everything for a distance of ten or twenty meters. It got into Algie's eyes and mouth and left a bitter taste that stuck to the roof of his mouth. Once he was able to wipe it from his eyes, he saw that he was covered completely in the white gritty powder. He looked like someone done up as a marble statue for a pantomime.

The esteemed doctor from Africa was also painted completely white. He removed his glasses and blinked at the sputtering remains of the fire.

"I would say that that was a successful test." He wiped his glasses with a pocket handkerchief and placed them back on his nose. "Thank you very much for your assistance."

"You're welcome," Algie muttered as he spit out more of the fire suppressant. "This isn't bad for you, is it?"

"Not in small doses."

Members of the bucket brigade that had been outside the cloud wet down the debris and pulled it away from the building as they could. Those who'd been close to the explosion had their own concerns.

The now-white people all around them were coughing and spitting up the noxious powder. Some splashed their faces from the fire buckets to clear their eyes. No one that had been caught in the cloud looked to be enjoying themselves. As they cleared their eyes of the grit, they cast them about to find the people responsible.

"They don't look too grateful, Dr. Cookworthy."

"They're not looking at the broader ramifications of this new discovery," the doctor replied. "And since the inhabitants of this caravanserai have an unfortunate tendency to riot, I would think it would be best if we left now."

Algie only nodded and started away without waiting for the doctor to catch up. He knew this would be something Dale Daring would do, if he had a brain in his head. The two of them didn't get very far before they found themselves bracketed by armed men in BC&I redcoats. A large number of the caravanserai locals were shouting and pointing at Algie and Cookworthy. It didn't take a Conversor's facility with languages to know they were shouting: "Those two."

A strong hand clamped around Algie's upper arm like a manacle and dragged him in the direction of the Governor's compound.

NINETEEN

7th of September 1889
Turfan Governor's
Mansion

Algie had never been in a
dungeon before and he
wanted to take full advantage
of his time there. It was far
better than dwelling on the
events of earlier. He made a
complete circuit of the mud
brick walls, tapping and listening for secret doors or hidden chambers. The search was
fruitless.

The rough flagstones that made up the floor were both massive and closely joined. Tunneling out that way would be a decades long undertaking like "The Count of Monte Cristo." Algie
found no sign of an *oubliette* or even shackles bolted into the
wall, and he was disappointed.

The only window in the chamber was over two meters above
the floor, just at the top of Algie's reach. If unobstructed, it
might be just large enough to let him slip out. Unfortunately, it
was covered over in an ornamental metal grate.

Still, there might be a way to loosen it if I could just get up close.

"Dr. Cookworthy," he called out over his shoulder, "could
you give me a boost up here?"

"No, I don't think so, young man."

The professor sat on one of the two wooden stools in the
chamber, still absorbed in the task of cleaning his face and his

clothes with a small, dry handkerchief. The results were spotty at best without the benefit of a hand mirror, but he scrubbed away in an attempt to regain his dignity.

Algie returned to the problem of the window. With a running start, he was able to leap up and grab the window ledge with his fingertips. The uneven bricks made it easy to scramble up the wall. Once he was able to rest his elbows on the ledge, Algie got his fingertips through the grate.

There was a tiny amount of play in the way the grate was seated in the wall. With several minutes uninterrupted, he could certainly work it loose. He rattled and forced the metal in its groove in the stone window sill. He paid no attention to the pair of ankles beyond the window grate until the guard attached to them shouted and struck at Algie's fingertips with a heavy stick.

Algie let go and fell backwards onto the flagstones. His buttocks took up most of the impact, so he still had an intact skull as he laid on the floor and looked up at Dr. Cookworthy.

"I warned you about that," the professor said as he scrubbed away on his neck and behind his ears.

"I had to try."

"Why don't you sit down before you fall again and break your neck?"

Algie laid against the cool stone and looked up at the ceiling. He tried to remember any of his penny dreadfuls that gave any helpful tips on escaping from a dungeon.

Keys rattled in the door lock.

Algie was galvanized. He rolled to his feet, scuttled across the floor to the vacant stool, and sat down. He tried his best to look like that had been what he'd been doing all afternoon.

The heavy door creaked open. Two lanky BC&I redcoats shuffled in, looking bored and tired. Probably fellow Britons to Algie's eye. They weren't so slack that they didn't have their revolvers in their fists and truncheons in their off hands.

"All right, you two," one of them grumbled. "The governor wants to see you now."

"Perhaps, you could get us some water and a hand mirror to clean up?" Even under suspicion of murder and mayhem, Dr.

Cookworthy embodied the spirit of courtesy.

"This isn't a cotillion," the other guard grunted. "Up on your feet."

Dr. Cookworthy stood up, pounding the white powder from his clothes as he did. Algie did the same and fell in at his right elbow. The guards motioned them up the dark corridor of whitewashed plaster with the barrels of their pistols.

"Remember this as an important lesson, Algernon, the next time you feel compelled to act as a hero," the professor said. "No good deed goes unpunished."

*

Zhao Guanting and Sun Lei glared poison and bad feeling at each other from opposite sides of the grand fireplace in the Governor's library. Master Zhao, as the regent empress's representative aboard the *Wu Zetian*, took the lead of the small group from the ship. He wore his red and gold court silk robes as if they were a shield of tradition and propriety for himself, Captain Strausser, Liu Jean-Pierre, and Mme. Streif.

Sun Lei, representative of the same regent and tasked with annoying Governor St. George and Boycott just as much, wore a Saville Row pinstripe suit with equal pomp and authority. His sheaves of reports and affidavits did the same to convey his authority as Zhao's signets, baton, and fan. The Governor stood impassive and unreadable behind his colored spectacles. Mr. Boycott fumed to the rear.

Both of the Chinese courtiers turned upon Algie and Dr. Cookworthy as they entered the room with identical expressions of contempt and annoyance. The Governor, the BC&I representative, and even Capt. Strausser displayed similar attitudes. What disturbed Algie was the look on Mme. Streif's face.

She generally terrified those around her, but she acted as a benevolent force of Nature, like a hurricane that might give a day's notice before destroying everything you held dear. Algie saw not a dram of benevolence nor mercy in that room. The last time he had been in an audience like this, he had been shipped off on a sheep ship to Australia.

"Good afternoon, Sirs. Madame," Algie murmured as

politely as he could.

"It has not been good at all," muttered Master Sun. "Did you have a good time?"

"I guess not." Algie did not have Feng Po's mastery of words, nor his support at the moment. Silence seemed to be the best course of action.

The Governor spoke to Dr. Cookworthy next, after referring to his own sheaf of notes.

"Doctor, could you please tell us what exactly happened this afternoon?"

The African took off his dusty spectacles and carefully wiped them with the tail of his dusty tunic before speaking.

"As far as I could tell, an airship crashed in the middle of the marketplace," he said evenly. "Some of the debris scattered to the residence hall where we were... arrested."

Mr. Boycott leaped on that statement:

"Crashed, do you say?"

"Well, it would have been the most regrettable landing imaginable."

"Other witnesses say that it was dropped," Boycott said, "Dropped by a dragon."

"Whether it crashed, or it was dropped and then crashed, there would be identical damage and loss of life."

"And the dragon?" Governor St. George prompted.

"I will admit that there was some flying construct that possessed an elongated flexible body, wings, head, and a tail," Cookworthy stated, "but if I were to go on the record to say that Turfan was attacked by a dragon, I might have my doctorate revoked."

"So, if this was not a dragon," Master Sun said in a voice as smooth as a serpent, "what would you think it was?"

"Since it was able to drop something with the mass of an airship and its power plant on your Central Market, it obviously was not an illusion, a projection, or a manifestation of mass hysteria."

"Well, that is painfully obvious and unhelpful," Mr. Boycott sneered.

"If we are going to unravel this mystery," Master Zhao

cautioned, "we must eliminate all possibilities."

Though it sounded like the royal representative was siding with the doctor, it may have been him only refusing to go along with Sun and his allies.

"Thank you." Dr. Cookworthy nodded to Master Zhao. "Considering all that I know of physical science and technology, I would say it was either a new type of airship or an immense automaton."

That set the cat loose amongst the pigeons in the library. A disciplined interrogation disintegrated into multiple rotating conversations. Algie spoke up, though no one had set to question him yet.

"It sounded like a *karakuri*." Though Algie kept his voice low, his statement cut through the noise. Most of the room's occupants went silent and looked upon Algie not at all kindly.

"What do you mean by that?" Mr. Boycott snapped.

"It flew right over my head," Algie said. "I could hear the metal plates move against each other. The control cables inside, they sound like the strings on a musical instrument."

His next remark he directed to Dr. Cookworthy:

"It sounded just like the caracal. You remember from the other night, sir?"

The doctor took on a distant look as he tried to recall the sounds of a raging dragon.

"You could be right... Though, I wasn't as close to it as you were, Master Piggrem."

"*Karakuri?*" St. George asked. "What is that?"

"An Asian form of automaton," Master Sun said. "A representative of the Kumari Kandam Automata Company, a Mr. Zdan Ag Ahar, was lodged here the last seven days. He was giving demonstrations of his *karakuri* hunting cat on the night of the riot. That gentleman left our caravanserai mere minutes before the attack."

"He did?" Algie was shocked Zdan had moved that quickly.

"Indeed, he did," Master Sun crooned. "But, don't worry, he left a package for you at your residence."

He placed a small parcel wrapped in brown paper and twine on the end table before St. George and Boycott.

Algie took a step forward and reached out for the package without thinking.

"May I?" he said.

"Don't be too quick about that," said Boycott as he snapped the package up. "I think we need to see what he left for you before you have a chance to conceal anything."

"You can't do that!" Algie exclaimed. "That's mine."

The loathsome smirk on Boycott's face declared that he could indeed do that, and he hummed to himself cheerfully as he did it.

A pen knife made quick work of the string and wrapping. After Boycott slipped back the cover of the wooden box, he extracted an intricate brass pendant on a gold chain and a folded slip of paper. He dangled it out of Algie's reach as he unfolded the note and read from it:

"British boy." Boycott sneered at the greeting. "Wear this close to your heart. You may find it of some use in the future. Then, there's his signature and a bunch of heathen scrawls."

Boycott held the paper towards Algie to show a line written in Arabic script, right to left. Algie squinted to make it out.

"I believe it says "May the love of Allah be with you"."

Master Sun's eyes narrowed as he looked down upon Algie.

"Are you a Moslem?" the courtier asked. He made the last word sound like an epithet.

"No," Algie replied, "but Zdan is. I have been taking lessons to learn Uyghur and Arabic since we landed here."

"Which was the same day as the attack by the Uyghur bandits at our west gate," Boycott said. "Isn't that the most amazing coincidence?"

Algie didn't really understand what the BC&I man was saying. The rest of the room's occupants all seemed to have their own opinions. Urgent, whispered conversations turned to arguments, and then reshuffled within seconds. It was like watching the *Lǎoshǔ* playing ball on the roof.

Master Zhao Guanting's voice cut through the babble:

"I believe we drifted completely away from our purpose here. Governor St. George, could you guide us back to something more productive, if such a thing is possible?"

The governor, his expression unreadable behind his spectacles, laid a restraining hand on Boycott's shoulder.

"Give the boy his things," he said.

He shifted his attention to Algie's cellmate.

"Dr. Cookworthy, where were you going when the airship... crashed on the market?"

"I was on my way to luncheon meeting with Mme. Streif and Mr. Liu. We were to discuss one of my inventions for development."

"So, it was simply a coincidence that you and the *Wu Zetian*'s boy-hero happened to be right there?"

"There aren't too many places to be in this caravanserai," Mme. Streif interjected. Algie didn't feel like she was leaping to his defense as much as instinctively attacking the governor's stupidity.

"Doctor?" Mr. St. George acted as if Mme. Streif had not spoken.

"It was three paths that happened to cross all in the same place. A topology puzzle like Euler's s Seven Bridges of Königsberg. I could plot it out for you, if you'd like."

"And where would you plot the two of you setting the second explosive charge?" Boycott asked.

"There was no second explosive!" Dr. Cookworthy exclaimed.

Master Sun raised an eyebrow, but said nothing.

"Well, yes," the doctor conceded. "There were explosives, but they are only used to disperse the fire suppressant powder."

"So you say," said Boycott.

"The residence hall was endangered by burning debris when Algie and I arrived. The fire was extinguished when we were through. You are all very welcome."

"While that fire may have gone out," the governor said, "I received multiple reports of eye irritation, chemical burns, and inhalation injuries around that hall. That is why we are not overly eager to believe that your invention is entirely benign."

"Noone took into account the chemicals and fumes from a burning airship with an unknown cargo?" Dr. Cookworthy's voice held a sharp note of frustration though he was doing his best still to treat his inquisitors with tact and diplomacy.

"No." Governor St George sounded the slightest bit deterred from his plan to have the doctor and Algie executed, but only a little bit.

"I don't trust this African poser any farther than I could throw him," snapped Boycott. "How the Hell could he invent anything?"

Dr. Cookworthy tried to act as if he hadn't heard the remark.

"I believe we have all heard just about enough," Mme. Streif said. She stepped forward, past Master Zhao, to stand practically nose to chest to the governor. "This gentleman—and this boy—stepped forward to save lives and property when no one else could. Now, you bring them up as scapegoats simply because you have no way of arresting the dragon."

She pushed past the governor to reached into Dr. Cookworthy's satchel without so much as a "by your leave" and removed a miniature version of his fire ball.

"As far as inventions go, Mr. Boycott, this is an elegant solution to a far-reaching problem that will save many lives and make him and I quite rich. Do let me know when you make a similar contribution to the welfare of humanity."

Mme. Streif aimed a steady glare at the BC&I representative, who shortly dropped his eyes like a whipped dog.

"And if you have problems believing that a man from Nigeria might be able to outdo the best minds of the British Empire, I could bring in Mister Liu to explain the science of these fire suppression spheres," Mme. Streif said coolly. "His English is quite good and he can speak very slowly if you have problems with the larger words."

Boycott fumed. Governor St George worked his jaws as if he were chewing through a manila rope.

"Is there anything else that needs to be discussed?" She smiled up at the governor, but there was no cheer in her expression. She was only displaying her sharp white teeth.

"There is one thing," the Governor said stiffly. "You and your... ship have been here for nearly three weeks. Your repairs should be complete. You will need to vacate your space in dry-dock for other airships that might need it."

Captain Strausser began some sort of angry response that sounded like only barking, but Mme. Streif cut him off with an upraised hand.

"Of course, we would not want to over-stay our welcome," she purred. "Though too many airships is not likely to be a problem you'll be having for the near future, considering what happened today. If I may take my people with me, we will all be packed and gone by the end of the week."

"I would be most appreciative."

Mme. Streif gestured for the doctor & Algie to collect up their things. She held up Dr. Cookworthy's little extinguishing sphere and moved it left to right and back. Master Sun and Mr. Boycott followed it hungrily with their eyes.

"It is so peculiar how valuable the smallest things can be. If you were to take this little marble to a competent chemist in Vienna or London, the secret of its manufacture could be teased out of it eventually. It might be worth ten thousand pounds sterling to a right-minded capitalist."

She tossed the sphere into the fire and glided swiftly towards the door. The sphere exploded with no more noise than a fire-cracker and snuffed out the burning logs. A minimal amount of grayish powder blew into the room. The rest ascended the chimney with the last of the smoke and heat. Algie once again could taste the bitterness on the back of his tongue as he in-haled.

Master Sun and Mr. Boycott stood gape-jawed as several thousand pounds of business potential went up the flue.

Algie left as quickly as decorum would allow. This time he had no desire to wave.

Mme. Streif waited at the door until all of her people had slipped though.

"It has been a most stimulating conversation," she said to the governor then. "Do have a pleasant evening."

*

Mrs. St George was waiting for them outside the library. Her hair and dress were a mess and her nerves were a frazzle. She scooped up Algie in a desperate embrace as soon as he was in reach.

"Oh, my poor sweet boy," she blubbered. "I was told that you were nearly killed."

The boy felt drowned in a sea of perfumed blonde curls and white lace. He pushed himself far enough away to clear his mouth.

"A lot of other people were hurt very badly," he said, "some of them died. I'm all right though."

She put her hands on his shoulders and held him at length to look him over. Mrs. St. George had a lopsided grin on her face.

"You are so brave. And compassionate, too." The governor's wife looked up at Mme. Streif, who hovered just over Algie's left shoulder. "I hope you appreciate what a special little boy you have here."

"I believe we are finally getting his true measure," Mme. Streif replied.

Though Algie didn't quite understand what she meant, he could hear that it wasn't meant the way it sounded. Mrs. St. George didn't seem to have the ear for it.

She gave him an exuberant kiss on the cheek and stood herself back up.

"You take good care of him," she told Mme. Streif.

"Don't worry, he will be taken care of."

The governor's wife gave her a perky nod and a good bye before flouncing her way into the library.

Algie could feel the temperature of the chamber dropping before he could turn and see the expression on the Silk Empress's face.

"I'm very sorry, Mme. Streif," he said, "for all the trouble."

She sniffed as she looked down on him.

"I'm sure you are."

Algie wished he could shrink down to the size of an ant rather than endure that look. Then he could disappear between the stone slabs of the floor.

"Have you learned anything of economics yet?" she asked.

Algie had never heard the word before, and he knew enough

to not even try to bluff his way through an answer. He mutely shook his head.

"It's the science of money," she said. "Of business and trade. Have you ever heard the term 'opportunity cost'?"

"No, ma'am."

"It is the price of not being available for a business opportunity. I was expecting to spend two more weeks at this caravanserai. Do you have any idea what kind of money I could have made in that time?"

Algie shook his head again.

"I would prefer answers that do not make you seem to be bereft of speech and reason."

"No, ma'am."

"Of course, you don't, because you don't understand economics," she said. "You will start new lessons tomorrow afternoon. Economics and cartography. Keijín is very good at both."

She gazed at him with a look that made him feel like a butterfly pinned to a card.

"Do you have any objections?" she asked.

"No, ma'am."

"Do not even begin to think you are out of trouble, young master Piggrem." Mme. Streif turned her back on him and was leaving already. "You and I will have to discuss whether you have a future aboard the *Wu Zetian* before we leave Turfan."

TWENTY

16th of February 1889
Capetown

Algie sprinted away from the docks like a madman. He dodged around fishmongers and stevedores, nearly toppling their crates as they avoided him. The men all looked more terrifying than First Mate Doyle: grim, beefy men with muscular arms and thick necks. More than one shouted at him as he passed, or even brandished

the truly fearsome cargo hooks hung on their belts. They were Africans and Chinese and unidentifiable brown-skinned men, all seeming perfectly at home in this alien city.

Algie was a pale, frail nuisance that stuck out like a white goose in a nunnery.

He cut through the warehouse where dour men in leather aprons hacked away at dead fish with razor sharp cleavers. They paid Algie no mind, and he sprinted past before they could. Several times, he barely avoiding an embarrassing fall in the blood and slime.

The far side of the building opened onto a cramped street filled with traffic of all kinds. He stopped in the broad doorway for a moment. The cheek to jowl parade of strange and un-friendly faces daunted him almost as much as the four-horse dray carts that thundered down the brick alley which passed mere feet away from the pedestrians. The sounds and smells settled over him like a heavy wet blanket.

A heavy steam tractor and trailer came from the other direction. The smoke and noise disturbed the horses, but the teamster kept them in check.

Algie, asking himself what Dale Daring would do, screwed up his courage and pushed his way into the flow of foot traffic. He first blundered in front of a peddler. The old man held a rack of his wares in his left hand, carved wooden spoons and other minor utilities. His right arm clung to a rag-wrapped crutch. Algie had jostled that and nearly toppled the peddler. The old man spat out more of that drunken-uncle language. Algie thought it was swearing. He could be sure it wasn't wishing him a Happy Christmas. The peddler hopped away with his naked stump dangling out of his cut-off pants leg. The gnarled flesh looked like a piece of old dead wood.

Algie set one foot in front of another, realizing that another stop could cause another frightful collision. Two men passed to his right: swarthy Indians with sleepy eyes, red turbans, and fierce bushy beards. They carried leather cases that could have hidden anything. He suspected poisoned daggers, cursed rubies, and sleeping cobras to guard them.

A boy shouted at him from behind. Algie turned and saw a ragged child who guided a knife-sharpener's cart through the crowd. The older man behind it pushed the heavy grindstone with the patience of an ox. His eyes were covered with dirty bandages. Algie cut quickly to his left, towards the center of the crowd, goaded by his sudden cringing fear. He jostled a young woman in ragged dress there. Unknown fruit fell from the basket she carried. She dropped to the bricks in a swirl of skirts to retrieve them and she hissed at Algie when he tried to help. Scars on either side of her mouth made it look that her head had nearly been cut in half long ago. Only a stump of a tongue showed when she hissed at him again.

Algie broke and ran.

He tried to slip between the peddlers and beggars, but he wasn't too worried at who he might bump as long as it got him *away*. He left a wake of chaos as he dashed the last twenty or thirty yards.

Algie broke clear and then hid himself behind an unattended horse cart. He took several seconds to calm down and grasp the lay of this new landscape.

The alley opened out onto an arcade, a space between two buildings filled with tents and stalls. Two floors lined with a series of arches fronted either building and those cool shadowed places were filled with even more people than the market. It looked to be permanent stores and restaurants behind those arches, places that charged far more and attracted customers without holes in their shoes and patches on their clothing.

A commotion in one of those archways attracted Algie's attention. Two men that looked like police dragged a young girl out of a store. Brightly colored scarves hung out of her blouse. She screamed the top of her head off as the officers plucked them away and returned them to the florid round-faced man that came scolding behind them.

Algie still couldn't understand a word of what they said, but he'd seen an arrest like this more than once on the streets of Portsmouth. As the men secured the young thief in the caged rear of their horse cart, he decided it would be best if he searched for his fellow fugitives somewhere else.

*

Algie didn't find any of his friends that morning. He didn't find them late into the afternoon. By then, he was sure that it would be more important to locate food, shelter, and warmth.

It was the end of summer in Capetown, but the day had been overshadowed with grey clouds and a steady cold drizzle in the late afternoon. Algie returned to the dark corners of the waterfront warehouses then. He didn't want to venture onto the streets and risk capture and pneumonia.

His past willingness to climb most anything from trees to curtains served him in good stead. A warehouse full of grain and dry goods provided several empty sacks which he took with him into the rafters. They made a nest that was relatively warm and out of sight. Curling up in it gave an opportunity to regroup his resources and contemplate his myriad errors.

His primary mistake was that he had no plan for how they would live after they got to shore. In his penny dreadfuls, there were always kind-hearted strangers that would help out the hero no matter how dire their situations. As he nursed his wounds, he recounted in his head the number of times a helpful native had arrived just in time to save Dale Daring's life. In real life, it would have required a network broader than the British China & India Company looking out for wayward boy adventurers.

To go out into a foreign city with no more than a pocket knife and a strong pair of legs was so stupid as to be suicidal. To lead all the others on that kind of a wish and a prayer was criminal. He only hoped that he could find his friends and get them someplace safe and warm. As he drifted off to sleep, he promised himself that he would one day have his own home, along with friends that would look out for each other and care for each other, no matter what befell them.

*

One thing Algie quickly discovered was that things broke pretty much the same way in Capetown as they did in Portsmouth, and he had a knack for fixing them. Starting off with Chauncey's penknife, he could tighten screws and trim away wood. He got a pair of pliers and a Phillips screwdriver in exchange for adjusting the blind knife sharpener's grindstone and cart. Fixing the spirit burner on the nut roaster's cart earned him an adjustable wrench and satchel for his tools. In a matter of a few days, he had become the acknowledged handyman of the lowest marketplace, trading his skills for tools, supplies and food. Though he'd learned only a few words of the local tongue, mechanics was a language all its own.

He had been wary the first few days after his escape, always keeping an eye out for Dolan and his crew of Irish child-snatchers, and the other eye out for his friends. There had been no sign of either for three days. In hiding from their keepers, the children had done an excellent job of avoiding Algie, too.

Keogh made his appearance first. Algie found him eating

from a trash can behind the fish-mongers. The younger boy was still black and grimy looking. The smell might have been his layer of camouflage paint, or it could have been the dead fish. Algie took him into his warehouse hideaway anyway.

The space he had made with discarded signs and broken crates in the rafters proved to be a bit close with the atmosphere that clung to Keogh. As the younger boy fell to gnawing at the store of hard tack and smoked cod, Algie quietly knocked out one of those walls to extend his shelter to the adjacent truss.

It took him a few days to find seven more of the children. Hannah, with the young Blake and Christine in tow, had become their own nomadic family when they stumbled across Algie. Deirdre, as the last of the child refugees, seemed to have done the best for herself when found. She wore a nice blue calico dress and woman's makeup. She wouldn't say what she had been doing in Capetown.

✳

All of the *Roscommon Venture* refugees bunked down in a single nest of nets and blankets in the rafters of the deserted warehouse. They slept in their clothes, partially for warmth, and partially in preparation to run if Dolan and his crew appeared.

On the morning of the seventh day, Algie woke to the sound of swearing. Keogh was just popping his head into their sanctuary like some foul-mouthed ground squirrel.

"Bloody Hell, you'd think those knuckle-dragging bastards would have someplace better to be by now."

Algie rolled out from under his home-made quilt of feed sacks and discarded trousers.

"Who?" he muttered. "What?"

"Those damned Irish sheep-defilers from the ship what brought us here," Keogh responded. His eyes were wide with panic. "I think they saw me, too."

That woke Algie up in an instant.

"Where did you see them?"

"Along the bloody arcade, where everybody in this town goes!" Keogh may have had something else important to say, but he disappeared down the ladder with a shriek of surprise.

Shouts and oaths and ejaculations of pain came up through the opening in the floor, but Algie could see nothing of the struggles below. He had a sudden damning realization that in his hurry to expand his little rafter nest to accommodate nine children, Algie had boarded up all his secondary exits. Their only way out of the warehouse would be through, or accompanied by, a contingent of angry Irish sailors.

Algie crawled sideways and backwards to where Deirdre and the others had been sleeping. They were bunched up like frightened livestock against the furthest truss. The group was evenly split between wild-eyed paralyzing panic, and frantic preparation to cut and run. Hannah was already searching for objects with sufficient heft to throw at a sailor's head.

Dolan himself, the original devil of the *Roscommon* crew, popped his head through the doorway with an infernal grin.

"So, all my little charges herded themselves up for us to catch," he called out. "Thank you oh so much for saving us the effort."

A chipped cereal bowl lofted across the tiny space to catch him on the forehead. It shattered into a hundred sharp fragments, but did little more than draw a bit of blood above his left eye. Dolan's hand shot up to the wound and then came down in front of his face to reveal the blood on his fingertips. Devilish glee turned to blazing fury in a moment.

"You little monsters! I would drown you myself if you weren't already bought and paid for!"

A spoon, a leather-bound book, an empty Bovril tin flew at his reddening face. They bounced off his upraised arm without further damage.

Dolan climbed up into the children's nest with a snarl and an oath in some unknown language. He hunkered down low to fill the space and held up his one arm to fend off whatever objects the children could pitch at him. His other arm lashed around like a serpent. He caught Blake, one of the smallest boys, by the wrist and twisted until the child stopped struggling.

"I just have to bring you in alive," Dolan shouted. "A few bumps and bruises that'll heal before we arrive in Australia won't drop your value."

The first mate swung the boy into the open air of the ladder way. A pair of dark greasy hands snatched him out of sight. Another crewman heaved his mass up into the chamber like a walrus pulling itself up onto the shore. He snatched at Algie's ankles, without luck. The other children screeched and flailed around him. Algie felt to be in the midst of a hurricane.

He was suddenly pulled back and up by his shirt collar. Even as he fought to turn around inside his own clothes, Algie felt himself being walked on the tips of his toes towards the gaping hole in the floor. Looking down, he saw hands, ropes and nets waiting for him.

"So, we've got the clever one here," Dolan boomed out from above. "We'll make sure you're trussed up extra tight for the trip to the ship, just like a Christmas goose."

Algie struggled against Dolan while walking up the face of the crewman below him. Just as he got both feet on top of the man's head, the first mate yanked him away. Algie had hoped he could run up the walls and over the top of his opponent as Dale Daring would often do in his stories. A few of the other children took the brunt of Algie's flailing feet.

Dolan switched off his grip to put his other hand all the way around Algie's throat. This put them face to face, and the boy kicked away at any soft spot he could find. The larger man squeezed shut his airways in return. He wrapped both hands around Algie's throat for the task.

"I've been thinking that maybe we don't actually have to bring you back alive, you little whelp."

Algie's sight was dimming quickly. The bedlam around him was nowhere near as loud until a ball of screaming fury hit Dolan high in the chest and began to climb him like a garden trellis.

"You let go of him, you sodding ape!"

From the skirts and shoes, Algie assumed it was one of the older girls, but her face was hidden in a cloud of light brown hair. Her hands were claws that raked at Dolan's face. Her feet kicked hard between his legs. The jolts ran through his body, bouncing Algie up and down with each blow.

Algie took the opportunity to twist towards the sailor so he might kick and punch a bit too.

Dolan spun and lunged to dislodge them. This threw Algie shoulders first against an angled truss. Pain flared through his back and red lights flashed before his eyes, but the boy held on. Dolan spun again and hit one of the recently added walls.

There was a cracking sound like thunder and then a sickening feeling as the bottom came up on his stomach. As the three of them fell into open space outside the nest, Algie silently cursed himself for not building better bracing into the new walls.

*

Algie awoke in a pile of debris on the warehouse floor. Dolan laid motionless underneath him. Deirdre laid with her back pressed to cold stone floor beneath the both of them. Neither girl nor sailor moved. Deirdre's eyes were open and stared upwards through the darkness.

Algie couldn't tell if they were dead or not. He didn't have time to investigate.

"There's the stupid bastard, over there," one of the other sailors shouted.

He threw off the wood and debris piled on his shoulders and put his feet underneath himself. Dolan made a plaintive noise as he stood on the man's kidneys, but there was no sign of life besides that. He took no time to check either of the prone bodies beneath him since a pair of the crewmen were already skinning it his way.

With no more than the clothes on his back, Chauncey's penknife in his pocket, and his shoes on his feet, Algie once again fled into the streets of Capetown.

*

The sky over Capetown looked to be a single sheet of steel in the hours before dawn and it felt like it was about to drop on Algie's head. The spaces of the open air market and the arcade were still empty with no crowds to provide him cover or the remotest chance of aid.

Algie kept running.

Closer to the wharves, some merchants staked out corners with food or drinks for the odd sailor or stevedore. He slowed to a winded walk as he saw Meg and a small crowd around her food cart. She called her fare "marsh birds", though he always suspected that they were actually roasted mice on a stick.

Her current lot of customers, all boys his age or a bit older it seemed, didn't seemed to care. They beamed as they gnawed at the little bits of skin and meat. They kept up a loud conversation in some foreign tongue, waving, gesturing, and tossing a red rubber ball from one to the other.

Algie skirted the group to put his back to the building and use them as a screen from the sight of the *Roscommon* sailors.

The red ball came flying at his face, but he caught it easily enough. As keyed up as he was right now, he wasn't going to get ambushed by a bit of rubber. The other boys cheered at his catch and begged in their babbling way for him to throw it back. He bobbled with it a bit, bouncing it from his bicep to his hand and back, before returning it.

The boys spread out, running circles around each other and falling into a complex game with no discernible rules. Algie watched their play as he tried to cast an eye in all directions for his pursuers.

The boys ran and whooped like wild animals. They drew him into this game with easy throws of the ball and quick slaps as tags to his shoulders and legs. Algie had to move within the circles they created to avoid being beaten or knocked down. The strange boys tightened their group around him and then spread out until they filled the entire courtyard. He ran along to keep up.

He saw the sailors come around the bend and Algie tried to break free of the formless mob. The boys were having none of it.

The first of the *Roscommon* crewmen came up on some of the boys from behind. The greasy bearded man snatched the brown boy out of the air the way a gull would catch a crust of bread. He held the urchin up by his upper arms pulled almost behind him. All the boy could do was kick and scream.

"I don't think this is one of ours," the sailor shouted out to his comrades.

"Doesn't matter," one of the others replied. "He'll replace the ones we lost."

The game stopped dead and the wild boys backed away from the child catchers. As the captive screamed in their shared language, they shouted back, either words of encouragement or curses at the sailors. Algie put himself into the middle of the crowd with hopes to disappear.

About that time, the warehouse door behind them opened. An odd man of middling height came out rolling a barrel along its bottom edge. He wore a low coachman's hat, along with striped canvas pants and hobnail boots. He topped that with a garish waistcoat of bright blue and gold decorated with red knotted cords, something that looked to have been salvaged from a dead Chinese courtier.

He settled the barrel on its base and pulled some sort of stick or baton from his belt. The top of the stick looked to be an ivory dragon. He brandished it at the *Roscommon Venture* crew and shouted something that sounded like the language of the Chinese that frequented the Capetown market.

The sailors gawped at him and then hurled insults, most in English, though hard to tell with their hoarse Irish accents.

The strange man laughed.

"So, you be English. I'll talk slow so's you can comprehend me: Put my boys down so you won't be harmed yourselves."

The sailors laughed amongst themselves. One of them yelled back:

"Sod you, we're Irish!"

"So sorry for the mistake." The stranger then launched into a string of foreign invective that must have singed the very air from the reaction of the sailors. Their faces burned red and what teeth they had were bared in snarls.

The boy was put down and sheath knives came out. A good half dozen of them to one wandering peacock with a stick seemed like a lethally mismatched fight.

He jabbered to the boys in what sounded like their own language as they gathered around him. He pointed his baton at the first of the sailors and gave a one word command:

"*Treppar!*"

It either translated out as "attack" or "swarm that lackwit like a hive of angry bees," because that is what happened. In the seconds it took for them to regroup and turn on the sailors, pipes, bricks, cobblestones, and shards of glass appeared in the boys' hands. All dozen or so of them made a mad rush for their target. He was knocked down and beaten bloody before he even had a chance to swing his knife.

The peacock engaged the nearest sailor. With a sudden sweep, he struck the knife out of the sailor's hand with his baton. After that, he made a quick inventory of all the bones in Irishman's face, skull, and arms before allowing him to drop to the ground. Another sailor, who made as if to stab the stranger in the kidneys, suffered a similar thrashing.

Three minutes later, there were only three sailors still on their feet, and they were taking to their heels. The boys were going through the pockets of the fallen for apples, bits of string, and copper coins. Several sheath knives became prized trophies.

The strange man in the gaudy waistcoat came up to Algie and questioned him in the native tongue of Capetown. The boy shrugged and replied:

"I'm sorry. I don't understand."

The stranger burst out laughing at the sound of Algie's voice. He tousled his hair and offered one of the pilfered apples thrown over by one of the wild boys.

"So, *you* are English. Maybe we should wake up these *wáng bā dàn* and give you back to them."

Algie's expression must have been amusing, because the stranger chuckled almost kindly.

"Were these men taking you away from your parents?"

"I have no parents anymore. Just the Friends of Children Home in Portsmouth, and they sold me to Australia."

"Don't worry," the man in the gaudy waistcoat said, "if you have no home, there's a place for you on the *Wu Zetian.*"

TWENTY-ONE

8th of September 1889
Turfan Caravanserai

"That will be all for your lessons today, Mr. Piggrem," Mssr. Patrouille said coolly in French. "I shall see you at the same time tomorrow for further lessons."

Just like Jakinda and the other Conversors an hour before, the writer had been polite and attentive, but not friendly. As a matter of fact, the writer had acted as if he didn't know Algie at all. Lounging on the red velvet settee while wearing a purple suit with a gold waistcoat, the *Wu Zetian*'s scholar and gentleman acted bored and pained listening to Algie's reading.

He would interrupt to correct pronunciation or diction, but with none of the sly play that marked their lessons in the past. In their Conversation period, he eviscerated the boy's conjugation of verbs and articles. The criticism lacked any commitment, as if he didn't give a fig if Algie learned or not. Just as with the Conversors, the total effect was a single word:

Disappointment.

Not being able to help himself, Algie had mumbled something about meeting Timothy Freemarch before it was too late.

"Freemarch?" Contempt dripped from the Frenchman's words. "For a boy once thought so promising, you are a bit thick, aren't you? I have been that damnable Timothy Freemarch all along and you have never caught on to the scent. Those insipid Dale Daring books have allowed me to accrue a small fortune from children with no wit or discernment."

He cocked his head sideways.

"So. Are you happy now?"

Algie was not. He collected his books and left.

*

First Mate McLaren was still in his hammock when Algie returned to their room. Though the gentleman did enjoy his kip time, it was highly irregular for him to be asleep just before lunch. Considering the call for all hands available to make the *Wu Zetian* airworthy in less than a fortnight, it was doubly concerning.

As he was putting his books back on top of his desk, Algie heard, no more likely felt, something rushing towards his head. He leaned away from it and let the object fly past. The red rubber ball hit the wall and bounced backwards across the desk. It was an easy catch for his left hand.

"So, you've been waiting for me?"

"Empress's orders," the first mate replied in Scots-tinted French.

Algie pitched the ball back. It struck the far wall, bounced across the corner, and came up upon Feng Po from behind to catch him in the head. His father's early lessons on billiards had stuck and, in the years since, Algie was able to apply them in three dimensions.

"Sorry," said Algie, "lucky shot."

"You have a certain genius for mayhem," the mate replied. "That is the reason you're not allowed loose in the caravanserai without proper armed supervision."

Feng Po rolled easily out of his hammock and pulled his wood & ivory baton from his belt in what looked to be one simple, circular motion. He came up behind Algie and gave him a sharp swat to the buttocks.

"Come along, now. We don't want you to be late for lessons."

*

The market in the Grand Plaza was all but shut up. The

steady stream of merchants and travelers that had previously flowed like a river from all points of the world, in every color, race, and fabric, now barely trickled.

The Uyghur rebels had attacked again the day before, and their encounter with the BC&I guards was more bloody and general. Three dozen had been injured or killed. The rebels left no clues as to their casualties. Short on the heels of the dragon attack, the populace was properly terrorized.

The people of the caravanserai mostly looked sullen and anxious. Many kept their eyes on the ground ahead of them as they trudged along, but flicked their eyes to the sky with the slightest shadow thrown by a passing cloud.

Feng Po and Algie fell in with the pedestrians and teamsters as they made their way to the Governor's mansion. The first mate assured Algie they would be able to cut across without using the elevated bridges.

The task suddenly became far too easy. The buzz of propellers and engines came from the southeast. A skein of aircraft approached in the distance. Sunlight flashed off their silver hulls like fire.

The travelers of the Low Silk Road scattered for cover. Some pressed against the clay brick buildings, cowering beneath the awnings. Many others piled up in the protective arches of the caravanserai's gateways. Oxen, horses, and automata jostled for positions of safety there. The same struggle, punctuated with cries of fear and anger, was fought on the covered arcades and porticoes.

One heavy draft horse broke through the wooden balustrades of a raised porch and fell sideways the meter or two to the ground. It rolled uninjured to its feet as it shook itself and shed its heavy packs. A steady stream of people and livestock were pressed out of the gap and then scuttled for cover.

"A damned skittish lot," Feng Po said to Algie. "You'd think they never saw an airship before."

"May I borrow your altitude mask?" Algie asked.

Feng Po slid it off the hook on his belt and handed it to the boy.

"Can't hurt to take a quick look."

Seven silver ships flew in close formation, their pennants and battle flags billowed behind them. Algie noticed the Union Jack amongst those. Each fish-like airframe looked to be perfectly symmetrical front to back and top to bottom, except for a railed walkway that ran around the center and the merest extension of fins and engines to the rear.

"Those are new," Algie murmured. He was suitably awed at the spectacle. He handed the mask back to Feng Po.

After a few moments of dithering with the focus wheels and close observation, the first mate stowed the mask and whistled softly.

"Those are the new *Pericles* class light cruisers," Feng Po said. "You British love your classical cultures... as long as you don't have to deal with the people who own them."

Algie started to protest, but stopped at his mentor's crooked smile.

"Armed to the teeth, they are," Feng Po said. "Eight one-pound guns evenly spread about the gunners' gallery, plus a Puckle Heavy Repeating Rifle at the tip. HRM Anglesea Laboratories' aluminum armor to cover them tight as a turtle and three Johnson rotary steam engines to push it all. Quite a parcel of the most modern technology available."

"You're not impressed?"

"It makes it look like they're trying too hard," Feng Po sneered. "Besides, I've seen one of those armored ships taken down by five Chinese *Qī Fēngzhēng*."

The flight of airships slowed and spread out into an arrowhead formation as they neared the caravanserai. The configuration was perfect for the showing of the colors... or a saturation bombing run. The locals and the traveling merchants acted as if it were the latter.

Men and women screamed as animals brayed in panic. They all tried to squeeze under the limited shelter provided by the mud brick buildings or cloth awnings. It did not go well.

"There is a preview of the Afterlife for you." Feng Po flicked his chin towards the pandemonium. "*Maharauravu*, the Hell of Great Screaming While Being Eaten by Animals."

Algie looked up as the flight made its circuit of the ancient city walls. The airships were no longer mirror-bright flares in the distance but impossibly solid metal platforms moving like sharks on the hunt. Their engines buzzed like a cloud of angry hornets. Even Algie was feeling an innate desire to run from these monsters.

When they began opening their bomb bay doors with loud mechanical clicks and grindings, Algie's legs started a retreat without his consent. Feng Po caught him by the upper arm before he made two paces.

"Don't be afraid, *chong wu*," he said. "These are the Governor's monsters. He won't be hurting anyone here with them."

The First Mate pointed out the guards on crest of the wall. The armed men in BC&I redcoats were calmly taking in the spectacle. Some even looked bored. The Governor and Mrs. St. George were ensconced on the highest tower. When she saw Algie and Feng Po in the open, she waved and pointed them out to her husband. Algie waved and Feng Po fired off a crisp salute, but the Governor went back to his inspection of the incoming aircraft without any sign of recognition.

"Come along, Pig. You have lessons to learn." First Mate McLaren looked around at the chaos inspired by the British aircraft's arrival. "That is, if your teachers all haven't run mad."

They slipped through the panicked crowds without incident, looking to their feet as the others pointed to the skies and screamed. Still, it took very little extra time for them to arrive at the Residence Hall's unburned rear door. Algie's Uyghur studies with Meryem were to be held in the gardens there. Ayotunde would be doing Mme. Streif's business elsewhere.

Meryem stood silently next to the stone table and chairs. She folded her hands in front of her and kept her eyes on the fine gravel of the path. Her forehead was still bandaged where she had been struck by burning debris.

"My instructions were precise," she said in English.

"As were mine, ma'am." Feng Po handed Algie off as if the boy were a Mermaid's Purse himself. "One of Mme. Streif's women will be here to acquire him in about an hour."

He made his goodbyes and disappeared as if under fire.

She gestured for Algie to be seated, and then she sat opposite him. The lessons started immediately.

Today she paid particular attention to etiquette, particularly amongst royalty and councils of war. She drilled him mercilessly until a woman in a tan walking dress appeared at the garden gate. The dark bars tattooed on her chin marked her as Keijín: Tlingit Indian, Conversor, cartographer, economist, and alleged scalper of young boys.

Meryem gathered her books and murmured her farewell. Only after she had passed the Conversor at the gate did Algie notice that a plate full of tamarind cookies had been left behind. He did his best to slip one from the plate and into his mouth before his next teacher could spoil his fun.

Keijín settled into the chair opposite and began her tuition without social small talk.

"What do you know of Power, Privilege, and Prestige?"

"I dunno," Algie replied. "They sound like good things to have."

"Exactly. They are the working fluids of a working society. Power is the ability to do things, a combination of Wealth and Personal or Political Capital. The last team, that would be your friends and favors owed you, alliances, and support."

"I think I see," said Algie, although he really didn't.

"Mme. Elizabeth Streif, upon careful examination," Keijín recited, "would be found to be a powerful woman."

"Now, I know I see."

"Privilege is a kind of power assigned to a person solely for the accidents of their birth: race, color, creed, or class. This is highly contextual, depending on the society within which you're engaged and your own traits."

"So..." Algie fumbled. "Mrs. St. George would have privilege in any drawing room in Europe, but would be considered an imbecile in one of Mme. Streif's salons?"

Keijín let out a whoop of laughter, but quickly covered her mouth with one gloved hand. Her eyes still glistened as she resettled her self-control around her shoulders.

"You have a quick and discerning eye," she said. "I can see why Mme. Streif had such interest in you."

Algie couldn't help but notice in French the past tense of

their mistress' interest. This set off a gnawing anxiety and a heartfelt need to please.

"The last is Prestige. This springs from things a person *does*: education, marriage, achievements in sports, science, or letters."

"Blowing up a airship full of *picaroons* and saving the lives of everyone on our ship?" Algie smiled as he said that, but he was beginning to think this was something he shouldn't be bragging about anymore.

The Conversor half-smiled and looked at him directly with her liquid-brown eyes and long lashes. She closed her eyes and nodded.

"Yes, that would be a source of Prestige." Keijín took a deep breath. "The problem with Prestige is that it can go stale so quickly."

"Stale?" That sounded to Algie more like bread or crackers.

"People will eventually forget acts of daring and other accomplishments. Later acts of failure or infamy might even cancel out the prestige value of earlier actions. Do you understand?"

Algie was beginning to understand all too well.

*

Keijín wrapped up her tutorial on production economics with Algie's eleven tamarind cookies.

"The owner of the bakery, he would get forty percent of the gross cost of the product."

She swept four cookies to the right side of the tray with tip of her closed fan.

"The distributors and retailers receive approximately fifty-five percent for their efforts."

Six more cookies joined the first group.

"Which leaves only about five percent to go to the silk laborers who actually bake the cookies." She slid the tip of her fan under the last cookie and then flipped it through the air for Algie to catch. "Enjoy your cookies, *chong wu* Pig."

With a too-wide grin, the Conversor packed up her books and the remaining cookies before guiding Algie back to Mme.

Streif's villa.

Algie was not enjoying this economics thing in the least.

TWENTY-TWO

9th of September 1889
Turfan Caravanserai

Algie imagined a plethora of horrifying fates when he was summoned to Mme. Streif's sitting room before supper. He walked iron erect and stately slow to her quarters. He didn't want to give her any more reasons to be irritated.

The *Lǎoshǔ* had no care for that. In the latest iteration of their ball game, Algie had somehow been declared the goal. The red rubber ball was lobbed at him twice as he crossed the central courtyard and arcades. He caught it both times before it struck him in the head.

His friends cheered with the catches, and with his return throws to Peng and Mateo. He guessed the cheers would have been even louder if the ball had hit him.

Another volley came through the open window as he ascended the stairs to the second floor. The sheer drapes which fluttered in the light breeze obscured its path, but still Algie caught it.

"*Treppar*," he shouted as he lobbed it out of the next window up. That was the Ships' Cant word that meant "attack," "bugger off," or "burn it to the ground," depending on the context.

A secondary rule must have been to keep the ball in the air at all times. Much shouting and splashing from the central fountain could be heard as the *Lǎoshǔ* went in pursuit.

*

There were no exterior windows to the hall just outside Mme. Streif's chambers. This gave Algie a feeling of peace as he faced down his moment of existential dread. He stood with both hands on the double doors' handles for a good twenty-five Picadillies before he worked up the courage to tap on the door,

"Come in," Mme. Streif called out gruffly in English. Her tone and choice of language did nothing to calm his overactive imagination.

Algie opened the doors and slipped through.

Mme. Streif and Mrs. St. George waited for him on the other side, a tray of tea and biscuits between them. The Governor's wife beamed at him. The Silk Empress just looked at him as if she were trying to discern what was soiling her fine Oriental rug.

"Good afternoon, ladies," he said.

"Please close the doors behind you, Master Piggrem," Mme. Streif replied.

He did so, even though he knew that was cutting off his best avenue of escape.

"Sit down." Mme. Streif pointed to the settee, which was more than an arm's length away from the tea cart.

He complied immediately, hands in his lap, spine straight.

"Do you understand why we called you here today?" Mme. Streif's voice was cool and measured.

"I would assume that it was to discuss my future, as I was told, ma'am."

"He is such a little gentleman," Mrs. St. George gushed.

"He is very much like men twice his age," the *Wu Zetian's* mistress stated. "That is what brings us to this situation."

"I would say that he is quite clever and resourceful," the Governor's wife replied. "That would be exactly the kind of candidate I would choose if I had an airship to crew."

"I'm sure." Mme. Streif took a leisurely sip from her teacup.

She turned her not entirely kind eye upon Algie. Her strained smile turned his insides to jelly.

"Perhaps, Mrs. St. George, you could share with young

Master Piggrem what you said to me just a while ago?"

"I feel no shame at all for repeating in that your presence. You are clever, and compassionate, and quite physically skilled. I have seen you playing ball on the rooftops with Mme. Streif's *other* children."

The tone to her voice as she said "other" conveyed a wealth of distaste and judgement that curdled the contents of Algie's stomach. Mme. Streif's expression remained serene.

"I believe that the life of a rigger aboard a merchant airship is a total waste for a young man with such potential."

"Well, thank you, ma'am."

Algie caught a flash of movement through the white sheer curtains out of the floor to ceiling windows behind Mrs. St George as the *Lǎoshǔ* positioned themselves for another Algie goal in their ball game. He wondered how he might be able to move out of their line of sight.

"My husband, the Governor, went to Tonbridge School, one of the finest private schools in the Empire. We would like to take you under our wing and see if we can get you in there too."

"Under your wing?" Algie repeated quietly.

"What Mrs. St. George is saying so imprecisely," Mme. Streif said, "is that they would like to adopt you."

"I would be your new mother," the pale, fluffy woman cooed.

Only his hours of training and practice with Nilenha at whist, faro, and protocol kept him from pulling a face of surprise and horror. Mrs. St. George was nice, courteous, even pleasant, but she was nowhere near what he remembered or required for a mother.

"The Governor, then, he would be my new father?"

Mrs. St. George bobbled her head with a curious smile:

"There's no avoiding that, my dear."

Algie was truly distressed, then. Whenever he thought of Governor St. George, he remembered the brazen automaton head that always seemed more lifelike than the flesh-and-blood personage.

"Well, thank you for the offer, ma'am," he said, "but I think I am quite content with my place aboard the *Wu Zetian* for the time being."

A muted *thwap* sound came from the casings between the two of the tall windows. The half-open windows rattled on their hinges. To Algie, it sounded like the rubber ball striking the outside wood frames at speed.

Again, his training kept him from startling, but Mrs. St. George nearly twisted her head off looking behind her. Mme. Streif held her composure.

"As we have said before," Mme. Streif murmured over the brim of her teacup, "your place on my airship is not guaranteed."

Algie's brain simply stopped.

"You don't want to spend your life on that horrid airship, anyway." The Governor's wife leaned across the arm of her settee to whisper to her host. "No offense intended."

"I'll consider the source."

Mrs. St. George turned back to Algie:

"You deserve a nice home, a good school, nice clothes, shoes even. You're a charming young man, not some ragged ship urchin that'll only grow up to be intemperate, illiterate cloudchaser."

Algie flicked his eyes towards Mme. Streif in what he hoped would be subtle. She caught him and almost smiled in response.

"So, you want to take me back to England?" Algie asked Mrs. St. George.

"Oh no," she replied. "Tristan is posted here to Turfan for at least the next five years. Tonbridge is a boarding school, but you could come back to visit with us here between terms, if you'd like."

"Oh, I see..." While the prospect was better than Australia, it wouldn't be anything like having a real mother. Even though it would be a guarantee of room, board, and warm clothing, Mrs. St. George's proposition was far less attractive than a berth on the *Wu Zetian*, gunshots and death by *picaroon* notwithstanding.

"I must say this, young man, before you make any decisions about your future," Mme. Streif declared, "that I see several flaws in your character that make it questionable that you will find yourself aboard my airship all the way to Vienna."

"Yes, ma'am." Algie clasped his hands and straightened his spine even as he saw the shadows of the *Lǎoshǔ* flitting past the windows.

"You are over-energetic, over-imaginative, and under-disciplined. If there is any form of trouble within a thousand meters of you, you have an unerring ability to triangulate its position and make it a hundred times worse."

"That is being awfully harsh," the governor's wife interjected.

The Silk Empress ignored her.

"The betting riot at the Grand Entertainment. The brigand raid at the caravanserai gate. That explosive ordinance at the market. Even our encounter with air pirates on the way here."

"None of that was my fault!"

Mme. Streif narrowed her eyes.

"I wouldn't be so sure. Sailors told stories of men that were refined bad luck, who could sink a ship just with their virulent presence. Men like that would find themselves thrown overboard and fed to very large fishes."

Mrs. St. George gasped at the implied threat.

"I would not let Captain Strausser be so cruel," Mme. Streif continued, "but I will not have my business interests be jeopardized by sentiment over an undergrown boy with no understanding of the harsh realities of this world. I have changed the course of history, young man. My money and influence guide the tides of trade and circumstance.

"One more incident, one more glorious disaster where I find you standing over the smoking remains of my plans, and I will put you off my ship so fast, parts of your shadow will be stuck to the bamboo decking."

Both Mrs. St. George and Algie were gobsmacked. Algie was smart enough to not show it.

"Yes, ma'am, I understand," he replied in as even a tone as he could muster.

"So, if you'd prefer to fly under my silks," she continued, her voice both serene and venomous, "you had best think carefully with every step you take. Another misstep will be from a great height and without a tether."

"Yes, ma'am."

Mrs. St. George leaned forward. She was on the edge of tears herself as she spoke:

"There's no need for you to make your decision right away. You just think about it."

"Thank you, Mrs. St. George."

"You may go now, Master Piggrem," Mme. Streif said.

"Yes, ma'am," Algie said. He'd repeated himself so much this afternoon that he felt like a wax cylinder recording.

As he stood and bowed his head to both his mistress and the governor's wife, he looked squarely into the gold filigree mirror. He saw Peng's face reflected from where the boy hung outside the window.

His friend squinted one eye closed and left the tip of his tongue out one side of his mouth, both signs of intense concentration. The red rubber ball was clenched in the one hand that Peng held high over his head.

Algie could see exactly what would unfold in the next few seconds, but could say or do nothing.

"*Olo parsima!*" Peng shouted.

Peng let fly with the rubber ball. It flew through the open gap of the tall windows and tossed aside one corner of a sheer curtain. The missile struck the mirror square in the center of the *Lǎoshǔ*'s reflection. The silver glass cracked into a spider web as the ball caromed down the mantle to knock delicate porcelain figures to the floor. It was deflected as it struck a red enamel and gilt urn. The ball sped across the sitting room behind Mme. Streif's head. The urn shattered on the floor and scattered porcelain shards and grey powder.

"Jeanne Pierre," Mme. Streif murmured. Her husband's name.

The ball bounced against the walls three more times, slowing only the slightest bit as breakables were encountered. Algie grasped it out of the air as it finally flew towards his face.

A cheer went up amongst the boys on the roof.

A tottering vase full of flowers on one of the side tables crashed to the floor. Everything else in the sitting room was silent. Mme. Streif had her eyes closed, and was either praying or counting under her breath. Mrs. St. George, in wide-eyed bovine shock, slowly took in the destruction.

"I'll pack my bags," Algie said.

TWENTY-THREE

14th of September 1889
Turfan Caravanserai

The *Wu Zetian* made a leisurely Bastard Turn to starboard as it left Turfan behind,
almost as if she were waving
goodbye to Algie. The intricate bamboo supports and
cross-tied rigging kept her stable, though at a half a kilometer away, he still could hear
her groaning under the strain.

The airship straightened up
and then executed the same
maneuver the other way. She ultimately took her place between
two of the gleaming silver Pericles airships set to escort her
safely on to the next stop on the High Silk Road.

Algie had gotten no real 'farewells' from Madame Streif or
her Conversors, but he had been in the next room with Mrs. St.
George when the governor and Boycott had levied the fees for
that armed escort. Mme. Streif had not raised her voice even as
she was compelled to pay one thousand pounds sterling. That,
on top of exorbitant rentals for living quarters and repair bays,
might have sent Mssr. Patrouille or First Mate McLaren into
sputtering paroxysms of righteous fury, but she had always
been the steady hand on the slow knife.

Just as she had been with Algie.

It was only the gunshot-like cracks of the Conversors' iron
fans that could be heard hear through the closed door as he
read.

Mrs. St. George had floated into the library after that with a slightly off-level smile on her face.

"Your Madame Streif and her women wanted me to tell you 'good bye,'" she said.

Algie looked up from the bland English history he'd picked up in the library. Mssr. Patrouille and the Conversors had taken back all the good books.

"Did they?" he responded.

Hannah St. George, not "Mother" as she would like to be called, widened her eyes and glanced off to the left. It was her "tell," the unthinking signal of a bluff or a lie Nilenha had taught him to suss out.

"Well… not in so many words." She fluttered verbally like a startled pigeon. "But I could tell that it was with heavy hearts that they all left you here in my keeping."

"It's all for the best, though. Isn't that what you told me?"

His new guardian's mood brightened significantly. He himself didn't really believe that was the case, but a white lie for a white lie seemed to be a fair exchange.

"I'm tired," he said. "May I go to my room?"

She stroked his hair and kissed his cheek and generally made him feel like a lap dog.

"Of course, you may, my sweet."

He ambled through the halls of the Governor's Mansion, his elegant new home for the foreseeable future, but his mind raced as fast as the *Lǎoshǔ* in the rigging. He couldn't help but feel like he was a chess piece in a game Mrs. St George had won.

That scene from three days ago with Mrs. St. George, Mme. Streif, and Jeanne Pierre's ashes played through his mind again and again, especially as he watched the red ship and floating fish lantern disappear into a sunset over the Taklamakan Desert. It had felt very cold standing alone on the western wall of the Turfan caravanserai.

*

Algie had no lessons the next day. No movement exercises to music in the courtyards. Though he saw Meryem around the Governor's mansion, she refused to speak to him aloud, in

English or Uyghur. By lunchtime, he was nearly mad from boredom. The babble that Mrs. St. George spewed—about his future school, family holidays, caravanserai gossip—inspired him to rush to the library afterwards. He began filling his personal notebook with descriptive French words like *fatuité, inexpérimentée,* and *inconscient*[19].

He missed the *Lǎoshǔ* and Feng Po, the Chinese crewman and the German engineers. The blustering Captain Strausser and the quivering Liu Jeanne-Pierre. The gaudy Mssr Patrouille. The absolutely fascinating while terrifying Conversors and even Mme. Streif, the unyielding Silk Empress.

All those characters were like a constant pantomime playing aboard the airship just for him. The Governor's Mansion seemed to be a cloying nursery, too-clean, too white, without any rough textures or sharp edges that might discomfit the children. Well-fed, pampered, totally unchallenged, he felt an aching need in his bones.

After much contemplation, he decided he needed a distraction.

Algie made the first few cuts on another wooden bird like the one he had given Peng as a farewell gift, but his heart really wasn't in it.

He decided to go through his trunk of possessions to see what he might have at hand. Though he had said he was packing his bags almost as soon as Mssr. Streif's ashes hit the floor, the process ultimately had been prolonged and communal. Everything he owned was pitched into the black lacquer and brass trunk by the first mate by the time Algie had made it to their shared quarters. After that, before he made the quick move to the Governor's Mansion, others picked through to retrieve books and other loaned items. The final result was a jumbled mess.

He attacked the task systematically, removing everything and sorting out into piles as he went. His tattered penny dreadfuls acquired at the Turfan marketplace, most not in English, made up one pile. His clothes, both normal trousers and shirts along with the robes inherited from that Indian prince, went to a larger pile. Assorted pencils, pads, notes, marbles, machine parts, and natural history specimens collected in the trunk's lid. At the very bottom Algie found another black lacquer box set flush with the trunk's bottom. Only a fine gap around edges marked it as separate from the trunk itself. He pried it free with Chauncey's old pocket knife. Once in his hands, the box proved to be the size of a Mermaids Purse.

He laid it on the fancy embroidered coverlet topping his bed.

Under the lid was a wrapping of black cloth that packed everything tight enough not to rattle when moved. A calling card was the first thing he found beneath that. On one side was printed: "Elizabeta Kaczmarek Streif." On the other side, handwritten in a tight but feminine style, was a single line of Uyghur: "There are things you need to look into." It was a peculiar phrase to find in a hidden box at the bottom of his trunk of possessions, but one that Meryem had taught him and Ayotunde specifically. He laid the card beside the box and dug further.

He found one book left behind from his lessons here in the caravanserai: "Hoyle's Book of Games" inscribed by Nilenha in Portuguese. He wasn't completely sure what it said, but he guessed it was one of her often-repeated warnings: "Never bet against the house. The house always wins."

Intriguing, but not clear. He set the book beside the card.

Next in the box was a pair of dark violet spectacles. They looked to be the pair Nilenha used as a signal for the wagering scam during Bigsby's boxing match. It also looked like the ones Governor St. George always wore.

Possibilities whirled in Algie's mind, but nothing connected. For a moment, he slipped the spectacles on the bridge of his nose. They proved too dark to see through and so he put them aside after a few moments.

A hand-sized sheet of white cardstock came up next. One of the fountains near the mansion was drawn on it in pencil. Keijín was a skilled artist as well as a cartographer and he had seen her do many sketches like that around Turfan. The caption on the back read: "The fountain where lovers and conspirators meet."

He was completely mystified by that.

A red rubber ball like the one's the *Lǎoshǔ* favored was next out of the box. He didn't even try to figure where that might fit into this mystery.

The last item in the secret box was a dragon's head, carved in ivory with red glittering stones for eyes. If he wasn't mad, Algie would say the carving was the top half of Feng Po McLaren's precious baton. No matter what, he would be wanting that back.

He turned the dragon's head over and over in his hands and felt it growing warm in his fingers. If Mme. Streif had Feng Po and her Conversors put together this rebus box of odds and ends for him to find, they truly must have had a plan in mind for him. He had actually been left behind on a secret mission instead of being simply foisted off on the St. Georges.

All that needed to be done was to decipher Mme. Streif's covert request. Her requests when spoken in the clear were obtuse enough, but he had an advantage.

Almost every one of the Dale Daring stories had a hidden message. Algie guessed Mssr. Patrouille, *neé* Timothy Freemarch, was addicted to them. If Mme. Streif wanted to send Algie a message, the Frenchman would have been the one to compose it.

Algie started with the book. He examined the covers for marks, along with the edges and spine. When that revealed nothing, he painstakingly flipped through the pages one by one.

A single playing card was tucked into the book on the first page of the section of the popular American card game Faro. It was a face card, the Queen of Hearts, with the exposed hair painted a golden blonde color. The top-to-bottom figure held a rose in her hand instead of a sword. Algie had a few guesses who she was intended to be, but he reserved judgement for later.

Two passages were underlined in that section. In the first paragraph, the underscored passage read: "Cheating in this game has become so prevalent that it is impossible to find an honest game in the U.S." Further in, two words were similarly marked: "*carde anglaise.*"

Those three exceedingly slim clues, along with the dark

glasses, convinced him that the Governor and his wife were the targets of inquiry. They were up to some double-dealing for the BC&I, or even the Crown.

Once Algie had gathered intelligence upon them, he was to meet someone at the fountain, bearing the carved ivory dragon as a token.

He still had no idea what the red rubber ball was for.

He bounced it once or twice, experimentally, but then slipped it in his pocket. Since the incident of Mssr. Streif's ashes, balls and other sporting equipment had been strictly forbidden.

He made his way to Mrs. St. George's sitting room and tapped on the door. One of the local servants opened it and peered curiously at him. He could see his new parent reclined on the couch behind her.

"I need some fresh air," Algie announced. "I was thinking I would take a walk through the gardens."

Mrs. St George blinked at him placidly.

"Oh, of course. A growing boy needs air and exercise." She took a discreet sip of her tea from a gilded china cup. "Don't leave the grounds. It's a dangerous world outside the walls."

Algie refrained from laughing. The *Wu Zetian* on payday was a dangerous place, but made him feel more safe and secure than this walled greenspace he now called home.

"I shall be careful."

He ambled through the halls and down the grand staircase to the double doors at the front entrance. Though he took in all of the paintings, sculptures, and trophies that lined the walls, he didn't give them serious consideration. If the St Georges were indeed villains, evidence of it would not be displayed as openly as the Ming vases and marble busts of Bacon.

The building and grounds were strangely deserted just before sunset. The shadows of the caravanserai walls and docking towers stretched over everything like a dark cloak. The local Moslems were no doubt finding someplace to spread their rugs and kneel to the west as the call to prayer came from the spiral minaret.

It was just him and the carefully pampered flora as he slowly made his way around the outside of the mansion. Clockwise, just in case the rules for mansions were the same as churches. The gentle babble of the fountains drowned out the bustling cries of the insects.

His mind was engaged in nothing more than wool-gathering as he wandered. Whereas Dale Daring, or August Vogel, or a dozen other boy-adventurers he read voraciously, would have a mystery thrust upon them by page ten and solved by fifty. Algie had no idea what was afoot or which way it ran.

Along the back of the white marble edifice, Algie examined every trellis, pillar, and balustrade, hoping there would be something obvious like a pirate flag or a red pointing arrow with a caption "Here be evil folk."

There was nothing like that, of course. Even Dale Daring never had it so easy.

There was a small flash of color that caught his eye. A bit of bright red against the stone painted pink by the sun's last light.

Three stories up, behind an elaborate marble balcony, were the French doors to the Governor's private quarters. He had seen it from the other side when given his personal tour of the building this week.

Wedged into the stonework above the balcony was a red rubber ball.

19 "fatuous, inexperienced, & unconscious" French

TWENTY-FOUR

14th of September 1889
Turfan Caravanserai

It was impossible to do any proper climbing in long pants and a button-down shirt. Algie stripped down below the balcony and tucked his folded shirt and trousers behind a rosebush along with his hard soled shoes. He would need his toes to grasp the vines and jutting stonework that became a ladder up to the third floor.

Under the cover of darkness, a good thing when wearing only his skivvies, he began his ascent. The creeping vines to the left got him to second story balcony, which he traversed quickly before anyone inside had a chance to see him. The intricate carvings of fruits and flowers gave him multiple foot and hand holds. In less than five minutes, he was standing on the carved stone railing. As he pressed himself against the wall for a secure grip, he calculated how to reach the ball wedged into the pinnacle of a twelve-foot arch.

Then, he heard voices coming from the lit bedroom just on the other side of the French doors and sheer curtains.

He padded down gently from the railing and worked himself into the dark corner near the glass as slow as sunset. There was a gap in the curtain that allowed him to peer inside the St. George's bedchamber.

Mrs. St. George stood with her back to the window and her hands wrapped around the bed-post of her canopy bed. She wore only her corset and a baggy pair of white lace knickers. One of her local maidservants stood directly behind her, doing something with her hands, but it was hard for Algie to make out. It looked like either a very physical game of cat's cradle or she was tightening her corset.

The boy allowed himself only a fraction of a second to take that in before he averted his eyes. The crewmen of the *Wu Zetian* often made jokes about nasty little men that crept outside women's bedroom windows, calling them *bìhŭ* or screaming lizards. Algie never saw the pleasure in it when he wound up outside Madame Billew's window. Just the thought of creeping outside the windows of the Conversors or Mme. Streif inspired terror in his young heart.

He didn't even want to think of his new mother dressed like that. Algie was preparing to crawl back down the face of the building when he heard voices down below. He hunkered down behind the heavy stone railing and peeked through railings.

A couple, man and woman, were locked in earnest conversation under the cover of one of the fruit trees three stories down. They were less than two meters away from his folded clothing. It didn't look like they intended to leave soon.

He sat down on the cold tiles of the balcony with his back to the window. He didn't want to look inside. Algie just sat and listened.

The conversation below went on for some time as equal parts love-making and angry ultimatums. Algie could hear Mrs. St. George at her vanity, puttering away with a multitude of glass bottles. He wondered if he might freeze to death if he fell asleep trapped between the two. Turfan on the edge of the desert grew frightfully cold at night.

It seemed like hours until the Governor entered Mrs. St. George's chambers. Their conversation seemed pleasant but distracted until finally Mrs. St. George said this:

"So, do you think they are dead yet?"

Algie instantly jolted to full alert.

"No, dear," the Governor replied. "The escorts are supposed to take them three day's journey out before leaving them to their fates. I don't want their corpses dropped on my doorstep."

"Too bad. I would love to display that awful woman's head. On a pike. Between my azaleas."

Algie wasn't entirely sure that was still the Governor's wife speaking. Her tone was grating and cruel, with a touch of cordial homicide he had never heard before.

"Now, now, dear... Don't get yourself so worked up."

"There is something about that woman that inspires, nearly requires, glorious outrage. She is arrogant, and imperious, and not at all a nice person. She doesn't deserve a boy like that."

"Are you actually that concerned with Master Algernon?"

"Lord, no!" Mrs. St George replied. "He was only something she had that I could pry from her claws. We send him off to your dreadful old boarding school and we'll never have to bother with him again."

Even though he had never wanted this place, or a new mother for that matter, it stung to hear that she never really wanted him. He pressed his ear to the window in spite of that. He needed to gather every word.

"Are you sure they won't reach the next caravanserai?" Mrs. St. George asked. "They took down two of Boycott's *picaroon* ships without too much trouble."

"The way that Chinese folly limped into our repair bays indicated that the *muhafez* were quite a bit of trouble." The Governor chuckled. "It would take a dozen airships to defeat those two armored light cruisers. Don't you worry my dear, that witch Streif and her whole crew are as good as dead."

Algie took a deep breath. He settled back against the white stone wall in the far corner of the balcony, away from the window and out of sight from the courtyard. As he did so, his hand settled down on top of yet another red rubber ball.

As he picked it up, he saw it was attached to a string which was hung over the stone railing and leading off across the face of the mansion. He had no idea where that might lead to, but it seemed important.

His guess was *this* was the thing Mme. Streif wanted him to look into.

*

The lovers were still chattering down below. They probably would not look up or notice him as he traversed the face of the building by fingertip and toenail, but he wouldn't risk that. He fumbled in the dark for something portable, but still light enough for him to pitch. He came upon a planter full of herbs.

Algie weighed the flower pot in his hands, figuring it to be two or three kilograms. He lofted it underhand over the railing with enough forward impetus to drop it in the center of the brickyard. After a few seconds, Algie heard a satisfying crash and a shriek like a little girl's. Hurried footsteps and hushed, angry words from the woman followed shortly.

Then, Algie was alone.

He crept up over the broad curved stone railing. Pressed close to the wall, holding tight by toe and fingertip, he followed the twine along the path of ledges, pillars, and carvings. He would have found the transit terrifying before spending his months in the rigging of the *Wu Zetian*. Now, it was simply the shortest path to where he needed to be.

The twine curved over another railing to end up tied to a leg of a wrought iron plant stand. Algie slipped onto the balcony and close to the new set of French doors. He pressed through, convinced any secrets were in this room instead of under the flower pot.

It was the Governor's office on the other side of the sheer curtains. Like most of the mansion, the chamber looked bright, sparse, and vaguely military, even when seen by the pale light coming through the windows. Algie had come in right behind the swivel chair pressed up to massive carved-wood desk that occupied much of the available space like a dark brown sleeping bull in a china shop.

Algie cast his eyes around the dimly lit room for the most likely cache for secrets. Most of the walls held glass-front book cases, with official portraits and weapons trophies hung between them. A cut-glass liquor service on a rolling tray and a meter-wide wooden globe caught his eye, but neither seemed to be his prize.

Returning to the hulk of the desk, he finally noticed the green-glass shaded oil lamp and the red leather casket, the type all officials in Dale Daring novels kept their sensitive papers. He lit the lamp and pulled the casket to him.

It was unlocked.

That was a likely result of being three stories up and inside a walled compound within the caravanserai's massive walls. The governor secured absolutely nothing. Algie extracted the papers a few at a time and skimmed over the cramped script that filled every page. His *Lǎoshǔ* friends could have gotten themselves into this office, but none of them could read more than the simplest food tin labels.

The first few papers were mundane letters from the Home Office, economic directives urging the governor to steal more cookies from others, in the way that Keijín described economics. Not likely to be incriminating. He put those in a pile for later consideration.

He next came upon a series of documents with airship names and listed range of actions. These were the letters of marque, like the one offered to Mme. Streif to hunt *picaroons*. Governor St. George had assembled a sizeable fleet of privateers, at least two dozen contracts from everywhere between the Levant and Indochina.

This was concerning, but all perfectly legal, if not moral. He made a new stack of those papers.

The next few papers looked promising. Various airships were listed as having passed through Turfan, and whether or not they paid a voluntary transit tax. Algie recognized many of the names of the ships that had refused. They were the ones recently taken down by *muhafez* raiders or the mysterious golden dragon. Every single one of them.

The Dowager Empress and her court would not be pleased if the Governor and the BC&I were killing off free passage along the High Silk Road. Treaties would be broken and franchises removed. Jakinda and Keijín had mentioned that in what seemed like idle conversation about economics before they had left. He folded up these papers flat and stowed them in his skivvies.

Algie kept looking, hoping for a bigger prize.

Mme. Streif's full name, just like the calling card in his trunk, was written large across the top of the next document. Mssr. Patrouille's name and all the Conversors were set down below it. The paragraph below declared them to be Enemies of the Crown and Western Civilization in general. A sizeable price in Pounds Sterling was placed on their heads.

It all looked very official and was dated to be effective three days in the future.

That piece of paper would pitch every privateer and every airship loyal to the Crown against the *Wu Zetian*. It was a death warrant.

He stashed that paper with the others in his shorts. The rest he stuffed back into the red leather casket and then blew out the lamp. He fled, moving as quickly as he safely could over the balcony and down to his hidden clothes

Once dressed, he ran to the fountain in Keijín's drawing. He hoped he had gotten that clue right, because the *Wu Zetian* and her crew didn't have too many spare moments for mistakes.

*

The little fountain and the marble gazebo that covered it were overshadowed by the caravanserai walls. Algie could hear the tinkle of falling water, but everything else was a silhouette.

No wonder conspirators met here after sunset.

He stepped out into the open, trusting that someone waited in the shadows for him. It took only a few moments to prove his assumption.

"*Assalaamu alaikum,*" Meryem said as she emerged from the bushes. The entirety of body and head were swathed in a black cloak, but her voice and almost-luminous green eyes were unmistakable.

"*Wa Alykom As-salam,*" he replied. He was pleased to see, to speak with her. Algie had not been allowed to speak to the servants since coming to live in the mansion. Their responses, when he tried anyway, were worthy of a very civil *karakuri*.

Algie began to stammer out a response in Uyghur, but she placed a single finger over her veiled lips and shushed him. He was glad for the effort she saved him; his mastery of her language was nowhere near his knowledge of English or French.

As Meryem slowly approached him, she raised her hand above her head and beckoned to someone behind her.

A second person wrapped in a dark cloak stepped out of the shadows. One of the Conversors left behind to meet with him, no doubt.

He hoped that it would be Nilenha or Jakinda, the two he liked best, and seemed to like him. Keijín would have done fine in a pinch, or even the under-sized and near incomprehensible Chabi. There was only one of the Conversors he dreaded mounting an adventure with, one who always seemed on the verge of selling him back to the Australians or worse.

The second woman pulled aside her cloak to reveal midnight dark skin and close-cropped black hair.

"*Assalaamu alaikum,*" Ayotunde said, and then followed in French. "I do hope you missed me."

TWENTY-FIVE

15th of September 1889
Outside Turfan

A steam tractor pulled a train of cargo trailers out to the Uyghur farms each morning before dawn. Local farmers loaded them full of grapes, melons, and other perishables for market. Algie, Ayotunde, and Meryem rode in one of those empty trailers, hidden from curious eyes by stacks of burlap bags.

"When exactly will you be explaining Mme. Streif's master plan?" he asked.

The empty freight train ran over a bump in the road and ground Algie's tailbone into the wooden floor with the impact.

"It's not so much a plan," the Conversor replied, in French, "as an over-arching goal and a set of up-close tactics."

"And what is the Silk Empress' over-arching goal?"

"To wake up tomorrow morning."

The land train rumbled on and Algie thought better than to disturb the silence again. Eventually, it stopped and the burlap bags were lifted off the passengers on the tips of bayonets.

"Hallo, hallo, hallo," came a voice on the other side of the rifle, "What have we got here?"

"Mice in the granary, seems to me," another voice replied. "Just like the governor warned us." Both spoke in English, in a thick accent that sounded like the Northlands.

Algie felt a little thrill that he understood what they were saying without having to identify and translate. That was replaced with a chill of terror when he realized what the words meant.

The bags were all pulled clear of their little nest and a lantern brought to light them. Though he could see little of the men with the light shining directly in his eyes, he was sure they were wearing red coats and black high hats like the British China and India Company did.

"You all can come out, now," one of them said.

Ayotunde showed no inclination to kill them with her fists or her fan, so Algie stood and followed her out the rear drop gate of the trailer. He got poked in the buttocks with something sharp as he stepped down to the packed dust that passed for a road.

He stepped away from the train and took in his surroundings. Though there was just a glimmer of light in the east, enough sunlight reflected from the whitewashed brick buildings for him to see.

The Uyghur village was green with trees in full leaf and potted plants in every space Algie could see. Water was not nearly so dear here as in the vast sea of sand he knew to lie to the south, thanks to *qanat* canal systems. The arcade behind them opened to cool warehouses filled with crates of fruits and vegetables. It would all be a pleasant place if not for the three ugly men with guns. He drifted towards the warehouse in small uncertain steps.

"We'll take them down to the Semaphore building and hold them until we get word what we should do with them," one of those men grumbled.

"That's enough of that, boy." Another thug put a hand on Algie's shoulder to keep him from moving farther. He pressed down until the boy's knees bent and finally touched to the ground. Another did the same to Ayotunde. She somehow allowed it.

The third redcoat had Meryem pressed back against the wooden wall of the trailer, an unpleasant grin displayed on his pock-marked face. The other two joined him close around her.

"They do grow them pretty around here, don't they, Randall?" one of them crooned.

The one called Randall nodded and flashed a yellow-brown smile. He leaned his rifle against the trailer to free both of his hands. Reaching out, he pushed her scarf off of Meryem's hair to fondle a strand of her strawberry blonde hair.

The bulk of the man's back covered in red wool blocked her face from view, but Algie could hear her fearful whimper. He looked over to Ayotunde, hoping for intervention from the Conversor. She stared straight ahead, motionless as a statue carved from teak. She held one hand out before her, her splayed fingers parallel with the earth. The fingertips bobbed up and down minutely, a silent signal used in his movement lessons which said: *Wait*.

The other BC&I thugs set aside their guns and pressed close to the native woman. They emitted low growls and mumbles that for them must have passed for pitching woo.

Ayotunde made a slow, gentle movement with her other hand; her furled iron fan slid out of that sleeve like slow-flowing water. She rose up from her knees quietly, almost floating as if she were an airship herself.

A minute or two later, Algie helped drag the unconscious bodies behind crates of melons and grapes. Ayotunde gave the rifles to the local stevedores who were already loading the train with produce. Algie kept one of the beaver high hats for himself.

Meryem took a little time to gather her wits about her and to wrap her scarf and shawl all around her. She murmured something and spit in the general direction of the warehouse.

"Now," she said in English, "I will take you to my people."

*

They rode in the back of a borrowed milk cart to the orchards that spread out to the west of Turfan. Algie's new hat kept sliding down over his eyes until Meryem rolled up one of her handkerchiefs into a bulky headband. This held his new badge of victory in place like a foil cap on a milk bottle.

The half hour trip passed pleasantly enough. Not having to conceal their presence, Meryem began singing children's songs. The old man who drove the cart would sometimes join in. To the boy's astonishment, the taciturn Ayotunde started singing along, too.

The milkman drove them past an orchard where mature orange trees stood in careful rows with their foliage nearly touching, across the edge of the desert, almost up to the foothills of the Flaming Mountains. He put them off along the line of *qanat* wells that ran from the mountains down to the irrigated fields of the Uyghurs.

Uyghur men armed with pruning hooks and grain flails stood around a steam-powered crane beside the nearest access shaft. Some sat on the low circular stone wall of the *qanat*, a perfect circle of finished sandstone ten meters across while others pretended to attend to the crane's platform and the stone and gravel stacked by it for maintenance. These fierce-looking men were all dressed in fine cloth & bright colors, exactly what Algie had been promised for *picaroons*.

Meryem waved him and Ayotunde in the Uyghurs' direction. Having no better place to go for help, they went. The armed men stood as they approached, surrounding the boy and Conversor at the edge of the wall.

Meryem gave a quick synopsis of what damage they had done to the Governor and the BC&I already, and the briefest of sketches of their plans. The rebels and brigands laughed easily at the stories, some even reaching out to tousle Algie's blonde hair. Two men pitched the rolled-up chain ladder over the edge with a whoop.

Algie went over the edge first, barely concerned with the twenty- to thirty-meter drop. Ayotunde took a moment to bind up her skirts in her belt before she climbed down after him. He paid more attention to the smooth clay tiles that covered the surface of the shaft and the electric cables and naked Edison bulbs that lit everything on his descent rather than dare to look up the Conversor's skirts.

Armed men waited for them in the arched tunnel at the bottom. It felt quite crowded at barely five meters across. Algie made a splash as he landed in the underground stream that ran through its center. The water came up to just over his ankles. He nearly tripped over the narrow-gauge iron rails that ran just below the surface.

The men who stood on the wood decking on either side of the stream made no show of protecting themselves with farmers' tools. They carried bolt action rifles and bandoliers of cartridges slung across their chests. Though Algie did not keep informed on firearms as much as aircraft, he guessed the long guns were Japanese *Muratas*.

Ayotunde and the Uyghurs came down shortly after him, all managing to land on the deck instead of the water. She gave one disapproving look at Algie's sodden appearance and fell to rearranging her skirts.

That's when the train arrived.

It could call itself a train by only the loosest of definitions. The engine was a basic rail truck that held a small spirit engine, controls, and a saddle for the engineer to mount. Walls, ceilings, and safety guards were a luxury the Uyghurs dispensed with for the sake of speed and stealth. The ten cars behind it looked to be nothing more that wooden flat-beds on rail trucks. An identical engine facing the other way brought up the rear.

Meryem exchanged words with one of the rifle bearers and they were waved onto the nearest car. The Conversor settled down with her legs folded under her orange and yellow ochre skirts. Algie did his best to emulate. The dozen or so Uyghurs who joined them on the moving platform, including Meryem, crouched down on one knee with a rifle butt or a hand on the deck. A stable pose, but one ready to leap up at a moment's notice. The engineer engaged in reverse gear and the train left the underground station with a lurch.

The engines wound up to a steady pace, perhaps as much as twenty-five kilometers per hour, and headed for the mountains. They passed beneath ten access shafts before the tracks veered off to the left in a new tunnel separate from the subterranean aqueduct. Bright new tile and Edison lights zipped by at a steady clip for several minutes.

It came as a total surprise when the tunnel opened out to a vast underground space the size of one of Turfan's airship repair hangars. The domed roof reached all the way to the surface at its apex. Algie recognized the camouflage nets that covered the opening there as the same type as the ones used in the ambush along the High Silk Road. Cables, cranes, and walkways filled the space between that gateway and the top of Algie's head. He felt a shiver run down his spine, and wondered if he had made a horrible mistake.

Four high-speed Von Siegling *Raubvogels* rested to his right some twenty or thirty meters in from the tracks. Stolen BC&I Magnus chiropters, their official logos defaced, waited beyond those. As Algie and Ayotunde rode on, more and more of the equipment from the raid on the Turfan appeared.

The flat-bed heavy lifter filled up the space at the end of tracks like a castle gate itself. Her gas envelope laid deflated over her like a shawl across a woman's shoulders. Camp chairs and what looked like a throne were arranged in a semi-circle on the wooden deck, each occupied by a gray-haired man or woman in bright colors. Algie assumed these were the elders of the Uyghur tribe that held court there. It looked like the kind of court which ordered frequent executions.

He and the Conversor disembarked and walked up to about three meters from them. Meryem stood just behind him with her hand resting lightly on his shoulder.

"Be brave," she murmured in French.

He wanted to be brave for her, even if that were the kind of thing Dale Daring might do.

Algie recognized the old warrior who sat on the throne. He was the leader of the market gate raid, the man that had been shot through the chest without seeming injury. He stared at Algie with unhidden suspicion and hostility. Algie thought to make a friendly gesture: He removed his hat, stepped forward, and bowed his head.

"*Assalaamu alaikum.*"

The old Uyghur did not alter his expression a whit. One younger man, possessed of a savage beard and red-rimmed eyes, cocked his head to one side like a hungry dog. Algie felt his stomach ache.

Meryem spoke up for them, calling the elder Boway Kashgari and the younger, Sardar Pakhirdin. Algie caught every fifth word, but he understood the story of how he had saved her from the fire and Ayotunde had saved her from the BC&I redcoats. The elders seemed to soften somewhat, but they weren't smiling.

Hushed conversations welled up in the ranks of the Uyghur clan. Algie comprehended even fewer of those words, but he did pick up the words for "British," "dog," and a few other unclean animals.

Ayotunde flipped open her fan and fluttered a breeze onto her face. She looked over the assembled elders one by one, and then she smiled sweetly. Algie didn't remember ever seeing her do that before.

She spoke slowly, a well-modulated ballad of Algie's adventures that rose and fell like the hills outside Turfan. He didn't understand a tenth of what she said, but he didn't need that. He felt the words in his chest, first fear shifting into blackest despair, then sparking irrational hope and even courage and pride.

Ayotunde gestured towards Algie and he felt that she was literally singing his praises. He stood straighter, feeling blood and heat rising in his cheeks and ears. The Uyghur audience was captivated. Their eyes glistened, they leaned forward, some even smiled. There was no applause as the Conversor finished, but Algie no longer feared for his life.

"You need to speak now," she said as she turned back to him. "I told them how you are a young hero, wise beyond your years, and a mighty warrior. They know you killed a whole ship-load of *picaroons* single-handed, and I've implied you will do the same to the Governor and Boycott."

"I can't do that!" he responded in an urgent whisper. Speaking in front of this group held more terror for him than fighting armed *muhafez*.

"If you want their help in time to save our friends, you will have to make a most eloquent argument. I will translate."

Ayotunde turned him to face the tribal elders and gently thrust him forward with both hands. As he stood there with his new top hat in his hands, she leaned in close and whispered into his ear:

"And make it in French. My English is inadequate."

The Uyghur elders looked at him in expectation. He felt the bottom of his stomach falling away, the same sensation as when he stood on the rail of the observation platform with a Mermaid's Purse in his hands. He would either leap into open space in this moment, or hang on the edge forever powerless.

He took the leap.

"As a child, I read nothing but stories of heroes," he began quietly. "They filled my dreams with adventures, glorious battles, and miraculous deeds. I wished to be like them more than anything else I could ever imagine."

He paused for Ayotunde to translate. His words sounded so much better in Uyghur with the Conversor's voice behind it.

"But I've come to learn that kind of hero is just vanity, and wishes, and a story used as a blindfold to keep us from seeing the villainy that is done by old men with their hands on the levers of power."

He let Ayotunde have her chance to translate. The audience seemed to appreciate her version of his words.

"But there is another kind of hero, the real kind. Honest people who are forced to do what is hard, who do it because it is terribly difficult, but not doing anything will be worse for more people, and for longer. The ones who will never be put down in the pages of a book or whispered of around campfires.

"I want to be that kind of hero, and I need your help to do it. The people aboard the *Wu Zetian* will be able to defang Governor St. George and Mr. Boycott, as long as I can warn them before they are killed. Just please get me to them in time!"

Ayotunde took a very long time wrapping up his speech, but the listeners were rapt. They rose and cheered as she finished her impassioned performance. Pakhirdin nodded and said something that sounded like an approval. The elder Kashgari glared at him, stood, and looked directly at Algie.

"I forbid this," he declared, a phrase Meryem had taught Algie in Uyghur. As the clan erupted in a myriad of small chattering cliques, the old man turned and disappeared into an ornate tent set up beside the airship. Ayotunde had a hushed fervent conversation with the red-bearded second-in-command. Before Algie saw what was happening to him, Meryem and the

Conversor had grasped him by his upper arms and marched him after Pakhirdin, who practically ran after the clan elder.

Kashgari stood with his back to the tent opening, but grumbled at them over one shoulder.

"I will not discuss this," Ayotunde translated for Algie's sake. "The boy is the governor's pet and I will not risk our men and our aircraft on his say-so."

"That is an astounding turnaround," Pakhirdin shouted, "considering the number of men we have lost in the last few weeks."

The old man turned and glared at him as if that alone would strike him dead. The younger man bowed his head and started again in a far more conciliatory tone:

"It doesn't need to be just for the sake of the boy."

Pakhirdin pointed at the open neck of Algie's shirt and spoke in English. "What is that enormous chunk of gold that hangs around your neck?"

Algie's hand moved to his throat of its own accord. His fingertips fell upon the leather lanyard and slipped down to Zdan's present. He pulled it out to show it off.

"I got this from a friend who is a wandering automaton peddler. It's called a Tuareg cross, and you can play it like a penny whistle."

Algie unhooked it and had it up to his lips before he heard the Uyghur leader cry out in distress. The high-pitched warbling tone drowned out everything else.

When he looked up, he was speechless. The Boway Kashgari was reaching out as if to swat the cross out of his hands, but was somehow frozen in the middle of the act. Everyone else in the chamber seemed frozen, too, but that was mere shock. That wore off quickly and the room filled with frightened and angry voices. Several crowded around their cataleptic leader and examined him for signs of life.

"What did you do?" Ayotunde asked in French.

"I don't know," Algie wailed. "All I did was play one note! Maybe if I play another..."

Algie immediately changed his fingering on the cross and blew again before anyone else could try to stop him.

The result was distressing.

The leader's head fell forward on a joint in the front of his throat. Panels opened up the back of his head like a beetle's wings. A golden light shone out of his brainpan. Algie could hear the delicate sound of plucked strings and vibrating metal plates.

"Bloody Hell," Algie muttered. "He's a *karakuri*!"

Meryem and Pakhirdin stood open-mouthed and staring. The Conversor recovered her equilibrium far more quickly.

"I suppose," Ayotunde murmured to Pakhirdin, "you won't be taking his orders anymore?"

*

A quick tribunal on succession of power convened in the tent with several other clan elders ushered in for the discussion. Algie and Ayotunde stood unnoticed in the corner as Pakhirdin was anointed new leader of the tribe. The former leader was laid down on a cot and covered over with an ornamental rug, still in his open form.

Meryem squeezed his hand and whispered into his ear:

"You did it. Pakhirdin has ordered that our pilots will take you out in the chiropters right away."

"Thank you," he replied. He was both elated, surprised, and, considering what he knew of Conversors, gnawingly suspicious. He crept up beside her as she repeatedly bowed to the Uyghurs who surrounded her. He bowed and thanked and spoke sidewise to Ayotunde:

"You didn't translate my speech at all, did you?"

"Ayub Khan gave a very inspirational speech before going to battle with the British in eighteen-eighty-two," she said. "It seemed far more appropriate."

Algie scowled in spite of himself. The Conversor looked down at him with a comical grimace on her face.

"Oh, don't be that way," she said in French. "We have a flight to catch."

TWENTY-SIX

7th of March 1889
Somewhere over China

Algie awoke in a tangle of limbs and knotted twine. It took him a while to orient himself in the dark. Whatever he laid on was gently swaying from side to side. A faint buzz came through the canvas walls of the chamber.

That last sensory clue brought it all together. He, and the dozen or so boys he had met in Capetown, were bunking in a cargo hold of an airship bound for Nanking, China. Feng Po McLaren had told him that it was the most economical way for his band of monkeys to travel from Macao.

Though the captain provided thirteen hammocks, it seemed the boys only used three. This was not so much huddling for warmth as gathering for defense. They seemed a bit feral, but had taken him in as one of their own. That is how he went to sleep alone in his hammock and awoke under a clump of them.

The fire door of the chamber cranked open and Feng Po McLaren stationed himself in the doorway. He held a stacking tray of breakfast bowls in one hand and his formidable baton in the other. The gaudy Chinaman tapped out a cadence on the wooden doorframe as he called out to them"

"*Olo parsima! Yeiban sush!* All hands, all eyes, up and at the world!"

The boys, Feng Po called them *law-shu,* tumbled to the deck in a spectacle half-way between a stampede and an avalanche. They clamored for their breakfast porridge like hungry puppies.

In the weeks he had spent on an Australian sheep ship, and subsequently hiding in an African warehouse, Algie had become a bit of a wild child. But his years of habitual grooming and self-care returned when the opportunity arose.

He rolled out of his bed, re-buttoning his shirt and pulling his trouser legs down to his ankles. Coming to the water tap and mirror that added to the pretense of this chamber being a passenger cabin, he moistened a washcloth and washed his hands, neck, and face. There was nothing he could do about his teeth except a quick rinse and spit. He simply surrendered to the state of his hair.

Feng Po held up the last porridge bowl high enough to discourage the others from snatching at it.

"You need to be quicker with this lot," he said in his odd Scottish accent. "They'll eat your lunch, before you you've noticed you missed breakfast."

"Thank you, sir," Algie said as he took the bowl from him.

"Be careful bandying around the "sir" word. It's reserved for officers and other mental deficients."

"But, I thought you were the First Mate?"

"That is a rumor propagated only to keep the Captain from throwing me off the airship at a great height."

"Oh."

Algie looked around at the other boys who devoured their oat porridge with their fingers and licked the remains out of the bowls.

"You wouldn't happen to have a spoon, would you... Mr. McLaren?"

The First Mate's eyebrows went up at the request.

"A spoon? No one's ever asked for that before. Mme. Streif and her Conversors will love meeting you."

*

Six women awaited them at the landing gantry in Nanking. The gray-haired woman in blue silk and black fringe was evidently Mme. Elizabeth Streif, his new employer. She seemed small and unimpressive at a distance of a hundred yards.

Something about his carriage must have conveyed his attitude to Mr. McLaren unspoken.

"You're a well-educated young man," The Chinese man said in his confusing Scots brogue. "You ever hear of Louis Pasteur?"

Algie had indeed. His mother had bought him a popular biography of the scientist a few years ago.

"Sure," he exclaimed. "He saved the French wine industry and invented the first vaccine for rabies."

"But do you remember anything about the French silk industry?"

"There was a French silk industry?"

"Indeed there was," Feng Po said with a nod. "When Mme. Streif was a mere slip of a lass, *pebrine* struck the silkworms of the French countryside. The government commissioned Dr. Pasteur to save the day. Out of the goodness of their hearts, Mme. and Mssr. Streif provided a private train to travel to all the silk-growers in the country."

"So… she's a philanthropist?"

"At least for anyone named Streif," Feng Po replied. "Pasteur travelled from plantation to plantation, pointing out the methods to separate diseased worms and starting up a new stock. What he didn't know was that the last car of their train was filled with *pebrine*-infected silkworms and her personal workers in charge of re-introducing the disease. Within a year, hers was the only plantation still raising domestic raw silk."

"Wicked!" Algie exclaimed.

"Many would make that estimation. The Silk Empress' machinations helped the armies of the China defeat the colonial powers at Palikao, as well as the defeat of the British at Khartoum."

Algie was speechless. Looking at the old woman again, he didn't see any sign of her being capable of such things. Which would be the image that someone capable of such things would want to cultivate.

Mme. Streif inspected the boys with a distant expression, in absolute silence as they approached. Up close, she struck him with a quiet kind of terror as he wondered what she might do with him if he didn't measure up. He clutched tight his only possession, a dog-eared copy of "Dale Daring & the Transatlantic Terrors" he had wheedled Feng Po into buying for him in Macau.

The other five woman gathered around and behind her like bodyguards to a Roman emperor, but most dressed in the finest dresses befitting royalty or stage actresses. One, the tallest, was a dark-skinned African in yellow. Her expression displayed that she had little love for children. Two were dark-skinned, but from all his readings Algie couldn't guess from which part of the world they hailed. One was red-headed with dark freckles and a red and black dress; she looked at the children through heavy-lidded eyes as if they might be new toys. The other wore a plain brown walking dress. She had dark hair and eyes and tattoos on her chin. That one was totally unreadable to Algie.

A tiny pale-skinned woman with jet-black hair stood next to the African. Her dress was sky-blue and silver. She smiled constantly, which concerned Algie for some intangible reason. Being shorter than even Algie, she looked ridiculous at the elbow of the largest, a woman that might have been taller than First Mate McLaren.

The last woman in green, close by the old woman's right hand, looked like a Spanish dancer with dark hair and bright red lips. She looked at Algie and his book, and he could see calculations going on behind her eyes.

Confronted by all six at once, one thought ran through Algie's mind:

Could Australia really have been all that bad?

"So, these are your auxiliary riggers, Mr. McLaren?" Mme. Streif asked. "They seem to be a bit... rough around the edges."

"They're just what we need. Smart, nimble, fearless," Feng Po replied. "And much too young to be spending their money on whiskey and women."

She made a small sound and sniffed.

"I am trusting you."

"And you won't regret it," he said with a smile.

The woman in green at her right indicated Algie with an elevation of her chin.

"What about this one?" she asked.

"This one, Miss Jakinda?" Feng Po asked as he placed a hand on Algie's head. "The clean one with a book?"

"Is he the one you told us about?"

"The genuine article."

She smiled at Algie and came up close to him. Her flowery perfume enveloped him.

"I have been told that you arranged an escape from a transport ship for two dozen children in Capetown harbor using empty supply barrels."

"Yes, ma'am." Algie wanted to be liked by this woman. She seemed nice.

"Did you see any of your friends after you got away from the ship?"

"We lived together in an abandoned warehouse for a few days, until the sailors found us. That's when Mr. McLaren rescued me." Algie saw Feng Po look quite pleased to be called his rescuer and "Mister." "I think they're all gone now."

"I'm very sorry," she said. "I know you have lost a great deal in your life."

"Thank you."

She reached out and tapped his book.

"Mr. McLaren tells me that he loaned you money to buy this."

"Before my mother died, I had all the Dale Daring books. I want to collect them all again."

"You'll have to be quick," she said, "he's always writing more."

Algie knew his eyes grew wide at her remark.

"Do you know the man who writes Dale Daring?"

Jakinda immediately looked embarrassed.

"I'm not sure I can say."

"Extraordinary," Mme. Streif interjected. "Mr. McLaren, you made an excellent choice. Try to keep him from killing himself."

She turned to be on her way, but threw one last request over her shoulder:

"And teach him the metric system, like a civilized human being."

TWENTY-SEVEN

15th of September 1889
Taklamakan Desert

To ride aboard a *Raubvogel* chiropter, one is wrapped up in something like a corset and left dangling parallel to the ground beneath the great bat wings and the ten-meter-long gas envelope.

The Uyghur air crew strapped Algie into the passenger's sling as Ehmet the pilot inspected the control surfaces and cables. He was a strapping young man with a flowing black beard who was full of jokes and bravado in a way that reminded Algie of the American ensigns on the *Wu Zetian*. He brushed back Algie's hair and slipped a tight flying cap onto his head. As Algie pulled the attached goggles over his eyes, Ehmet handed him a colorful silk scarf. As he showed him how to wrap it over the lower half of his face, he said something in Uyghur.

"Don't eat bugs," was what Algie thought he said.

Bundled up properly, he clutched the cables that held his torso and swung his legs into the loop to the rear of the craft. Now, he was strung up like a Christmas goose in a butcher shop window. His primary view was dirt and the ground crew's boot-clad feet.

A pair of women's brown high-button shoes came into sight, topped by the cuffs of red woolen pants. Algie craned his neck to see the rest of that person's outfit. Ayotunde had abandoned her orange and yellow silk walking dress for Uyghur men's clothing: white embroidered shirt, red vest covered with hand-stitched flowers, the red trousers with decorations down either side. The two pilots looked absolutely drab in the greenish-brown coveralls favored by European airship engineers. The men who normally wore Ayotunde's new clothes stood and stared as she worked herself into the sling of the adjacent craft.

Algie was not so easily scandalized; he'd seen her exercising in blue silk pajamas.

"*Inshallah*[20]," Ehmet chuckled as he slid into his own sling and harness with control loops for each hand and foot. With the weight of the two of them hung from the chiropter, it dropped towards the ground a foot or two, and then bounced upwards until it hit the ends of its tethers. The motion was rather like flying already.

"Fire it up!" The other pilot shouted once he was in place. The ground teams did just that. The Von Siegling's spirit engines roared into life and then revved up to a mosquito-like whine. The pusher props thrust the aircraft forward against their anchor cables and then abated.

Algie heard the sounds of blocks and ropes and grunting men as the camouflage netting above them was pulled back. He had to trust to his ears as all he could really see was dirt.

The attendants disconnected the aircraft from their tether cables and then walked them to the clear space in the center of the dome, holding the edges of wings well over their heads. They turned them loose like birds as open air was reached.

Ehmet grinned at Algie as he cranked the throttle down hard. The ungainly contraption of phlogiston, wings, and motors whined shrilly as it made tight rising circles underground. They avoided numerous cables and walkways until they rose up through the breach in the earth and headed west in pursuit of the *Wu Zetian*.

*

The Von Siegling craft were built to be high-speed couriers, when not buzzing guards off of city walls. They held auxiliary fuel tanks which would let them run for twenty-four hours at top speed, which was good because it would take eighteen to catch up with the *Wu Zetian* at its dawdling pace over the last two days.

The Uyghurs had hung pouches from the vehicle's wooden frame around the pilot and passenger. These were filled with canteens of water, and packages of dried fruit, cheese, and bread. The only thing they had not made arrangements for was a lavatory.

Algie realized this oversight about six hours into the journey. He tried to yell at Ehmet, pulling his scarf down around his neck, but the sound of the wind and the engines made conversation impossible. He shouted *"Hajätxana qayärdä?"* —what one yells when looking for a Uyghur water closet, anyway.

He caught the pilot's attention ultimately by bouncing an ear-like chunk of dried peach off of his forehead. Once the bearded man looked his way, Algie did his best to communicate his situation without words. First, Algie opened his eyes very wide, then tugged at the front of his trousers, and then crossed his legs in the loop they hung from.

Ehmet caught on fast as lightning and nodded.

Algie pointed to the ground, indicated that they should land, preferably near a large desiccated bush that might provide cover.

The pilot frowned and shook his head with great vigor. Then, he pantomimed back an answer: Algie should simply undo his trousers and relieve his bladder upon the desert like a gentle rain. His waggling fingers conveyed the sense of falling fluids vividly.

This was not an entirely new concept to Algie. There were no water closets in the rigging of an airship. There were also no women around to see that sort of thing. Algie glimpsed over to the starboard where Ayotunde's craft kept a pace with them only ten or twenty meters away.

Ehmet saw Algie's apprehension and did something about it right away. He dropped their chiropter down about thirty meters, putting the craft's wings and gas envelope between the Conversor and any embarrassing bodily functions.

Algie undid his fly and irrigated the thirsty sands below. Once he was finished and fastened, Ehmet brought the chiropter back up to parallel the other. They flew on through the twilight, towards distant lights that could be either ship's lanterns or fires.

*

They had been fires.

It took them perhaps four hours to catch up, but finally the two British escort ships appeared on the horizon. They flew close to the desert floor so as to have that much less distance to crash, sticking to the line of semaphore towers that ran along the main course of the High Silk Road. The lights from below let Algie see some of the damage. The fires had been dowsed, but many breaches in their silver hulls still spat smoke. The external walkways were deserted as the two warships limped back towards Turfan.

Algie made a sign to circle around them and close in. Ehmet tapped his forehead with his fist to show he thought the boy was mad, or had a head made of wood. The two went back and forth symbolically for several seconds, but then the other Uyghur craft swooped low to match altitude with the crippled destroyers. Ayotunde was no doubt more persuasive than Algie.

Without further pointing and shouting, Ehmet banked the chiropter down to take a closer look. The sight sickened Algie. The gleaming armored aircraft were covered with greasy patches of soot and char. He saw a shocking number of holes punched clean through the hull. Something like a human body dangled from the cables and struts that supported one sputtering engine, though it could have been a tangle of signal flags. As they drew close, Algie still couldn't see any positive proof of survivors on the vessel.

"Keep your distance, you bloody savages," an electrically-amplified voice declared, "or we will blow you out of the sky!"

Ehmet looked to Algie for a translation. Algie didn't have the words available in the other man's language, so he fell back on pantomime. He grimaced with rage and then, turning his fingers into symbolic pistols, shot in all directions. The pilot caught on and shrugged with a comprehending smirk. He would be in that bad a mood if he had been that badly shot up.

Algie tapped his ear and pointed at the motor. Ehmet was able to throttle back the engine from an ear-piercing whine to a dyspeptic grumble. Cupping his hands around his mouth, he shouted what he thought to be the safest thing to yell at a damaged airship filled with angry British Marines:

"God save the Queen!"

"What did you say?" the electric voice responded.

"God save the Queen! I'm a citizen of the Crown!"

"What the blazes are you doing out here?"

Algie had a sudden intuition that telling them why they were aboard two Uyghur pirate craft would likely get them blown out of the sky. He chose to tell about one-tenth of the Truth.

"I've just come from the Governor of Turfan's mansion." Algie waited a few moments for incoming gun or missile fire. "What happened to you, sir?"

"That mad woman Streif, she ambushed us."

Algie highly doubted that. From what he had heard, and what he had read, at the Governor's mansion, he was sure it had been the other way around. Also, considering that there remained a few inventions from the Liu Chemical Works he had not yet seen, he was sure it was the *Wu Zetian* that had crippled them in a stroke. He couldn't sound too pleased at that.

"Is her airship still in the air?" he asked.

"Don't know," the voice said. "Don't care."

With that, Algie knew the interview would be over.

"Godspeed!" he shouted. "We have to complete our mission."

The British warships did not reply.

Algie gestured for Ehmet to ascend and return to their original course. Before he pulled his face scarf back over his mouth, he shouted:

"I must fly like arrows!"

He hoped he got the Uyghur grammar right.

20 "To God's ears", Arabic

TWENTY-EIGHT

16th of September 1889
Taklamakan Desert

They flew through the night without further incident. Algie may have dozed for a few minutes in spite of the dreadful whine of the engine. The noise worked its way into his nightmares as swarms of shrieking black flies that swarmed around him as he ran for shelter. Suddenly he broke open like *karakuri* and the flies filled up his exposed insides.

That's when he jerked awake.

He was still hanging from the passenger sling, rocking from side to side. The aircraft yawed sharply from starboard back to port and Algie realized that Ehmet was jerking them back and forth to wake him.

The pilot grinned when he saw Algie's eyes were open. He pointed down the High Silk Road towards the horizon. The tiny red dot at the far range of Algie's sight was the *Wu Zetian*. With the rising sun behind him, she looked lop-sided, as if her wings and engine outriggers had taken a beating from the two warships. He'd have to wait until they caught up to see.

It still took hours of flight to catch the wallowing merchant ship. As the sun rose up close to the meridian, Ehmet ran a little mad and revved the chiropter's spirit engine to its maximum. He gesticulated and whooped at the other pilot, challenging him to be the first to their target. It felt like riding a hawk stooping to catch a slow fat pigeon.

Algie was having the time of his life. It was hard for Algie to tell with her dangling on the far side of the other pilot, but he thought he saw Ayotunde laughing.

Algie wondered if Mme. Streif would be pleased to have him back, with or without the Governor's papers. He wondered if there was still a place for him amongst the *Lǎoshǔ*, the Conversors, and the Silk Empress' collection of human oddities.

He also wondered how he was going to get back on the airship.

The sensible method would be for all of them to touch down in the desert and have Algie and Ayotunde simply stroll over to the *Wu Zetian*. But the Von Siegling *Raubvogels* were balky craft. Landing face down while slung like a baby kangaroo in a pouch would be difficult, even painful, in even the softest sand. From what Algie had seen, they needed a full ground crew to launch. Algie had no idea if the chiropters could ever take off once they landed.

The next simplest plan would have Mme. Streif's vessel settle down to the ground along a soft and inviting dune. Then, he and Ayotunde could leap from the chiropters as they flew by at minimal speed to tumble heels over teakettle until they come to undignified halt. Again, some sensible strolling plus a bit of dusting off would follow.

All other plans which came to mind would be only suitable for a Dale Daring story.

Ayotunde's chiropter dropped to the *Wu Zetian*'s level and approached. Algie wondered how she intended to communicate with their people on the airship. Then, with chiropter and flying folly only a few hundred meters apart, he heard her shout. Over the sounds of both sets of engines, over the near to a kilometer's distance between them, he heard her yelling directions in French. He had almost forgotten that night of the Grand Entertainment and how inhumanly loud the Conversors could be. He didn't envy the other pilot for the headache he'd be getting from that.

His chiropter cut a lazy circle around the *Wu Zetian* as the

Conversors shouted back and forth like public address systems. As Ehmet held back and shook his head, Algie watched the *Lǎoshǔ* and other crewman break off their repair work to collect on the starboard side. Hawsers, deadeyes, and cargo nets were pulled out of stores and laid out on the mid-deck.

It looked like a Dale Daring solution was the order of the day. Algie wanted to engage in a long talk with Mssr. Patrouille about his bad influence on the airship.

Feng Po began shouting orders and gesticulating. As he did so, a triangular capture net took shape between the engine struts amidships, along the starboard railing to just below the flying bridge on the Texas deck. The *Lǎoshǔ* wove the odd pieces together, flitting about like an odd combination of spiders and monkeys.

The *Wu Zetian* cut her engines fifteen minutes later as the final touches were cinched down tight. Both of the Uyghur aircraft had idled their engines to conserve fuel. They circled the larger airship like vultures. By then, Ayotunde had shared with him the Conversors' plan: Both she and Algie would disengage from their slings and leap into the capture net as the chiropters flew low and slow along the starboard side. He'd done riskier things in the rigging of the *Wu Zetian*, but Algie was going to enjoy seeing Ayotunde take that dive.

The process of extricating herself while still in flight proved to be highly entertaining. Her chiropter made a close approach in the space between the ship's engines and wings, and the massive gas envelope like threading a needle. The Conversor leaped off at the right moment and landed squarely in the center of the net. Once she rolled her way to her feet in the garden of pagodas and silk flowers, she handed the stolen papers and Feng Po's ivory dragon head to Mme. Streif.

Then, she waved broadly to Algie for him to follow. Algie squirmed free of the passenger sling, being careful to hang on tight, as Ehmet circled around again make a bow to stern run along the side of the *Wu Zetian*.

That's when Ehmet pointed towards the western horizon and screamed.

Algie followed the pointing finger while trying to remember

what the Uyghur phrase meant. Something about a dog's mother.

Then Algie saw the dragon bearing down on the other Von Siegling chiropter.

It didn't entirely register as "dragon" at first. His eyes took in the enormous brass wings that seemed to block out the whole horizon and the maw the size of a repair hangar's front door. The glint of sunlight brought his attention to the serrated blades that acted as teeth for it.

Then, his brain said: *dragon*.

Next, his brain told him: *Dragon just ate chiropter*.

The gigantic jaws snapped shut around the Von Siegling, severing the wings and deflating the envelope in a single stroke. It popped inside the metallic mouth like a firecracker. Bits of wood, fabric, and pilot rained down on the desert.

Algie stopped extricating himself from his sling and concentrated his energies into screaming at Ehmet while gesticulating wildly. Ehmet clenched his jaw and opened the throttle. With a few quick tugs on the control loops, he put the aircraft into an impossibly sharp bank to port. The great metallic beast was suddenly beneath them. Algie's sling now hung down towards the pilot and he had to guard carefully against kicking him in the ribs.

Algie wrapped his arms around the straps of his harness and held on for dear life. Since Ehmet was now quite aware of the situation, he felt no need to scream anymore.

The chiropter levelled out from its banking turn and shot into sharp ascent. The engine screamed like a banshee. As Algie looked down again, he saw that their veering away from the *Wu Zetian* had caught the dragon's eye. It coiled back on itself like a question mark as it turned in mid-flight. Two flaps of its gigantic wings began to straighten it out and send it after Algie and Ehmet.

Algie thought to scream another warning, but decided that Ehmet had a good idea of what was coming.

The chiropter topped off its climb and went into an equally sharp descent. For a moment, Algie floated parallel to the craft, weightless, connected to it only by his death grip on the sling straps.

They picked up speed and Ehmet made another excruciating banked turn. Again, they moved away from the *Wu Zetian*. Ehmet must have already done the arithmetic of two lives against several dozen while Algie was panicking over being chewed up and swallowed. He shouted "Hold tight!" in Uyghur as he executed another maneuver that felt like the chiropter flipped all the way over. Their wild flight continued to lead the dragon away from the damaged merchant ship.

The great metallic beast twisted in the air again and snapped its jaws after the chiropter mere meters away from its tail rudder. They flew on past the dragon's enormous glass eye and its ornate horns, ears, and dorsal fins. Algie was close enough to hear the musical sounds its internal mechanisms made as it moved.

He also saw the makers mark embossed in the metal behind its right ear. It was an intricate eight-pointed running cross, a symbol he'd seen before on the neck of the *karakuri* caracal, along with every other clockwork creature his friend Zdan had in his entourage.

A glimmer of an idea formed in Algie's mind, but he didn't have the time to complete it.

One gigantic brass wing struck out at them, not coming near enough to knock them out of the sky. The storm-force winds it generated did the job, though.

The chiropter was thrown into a loop by the buffeting wind. Algie heard the wings wooden ribs snap as the engine strangled and died. The final twist of the craft threw him free of the passenger sling into free flight. He saw the dragon's serpent-like neck twist around after them. A terrifying set of brass teeth bore down upon them.

The jaws shot past him and closed around the Von Siegling chiropter. Algie flew on until he collided head-on with the angry ridge of scales right between the red-glowing glass eyes. He bounced off of the bridge of its nose and slid half-way down its ten-meter snout. Algie stopped sliding once he slipped his fingers under the metal scales and held on even more tightly than he had on the chiropter.

The creature's gigantic head bounced up and down for a few moments as it chewed and then swallowed. Then, it finally noticed that it had a stowaway on its snout. The eyes crossed their focus to see Algie, an effect that was both laughable and horrifying.

It vocalized, a sound Algie could only describe as a metallic grunt, like sledges against the hull of a Portsmouth ironclad, but angry. It shook its head to dislodge him, but Algie stuck tight like a magnetic mine. Algie heard pumps working inside the automaton's throat followed by the sound of rushing fluid. Wind and flames surged out of the mouth and nostrils.

Though some of the flames came close to scorching his hair and clothes, Algie held tight. The *karakuri* dragon lost interest in its little parasite and cast its head about to find the *Wu Zetian*. With its head twisted back over its left wing, it finally caught sight of the airship. She was several kilometers away by now, but that would be only a few minutes' flight.

The dragon bellowed, a totally different and devastating metallic sound, and blew a gout of flame her way. The dragon uncoiled itself to pursue.

Poor Ehmet had given his life to lead the dragon away, to no use in the end. Only Algie could save them now.

The thought he had begun earlier came to Algie fully formed. It was a stupid idea, but probably as effective as his Mermaid's Purse stratagem. Surviving it would be the part he hadn't worked out yet.

He pulled the Tuareg cross from inside his shirt and blew a tone on it. The effect was immediate. The dragon froze on the down stroke of its massive wings with its neck arched forward and jaws gaping.

Algie and the dragon fell slowly at first, as if the huge mass of metal had to be convinced that gravity still held sway at these altitudes. They gradually picked up speed. Algie was convinced the fall would be enough to kill them both.

Algie blew on the cross again, the same way he did with the Uyghur elder. Access panels swung open all across the automaton's head, neck, and body with an anguished screech. Like the other *karakuri* he had seen before, it was filled with amber cogs and golden light. At the base of the neck, he found what else he had expected: a huge cluster of fabric gas envelopes. The phlogiston inside wouldn't keep this much metal aloft, but it would reduce the amount of power the automaton would expend in flying.

Algie climbed up the dragon's head and down its neck to tuck himself between the gas balloons. It was the best and worst place to be when this whole contraption struck the earth. The envelopes would most likely act as cushions and protect him from the worst of the impact. They also happened to be filled with highly flammable gas that would most likely incinerate him.

Those were the best odds the house was offering, he thought, recalling how often Nilenha had used that phrase. He tucked his limbs under the broad canvas straps that secured the bladders and waited for the crash.

TWENTY-NINE

Unknown
Unknown

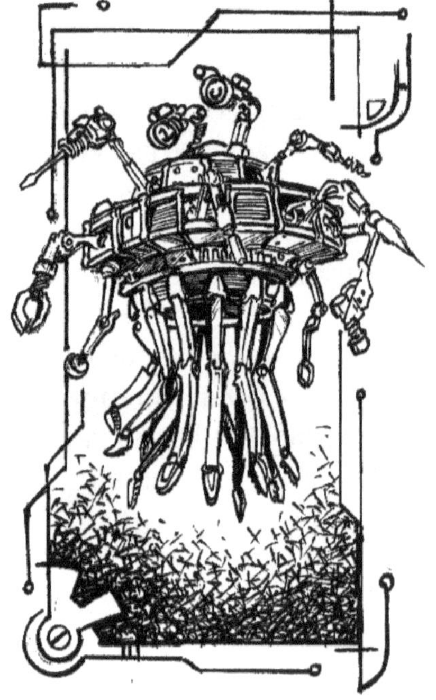

Algie awoke in darkness. His head felt thick, like it was filled with cotton batting. His mouth was dry and coated with something sticky and foul. He smacked his lips, rigid scaly things, and worked his tongue against the back of his teeth. He thought he felt gritty sharp edges.

A thunderous noise came to him, what he assumed to be the slow opening of enormous metal doors. He let his head loll off to that side. Bleary eyes made out a huge mound of gleaming metal in the dark chamber beyond. He blinked and squinted until he made out the broken corpse of the *karakuri* dragon laying on the dark stone floor.

He hurt.

His right leg felt to be filled with blades and broken glass. One of his arms ached to the bones from shoulder to fingertips; he couldn't feel or move the other. A slow catalogue of all his injuries actually made him chuckle.

I should be happy to hurt so much, he thought. *You don't feel anything when you're dead.*

He was distracted from his philosophizing by a new sound: thousands of footsteps on the stone floor. Hundreds of golden men gathered around the damaged automaton. Some probed it with their fingers, looking for hand holds. Others crouched low to wedge their shoulders beneath its bulk. None of these metallic workers had heads, just like Zdan's palanquin bearers. After several minutes of wordless jostling, they lifted the remains of the brass dragon and began to carry it away. The slow shuffling procession took a very long time. Eventually, the headless men and the broken dragon disappeared from his sight.

He heard the doors close and the overhead lights shut off with a mechanical "clunk" one by one. Algie was left alone in the darkness on a pile of what felt like discarded gas bladder skins and canvas straps. No one and nothing was coming back for him soon.

Hushed noise in the distance told him that there were things moving in the darkness, though they could have as easily been rats as more clockwork servants.

He called out in Uyghur, since he had still been above their lands when he had fallen from the sky. There was no response to his cries, really little more than whispers.

His halting Chinese did no better.

It made no sense for him to try English. The High Silk Road had little space for the language of empire. Algie tried anyway.

"Hello, is there anybody out there?"

All he heard in response was a faint echo of his own voice. The huge lightless chamber fell completely silent. It felt like whatever waited in the darkness was holding its breath.

"I'm frightened," he said. "Please, help me."

The burning of his eyes told him he was crying. Tears welled over and ran down the sides of his face. He was terrified, pained, and helpless.

He felt a weight on his chest and realized it was his Tuareg cross still hung around his neck after the crash. He picked it up with his good right arm and put it to his lips to blow. If there was anyone here in the darkness, the shrill sounds of the whistle should reach them.

Sharp sounds, like light, swift footfalls, came out of the dark. As they drew closer, the sound of metal dragged over stone grew louder. Whoever it was, they sounded to be whistling back.

*

Algie awoke again on a red leather couch. He could see light when he opened his eyes this time, the warm glow of an electric light. This room looked like it could be a room in the Turfan Governor's mansion. The furniture was equal parts British Empire and Uyghur handcraft. Now that his eyes could focus, he made out that the walls were hand-carved stone in the busy geometric style of the Moslems with much of the stone covered with Oriental woven tapestries. It was a much better experience than waking up on a cold trash heap.

He tried to sit up and felt a weight on his left side. His arm was immobilized in a mechanical brace made of the same golden brass metals as the caracal and the dragon. It was bound tight to his chest by a sling reclaimed from canvas strapping.

He flexed his fingers in an experimental fashion. Though stiff and achy, they responded. The arm itself was many disturbing colors from blood red and purple to jaundiced yellow towards the fringes. Black metal pins from the brace actually pierced his skin and looked to be anchored in the bone.

So, he thought, *while I was unconscious, someone picked me up and did major dry-dock repairs.*

He grasped the edge of the table beside him and pulled himself to sitting. This gave him a clear view of the little room, no more than five meters on a side, which looked like a typical doctor's treatment room. It had book shelves, glass cases of medical supplies, and rolling trays of shiny instruments. Photographs of various people and paper notes filled the odd spaces. He calculated the chances of his having been transported back to Turfan after his dragon crashed.

The odds were not good. If the Governor and his redcoats *had* found him in the desert, the best he could expect would be a shallow grave. If they were being particularly compassionate, they might kill him first.

Algie felt like exploring.

He swiveled his legs off the edge of the couch, slowly since they felt to be made of lead. His right leg made a loud metallic "clunk" as it struck the floor. Algie pulled up a pant leg to take a look.

The first thing that he noticed was that he was wearing new pants. They were stitched together from the scrap gas envelope fabric. Once he looked carefully, he saw why they were needed: his right leg, the one that had hurt him so much earlier, looked to be twice the size of his left. As he pulled up the right pant leg, Algie could see his leg was encased in a brace like the one on his arm.

Major repairs, he thought to himself with a smirk and a twitch. *And then they left me completely alone.*

With a push from his good hand, and no little trepidation, Algie rose to standing. He heard and felt a gentle hum coming from his leg brace. He felt the device literally pulling its weight so that his leg moved as if uninjured and unencumbered.

Algie was both impressed and pleased.

He was also feeling fairly thirsty.

A decanter and glasses sat on a tray on the table. Assuming that it was filled with water instead of stronger spirits, he began the slow circumnavigation of the couch to reach it. Algie took one slow step after another with his free arm held out before him in case of a slip. He reached the tray and poured himself a large glass of what did prove to be water.

He took small sips, remembering one of the August Vogel stories set in the Empty Quarter of Saudi Arabia that warned that a dehydrated man could founder if he drank to deeply. He savored it as it flowed over his mouth and throat, counteracting his headache almost immediately.

As he took deeper drinks, he smacked his lips and hummed to himself in satisfaction.

The double doors on the other side of the chamber pushed open and a tea tray rolled through the gap.

Algie saw nobody pushing the tea tray.

In the scheme of themes, considering everything he had seen in the last few days, it was a minor incongruity. Still, it gave him pause. He set down the water glass and called out to the tea tray:

"Hello?"

The tea tray did not respond, but it did stop.

Then, something came out from behind the cart.

It was obviously an automaton, a collection of limbs and tool extensions attached to a circular body, the size and shape of an inverted bushel basket. Its rolling stride on scythe-like legs moved it along quite briskly. It skittered around the couch to get a clear line of sight on Algie. Glassy eyes extended on multiple delicate arms to look him up and down.

"Conscious," it said in a vibrating brassy voice. "Mobile."

Algie was nonplussed. Was this thing on the floor an intelligent being or nothing more than an over-large multiplex knife? How should he treat it? He decided cordiality was probably the best course.

"May I ask your name?"

"Affirmative." The device settled down on its limbs and said nothing more.

Algie tried another tack.

"Who, or what, are you? If that isn't too rude to ask?"

The automaton flexed and resettled several of its limbs, as if it were shuffling its feet while thinking.

"Repair," it said. "Urgent."

That made the assorted wrench and clasper limbs sensible to Algie. It *was* a walking toolbox.

"Did you fix me?" The thing looked more adapted to metalwork than surgery, but Algie didn't want to be narrow-minded.

"Affirmative," it replied after a moment's silence.

Algie touched his braced-up arm, feeling how the pins sank into his flesh. It was all strangely painless.

"Well, thank you."

The device sat motionless on the floor. Algie didn't think it was being rude, but it may not have had a lot of experience with social niceties.

"You say 'You're welcome,' then."

The automaton remain silent and still for a few more moments. It rose to its many feet and said:

"You are welcome."

It skittered over to its original spot behind the tea tray. It pushed the cart to a position beside the couch and then moved away to face Algie again.

"You must eat food."

Algie realized that he really must. He sat on the couch and lifted the silver cloche from the plates. Breakfast consisted of some sort of curry, porridge, and flatbreads, a meal that called no single continent its home. His empty stomach didn't care to argue. He began shoveling food down his gullet with his fingers like the *Lǎoshǔ*.

"What should I call you?" Algie asked in a brief pause between mouthfuls.

"You called for help."

Algie supposed he had. He didn't really expect anyone to hear, though.

"No, I mean what is your name?"

The brass automaton spun in place a half turn counter-clockwise, and then a full turn the other way. After a thoughtful clenching and relaxing of several tool clusters, it settled down on its metallic haunches.

"I have no name." It sounded almost sad. "Urgent repair."

"That's not a name. That's your job."

"I am repair."

As if to prove it, the *karakuri* slid under the tea tray and began making fine adjustments on the ankle joint of Algie's leg brace. Multiple arms worked to loosen the laces that held that leg of his trousers closed. The complete lack of concern for his dignity and modesty made him think for a moment that he was back on the *Wu Zetian*.

The Wu Zetian.

Being injured and unconscious, he hadn't thought about his friends, his ship. In the moments before he and the dragon struck the desert floor, he remembered catching sight of the flying folly. The dragon had somehow damaged her even more than the British warships had done. He caught only a few seconds' sight of her limping back the way she had come.

"I need to get to Turfan," he blurted. "Can you help me?"

The mechanical repairman did up his trousers leg and scurried out into the open floor.

"Rapid transit?" it said brightly.

Algie repeated the words back to the machine. That would

be exactly what he would be needing to save his shipmates and the Uyghurs from whatever unpleasantness the Governor might be planning. He nodded and murmured thanks.

The automaton scurried towards the open doors with almost a spring in its insect-like step. Algie followed along behind as he tried to clear his mind.

He stopped short as he noticed a set of photographs on the wall that looked very familiar. One of the photos was of the Uyghur Elder Boway Kashgari standing in front of one of the local houses festooned with potted plants. Posted beneath that were extensive notes and mechanical specifications that all made a certain amount of sense after he'd seen the old man split open like a *karakuri*.

Beside that photo was one taken in the gardens of the Turfan Governor's Mansion. Algie recognized the spot. In the photo, he saw his new parents Governor and Mrs. St. George with the appropriate biological and mechanical notes hanging below, at least that's how he interpreted the mass of squiggles and hieroglyphs.

The automaton returned to stop behind Algie. It tapped its little metallic feet in impatience.

"Rapid transit?" it asked.

Algie barely heard. There were more paired photographs on the wall: an American Indian of the Plains with a Union Army General; an African tribesman bearing a leather shield and war-club with a British cavalry colonel; a Mongol horseman paired with a richly dressed Chinese courtier. These all figured in his penny dreadfuls as villains and heroes in exotic locales. Several more pairs hung there that Algie couldn't identify.

"Wh-what is all this?" Algie stammered as he tried to take it all in. "Who are these people?"

"Previous guests," the machine replied.

Algie's mind just stopped. A thousand questions should be asked and answered as he looked at what hung on this wall. Bookshelves and file cabinets stood right at his fingertips that he should have rifled. Dale Daring would have done it in a minute, even if bleeding and pursued by a villain's armed minions.

Algie couldn't make sense of it.

He needed to get back to Turfan. To find help from someone much older and bring them back here. Mssr. Patrouille and Mme. Streif came first to mind as experts in scheming.

He grabbed the picture of the St. Georges & their attached notes.

"We need to go," Algie said as he turned on his heel.

The automaton wheeled around and led him down the hall to wherever "Rapid Transit" was.

*

Like the Governor's Mansion, nothing in this place was clean or spare or functional. All the stone walls of the long hallway were either intricately carved or covered in luxurious tapestries. Every ten meters or so, little islands of habitation sprung up in the middle of the broad boulevards of polished stone. Furniture and equipment were laid out over an oriental rug in each of these, like sitting rooms just grown there like mushrooms. Some were small workshops, one even a smaller version of the medical bay he had awakened in a little while ago. Each seemed to have come from its own corner of the world.

Not a single person could be seen in the long hallways or the great round arches that pierced the walls. Just a battered boy and a somewhat crazed *karakuri* on a quest of indefinite distance.

Eventually, the little machine made a right turn through an arch way into a dark cavernous space. Algie followed it, but slowed to a cautious crawl as he lost sight of his feet.

"Into center," it urged when it saw his hesitation. "Automatic."

"Automatic? What's automatic?"

The overhead lights engaged with a startling electric sound he felt in his gut as much as heard. They revealed a broad stone chamber that could easily have held four or five soccer pitches. Little kiosks and the furniture groups were scattered along the perimeter. The far side of the room was dominated by a large stone globe and what seemed to be a world map laid into the wall with brass and semi-precious stones. Railway tracks cut through that wall behind it in parallel behind that map and led to tunnels going either way. A sleek teak wood and brass car waited on the nearest track

Algie walked over to that wall, squinting to make out all the stopping points and rail lines the map displayed. The brace on his injured leg seemed to be getting more efficient as he went along, with the device doing most of the work and him just coming along for the ride.

He recognized the rough outlines of the world continents. Some of the lines, if that was what they were, followed the High Silk Road connecting Eastern China with Europe, while others stretched south into India and north into Siberia. There seemed to be writing labelling all of it, a set of squiggles totally incomprehensible to him. It reminded him of the language he had seen amongst the Hindus or Indochinese. Points on the tracks were marked with the eight-point running cross he had seen as a maker's mark on the caracal and dragon.

Perhaps, those are other stations like this one, he thought.

A particularly large symbol marked the island of Ceylon, south of the tip of India. Algie recognized it from charts; he had stopped there with Feng Po and his charges on their way from Capetown. Running his finger over the design, the slightest pressure slipped it into the stone face with a click.

The running cross glowed with light from behind, along with the line that led to the tiny island on the map. A low hum came from the brass and wood carriage on the track to his right. Running and interior electric lights switched on with mechanical sounds. The motor made a noise that made him fear for an explosion. He tapped the symbol again before anything untoward could happen.

Algie looked over his shoulder at the automaton that sat on the stone floor behind him.

"Rapid transit?"

"Affirmative."

Algie supposed that if he were to get into that vehicle and hit the right controls, it would shoot into the nearest tunnel and careen off to Ceylon.

But he didn't want to go to Ceylon.

He re-traced the line that lead to Ceylon to find the starting point. If the system followed logical rules, that would be the marker for "You Are Here." Operating on the assumption that he was somewhere in or underneath the Taklamakan Desert, the track that crossed west to east would next stop at Turfan.

It was an incredible leap of logic, but it was at least some kind of action, and far better than sitting here just talking to an ambulatory toolbox. He pressed the button and held his breath as the carriage activated again with a building hum of power. A door opened in its side automatically.

It was time to leave.

"Would you mind if I gave you a name?" Algie asked the automaton.

"No objection."

Algie was thinking of a rat terrier his father had brought home many years ago. It was in the habit of chasing its own tail frequently, inspiring him to name it after the spinning ball speed governors on most steam engines.

"I'm going to call you Flyball.' Is that all right with you?"

The *karakuri* fidgeted its multiple limbs and tools as it contemplated the suggestion. It stopped and replied:

"Affirmative."

Algie climbed into the carriage and looked over the control panel. It was labeled in more squiggles and a few buttons and levers. Very simple, but complex enough to make it a risk to life and limb if he started activating them at random.

"I need to get back to Turfan," he said. "I will probably need a friend's help to do that. You coming along, Flyball?"

The automaton scampered over to the edge of the stone floor and stretched its limbs to step into the carriage. It climbed up onto seat beside Algie. "Affirmative," Flyball said as it tapped the controls, which closed the door and directed the vehicle to slowly advance down the tracks into the tunnels.

THIRTY

17th of September 1889
Beneath Turfan

There were quite a few ways to measure speed aboard an airship: calculating from time between mile posts; a wind sock and a spring scale, even an anemometer. None were of any use in the tunnel carriage. The best Algie could do was to hold up his hand outside the glass windscreen and calculate by touch.

The breeze felt roughly twice as strong as what he experienced in the Uyghur chiropter. Those were rated at a top airspeed of thirty-five knots. The rough maths Algie did in his head put their velocity at over one-hundred and twenty kilometers per hour. He didn't know before this that humans could survive such speeds.

"Rapid transit," he told his new mechanical companion.

"Affirmative," Flyball replied.

The marker lights imbedded in the smooth stone ceiling whisked by faster and faster. It took them roughly five hours to get to their next stop.

*

The carriage slowed to a stop with a squeal of brakes and a hiss of hydraulics. Of their own accord, the doors opened on either side.

Algie stepped up onto the stone platform of this station, moving tenderly due to his injuries and the stiffening of his joints from a long sedentary period. Bright lights imbedded in the walls and ceiling illuminated the vaulted chamber, but still he was concerned with what might be waiting for him here. Flyball, with no such concerns built into its clockwork brain, hopped out of the carriage and made a quick circuit of the perimeter.

Three ornately carved arches in the wall opposite the tracks led to their own spiral staircases. Algie stopped in front of them, feeling bemused.

"So, which one should we take?" he asked Flyball.

The *karakuri* examined the floors and lower steps of each of the three foyers. It stationed itself in the rightmost archway and declared in a voice like a fuzzy trumpet:

"More people here."

"You're saying more people went up and down those stairs than the others?"

"Affirmative."

"Hmmm."

Flyball pit-a-patted from one archway to another with its eyestalks slowly leaning this way and that. It seemed to be killing time as Algie ruminated.

"Is more better?" it asked.

Flyball may have had a point. More people, wearing their tracks deeper into the stone and metal of the stairway, were probably going to a place they counted to be more important. But more people would be more likely to see Algie and Flyball. He didn't know about the little automaton, but Algie was sure he himself was not ready for fight or flight.

If there were only two choices, he would have flipped a coin. If he still had a copper to his name, that is. Mssr. Patrouille had often said that more was better. He would trust that the French peacock knew something that he did not

"We'll go this way," Algie said, pointing to the right.

Flyball skittered over to the bottom step and leaned over on its side. The half-meter core of its body was wide enough to take the steps easily. With the multiple legs and limbs working in coordination, it clambered up the stairs with great rapidity. Algie found himself striving with some effort to keep up the pace.

*

It took them eight flights of stairs to reach the first exit. Six times, there were long, featureless hallways which led to the next staircase. Algie had no idea where he was when he got off the underground railway car. He felt even more lost by the time he reached that first door.

The door itself was made of steel, but decorated as ornately as the stonework in the tramway underground. Algie took hold of the bar handle embossed with floral patterns, turned it to disengage the latch, and slid it into its pocket in the stone wall.

He saw only darkness on the other side. Faint streaks of light glinted in the distance like cracks in a wall. The only certainty was the rough-hewn stone floor that remained visible two or three meters past the door. The possibility of traps and pitfalls seemed high. He looked down at the automaton which was slowly advancing into the passageway, one insectoid limb at a time.

"So, what do you think?" he asked. "Do we make our way down to the other end by touch?"

Flyball extended one of its tool extensions, a small bulb of brass and crystal.

"Illuminate!"

A bright light shone from the bulb that made the carved stone shaft nearly bright as day. The *karakuri* scampered forward with confidence.

"After you," Algie muttered to himself.

As he followed his clockwork friend, the door slid closed behind them. He devoutly hoped that whatever blocked off the other end of this tunnel could be opened.

It took only a minute or two for Flyball to reach the barrier on the other end. It climbed halfway up the crude wood surface as it probed for locks and handles with dozens of tools and pincers. Making quick work, it clicked the latch and pushed the door open outwards into a dimly lit underground hallway. They quickly slid through and pressed the door closed again, not knowing who might be there to catch them in the act. Flyball dimmed his light.

Once Algie was confident that there were no witnesses, he took a moment to examine his surroundings. What had looked like a plain wooden door on the inside was disguised as the front of several stacked moving crates on this side. The hall they stood in was lined in crates, an impromptu storage space filled with odds and ends. The dusty walls and floor somehow seemed familiar, though.

"Come this way," he told the *karakuri*.

They advanced around a bend in the hall and crept along close to the wall until they reached a door that most likely led to a basement storeroom. It looked exactly like the one he had been locked behind not so many days ago. He thought he heard a little dog barking on the other side of it.

"Can you open this lock?" Algie asked Flyball.

He heard a familiar woman's voice call out over the barking:

"Oh, I wish you would, Master Piggrem."

Algie stood there, for a moment gobsmacked. Then, he waved towards the ancient lock.

"If you would, please?"

"Affirmative."

Flyball unfolded a set of picks and went to work. The door clicked open within seconds.

Mme. Streif sat primly on a low stool with her skirts pulled tight around her ankles. Kosciusko, her black and white little dog vibrated with contained fury on her lap. It became totally unhinged upon seeing the *karakuri*. Mme. Streif seized the scruff of its fluffy neck with one hand which silenced it.

"Don't be so rude to our saviors," she said. "What brings you to our elegant retreat, Master Piggrem?"

He thought over the various modes of transport which had brought him there: powered chiropter, falling clockwork dragon, automatic underground tram. It was altogether too much to discuss in less than five hours.

"I believe this is the same room that the Governor had me

locked in."

"Well, he always struck me as lacking originality." She let the dog hop down to the floor and held up a hand to Algie. "Please help an old woman to her feet."

He was afraid at first that she expected him to lift her weight, but all that was necessary was for him to provide a steady anchor for her to pull against. Again, that thing about her spine not bending in certain conditions.

"Thank you," she said. "The first few inches rising up out of your seat are the hardest."

"You're welcome," he said. "Where is everyone else?"

"They are confined on the ship, in one of the repair bays. The Governor wanted me here as his personal guest. He's pressing piracy charges."

"I think that might be Mrs. St. George's doing. She hates you, you know."

The old woman settled her skirts in their proper places and then blinked at him with barely concealed amusement.

"The world is full of surprises, don't you think?" She held up a finger. "As an example, you should be dead. We saw the dragon devour your little aircraft before it crashed into the desert. So, I was quite surprised to hear you at my door. Pleased, but surprised nonetheless."

Her dog crept out from behind her skirts and threatened Flyball with a low, throaty growl.

"And what is this elegant little device?" she asked.

"This is Flyball." Algie tapped his arm brace with his knuckles. "It fixes things."

"Urgent repair," the *karakuri* said. "Rapid transit."

The dog barked urgently.

"Noisy canine."

Algie took in the dusty improvised dungeon. It had seemed like a bit of adventure to be imprisoned here with Dr. Cookworthy. It was absolutely unacceptable for the Silk Empress.

"We need to get you out of here."

"I concur. Where can you put me?"

The dog could restrain itself no longer. It broke out in a fierce spate of barking aimed at the brass automaton.

Flyball swiftly extended all its limbs and extensions to make it three times its normal size. It backed up the threat display with a sound like a warning klaxon that hurt Algie's ears.

The dog wet the stone floor beneath it and retreated beneath Mme. Streif's dress, squealing all the way.

"Now we need to get out of here *immediately*." Algie leaned over to speak with Flyball. "Do *not* do that again!"

"Self-preservation." The automaton sounded contrite, though a little defensive.

"Just don't!"

He turned back to Mme. Streif.

"I'm sure somebody heard that, and they'll be down here to check it out."

"Lead on, Master Piggrem." She scooped up her quivering lapdog as she spoke.

As luck would have it, he had been spending a good deal of his time exploring the Governor's Mansion after the *Wu Zetian* left. He'd found the servants' hidden passages and doors between the walls that led everywhere in the building. Even down to the basement.

Algie led her and Flyball to the basement pantry, which had its own dedicated stairway up to the kitchens. There was no one there and so they ascended the stairs and slipped past the few local servants working the stoves and cook fires. The scent of roasting meat and fresh bread nearly turned Algie away from his goal. Instead, he barreled down the long tile-floored hallway that led over to the residential wing.

"It would seem," Mme. Streif said between heavy breaths, "from your pace that you have somewhere specific you are taking us."

"Definitely. I've been gone for a few days, so the one place no one will be looking for anyone would be my room."

They made a quick left turn into the stairwell leading up to the backside of his old room. A young woman with flaxen hair and hazel eyes practically collided head-first with them. Everyone froze not knowing what, if anything, should be said. Algie was the first to break the silence.

"I think we met before," he said in Uyghur. "I sure you

surprised to see I not dead."

THIRTY-ONE

17th of September 1889
Turfan

Fortunately for all involved, the Governor inspired loyalty even less than he inspired love. The Uyghur housemaid, Aynur was her name, swiftly and silently guided them to Algie's quarters. Tea and biscuits arrived soon after they did.

The local servants started to gather there, most with helpful items in hand. Hot water and soap, bandages, and fresh clothes poured in. A painted screen came in to separate Algie from Mme. Streif.

Algie stripped down to his skivvies and cleaned up with the help of the maids. Once again, his leg was problematic. None of his trousers would go over the brace. One of the Indian princeling's robes still lurked in the bottom of his trunk. He was relieved that this one was dark blue with a minimal amount of tarnished silver braid, something that wouldn't embarrass him too much in front of his shipmates.

The screens came down like the walls of Jericho to reveal Mme. Streif in a white and red embroidered Uyghur dress. It hung strangely off her corset and bunched up around her bustle.

"At least," she said with a wry smile, "it's clean."

The locals chattered amongst themselves, and to Algie and Mme. Streif, completely forgetting their stations. It seemed that in rebelling against the Empire and crippling two armored British airships, Mme. Streif had become a bit of a folk hero. Freeing her from the Governor's inadequate dungeon allowed Algie to bask in some of that glory.

Sufficiently sated on black tea and tamarind cookies, Algie finally got around to questioning Mme. Streif.

"What exactly happened with your escort ships? I saw what was left of them on my way to meet you."

"They betrayed us, of course," she said after a sip of tea. "Or, they intended to. Captain Strausser and Mister McLaren were keeping a weather eye on them and unveiled Master Liu's latest surprise just as they were opening their gunports."

"The Mermaid's Purse?"

"No, this was something Mister McLaren never had a chance to show you." The old woman gave a rather dark chuckle. "It's called the Monkey King. It's an incendiary device with a clever bit of clockwork that lets it climb a cable up to its target quite quickly."

"And how did you get cables attached to two aluminum-armored gunships before they blew you out of the sky?"

"Mistress Chabi is a most excellent archer. Dr. Cookworthy is also surprisingly good. College intramurals, he said." Mme. Streif favored him with a malevolent smile which told the whole story of that battle. Then she turned her attention to the biscuit tray. "These little tamarind tarts really are excellent. I can see why they're your favorites."

Algie knew that was all of that story he would get until he had a chance to see Feng Po. He took his turn to relate to her everything that had happened to him since he'd found her cryptic message in the bottom of his trunk. The dozen or so Uyghurs in the room discreetly ignored him. Or, perhaps they didn't speak French.

"We are now in need of a plan to get you, me, and the *Wu Zetian* out of Turfan," Algie declared once he had summed up. "Do you have any ideas, ma'am?"

"Only the broadest of sketches," she said. "You?"

"I was hoping for something simple. Perhaps, slink out the back servants' quarters exit, run for our lives back to our airship, and then fly away, very fast."

Mme. Streif shook her head.

"Our crippled fish is not flying anywhere at any speed."

"What's damaged? The gas envelope? The maneuvering wings?"

"The spirit engines. The armed guards on the forecastle deck probably won't allow our crew a free hand at the repairs."

Algie thought upon the situation for a short while. An inspiration struck him.

"Flyball!" he called out.

The little automaton was straining to look out the window, several of its insectoid legs perched on the windowsill. It seemed to be watching birds. It plopped down to the floor and skittered over to Algie's feet. The Uyghurs gave it a wide berth.

"Request, Algie?" Flyball had developed a pleased tone to its metallic voice. "Urgent repair?"

"Could you repair a damaged alcohol spirit turbine?"

"Affirmative."

"All right," he said to Mme. Streif. "I think we have a working plan."

Mme. Streif allowed herself to express the slightest amount of distress in her stoic expression.

"You intend to unleash that device on my airship? What makes you think we can trust it?"

"It braced up my wounds," Algie explained. "I think it was repairing the fallen dragon."

"I wouldn't take that as a recommendation. Why does it obey your orders?"

He had to stop and think about that. He had never considered why the little *karakuri* had behaved like a friend; he had just so desperately needed one. He believed that Flyball had bonded to him like a puppy when it could have just as easily disassembled him in his sleep.

"Flyball," Algie said.

It looked up at him with earnestly extended eyestalks and pliers and pincers limbs pressed together in attitude almost like prayer. It made a soft metallic sound like a gentle gong.

"Why do you take my orders?" he continued. "Why did you

follow me from the caverns?"

"Urgent request," it chimed. "English command."

Algie knew he was going to need a long rest in a quiet place for the number of times this day he had been struck speechless.

"You mean, you follow me because you are built to take orders in English?"

"Affirmative," the automaton replied. "Gave override."

It repeated the random whistling noises Algie first made with the cross in that cavern under the desert. They must have been some sort of accidental command besides.

Algie swiveled his head back to Mme. Streif. Her expression was mild, but detached.

"Why on Earth would a mechanism that operates in a cavern underneath the Western Chinese desert be designed to accept commands in English?" he asked.

"I am mystified. I am very good at rooting out the secrets of men's hearts, but this..." she stretched out an open palm towards the clockwork device. "This might as well be something living on the moon."

Algie bit his lip. He had just registered that he had been alternating between English for Flyball and French for Mme. Streif in this conversation. He was going to be needing a long, long rest when this was all done.

"This seemed like a good idea five seconds ago."

"Don't dare to start that now, young Master Piggrem. Your intuition and quick-thinking have carried you through circumstances few adults except my Conversors could hope to survive. I am depending upon you to do something both brilliant and short-sighted."

Algie couldn't recall Dale Daring having a day like this. Not even August Vogel, who was far more bookish and subject to bouts of melancholy. The fear he was feeling now, the restrictive doubt, that wasn't something boy adventurers succumbed to. It happened to him because he had stopped to think. The only way forward was to stop thinking.

"If you trust me," he told Mme. Streif, "I believe I can make this work."

"I never for a moment stopped trusting you," she replied. "I just needed a good excuse to leave you behind with that horrible St. George woman."

*

They'd hid Mme. Streif in his quarters as well as one could with a woman her age and then dispersed. Even one servant attending to a vacant room would cause suspicions. Algie and Flyball slid into the service corridors, down the internal stairs, and out of the mansion through the kitchens. He wore a Uyghur dress and headscarf as he rushed to the milk cart Aynur held at the gate. Flyball was covered with a bag of turnips Algie pretended to carry. It was an imperfect disguise, but worked for the few seconds needed.

None of the Governor's guards or BC&I red coats showed themselves in this back corner. Aynur waited not a second to give them to appear. She whipped up the cart and they were into the stream of traffic that led to the repair shops to the west.

The river of humanity that always flowed through the heart of Turfan most days had dried up to the level of a piddling creek. The drop off made for quick passage through the caravanserai, but it also saddened Algie to see it. The *picaroons* and the karakuri dragon had almost shut down the flow of commerce along the High Silk Road. The poor merchants and workers of Turfan that depended upon them were suffering the most for it.

Even the usually bustling airship repair shops were only operating at one-quarter capacity. Times were hard for most everyone in Turfan, except the Governor, Boycott, and their lot. Very little interfered with Aynur and Algie until they got to the base of the repair elevator where the *Wu Zetian* was moored.

A single redcoat, gaunt and tanned like an old shoe, stood just outside the elevator cage for repair workers. He did not seem particularly attentive, but his size and the musket he carried guaranteed that no one would get past him without a struggle.

Algie and the Uyghur woman exchanged nervous glances, but said nothing. She pulled the bottom part of her headscarf across her face and secured it as a veil, in the fashion of the most devout Moslems. She gestured for Algie to do the same. With it in place, he hoped he would pass for a harmless little girl.

"You stay here," he told Flyball in English.

Algie and Aynur took up their covered baskets of baked goods and strolled over to the armed guard. They had no real plan except that Algie would get them into the elevator.

"Bugger off, you two," the guard shouted, "nobody's allowed around here!"

Aynur responded with a string of babble in her native tongue. Though it sounded cheerful and friendly, it was a laundry list of insults reserved for the British invaders. Algie joined in, though his remarks were more personal, like: "It's a shame that your parents didn't have any children that lived."

Algie moved in a steady straight line for the wrought iron gate. The guard made to stop him with a heavy hand clamped on his shoulder. Algie dropped his basket and clamped both hands around the big man's wrist. He had no intention to inflict pain, but his weeks of movement training had taught him how the laws of human nature and physics could do all the inflicting for him.

The boy, instead of pulling away as would have been natural, gently pushed back and drove his opponent backwards off his point of balance. The larger man snarled and shoved back, hard. Algie planted himself as a fulcrum to lever the other's mass around and over in a single seamless curve.

The redcoat guard struck the tarmac teeth first.

Algie quickly rolled the moaning man over onto his back. Jakinda had taught him several blows to the chin, jaws, and throat that would incapacitate a man without killing him. The moaning stopped shortly thereafter.

Algie stood up, straightened his dress, and took up his basket of goodies. Aynur, still veiled, stared at him with eyes large and round as silver dollars. She rocked slightly from side to side as if she were deciding whether to follow or run away screaming.

"Here, could you help me drag him away?" Algie asked in Uyghur. "We cannot just leave him where someone could see him."

The woman shook herself out of her paralysis and grabbed the fallen guard by one shoulder of his uniform. Together, they hid him behind the elevator shaft and covered him with some empty cement and asphalt bags.

"Come along, Flyball!" Algie shouted as he pressed the button to summon the elevator car from its upper levels. The automaton leaped and scampered over to him as the car noisily descended.

Aynur was getting back into the dogcart when he looked her way. She shouted something as she pulled away, something about her bringing him more of something, though he couldn't work out what that might be.

In the minute or so it took the elevator to come to him on the ground level, Algie sketched out vaporous plans for how he might not be shot by the next set of guards.

THIRTY-TWO

17th of September 1889
Turfan Caravanserai

The elevated repair platform, some thirty meters from the ground, made for an escape-proof prison camp. The eighty or so crew and passengers of the airship sat on the platform adjoining the repair cradle. They were only partially shaded from the midday sun by *Wu Zetian's* enormous gas envelope. The Conversors had their parasols and fans to keep them cool, but most of the others looked to be melting. The American bridge crew had shed their woolen uniform tunics and the Chinese men had simply stripped down to the waist. Poor Chen Bolin had his metal hand taken away as a possible weapon.

Looking out from the elevator car, Algie counted eight armed guards on the platform. They stood spread out around the edges of the platform, no two any closer than ten meters apart. With the long guns they carried, seven of them could shoot Algie as he engaged the eighth. He had been shot once already this year, and he'd like to keep it that way at least until Christmas.

The sound of bamboo struts striking rigging caught his attention. He finally noticed the local workmen that swarmed over the airship, securing her for storage and venting away the phlogiston for safety. There might have been as many as two dozen of the locals surrounding the guards surrounding his friends. Their chances didn't look good when armed with only sheath knives and spanners.

But the guards, Algie thought to himself, *did look terribly hungry.*

"Stay right here," he told Flyball, "and don't make a sound."

The automaton nodded an affirmative with multiple limbs.

Algie secured the lower half of his headscarf across his lower face and opened the folding elevator gate.

"*Assalaamu alaikum*," he shouted in his highest, most girlish voice. He waved at the nearest guard and held up the basket with his good arm. Pretty much everyone was staring at him wearing a dress now. He screwed his courage to a sticking place and walked over to the redcoat. He emphasized his limp to seem even more harmless.

"What are you doing up here, Miss?" the guard grumbled. "Johnson shouldn't have let you pass."

Algie could have told him that Johnson had let him pass because he was unconscious and bleeding from the nose, but that would not have advanced his plan. Instead, he waved the basket of baked goods under the older man's nose and said:

"Food!"

Algie said it in English, but in a way that he hoped would sound like he didn't speak the Queen's English. He added:

"Food from mansion."

The guard took the basket in both hands as Algie pulled the checked cloth off to uncover some of Meryem's best baking: bread, and rolls, and tamarind cookies, and treacle tarts. The scent wafted up into the guard's nostrils and drove away all sense and caution. He waved over his companions to join him.

"Hey, Archie! C'mere and see what the little girl brought us!"

Shortly, all eight were gathered around the basket and wolfing down treats. The Uyghurs who had been working above them had stopped to watch. Algie moved towards them and called out in their language:

"Please tell me these men are as stupid as they seem."

The workmen tending to the airship's gasbag, acted startled by his remark, but they smiled and nodded agreeably. Several shouted back:

"Who are you?"

"I am the boy called Pig," he replied in a high clear sing-song which he hoped would convince the guards he was a Moslem girl. "I used to fly on this ship. I served the Silk Empress in opposing the governor here."

Ayotunde evidently heard and understood. She stood, discarding her parasol and folding her fan. Most of the guards had their backs to her. The others were too busy feeding their faces to care.

"I met with your *Boway* Kashgari and *Sardar* Pakhirdin in their retreat in the *qanats*. They gave me help to return to this ship before the British warships could shoot them down."

Algie had their complete attention. Some were already making secure their belay lines to descend. The other Conversors were following the African woman's lead while, at the same time, silently urging the others to stay low to avoid bullets. Ayotunde began to creep up on the guards like a cat stalking a bird.

"That scary old woman was a prisoner in the caravanserai," Algie said. He didn't dare use her name for fear the guards might recognize it. "Up until twenty minutes ago. Now she is in hiding and waiting for this ship to make her escape."

That amused the Uyghurs quite a bit. Algie could see from the corner of his eye that the Conversors were surrounding the gorging guards in slow and stealthy steps.

"We need this ship ready for the air again. We need the guards restrained," he continued. "Will you please help us?"

The workmen looked amongst themselves. With a laugh, they dispersed across the superstructure of the airship. Algie felt his stomach drop, convinced as he was that he had failed.

He was still trying to formulate a new plan when several ropes dropped from above. The dock workers slid down those ropes to land around the guards. The commotion finally distracted the redcoats from their eating. As they looked up, the Conversors closed the distance and peeled away the long guns slung over their shoulders. The Uyghurs, armed with wrenches and blunt implements, pressed in as a wall of disapproving muscle. Those in the center quickly realized the sudden reversal of their fortunes and surrendered.

The whole lot of BC&I men were wrapped up and gagged within five minutes. The Conversors gently laid them out in a row like a prize catch from a good day's fishing. With the Governor's lackeys properly squared away, the *Wu Zetian* prisoners began to rise to their feet and surround the unknown girl in the head scarf and veil. Ayotunde, the only one of Mme. Streif's women who understood Algie's speech, put a hand on his shoulder.

"Excellent work, Pig," she said in French. She quickly corrected herself. "I'm sorry. Algie. We were not expecting you to come to our rescue."

Nilenha playfully tugged on the end of his headscarf to reveal his face.

"Come on and show us your pretty face, Ma'mselle. *Chopon!*"

He felt a blush rising in his cheeks, but he uncovered his face in spite of that. The sound of two dozen shocked conversations swept the platform as his shipmates finally saw his face. The *Lǎoshǔ* raised a triumphant roar and swarmed Algie from all sides. He bent a knee to avoid going down under their weight with a broken leg.

The adults around him peeled off the other boys one by one.

"Get off of him, you heathens!" Feng Po McLaren roared as he held Peng and Mateo aloft in either hand. "We have time enough for this later."

The *Lǎoshǔ* dispersed and regathered in pursuit of a red rubber ball he rolled in the direction of the American bridge crew.

"I'm quite pleased to have you back from the dead, Pig." Feng Po said. "You didn't happen to see my sainted mother, did you?"

"I wasn't dead," Algie said flatly.

"Pity. I have missed her."

Jakinda exchanged a dubious look with him.

"What message do you bring from Mme. Streif?" she asked. "What does she need?"

"We need to get the *Wu Zetian* air-worthy immediately," he

replied. "Could we have Jean-Pierre and Dietrich brought over here?"

As the two engineers were retrieved, Ayotunde organized the disposal of the guards. The Uyghur dockworkers placed them in one of the clapboard storerooms to one side of the platform and nailed the door shut.

Liu Jean-Pierre looked over-stressed and disheveled like a parrot about to go into molt. The German looked mildly amused as always, and pleased to once again to be in the company of the Conversors.

"What does the ship need to fly again?" Algie asked them.

"A week in dry-dock," was Jean-Pierre's dour response. Dietrich guffawed and then fell silent under warning looks from the Conversors.

"The absolute minimum? What would get us to the next caravanserai?"

"Rebuild the starboard engine and struts," Jean-Pierre said. "Emergency repairs to the rigging and the new control ring."

"If you were to get help, could you get that all done in a couple of hours?"

Young Mr. Liu goggled at him for a moment.

"That depends on what sort of help you could get up here on short notice."

"You should appreciate this," Algie said with a smile. "Flyball!"

The accordion gate flew open with a clatter and the automaton emerged at a flat run. It normally skittered sideways like a crab, but it spun on its axis on a multitude of metal legs at higher speeds. The impression was that of a sawblade on the loose.

Liu Jean-Pierre slid uneasily behind Algie and Dietrich as the mechanism approached.

"What is this *dingsum*[21]?" Dietrich asked, still calm and bemused.

By then, it had arrived.

"Urgent request?" Flyball intoned in a brassy voice.

"Gentlemen, this is Flyball. It does repairs on things." He pulled up the hem of his dress to display the calf and ankle of his leg and its brace. As he flexed his ankle, brazen plates and cogs moved in intricate interplay.

"Is that your leg?" Jean-Pierre sounded on the edge fainting.

"No. It's just a brace." Algie spoke to the automaton now. "These are two of my friends. They need to make some urgent repairs."

"Urgent repairs?" Flyball's metallic voice sounded like a trumpet fanfare.

"Most urgent. Could you help them with that while I take care of a few things?"

It twitched its eyestalks from side to side as if thinking deeply.

"Affirmative."

The automaton scrambled up the *Wu Zetian*'s hull and across the struts of the starboard engine to disassemble the bullet-riddled cowling.

"Am I supposed to trust this thing?" Jean-Pierre asked.

"I'll keep an eye on this, *reparatursache,*[22]" Dietrich chuckled. "Hit it with a monkey wrench if it causes any trouble."

The three of them were distracted by the sound of the massive cargo elevator arriving at the platform. A good dozen dock men and technicians rode the open platform, escorted by Aynur. She directed them towards the airship with shouts and gestures.

"That should be enough help, don't you think?" Algie said.

Liu Jean-Pierre blinked at him until he jerked himself out of his nervous paralysis.

"I'll get right on this." The Chinese engineer rushed to intercept the crew headed for his airship. Dietrich jogged to catch up, and Flyball ran in tight little circles around them both.

"Give him orders in English!" he shouted after them. "He likes that!"

"And now, to retrieve our Silk Empress," Algie said to himself.

He turned towards the elevator and found Feng Po and two of the Conversors standing in his way.

"Not without us, you won't," Jakinda said.

21 "whatchamacallit" German
22 "Repair device" German

THIRTY-THREE

17th of September 1889
Turfan Caravanserai

Algie, familiar through his mother with the intricacies of modern women's dress, had been impressed with how quickly Ayotunde and Jakinda had changed into servants' uniforms provided by Aynur. Once in costume, the Conversors put their heads down and the three of them melted into the stream of female servants at the Governor's Mansion. They left Feng Po in the kitchen to keep a watch on their path of escape and the output of the bakery.

Algie had tried to tell the Conversors everything he had seen and heard in the underground realm of the *karakuri*. When his intelligence ran out, so did his courage. He longed to speak with the women, to discuss their plan, and his place in their future plans. He was too frightened to open his mouth, and it wasn't for fear of discovery. He instead held fast the loose end of his veil with his braced hand as he carried the enamel night-soil pot with the other.

The two Conversors followed swift on his heels with arm-loads of linens. Their lower faces were covered, too. The few times he looked over his shoulder as they traversed the stairs and hallways, the women's eyes looked determined, even murderous.

The between the walls traffic slowed to a crawl as they came up to the floor of Algie's old quarters. The three had a hushed conversation in French. Algie pointed out the final direction and Ayotunde led their little group. She brought them to the door of the resident's hallway like an angry icebreaker in pursuit of the Northwest Passage.

Everything stopped there.

Though Algie could see nothing, because even the average Uyghur woman was still taller than him, he could hear their whispers:

"The infamous Lady Streif escaped and is now re-captured. Not even she can outwit Boycott and the Governor."

He wriggled between the women until he got a clear line of sight on the door to his room. Sullen men in redcoats flanked Mme. Streif and her dog as they were coming out. The guards held pistols in their fists and looked to have no qualms in using them. As they approached Algie, he felt himself being pulled backwards into the crowd. Honestly, the number of times this happened in the presence of the Conversors, he considered having reinforced handles sewn into his clothing.

"We need to choose our field of battle wisely," Jakinda whispered in his ear. "Innocent people might get shot in a close-quarters scuffle. Or even us..."

They waited until Mme. Streif and her armed escort had passed. After that, they didn't as much follow them as allowed themselves to be buoyed along by the crowd of servants who did.

The trip wasn't very far. Mme. Streif and her yapping dog were taken to the Governor's Library. Algie heard the Governor's and Boycott's voices in conversation when the doors were opened. Four of the armed men took up posts outside as the rest turned the corner.

"They're probably going to stake out the servants' entrance to the library," Algie whispered.

"No doubt," Ayotunde responded.

"So, what do we do?"

Ayotunde looked thoughtful, then told Jakinda:

"I defer to your age and experience."

"I will not rise to the bait of a reference to my age," Jakinda replied with hushed serenity, "but I do believe I have a plan."

*

Ayotunde quickly acquired a serving tray, champagne in a bucket, and all the necessary accoutrements. These she placed in Algie's hands and then pointed him towards the servants' corridor that backed up to the library. Four more of the BC&I guards stood about the door to the library. This lot didn't look as sullen or dangerous as most of them.

Algie had not been in this corner of the mansion before. He was surprised to see another elevator cage that led to the lower levels. He had no chance to point this out as he approached the door with a Conversor on either shoulder.

"Not to be rude," said one of the guards, "but the Governor doesn't want to be disturbed, he doesn't want any refreshments, and he doesn't want *you*. Please, move along."

"But you don't understand," Jakinda said, exuding that deviltry she specialized in. "This is all a ruse."

Algie nearly twisted his head off his neck looking over his shoulder.

"What?"

Ayotunde nodded in agreement with a smile that troubled Algie more than the suspicious looks from the men with guns.

"Yes, we're deadly female assassins in the employ of Mme. Streif," Jakinda continued, "and we're here to free her."

She started speaking to the guards in the same sultry, flirting manner she used on Mssr. Patrouille so often.

"But, now that we see that there are four of you of such obvious strength and competence, there is no other option than for us to surrender."

"There isn't?" Algie said, out loud in spite of himself.

"I don't know what you're playing at, little girl," one of the other guards started.

Jakinda cut him off.

"Just take us in to your boss at gunpoint. He'll be happy to see us, and it will save so much unpleasantness."

The guards at least agreed on the gunpoint part of the proposition. They raised their weapons, though not necessarily aimed at anyone's vital organs.

The polite guard seemed to be the intellectual leader of the squad.

"This has got to be some kind of trick," he said.

"Of course, it's a trick," another guard said. "These are women. Listen to them long enough, and they'll have us married off and working as respectable bank clerks."

Algie didn't think there was any real danger of that, but the way they waved their guns around as they spoke could lead to an accidental discharge.

"You know that I'm already married, Clive," the polite guard replied. "I wouldn't be doing something like that to my Nancy."

"I know that," Clive snarled. "What I was saying, Trevor, is that they're cunning and should not be trusted. We should just shoot them now."

Trevor shook his head with vehemence.

"We have strict orders against shooting the locals. There's a hundred thousand of them and only five hundred of us. I've heard about what happened with the Zulus at Rorke's Drift."

"Then we take them downstairs for the commissar of the gate to sort them out, then."

"All four of us? That would leave our post unguarded," said Trevor. "That could be another trick."

He looked fearful at the prospect. The other two who had remained out of the conversation merely looked fatigued.

"Then we split up," Clive said with barely controlled fury. "Two of us take them downstairs, while two stay here to guard the doors."

The two others held up their non-gun bearing hands to volunteer to stay.

"But that's dividing our forces. Three of them against just two of us."

"BLOODY HELL, TREVOR!" Clive exploded in frustration and rage. No doubt this is how conversations with Trevor frequently went. "They are just women. One of them is just a little girl."

Algie spoke up in English:

"Actually, I'm a little boy." He directed himself then to Jakinda. "Can I take this off now? It's terribly hot and I think our whole deception plan is unraveling."

"Certainly, Pig, once we get inside."

The guards swiveled their heads every which way trying to make sense of their situation. The library doors burst open with a scowling Aramis Boycott just on the other side. The BC&I guards snapped to sharply.

"What kind of Bedlam are you idjiots raising out here?" he snapped. "We can barely hear ourselves think in here!"

"Good, we are still in time for the interrogation," Jakinda said cheerfully. "Thank you for holding the door."

"What?" Boycott sounded to be working things out in his agitated mind.

"They're here to rescue that Streif woman," Trevor said. "They wanted us to arrest them and bring them to you."

"Well... then... come in... All of you!" Boycott held the door wide and waved them through.

Algie pressed forward first. The tray of champagne was getting heavy, even with the brace taking up most of the weight.

"Thank you, Mr. Boycott!"

Algie saw the surprise on the man's face upon hearing his normal voice.

"I'm the Governor's adopted son Algernon," Algie explained. "I'm sure he's been looking for me."

*

The library was laid out like a pantomime tableau. Mme. Streif sat bolt upright in her stiff-backed chair with her back to the fire. Sun Lei in his pinstripe gray businessman's suit stood near the massive globe in the corner. He held a clipboard and a sheaf of papers in his hands, and kept his eyes on the third person in the room. The Governor slouched at the little bar with a tumbler in one hand and a whisky decanter in the other. No one moved from their stations as Algie, the Conversors, and their armed escorts entered the room.

Algie glided in and set the tray on the low table before Mme. Streif's chair.

"I appreciate your sense of hospitality, Governor St. George," she said. "What vintage best matches interrogation and blunt threats against my life?"

"The label reads 'Bollinger 1881'," Algie said. "Is that a good year for champagne?"

The formidable old woman raised an eyebrow and nearly smiled.

"Young Master Piggrem," she said. "You are just full of surprises. You've come to my rescue and brought with you an excellent vintage of champagne. Is there any caviar and toast there on your tray?"

"We didn't have time for that, Madame," Jakinda murmured. "Sorry."

Mme. Streif craned her neck to see the Conversors bracketed by men and handguns.

"Ladies! So pleased to see you made it also." Mme. Streif waved her hand airily. "*Que le Grand Salon commence!*"[19]

The Governor poured a drink and strode purposefully over to stand near her. Her little dog erupted in a furious spate of barks and snarls. Governor St. George stepped back, but noise only ended when she laid one hand over its tiny head and pinched its snout closed with the other.

"Shhh. Quiet down," she cooed. "You don't need to tell him that he's an evil man. He already knows."

"You'd best make that little pest behave," the Governor responded, "before I grab him by the scruff of the neck and pitch him out of a third-story window."

Mr. Sun stepped between them and scowled.

"We are here to discuss a capital charge of air piracy that you have levied against Madame Elizabeta Streif."

Boycott let out a self-satisfied chuckle as he settled into one of the couches. Mr. Sun glared at him as if he had just defecated on the rug.

"We will treat them with the severity and dignity they deserve," the Dowager Empress' representative continued. "I have read the affidavits from the captains of the two ships attacked. Is there any other testimony?"

"We have the reports of the battle west of Hami, along with extensive records of her illicit business activities from London to Peiping."

Sun Lei shook his head.

"Since the attack you reference would be considered against *other picaroons* at best, there is no room for examination of that incident at this time."

Boycott snorted in derision and Sun Lei responded silently in kind.

"As to her business activities..."

Mr. Sun pinned the Governor with a smoldering angry look.

"Mme. Streif and her late husband over the last twelve years capitalized several vital industries and facilitated access to important processes and patents. The culmination of this economic campaign was the battle of Palikao, where the forces of my government soundly defeated the forces of *your* government." Though Sun had spoken with restraint up until this point, the tiniest bit of passion crept into his voice, now. "And that explains why you possess a few hectares of farmland and market stalls on the spine of the High Silk Road, instead of the entire Xingjian province."

He sniffed and nodded his head to acknowledge Mme. Streif. She remained utterly composed, but focused her eyes on some point other than the men speaking in the room.

"I can very well understand why you would like to have her shot," the Empress' representative continued, "but her crime seems to be the very reason that the Dowager Empress Cixi gifted her an over-decorated dragon boat suspended beneath an enormous red fish filled with phlogiston."

Jakinda and Ayotunde concealed their smiles at the remark behind open fans. Their Silk Empress sat and blinked in her chair like a large grey cat who had just finished her cream.

"There will be no seizures or executions today," Sun Lei concluded.

"To Hell with that!" Mr. Boycott shouted.

"Pardon me?" Mr. Sun expression was very much like a startled owl through his rounded spectacles.

"What he means," Governor St. George interjected, "is that we have this woman here, and the regent is in the Forbidden Palace several days away. So, I will seize her ship and all its chattel, and have her rightfully shot at dawn. We can sort things out in the aftermath"

The big man looked over towards Algie, and his lip curled in disgust.

"And you, Algernon, take off that dress right away! Your mother would be appalled."

"My mother is dead! Your *wife* wanted Madame. Streif's head displayed on a pike between the azaleas. I don't care what appalls her."

The Governor blanched with his remark. Certainly, not many people were allowed to know of Mrs. St. George's spiteful and bloodthirsty attitudes.

Algie tried to shed the serving girl's dress with some care for its owner, but it tore going around his mechanical braces. Quickly enough, he was down to his blue tunic and canvas pants.

"While we are laying out crimes before the regent's magistrate, *Father*, may I tell him what you have been doing?"

Governor St. George's eyes narrowed as he stared down his nose at Algie.

"What ridiculous piece of nonsense did you make up now?"

Every eye in the room turned upon Algie at that moment, and he could feel the weight of their gaze.

"It's not made up! It's all true..."

Algie suddenly was almost too nervous to speak. He couldn't understand why these men frightened him more than *picaroons* and incendiaries. However, Jakinda, Ayotunde, and Mme. Streif were there with him, amongst the same men as he was, but showed not the slightest care.

He thought he'd at least imitate their courage, until the real thing snuck up on him.

"I found your papers in your office, in the red dispatch case," Algie declared.

"What papers?" Boycott asked. "What did they say? Don't lie."

Algie flinched, but continued.

"The Governor was charging a 'voluntary passage fee.' Except it wasn't, really." Algie took a deep breath. "Those ships that didn't pay, they didn't make it past the *picaroons*. None of them."

"That's nonsense," Governor St. George disparaged.

"No," said Algie. "That is graft. And corruption. And murder..."

St. George took another drink. He seemed to have the slightest problem swallowing.

"And where are those papers?" he asked. "You can't make an accusation like that, boy, without proof."

"He's just a prattling child with an over-active imagination," Boycott told Sun Lei. "His feverish brain has been poisoned by a constant diet of women's gossip and penny dreadfuls."

"I am not!" Algie shouted. "I am not a stupid, little boy... Not anymore..."

He took a moment to master himself and calm his breathing.

Mme. Streif gave him a minuscule, though still reassuring, nod.

"Continue, Master Piggrem."

"I stole the papers from his office," he told Sun Lei, "and then I gave them to the Conversor Ayotunde. The *Wu Zetian* had left Turfan for nearly a day before I had found out my foster parents' crimes. When we caught up to the ship, I'm told that Ayotunde gave them to Madame Streif."

"This is all a demented fantasy," the Governor declared. "We searched that ship from top to bottom and there were no papers."

"And why would anyone search for papers that do not exist?" Mme. Streif asked the room in general.

Sun Lei raised his eyebrows at the question, and then without words asked it of the Governor, who had no response. Mr. Sun turned his attention to Algie.

"*Caught up* with an airship with a day's head start?" He sounded intrigued.

The Conversors consulted in a quick conversation of whispers. Ayotunde made a few quick sharp remarks to Sun Lei in his native tongue. Jakinda translated for benefit of the others in the room:

"That is a very exciting tale that would sadly distract the more important issues before us today. I have something much more vital to show you"

She began unbuttoning the front closures of the embroidered Uyghur blouse she wore. Every male eye was upon her. She pulled it open and untucked it from her skirt, which revealed her white linen corset cover. She slipped a hand inside that garment and removed... a dark oilskin packet.

She offered it to the Empress Cixi's representative.

"I believe this is what everyone here has been seeking."

Opening the packet revealed a bundle of papers which he skimmed through for a minute or two. When he looked up, Sun Lei was quiet and thoughtful. He cleaned his eyeglasses with a white handkerchief and, after placing them back upon his nose, locked eyes with Governor St. George.

"We are in a most peculiar situation, Governor. Each of us represents a Queen and each can call upon millions of loyal subjects to do their bidding. But, of the four guns in this room, all of their wielders pledge loyalty to your Queen Victoria."

Boycott cleared his throat and pulled a small ivory-handled Derringer from his waistcoat pocket, which he laid on the seat cushion beside him.

"Five," he said with a chuckle.

"Yes," Mr. Sun agreed. "Five."

He looked over the papers again.

"Do you really see any kind of long-term success for your schemes? You may avoid immediate prosecution by suppressing evidence..."

"I'll take those, if you don't mind," the Governor said as he slipped the papers from Mr. Sun's grip.

"You can suppress *this* evidence, but the Dowager Empress and my humble self will be watching everything that passes through Turfan. You will eventually lose the favor of both crowns and be shipped home with your possessions in some discomfort."

"I neither believe nor care anymore," Governor St. George

said.

"Of course, you don't," Mme. Streif said. "I wouldn't either, if I were in your position. Master Piggrem, tell them all the interesting part."

"Which part?" There was so much that had happened since she had left Turfan, Algie couldn't be sure what she counted as interesting.

"You remember." She made an airy gesture with the hand not restraining her little dog. "What you found underground after you slew the dragon."

Sun Lei blinked at him, plainly amazed.

"The dragon was real?"

"It was a *karakuri*. And I disabled it. You can't really 'slay' a machine."

"Go on," Jakinda urged. "But be brief. We don't have much time. The equilibrium of the room is unstable."

"It crashed and I was there with it, in the place under the desert where they make repairs. There was a special room for people. It was like an infirmary, or a repair shop."

Algie went over all the things in his head which he had seen in the last twenty-four hours. He had to relate the most important things first.

"There were pictures on the walls, pairs of enemies. African warriors and British generals. American Indians and an American general. I recognized them from my magazines."

A tactical insight flashed into Algie's mind, that Governor St. George could take two steps and grab him by the throat. He began to slowly back around the love seat.

"Boway Kashgari, the head of the Uyghur rebels, had his picture in that infirmary under the desert."

"So, you saw a picture?" Boycott snapped. "So what?"

Algie flinched at his tone and backed away just a little bit faster.

Mme. Streif snapped back at him.

"You are a rude and boorish man, Mr. Boycott. There's no need to be cruel to the boy."

"I can talk anyway I want to," he replied. "I'm not the one with my neck in a noose."

"Could you please let me finish," Algie pleaded. What little fake courage he had was about to fail him. "I saw the Uyghur leader at the head of a raiding party on the day I came to Turfan. He was shot at least once through the chest without bleeding, or dying. He granted us an audience two days ago, but he wouldn't help us in our fight with the Governor. At the time I thought he was frightened, but that didn't make sense, because his people continued to attack Turfan no matter how many of their people they lost."

"They have proven to be relentless." Governor St. George took the opportunity to lay down the papers on the bar behind him. "But what is so special about that old man?"

Algie moved even further away from both Boycott and the Governor before he pulled the Tuareg Cross out from under his shirt. This was about to be a grand theatrical gesture, or it would make him look like an idiot.

"I guess it's what happened when I did this," he said as he blew a tone on the cross.

Governor St. George froze like a statue. Boycott froze too, confused but irritable.

Ayotunde spoke up in French:

"Yes, that's exactly how it looked."

Algie blew a second trilling tone, and the Governor came undone. His head swiveled forward from a hinge below his jaw as plates along his ribs and spine spread wide, tearing his shirt to shreds as they did. The golden light common to all the *karakuri* came from his exposed insides.

"Extraordinary," said Jakinda.

"Yes," Mme. Streif replied. "What better way to guarantee eternal carnage and destruction than to control both sides of a war."

"You said you saw pictures of warriors from all around the world in that preparation room?" Ayotunde asked Algie.

"Yes. I recognized many of them from illustrations in my August Vogel books..." Algie broke off as he heard a commotion outside in the hall. "What on Earth is that?"

The white double doors exploded inwards, splintering as Mrs. St. George pushed her way through. Algie froze with the cross in his hand, but he could see Jakinda and Ayotunde converging on Mme. Streif to protect her.

"You ungrateful little pig!" she screamed. "You've ruined everything!"

She picked up a life-size plaster bust of Disraeli and lofted it at Algie with a speed he had only seen in ship-to-ship rockets. Algie ducked out of its way, from weeks of practice with the *Lǎoshǔ* and their red rubber ball, but she was on top of him before he could make another move.

She wrenched the cross from his hands and snapped its leather thong. With a mere flick of her wrist, she cast it out through the closed windows.

"I'll deal with you later," and threw Algie at Boycott on the couch.

She sped over to her husband and tapped various spots on his neck and spine until he reassembled himself.

"Everything is lost," she told him. "Return to Agartha and collapse the tunnels behind you."

Blinking stupidly, he pulled together his clothing and dignity before disappearing through the back door to the servant's corridors.

The Governor's clockwork wife, now an angry cloud of white frills and blonde hair, focused her attention on Mme. Streif.

"Now there isn't any reason at all for me to not pull your head off of your shoulders."

23 "Let the Grand Salon begin!", French

THIRTY-FOUR

17th of September 1889
Turfan

As Algie untangled himself from Mr. Boycott on the couch, the Conversors swiftly bracketed Mme. Streif's high back chair. They in unison leaned it back and dumped her unceremoniously from her seat. Either she or her dog Kozzie yelped in surprise.

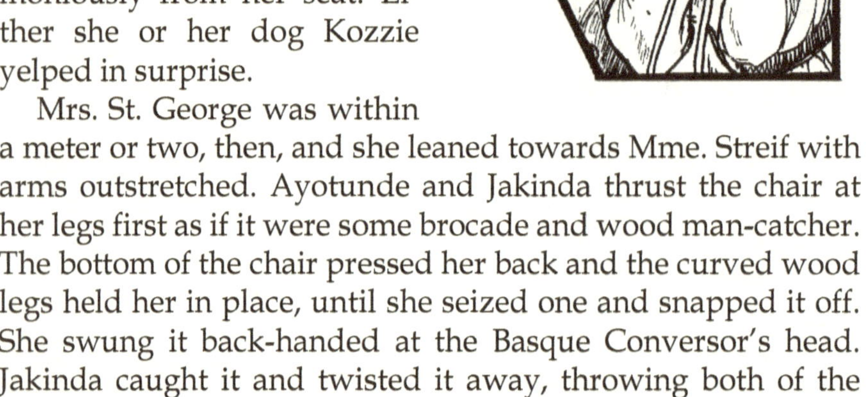

Mrs. St. George was within a meter or two, then, and she leaned towards Mme. Streif with arms outstretched. Ayotunde and Jakinda thrust the chair at her legs first as if it were some brocade and wood man-catcher. The bottom of the chair pressed her back and the curved wood legs held her in place, until she seized one and snapped it off. She swung it back-handed at the Basque Conversor's head. Jakinda caught it and twisted it away, throwing both of the combatants off balance.

All three fell in a twisted pile. The highbacked chair broke with a resounding crack. The Conversors and the *karakuri* continued to wrestle amongst the wreckage.

Algie got on his feet behind the settee. On the other side of that writhing knot, Mme. Streif crept away on her hands and knees as quickly as you might expect an old woman to do.

Mrs. St George broke free of Ayotunde's grip and lofted her across the room to ricochet off the globe, setting it spinning. Jakinda clamped a chokehold on her using her exposed thighs.

Algie averted his eyes.

Boycott, who had taken a little longer to get his feet underneath him, stood next to Algie and stared aghast. So did the four guards, who evidently had no clue as far as what to do.

"Don't just stand there taking in the show," Boycott shouted. "Help her!"

The red coats holstered their handguns and waded into the catfight. By then, Ayotunde had returned to the fray with her folded fan in her fist. She dropped the guards before they realized they had been in a fight, even as the *karakuri* in the frilly dress arched her back and squeezed her way out of Jakinda's leg grip.

Ayotunde laid both hands on one of Mrs. St. George's arms to prevent her from chasing down Mme. Streif. She in return grasped the African's right wrist and twisted. Algie could have sworn he heard the arm pop as it went limp.

She screamed from the pain, then gritted her teeth and dropped low to execute a leg sweep. As Mrs. St. George dropped on her back like a sack of hammers, Jakinda took up the broken chair leg and smote her between her glassy blue eyes.

The chair leg splintered and the *karakuri* grabbed her by the throat. All three women collapsed into a pile of thrashing limbs.

For all their elegance in movement class, this fight with an angry clockwork opponent looked like three drunken sailors wrestling on a slippery gangplank. There was no way the Conversors could prevail. He doubted they could even survive.

"You keep her busy," Algie shouted quite loudly, more for his foster mother's benefit than the Conversors'. "I'll go get my Tuareg cross. That'll fix her."

Then he sprinted towards the window.

From the screeching and crashing, he assumed Mrs. St. George was breaking loose and coming after him. He stooped to pick up the plaster bust and lobbed it with both hands through the window already broken by his cross. He was surprised how much of the statue's weight was taken up by the mechanical brace on his arm.

He had about a quarter second to appreciate that before he

leaped and hit the white lace curtains that covered the remaining jagged glass. With his left arm up to protect his face and his right knee forward to break the glass, he went through the window without major injury.

Thankfully, there was a balcony outside this window.

He dropped to one metal-encased knee to search for the cross on the tile floor. It wasn't there. Most likely it flew out over the stone balustrade and into the gardens. Tearing off the shredded remains of his embroidered robes, Algie started working out the best way down from the third floor.

The sound from inside was like an attempt to boil live cats. He knew he had scant seconds before the violent mechanism that wanted him to call it "Mum" would be coming through that window.

Up and over the railing he went and dangled from the ledge until he could drop safely to the balcony below.

"Algie! You come back here, right now!" Mrs. St. George screamed. She may have still been inside the library, but that was going to be a matter of very little time.

From the second story balcony, Algie assessed his situation.

It was bleak. The garden gates were closed, most likely locked, and armed guards stood outside and also inside the garden near the doors. He would be snatched up as soon as he hit the ground down there.

On the other hand, the garden wall attached to the side of the building two floors down and two balconies to the right. Once he got down there, he could run along the three-meter-high wall to the street while remaining out of reach.

Once he got clear of the Governor's mansion, he would have to improvise.

"Algernon Chauncey Piggrem St. George!" the Governor's wife screeched. "You come back here this instant!"

Algie's first thought was to climb along the ledge to get to the next balcony, but his time for that had run out. He climbed on top of the stone railing and prepared to leap the distance. He had made jumps like this before in the rigging of the *Wu Zetian*, but he hadn't been injured before, or weighed down with mechanical braces.

He chose to stop thinking and just put all his strength into it. He hoped it wasn't something that Dale Daring would do.

Just as the arm brace took up much of the weight he lifted, the leg brace added force to his jump. Not only did he make it to railing of the next balcony over, he sailed over it and landed on top of the far side. Only luck and a death grip born of fear kept him from tipping headfirst over that rail.

He would have been impressed if it hadn't nearly killed him.

The crash of glass and wood sounded above him and Mrs. St. George burst out onto the balcony above. Her fine white dress hung off her in tatters. Her disarrayed hair flopped around her face like a mound of candy floss. A cut on her forehead exposed the brass under her skin.

"Come back here, you little pig."

Algie made the leap over to the next balcony with better aim. He tried to climb down to the garden wall before she saw him. Only when he landed on top of the white-washed stone and was able to move to hide behind a tree's foliage did he look up.

Mrs. St. George had climbed out over the railing and was crawling across the mansion's outer wall like a spider. Algie gasped at the sight. Her head cocked down towards him when she heard.

"I see you, too," she said. "Stay there and I'll come to you."

He was about to run away in a blind panic towards the street when he heard a voice call out from the garden:

"Oy, Pig!"

It was Feng Po McLaren, straight from the kitchens, and he had the Tuareg cross in his hand.

"*Olo parsima!*" He called out as he pitched it up to Algie. It landed in his right hand with only the slightest effort to catch. The weight felt good. He quickly thrust it behind his back to conceal it as a plan came to him fully formed.

Now he would have to do something Dale Daring would do: stand his ground and taunt the enemy.

"If you want me so bad," Algie shouted, "come and get me, you raggedy old hag."

Already on one of the second story balconies, she shrieked and leaped into space towards him. Algie calculated she would land on top of the wall only a meter from where he stood.

He waited for a few terrifying seconds, until he was sure she would be within range of the whistle's sound. Then he put the Tuareg cross to his lips.

Her eyes went wide with terror as he blew the wavering tone, then her head lolled forward on its internal joint and her torso unfolded like a bird's spreading wings. She struck the top of the stone wall in her fragile state, shattered and fell mostly outside the garden.

He went up to where she had struck the wall and kicked off the few bits of brass and amber cogs left behind. Exhausted in multiple ways, he folded over with his head down and his hands resting on his knees.

"Nicely played, Pig," Feng Po called up. "Do you know any other tunes?"

"Thank you," Algie puffed. "How'd you know I'd need that?"

"Had no idea. But I heard the commotion up there, and when I came to take a look, your cherished possession was just lying here on the bricks. I figured it might be useful."

Algie took a moment to catch his breath.

"That is why you're the First Mate, and I, I am... whatever I am..."

"Third Mate, plenipotentiary, I was thinking," Feng Po said. "We've never had one of those before."

As Algie mulled over his imminent promotion, Feng Po looked over the fractured remains of the Hannah St. George *karakuri*.

"May she wind up in Mahapadma, the Great Lotus Hell Where One Freezes until the Body Falls Apart." The First Mate kicked at some of the amber clockworks at his feet.

"Machines don't deserve to go to Hell," Algie said. "And we have no idea what happened to the real Mrs. St. George."

Algie finally registered the sound of screams and crashes coming from inside the mansion. The struggle in the library must have grown more widespread and general across the residential floors.

A low rumbling sound came from the lower levels of the

mansion. The hanging flower pots on the balconies swung gently from side to side and dust shook loose from the stonework. Activity lulled for a moment, then the screaming inside redoubled and alarm klaxons blared from all corners.

"We'd best get the women out of there, immediately," Feng Po suggested.

"What was that?"

The First Mate was already running towards the kitchen exit.

"Don't know. Don't care," he shouted over one shoulder. "Try to keep up, *chong wu.*"

Algie ran the circuit of the garden on top of the wall. The path kept him clear of plants and troublesome guards. Though it looked to be nearly twice the distance, he did nearly keep up with Feng Po, especially with his flying dismount into the kitchen garden. He tumbled through the tomato trellis and pole beans and came to his feet just short of the brick paved sidewalk.

The walk was packed shoulder to shoulder with servants, guards, and government functionaries. They rushed out through the doors at nearly a dead run, but slowing down to turn and gawk no more than twenty meters past the bottom step.

Though it was difficult to hear over the panicked masses, another deep rumble came out of the lowest levels. From his experience, it sounded like an explosion to Algie.

Feng Po somehow wound up on the other side of the sidewalk. Algie stood on tip-toe and waved his good arm over his head to catch his attention.

"We've got to get these people away from the building!"

Feng Po pulled his command baton from his belt.

"Out of the mouths of babes," he shouted as he began herding and prodding.

Algie concentrated on the Uyghurs. He didn't know the words for "bomb" or "explosion," but the local words for "fire" and "death," matched with a wide-eyed expression of terror, seemed to convey the right message.

The crowd filtered slowly through the garden gate. The cluster packing the doorway thinned significantly.

Jakinda, Ayotunde, and Mme. Streif still had not left the building, and Algie was afraid they weren't going to. As the door from the kitchen cleared, Algie rushed inside. He heard a desperate and frustrated cry of "Pig!" behind him as he ran.

He wound his way through the kitchen and servants' corridors. He caught up with them halfway down the stairs from the second floor. The Conversors carried their employer in an improvised palanquin with their hands locked beneath her.

It was slow going as both young women had been badly beaten by his now ex-foster mother. Ayotunde used only her right arm, as her injured arm was wedged into the bodice of her dress. She stumbled and nearly dropped Mme. Streif head-first down the stairs.

Algie stepped in close, expecting at any moment to be crushed by the collapsing roof.

"Let me help," he said.

"No," Jakinda snapped. "You're injured."

Ayotunde's wide-eyed glare said the same thing.

"We're all injured," Algie replied.

A much louder series of explosions echoed from the sub-basement of the mansion. Algie guessed the subway tunnels to the Taklamakan desert were collapsing beneath them. Dust and debris showered down from the ceilings. The windows of the stairwell shattered.

"We don't have time for a debate," Mme. Streif pointed out.

"No, we don't." Algie moved around to get his left side next to her. "These braces are the same machinery as the *karakuri.* They're stronger than you are."

To demonstrate, he slipped his braced arm under Mme. Streif's hindquarters and lifted her up a few inches.

She let out a squeal of surprise and distress as her little dog began barking up a storm.

"Excuse me," he murmured. "I got excited."

"We'll discuss laying hands on women later," Jakinda said in grim determination. "We should leave before we are buried."

They locked hands and speed-walked their way down the stairs and out through the kitchen. As they made the last few meters, the center of the mansion collapsed completely. A cloud of dust, debris, and papers blew the three of them out the back door like a rocket leaving a launching tube.

Feng Po helped them to their feet as the others ran away in a mad panic. The four of them hobbled towards the garden gate, where they stopped to take in the spectacle. As he stood between Jakinda and Ayotunde, he patted the ivory head of his command baton thoughtfully.

"I hadn't had a chance to thank you for returning her to me, Pig," the First Mate told Algie. "I missed her something terrible."

"All in a day's work," Algie replied. "You're welcome."

Multiple explosions rocked the building and threw clouds of smoke and detritus high in the air. The Governor's Mansion disappeared in that cloud with a roar.

Mme. Streif laid a hand on Algie's naked shoulder.

"Well, congratulations, young Master Piggrem. Your record for disaster remains unblemished."

THIRTY-FIVE

20th of September 1889
The High Silk Road,
west of Turfan

Ayotunde escorted Algie down the passageway to the forbidden region, Mme. Streif's personal quarters. Flyball stuck close to his heels, as it always did. Though it did do wonders at rebuilding the ship's spirit engines on short notice, it had developed the disturbing habit of disassembling all machinery it encountered. The Germans and Americans insisted he keep the *karakuri* under his supervision at all times.

The transition to "women's country" was visible as they crossed a structural bulkhead moving forward. The lacquer red walls, marked only with black and yellow signs in French and Chinese script elsewhere in the ship, were painted in pastel landscapes bordered in flowers and foliage. Silk flowers twined around the open bamboo supports. Even the air smelled to be filled with flowers. Algie could believe the stories that this had originally been a pleasure craft of the Dowager Empress Cixi.

They stopped at the door at the end of the passage. It was decorated with a mountainous scene that looked more European than the others in the corridor. Above that was her full name in gilt lettering: Elizabeta Kaczmarek Streif.

Ayotunde tapped on it with the knuckles of her good arm.

"Enter," Mme. Streif called out in French.

Sliding the stiffened silk door into the wall, Ayotunde ushered Algie and his automaton into Mme. Streif's inner sanctum.

The silk-bedecked chambers were pretty much what he had always imagined. Red and gold brocades backed the high throne-like wicker chair the Silk Empress occupied. She looked imperial and bemused as always.

Her silver and steel-colored hair fell over her shoulders and down the front of her glistening blue dressing gown. Kosciusko arose from its perch on her lap as Algie crossed over the threshold. He tensed his every muscle; a fierce but tiny growl rose out of his throat that overflowed into a stream of ferocious barks.

"*Zamknij usta!*[24]" she snapped at the animal. The command was in yet another language Algie couldn't identify.

The chastised lapdog leapt to the deck and pit-a-patted to the door. Its path drew a wide arc around Algie and Flyball. At the hem of Ayotunde's skirts, it barked twice in a request to be picked up.

Ayotunde gave it the same dour frown she often used on Algie. The dog slinked into the passageway. Without a word, the Conversor slid the door shut behind her.

Flyball, left unattended for mere seconds, was examining the self-serving coffee samovar with great care. Drills and cutting tools extruded from its arms for material sampling.

"Be good," Algie muttered in English. "Settle down."

"Education," the *karakuri* replied.

"Just don't."

Flyball responded with an irate metallic tone and pulled its myriad limbs and feelers into its body.

"Come. Sit with me." Mme. Streif indicated a padded stool at her feet. "We need to talk and come to an accommodation."

That was always a remark filled with foreboding and imminent disaster. The last "talk" the two of them had had put him in the custody of a clockwork harridan.

"Yes, ma'am," he said oh-so-politely.

"Oh, don't be that way. Have some chocolate."

He filled a cup from the brass serving pitcher and took a sip. It tasted sweet and luxurious, even in the close warmth of her chambers. He and the Silk Empress sat and drank in amiable silence.

"I am sure you believe that I have always been an old

woman, but I really was as young as you once."

Algie was silent for at least three seconds.

"You're not that old," he finally said.

"My Lady Conversors have taught you diplomacy as another form of self-defense." She chuckled.

Algie drank more of his chocolate. It was very good.

"When I was only two years older than you, I had to flee my home. The Prussians were murdering the Poles, and doing even worse to young girls. My family sent me to Alsatia, where others from our village had gone before. They wanted me to be safe."

"Did you ever hear from them again?" Algie asked.

"Oh no," she said. "They were all killed, or went into hiding. I may still have a second cousin in South America, but we're not close.

"I eventually came to land in the Streif household, where I was employed as a maid and a seamstress. That's where I met my beloved Jean-Pierre."

She looked over to Algie, who hoped he was keeping an attentive expression on his face. Her expression indicated that it may have slipped a bit.

"I could go on forever about that, but it is evident that I shouldn't. The important points were that I was penniless and he was the middle son of a coal- and iron-monger. I had no parents or immediate family; he had an extensive crop of parents, siblings, and cousins, all of them alive and disapproving."

She sighed and a corner of her mouth curled up into a bittersweet smile.

"Anyhow, we were married by my nineteenth birthday. By my twenty-first, we had carved out a tiny empire in textiles, dyes, and chemicals. On my thirtieth, I was dancing on the graves of quite a few Prussian industrialists."

She stopped with a hitch in her voice.

"It was just a little after my thirty-second birthday that my darling Jean-Pierre succumbed to cancer, one that was common to chemical workers." Another mirthless chuckle. "He always told me we shouldn't be afraid to get our hands dirty in our business."

She paused to pull the stopper from the whiskey decanter and topped off the hot chocolate in her own cup.

"The point of that whole tawdry confession was to relate to you, Master Piggrem, that I know where you have been. With a little bit of luck, I might even be able to see where you are going."

"Thank you, ma'am," said Algie, though he wasn't sure if gratitude was the primary emotion he felt.

"When I was your age, I still had no idea who I really was, who I wanted to be. It's what the great thinkers now call 'self-discovery.' But it's not a journey, you're not following a map from point to point. Discovering your Self is a process of testing, pushing up against boundaries and opponents to see how you measure up."

She fixed him with a deadpan-but-playful look.

"In your case, it has been what the Liu company engineers call 'testing to destruction.'"

Algie had to admit that he'd left a lot of smoking wreckage in the wake of his twelve years on Earth, but he wasn't getting the point of this conversation.

"What is this 'accommodation' you spoke of earlier?" Perhaps he was being too blunt, but he felt he had earned the right to it in the last week.

"I understand that I offered you a home aboard my ship and then abused your trust to achieve my ends."

Algie hadn't been able to pinpoint exactly why he had been upset up until that moment, but that seemed to be as good a description as any.

"Yes, I suppose you did."

She shrugged and put down her china cup.

"I'm old. I am rich, and I am ambitious. It's what I do," she said. "For decades."

"Are you saying you're sorry?"

"Not if I can escape with an implicit apology."

Algie frowned. This conversation seemed to be devolving into a tennis match.

"One doesn't earn the sobriquet 'Silk Empress' by being conciliatory." She laid a hand on his forearm as he set down his chocolate. "However, I have wronged you, and I am sorry."

Algie carefully considered her apology for several long seconds.

"So, am I forgiven?" Mme. Streif asked in a very grandmotherly tone.

"You have done a lot for me, and I am grateful," he replied. "So, yes, you are forgiven. But I've been warned that you still want something from me."

"Why would you say that?"

"Feng Po told me the answer to that is: 'Because you're still breathing.'"

She choked the slightest bit at that, even though she wasn't drinking her chocolate at the time.

"He said *that*, did he?"

"That was the most polite thing he said."

"There is something that I want." She stole a glance at the inert Flyball, no doubt checking if it was safe. "Agartha."

"Oh."

"It is referenced in Theosophical circles as a remnant of the prediluvian Lemurians which, like Atlantis, sank beneath the Indian Ocean at the height of its technology." Mme. Streif shrugged. "Or, it could be a cabal of rich, evil men that like to play act."

Algie and the Conversors had spent the last few days teasing out every detail from his memory of what he had seen in the underground realm. Jakinda's book of Isilmandatu contained several chapters on mind and memory beyond its lessons on movement and combat. Its application had produced a thick volume of notes under the label "Agartha", the term Mrs. St. George had used with the Governor in their last conversation. Keijín, the ship's cartographer, was reconstructing the map of the automatic tramway.

"I have spent the last three, perhaps four decades, trying to use my money and influence to make the world a better place." Her voice sounded ancient now. "It was at least twenty years ago that I had realized that there was far greater advantage to doing business with other nations from their own position of power and privilege, than as slaves under guns and opium."

She waved her hand to take in her lush surroundings.

"Out of that ridiculous proposition, came all this. That, and a few million people have better lives to show for it, too."

"I guess that makes you some kind of hero, too," Algie said.

The old woman smiled, but her eyes were moist and her head beginning to bow.

"Those people from Agartha, with their clockwork monstrosities, are trying to take all that away. They are pitting the helpless against the empire-builders to guarantee that both are destroyed, and unleashing monsters to eat the survivors. I won't have it!"

Algie finished his hot chocolate and set down his cup and saucer.

"So, what will you be needing from me?"

"As Mssr. Patrouille can tell you, a boy adventurer is a valuable asset. Besides revenue, he provides privilege, prestige, access to circles of powerful people which don't have the foresight and wherewithal to manufacture their own heroes."

"And inspiration for the masses?" Algie added.

"Always a job requirement." She bobbed her head sideways in an ironic gesture. "I may also, from time to time, require you to jump out of an airship with explosives clutched in your teeth."

Algie laughed.

"I believe that is being written into the job description of Third Mate, plenipotentiary. I'll sign on, if you'll have me, ma'am."

Mme. Streif extended a hand to be clasped and he took it. He had only seen her shake hands with the Governor and his equals before.

"Welcome back aboard the *Wu Zetian*, Master Piggrem," she said.

*

Algie and Mssr. Patrouille walked down the corridor of bamboo and stiffened silk side by side.

"So you're saying the villain destroyed their home and base of operations to prevent you from pursuing them?" Mssr.

Patrouille tweaked the end of one of his waxed mustaches, a sign that he was lapsing into writer's composition mode.

"Or the Governor was just trying to kill us," Algie replied.

"Either way, that is fascinating. I don't recall reading anything like that before."

They picked up their pace down the *Wu Zetian*'s corridors to accommodate the writer's urge to compile notes. As they reached his sliding door, Patrouille gestured towards it.

"If you have a moment, Algie, I have a little present for you."

Mssr. Patrouille slipped inside and returned with a plain pasteboard box of the kind that manuscripts were shipped. He pulled off the lid to reveal the manuscript of his latest novel. The handwritten title page read: *The Adventures of Algernon Pilgrim*.

"I am honored," Algie said after a moment's thought, "but why 'Pilgrim?'"

Patrouille grimaced, which set his mustaches twitching about his mouth.

"There is that unfortunate 'pig' association," he said. "Besides, 'Pilgrim' implies a virtuous young man in pursuit of a higher truth."

Algie couldn't believe that really described him, but still he said:

"Thank you."

"I can't really let you have this until I have completed it, but I thought you would like to see the first page."

Algie peeled the first page off of the top of the stack and held it up to read. The writer looked as excited as one of the *Lǎoshǔ* with a new rubber ball.

"I wanted to wait, but I couldn't help myself," Patrouille said. "I think you will be an inspiration to young boys for years to come. And quite commercial."

"Well, let's see what kind of adventures I've been having," Algie said as he took up Patrouille's version of his own life story.

*

Algernon Pilgrim stood resolute on the prow of the airship Égalité and scanned the western horizon for air pirates. The dissolute First Mate McPherson squatted on the deck playing mumbley-peg.

As the sun set over this stretch of the High Silk Road, he caught sight of three airships lying in wait for them in the west China sky. Their bright banners and flamboyant clothes belied the grim black flags with skull and crossbones they flew.

Fifteen merchant ships had been taken by the Afghan brigands in the last month, and he swore an oath on his mother's grave that his airship would not be number sixteen. Never again would a friend or crewmate die due to his error or inaction.

"Nǐ hǎo, muhafez," he muttered as he silently signaled the bridge to prepare for battle.

20 "Shut your mouth" Polish

Josef Matulich is a writer, artist, and retired mime. His written works include four horror/comedy novels, several short plays and flash fiction, and one poor screenplay perhaps trapped forever in Development Hell.

He has built monsters for movies, slit throats on video, and provided magick amulets on the spot. His jobs have ranged from ditchdigging and setting explosives to operating a mass spectrometer in an EPA lab, not to mention several dozen children's parties

Josef lives with his lovely wife Kit in a deer-infested suburb of Columbus Ohio. Together, they also own a semi-haunted vintage and costume shop.